Cuckoo in the Nest

Nora Kay

Hodder & Stoughton

Copyright © 2003 by Nora Kay

First published in Great Britain in 2003 by Hodder and Stoughton
A division of Hodder Headline

The right of Nora Kay to be identified as the Author
of the Work has been asserted by her in accordance
with the Copyright, Designs and Patents Act 1988.

1 3 5 7 9 10 8 6 4 2

A CIP catalogue record for this title
is available from the British Library

ISBN 0 340 82365 8

Typeset in Plantin by Hewer Text Ltd, Edinburgh
Printed and bound in Great Britain by
Clays Ltd, St Ives plc

Hodder and Stoughton
A division of Hodder Headline
338 Euston Road
London NW1 3BH

For Bill and Raymond

I

When the post arrived Linda Chalmers' husband had left for the office and the children for school. There was only one letter and it was addressed to her, to Mrs Linda Chalmers. It was typed and to Linda it appeared to be a business letter. She wondered what it could be and why it should be addressed to her and not to Matthew. She took it through to the kitchen and sat down at the table. Finding a clean knife among the breakfast dishes, Linda slit open the envelope and drew out two pages. Only a few lines were typed on the second page and under them was a scrawled signature. From the heading she saw that the letter had come from a firm of solicitors in Inverness.

As she began to read her eyes widened in shock and horror. The letter was to inform her that their late client, Elizabeth Marshall, and her husband, Robert, had been killed when their car went out of control. The letter went on to say that no other car had been involved and that their daughter, Jennifer, a back-seat passenger, had escaped with bruising and was at present being cared for by a neighbour.

Horrified though she was Linda was mystified as to why she was being informed. As she read on the reason became clear and she stared at the words in total disbelief. This couldn't be, it couldn't. She read that part again to make sure she wasn't mistaken. She wasn't.

Linda wished that her husband was beside her. Matthew would deal with everything. Matthew who was always so calm, so reasonable, so dependable. It was very tempting to phone the office but she wouldn't. She wasn't one of those women who phoned their husband at every crisis or imagined crisis. Matthew, she knew, would not appreciate it if he was called away from an important meeting unless it was life or death and it was hardly that. He wouldn't want to upset those in authority. The nineteen eighties was a difficult time. Job security was a thing of the past and there was no such thing as a safe job or a job for life. Her news would have to wait until Matthew came home.

The housework got done in fits and starts and at midday she made herself a snack lunch then stared at the plate with unseeing eyes. In the afternoon she prepared the vegetables for the evening meal and tried to keep her mind on what she was doing. The day dragged on. She could have phoned or gone to see her mother. She could have phoned her sister, Helen, although the likelihood of her being at home was small. Helen led a busy life. As well as looking after her husband and two teenage sons, she served on various committees and in her usual brisk manner, organised everything and everybody. No one seemed to mind too much. Helen could be overbearing and annoying at times but she was good to have around in times of trouble. There were plenty of folk who offered sympathy but Helen did much more. She would drive over to wherever it was with prepared food for the invalid and the family, too, should that be necessary.

Certainly her mother and Helen would have to be told at some point but not yet. This was something she and Matthew would have to discuss and she was becoming ever more nervous.

When Matthew did arrive home, Linda strove to act normally. Since she had waited this long she could hold out until the meal was over and the children upstairs doing their homework or busy with their own pursuits. They knew not to disturb their parents. Coffee in the sitting-room after the meal was their time to be together and relax. It was a time they both enjoyed.

Matthew drank some of his coffee and was looking at his wife curiously. He was a tall man with broad shoulders, not handsome in the conventional sense, but attractive for all that. He had thick, dark brown hair showing some grey and his eyes were blue-grey.

'Has something happened? You seem a bit on edge.'

'I am, though I thought I had hidden it.'

'Not from me, I know you too well.' He gave the slow smile she loved.

They made an attractive couple. Linda was a nice-looking woman of above average height. She had a neat figure with small firm breasts and she was blessed with long shapely legs. Her fair hair was curly and cut short. Linda was thirty-five, two years younger than her husband. The letter was to hand and she gave it to him.

'That came after you left for the office.'

First he studied the envelope, turning it over. Linda closed her eyes for a moment. It was typical Matthew and it was infuriating. She would have had the letter out of its envelope and half read by this time.

'What, tell me, is a firm of solicitors in Inverness doing writing to my wife? Has some long lost relative left you a fortune?'

'If only,' she said and managed the ghost of a smile.

When he began reading the letter, Linda studied his face but it gave nothing away. He did, however, go back to read part of it again. Only then did he look up.

'Poor souls, what a dreadful end. Had the man lost his concentration or what?'

'He must have, I suppose.'

'You had better tell me something about this Elizabeth and Robert.'

'Betty. She was always called Betty. She was my best friend, you should remember that.'

'I think I do but vaguely. You lost touch?'

'Yes.'

'Did I ever meet her? I don't seem to remember.'

Linda smiled. 'No, you didn't meet Betty. We, you and I, had just started to go steady when we got the invitation to their wedding. I had to go alone.'

'Why was that?'

'A week before the wedding you managed to break your leg playing rugby.'

He grinned. 'Of course, I remember now. I remember it very well. My game was never the same after that.'

Linda worried her lower lip. 'What are we to do, Matthew?'

'I'm leaving it to you.'

Her eyes widened in shock. She hadn't expected that. 'Matthew, that isn't fair. I can't decide something like this on my own.'

'I didn't know you had a goddaughter,' he said quietly.

'Neither did I.'

'What?'

'It's true, Matthew. I have absolutely no idea why this letter was sent to me. Why me?'

'Linda, you must have been asked. Betty must have asked you.'

Linda was getting angry. 'I'm telling you I wasn't.' She was almost shouting and put a shaking hand over her mouth.

'Calm down, darling. This isn't making sense to either of us but remember I know nothing at all. Tell me what you remember and take your time. I'll pour us both more coffee and you can begin by telling me about your best friend from your college days. That will give you a starting point.'

She nodded. 'I'm sorry I shouted, Matthew, but it was all getting on top of me.'

'I'm not surprised. You have been worrying about it all day.'

'I have. I nearly phoned you but I didn't.'

'There wasn't much I could have done.'

'I knew that.' She took a deep breath. 'I am going to get this hopelessly mixed up.'

'Not to worry, we'll sort it out.'

She took another deep breath. 'Betty was very pretty, easily the best-looking girl in our year. She wasn't conceited about her looks. She was just a very nice person and the two of us got on great.'

'A very popular young woman?'

'Very and, of course, the boys were all over her. She dated a few but it was Alan Stephenson she began to go out with regularly. Alan was crazy about her and he was genuinely nice. When they got engaged we were all delighted and Betty was so happy.' She stopped.

'Go on. This is when things went wrong, I imagine?'

She nodded. 'It happened when Robert Marshall came on the scene. He was a bit older than our crowd and he was handsome. Really, really handsome, Matthew, and he had the charm to go with it.' She paused to drink some of her coffee. 'The moment he set eyes on Betty he wouldn't leave her alone. She was flattered but she didn't take him seriously. After all she was engaged to Alan and they were making plans for their wedding. Then suddenly the engagement was broken off . . .'

'Did you have an inkling of what was going on? Did Betty confide in you?'

'No, she didn't. It was obvious to us that she was keyed up and nervous but we put it down to pre-wedding nerves. Then it was all out in the open. She had fallen in love with Robert and broken off her engagement to Alan.'

'How did Alan take it, being thrown over?'

'How do you expect? He was devastated but there was a quiet strength to Alan. He didn't make things more difficult for

Betty. He accepted that she didn't want to marry him and decided he should disappear from the scene.'

'Which he did?'

'Yes.'

'And, as is now obvious, she married the other bloke?'

'Yes.' Linda sighed.

'What did you think of him?'

'I didn't like Robert, I didn't trust him. I know we shouldn't speak ill of the dead . . .'

'Why not? I never understood the sense of that. A person was what he was.'

She smiled. 'Robert was a bighead and thought himself wonderful.'

'Did you suggest to Betty that he could be less than perfect?'

'No, I did not. Don't be silly, Matthew, Betty was on cloud nine.'

'To say anything to Betty would have put your friendship at risk?'

'The friendship might have survived but it would have been damaged.'

'Sorry, I shouldn't have interrupted. Go on.'

'Have you finished?' she said, looking into his coffee cup.

'Yes, thank you.'

'Perhaps you would put the coffee table back and we'll get more room for our legs.'

Matthew got up to put the table back in its position.

'Thank you, dear.' She made herself more comfortable in the chair. 'We invited them to our wedding but they didn't come, which didn't surprise me. I don't think Robert had much in the way of qualifications but he had managed to get a job down south. They were settling in to a new house and Betty was expecting a baby.'

'You kept in touch?'

'Yes, we did but the letters were few and far between.'

'You wouldn't have known if the marriage was working out?'

'Betty said nothing to suggest it wasn't but reading between the lines I didn't think she was happy. Robert never stuck for long in one job and Betty was working part time to help out. She couldn't do full time, not with a baby to look after. Then they decided to take over a shop and small tearoom and for a while that was doing well then that failed too.'

'Did you hear anything after that?'

Linda was becoming exasperated with Matthew. 'Any letters I got were left for you to read.'

'A personal letter – I might not have read that.'

'You were given the chance. I never had any secrets from you.'

'I wasn't suggesting that. Let us get back on track. Was that the last you heard from your friend?'

'No. She did write and apologised for the long delay in replying to my letter and to tell me that they were coming back to Scotland. She seemed to be happy about that and I thought we might manage to meet.' Linda paused. 'I wanted that but I am not sure that Betty did. She knew we were very happy . . .'

'And if she wasn't, she didn't want you to know.'

'I suppose that is possible. Anyway time went on and no letter. I couldn't get in touch even if I wanted to because she hadn't given me her address. And that, Matthew, is all I can tell you.'

He was silent for a few moments. 'Don't jump down my throat, but when the baby was born did she suggest . . .'

'That I should be the baby's godmother? No, Matthew, and I repeat no. I can't make it plainer than that. Heavens! It isn't the kind of thing one would forget.'

'Had she asked you to be godmother to her daughter what would have been your answer?'

Linda thought for a few moments. 'Had Betty asked me,'

she said slowly, 'I would have considered it an honour. It is an honour. Yes, Matthew, I would have agreed and you would have known about it.' She moistened her lips. 'Did you have a godparent?'

'No.'

'Neither did I. I think long ago it was the custom in some families but not so much now.'

'It is not exactly a written agreement. I mean there is nothing binding about it.'

'I have to disagree with you there, Matthew,' Linda said shaking her head. 'It is binding when you give your word.'

'Quite,' he said in a clipped voice, 'but you didn't.'

'That's right, I didn't.'

'Not many godparents are called upon to do much more than remember birthdays and Christmas.'

Linda shivered.

'You're cold?'

'No, I'm not. I was thinking of that poor child. How must she be feeling? Matthew, she has just lost both parents and apart from the pain of loss she must be feeling very scared. Neighbours cannot be expected to take care of her indefinitely.'

'Does that mean you have made up your mind to take her?'

'No, it doesn't. If you want to know, I feel hard done by. Jennifer is not my responsibility yet I am made to believe she is.'

'The letter does not suggest anything of the kind. You are being informed of the position, that the girl is at present being cared for by a neighbour.'

'And I have been mentioned as godmother which is as much as saying that I should take some responsibility.'

'You are reading too much in to it. At the moment you are too emotional to think clearly.'

'Which is why I need to talk about it with you.'

Matthew didn't think there was anything to talk about. The godmother bit was obviously some sort of misunderstanding and all Linda had to do was phone or write to this solicitor, express sorrow over what had happened to her old friend and her husband and then state very clearly that she was not in a position to offer the girl a home. Only, of course, being Linda she would be incapable of doing that. Hers was always the helping hand. He groaned inwardly.

'How old is this girl?'

'I've been working that out. Jennifer must be fifteen.'

'Fifteen,' he almost spluttered, 'I thought we were talking about a nine- or ten-year-old. At that age she is able to take some responsibility for herself.'

'Would you like to think of ours taking responsibility for themselves at that age?'

'Not quite the same.'

'I think it is.'

'I meant she must know about her own relations.'

'Not if she doesn't have any, or I should say anyone prepared to give her a home for a few years.' Linda let out a shaky breath. 'Matthew, we don't know what state she is in.'

'She got off with cuts and bruises.'

'What about the mental damage?'

'She will have been seen by doctors.'

'That sort of damage doesn't always show up.'

'Another problem if and when it does.'

'I don't see it that way.'

Matthew was fast losing patience. 'What way do you see it?'

'I think Jennifer might be in need of a bit of loving care.'

'Which you are going to provide.'

'No, I wouldn't take that on myself.'

'You think we can give it?'

'I would like to think so,' Linda said quietly.

'Did you meet any of Betty's family when you were at college?'

She nodded. 'Her grandmother. Betty's parents died when she was small and she was brought up by her grandmother. On the one occasion I was in her company I can remember thinking her quite old then.'

'We can forget about her.'

'I think so. Wouldn't the solicitor know about relatives? No, of course not, not unless he was told,' she answered herself.

'It would appear yours is the only name he has.'

'Why Betty should have given my name I can't imagine. It just doesn't make sense. What do you make of it, Matthew?'

'I could be way out but I believe it might have happened this way.' He put one long leg over the arm of the chair which usually earned him a rebuke but if Linda noticed she made no comment. 'Betty could have been feeling a bit depressed, the marriage going through a bad time and she had begun to worry about the future. Maybe her health wasn't so good and she got to wondering that if something were to happen to her, what was to become of Jennifer? I gather she didn't have a lot of confidence in her husband.'

'Robert would be duty-bound to look after his own daughter.'

'He wouldn't be the first to conveniently forget his responsibilities and clear out.'

'If it was that, how awful and poor Betty.'

'That was only a thought. It might not have been anything like that.'

'On the other hand you could be right.'

'She could have been thinking that way when you came in to her mind. Her best friend, someone she could trust.'

'Fair enough, I could go along with that but surely I should have been asked?'

'No doubt that was her intention but she kept putting it off and as time went on it was forgotten altogether.'

Linda nodded.

'What about our three? They should have their say. Taking a stranger into our midst would be a big upheaval in their lives.'

'They would quickly get used to it.'

'Don't be so sure.'

'I agree they should have their say.'

'No time like the present. Get them down here and we'll find out.'

'Matthew, it is too soon,' Linda protested. 'We need to discuss this further before we involve the children. And I would like to talk it over with Mother and Helen, find out what they think.'

Matthew was frowning. 'With due respect, what they think is not important. This isn't going to affect them.'

'Thank you very much,' she said huffily.

'Of course talk it over with them, but there is no hurry.'

Linda got up. 'I'll call the children.' She went to the foot of the stairs. 'Hannah, Heather and Robin, come downstairs. Daddy and I want to talk to you.'

2

'What about? Can't it wait?'

'No.'

'What is so urgent?'

'You'll find that out, Hannah, when you come down.'

'This isn't at all convenient, you know. I am working on something serious and stopping in the middle of it is going to break my concentration.'

'You'll get your concentration back just as you always do when your friend, Julie, phones,' Linda said drily. The girls lived within easy walking distance of each other, they saw each other at school, yet still found it necessary to phone.

Silence.

'I want the three of you downstairs now. That is an order,' she said in her 'I am not standing any nonsense' voice.

Linda went back to the sitting-room and there was the clatter of feet on the stairs. Robin, in grey trousers and a light grey shirt was first down and sat cross-legged on the floor. Hannah was behind him and frowning. She sat on the sofa and crossed her long skinny legs. At thirteen years of age, Hannah was very conscious of her appearance and it didn't please her one little bit. The other two had all the luck. They had their mother's fair curly hair whereas hers was light brown and dead straight. She couldn't leave it alone. Either she was stretching strands of it across her mouth or tucking it behind her ears.

Linda could see the promise of beauty and told her so but

Hannah was having none of it. She was never going to get a boyfriend, she was convinced of that.

Heather, on the plump side and pretty, joined her sister on the sofa but sat as far away as possible.

Linda was frowning and shaking her head. 'Robin, we do stretch to chairs in this house.'

The boy made no effort to get up. 'I like sitting on the floor.'

'Robin,' his father roared. 'You heard your mother. Sit on a chair and do as you are told.'

The child's lips trembled. His daddy never spoke like that to him and Linda was looking at her husband in surprise. The prospect of having Jennifer to live with them must be upsetting him more than she thought. She was finding it upsetting too. Matthew was going about this in the wrong way.

She pulled the leather pouffé nearer to her chair and Robin sat down quickly. The thumb went in to his mouth. Robin was eight years of age and he had almost outgrown that bad habit. It only happened when he was distressed. Linda gently removed Robin's thumb from his mouth and put a protective hand on his shoulder. If Matthew was to call him a baby that would be the last straw.

'Daddy, I think I know what it is. You've lost your job.'

'No, Heather, I haven't. Why should I have lost my job?'

'Mary McKenzie's daddy was paid off. She was crying in school because they won't have any money.'

'I'm glad to say my job seems safe enough at present.' He paused. 'Your mother has something she wants to tell you.'

Linda could have wished for more time to prepare herself. In this kind of situation the right words were important. She would keep it short and simple and hope for the best. When she got to the end both girls remained silent. Robin twisted round on the pouffé to look at his mother. He was a tender-hearted little boy, too tenderhearted Linda often thought, and she worried about him. Matthew said he would toughen up but not if she fought his battles for him.

'If that girl has no place to live she will have to come and stay with us.'

That was a relief. 'You would like that?'

'Not much,' he said gloomily and Matthew grinned.

'Does that mean you don't want her to live with us?'

'No, Mummy, I never said that. She . . .'

'Jennifer. I think we should give the girl her name.'

'She – Jennifer – can come but I wish she was a boy. I would like a big brother.'

'Where would she sleep?' Hannah said abruptly.

'Hannah, I hadn't got to thinking that far.' And neither had she. 'I suppose you and Heather could share . . .'

'Oh, no, nothing doing,' Hannah said, sitting bolt upright and looking outraged. 'I thought it might be that and I am telling you here and now that I am not having it. And that is final,' she said in case any doubt still remained.

'Well! Well!' Linda said, taken aback.

'And that goes for me too, I'm not sharing with Hannah,' Heather said with a toss of her head. 'If she has to come here we will have to move to a bigger house.'

'I like it here, I don't want to go away,' Robin said fearfully.

'Don't worry, son, we will not be moving,' Matthew said firmly. He looked at Heather then turned his attention to Linda. She took the hint.

'This is our home, Heather, and as Daddy says this is where we stay. Moving house is not an option.'

Linda was remembering the time when they bought the house. With the arrival of Robin, the four-apartment bungalow had been too small for their needs. They required an extra bedroom, two extra bedrooms, in fact. Before long the girls would want their own rooms. She smiled thinking of the excitement when that day had come. The smile faded when she thought of what she was asking. No wonder Hannah was rebelling, and Heather too, although not quite so forcefully.

She was asking a lot and they were only children. How would she have felt if at Hannah's age she had been asked to share her bedroom? Not at all happy, that was for sure. Very likely she, too, would have rebelled. Hannah was making her position very clear. There was no way she was going to share, not with her sister and most certainly not with a strange girl.

Linda could see no answer to her problem. She could, of course, be worrying about something that wouldn't happen. Some long-lost relative might already have appeared on the scene.

Her thoughts drifted back to their home. Matthew and she had all but decided to reserve one of the bigger houses being built on the new estate and there was no reason at all why they should have gone to view Hillcrest. The stone-built family house was situated in a quiet cul-de-sac in Abbotsfield, a pleasant little village not far from Dundee. It was beyond their means. Matthew said it was unfair to put the occupants to the trouble of showing them around when they were in no position to put in a reasonable offer. Linda had agreed with every word Matthew said but in spite of that they had gone to view the house.

It was madness. Linda fell in love with Hillcrest the moment she stepped inside and Matthew was very favourably impressed. They went home to do more calculations but the result was the same. There was no way they could afford it. And that might have been the end of the matter if Linda's mother hadn't come to the rescue. When her time came, she told them, all she had would be divided between her two daughters. Helen's husband, George, was an architect, a successful one, and in no need of financial help. Their share would come to them in the fullness of time. 'Believe me, my dears,' she had said, 'I am not depriving myself of anything in order to help you out. I have all I could ever want. My small comfortable cottage is ideal, my car might be old but it is very reliable and there is more than enough for me to live on.'

Matthew was shaking his head. He didn't have George's kind of money it was true but he did hold down a responsible position with the well-established engineering firm of Charles Rattray & Sons. He was clever and conscientious and promotion was in his sights. The future should be bright but nothing these days was certain. There could be a slump in trade. Matthew had a horror of debt and it required a lot of persuasion but eventually his mother-in-law talked him in to it.

'You need the money now not later,' Kirsty had told him gently. 'To find the house of your dreams is rather wonderful. Please don't let pride stand in the way.'

He had smiled at that. 'All right, you win,' Matthew said, getting up to give his mother-in-law a kiss on the cheek. 'This is very generous of you, Kirsty,' he said huskily.

George, her other son-in-law, called her Ma which she heartily disliked. She ought to have said so at the start but she hadn't and now it was too late. Matthew said he wasn't going to call her Ma or Mother-in-law. If she had no objections, he would use her Christian name. Kirsty assured him she had none and that to be called Kirsty by a handsome young man would make her forget her age.

'I'm just so glad I can be of help.'

'This will be repaid as soon as possible,' Matthew's voice was firm.

'There is absolutely no hurry.' There was the faintest touch of annoyance in her voice. She knew Matthew wouldn't be happy until the debt was repaid in full. In the event promotion had come quickly and before they could have expected it, Kirsty's money was returned to her with grateful thanks. Hillcrest was the kind of house where a young couple would want to put down roots and bring up a family and they would be forever grateful to Kirsty for making it possible.

The old couple who were selling the house had taken a liking to Linda and Matthew. There was a lot of interest in the house and they could have held out for more but they accepted what they considered a fair price. The sweet-faced lady had loved her house and she wanted it to go to someone who would care for it the way she had. Linda would, she was sure. They were moving to a much smaller house and the heavy furniture would look out of place. If the young couple should want it they were very welcome. It would give them a start and the children would have their freedom. Most little ones were boisterous at times and heavy furniture didn't show the damage. Linda and Matthew were delighted. Solid pieces like that were in demand and would have fetched a good price in the saleroom. As a thank you gift, Linda had found out their new address and arranged for the delivery of a handsome bouquet of flowers and a card to wish them health and happiness in their new home.

Linda's thoughts had returned to the present.

Hannah looked glum. She *was* glum. She didn't want to be thought of as selfish and she didn't think she was. Being the eldest of the family gave her status. Jennifer, whatever her second name was, was not family but Mum would make sure that she was treated the same. No, not the same, better than family. There would be a big fuss made of her and she and Heather would be told to be especially nice and make her feel welcome and wanted. Hannah felt a rush of anger. Robin, being the boy, was safe enough, he didn't have to share. In any case his bedroom, which was much smaller than theirs, couldn't accommodate two single beds. And as for Mum and Dad, it wouldn't affect them. Married couples shared a bedroom or most of them did. Julie's parents didn't, their daughter told Hannah in confidence. They had separate rooms. And it wasn't because they weren't on speaking terms, it was nothing like that. Her dad snored. He always had but it was getting worse. And it kept her mum from sleeping. Julie had giggled. She hadn't known if her mother had meant it or not but she had said it was separate rooms or a divorce.

I don't want that girl, Jennifer, here, Hannah thought miserably but it was going to happen. She knew it was.

'Mum.'

'Yes, Hannah?'

'I am not trying to be difficult but I do have rights.'

'And what are those rights, Hannah?'

'As the eldest of this family I am surely entitled to have my own bedroom.'

Linda didn't answer.

'How old is she?' eleven-year-old Heather asked.

'Fifteen.'

Hannah stared at her mother. This was worse than ever.

'If she comes she will be the eldest,' Heather said triumphantly.

'No, she won't, she isn't family, she doesn't count,' Hannah said furiously.

'Will you two stop it? Really, I have to say I am disappointed. I had thought better of you both.'

Linda waited for some support from Matthew. She tried to catch his eye, but he pretended not to notice.

Robin was getting bored and was amusing himself by tilting the pouffé until he fell off.

'She can come, I don't mind,' he said, hoping to hurry matters along so that he could get back to playing with his Dinky toys that Aunt Helen had said he could have. She had been in her attic giving it a good clean and come across the toy box. Her boys were well beyond that stage and Robin had been told to choose what he wanted. It had been a difficult choice, too difficult for Robin, and it had ended as he had hoped it would. His daddy brought the lot home in the boot of the car.

'I know you don't, dear, you are a very kind boy.'

'Oh, a very kind boy, is he? Easy enough for him, I would say. He isn't being asked to share his bedroom. This won't affect him hardly at all and that goes for you and Dad too.'

Linda gasped.

'Hannah has a point, Linda. She is voicing her thoughts, which is what we wanted, so leave it there.'

Hannah gave her father a grateful look.

'I declare this meeting over,' Matthew announced. 'We were merely sounding you out and remember, it may never happen.'

'Don't kid yourself, Dad, it will. Mum will give her—'

'Jennifer,' Linda said gently.

'Mum will give Jennifer a home, she will see it as her duty or she will have sleepless nights worrying about her.'

'I have something to say, I'm not finished,' Heather said.

'Hurry up then and say what you have to,' Matthew said, looking at the clock.

'There is a solution to this and a very easy one.' She stopped and looked at everyone.

'And what is this easy solution?'

'Dad, why didn't you think of it? You could have an extension built on the back of the house.'

'No.'

It was an emphatic no, but Heather went on.

'I could find out from Geraldine Grainger how much it would cost. They built one on for a playroom and it's super.'

'No,' Matthew repeated.

'OK, since you can't afford an extension I'll be very noble. Jennifer can share my bedroom but not my wardrobe, she will have to get one of her own.'

'Not a problem,' Linda smiled.

'I won't say I am going to like it but I am not selfish like someone I could name.' The sisters glared at each other.

Hannah did feel uncomfortable. She didn't see herself as being selfish. Rather she was being firm. One had to look out for oneself in this world, she told herself. She remembered her dad saying that and that was all she was doing.

Matthew had grunted something and left the room.

'The three of you can go upstairs and carry on with what you were doing.'

'What about the dishes?'

'I'm letting you both off, Heather. For this once I'll see to everything myself.'

'Great.' There was a noisy exodus.

Linda was taking a very long time to clear the table and to do the washing-up. It was deliberate and a way of keeping her in the kitchen. Enough had been said on the subject but she couldn't trust herself to keep quiet if she was sitting with Matthew.

Just before everything was tidied away Matthew popped his head round the door. 'You still at it, dear?'

'Finished now.'

'That was a mistake letting them off.'

'No, it wasn't and I didn't mind.'

'You wanted peace to do more thinking.'

'Perhaps.'

'Try and forget it and remember you do not have to get involved,' he said pointedly.

'I know, Matthew, but it doesn't seem to help.'

'I'm off to the garage. Just remembered I'm low on petrol and if I get a move on I'll be there before it closes.'

'On you go then.'

'Maybe I'll stop for a drink on the way back.'

'Good idea,' she smiled.

Matthew wasn't a regular at the local but he was probably feeling like a beer and a chat with whoever was there. Men didn't have to know each other to get in to conversation.

It was mid-September and they had been enjoying a particularly mild spell. In another week or two, or before that if the weather changed, the heating would have to go on. Radiators made for less work and were efficient. Fine for the rest of the house, Linda and Matthew agreed, but not for the sitting-room. They had retained the original fireplace and never regretted it. A coal fire topped with logs gave out a good heat and added the homely touch. Linda didn't grumble about the work involved though her sister, Helen, thought she was mad. She and George were more than happy with their stylish log-effect fire. Kirsty had her coal fire and agreed with Linda that there was nothing to beat the real thing.

In the sitting-room Linda sat back in the chair and closed her eyes. If she was honest with herself she was disappointed in Matthew. She saw him as being less than helpful. Why couldn't he have been decisive as he usually was? What she had been looking for from him was a definite yes, the girl can stay here, make her home with us, or an equally definite no, she cannot come, it is out of the question. Then she would have known where she stood. The matter would have been out of her hands. Only Matthew wasn't playing it that way. Like the girls he was seeing Jennifer as a threat to their family life but he wasn't coming right out and saying it. As far as Matthew was concerned this was his wife's problem and it was up to her to sort it out. What should she do? She was torn both ways. This girl, Betty's daughter and recently orphaned, needed her or needed someone. There was little doubt her need was greatest but the price to pay might be too high. They were a normal happy family who occasionally squabbled but nothing more serious than that. Jennifer was an unknown, how would she fit in?

Hannah was going to be a problem. Linda had expected some opposition but not this amount of hostility. Her elder daughter wasn't selfish by nature and she was acting out of character. Was she afraid? Did she see Jennifer as a threat to her own security? If so she was being very silly. There was enough love to go around, no one was being deprived. Linda adored her family and they must know that. She sighed at the enormity of the problem. If it were true that the girl had no one, what would happen to her? A foster home for a few years – some were good, some were not.

Linda and Matthew were in bed with the light out when Linda again brought up the subject.

'Matthew, what am I to do?'

'Go to sleep.'

'I can't, not with this on my mind.'

'Throw away the letter, pretend you didn't get it.'

'Matthew, be serious.'

'Maybe that is what I am being.' He drew her closer and she snuggled in. The warmth of his body was reassuring and as always when he was near, she felt safe and cherished. It was easier to talk in the darkness when faces were hidden. Expressions could give so much away. 'Seriously, darling,' he said after a pause, 'I think you are asking a lot of the kids. That is what they are, just kids, and they don't want their well-ordered life to change. This is a stranger, not someone they know. And not for a visit. If they weren't too happy with the visitor at least the end would be in sight.'

'You are making Jennifer sound like a monster.'

'We know nothing about her.'

'She is Betty's daughter.'

'She is also her father's daughter and you didn't think much of him. Sleep on it. Tomorrow is another day.'

'You don't want her to come here but you won't come right out and say it.'

'Is that what you want me to do? Linda, I am sorry for the girl, who wouldn't be, but face facts. Not a day goes by without a tragedy somewhere. If you want my suggestion . . .'

'You know I do.'

'Ring this solicitor in Inverness. Put him fully in the picture and I think he will agree that Jennifer is not your responsibility.'

'If I walk away, what will become of her?'

'She won't be abandoned. Qualified people will assess the situation and do what they think best. We don't know but there could be a bit of money . . .'

'Highly unlikely. Robert was quite often unemployed.'

'A solicitor is involved so there has to be something.'

'Robert's name wasn't mentioned, just Betty. Maybe her grandmother left money . . .'

'Darling, could we give it a rest. I do have to work tomorrow and I need some sleep.'

'Sorry.' She yawned. 'Before I ring the solicitor I'll get in touch with Mother.'

'Do that.' He turned away and in a few minutes she heard his steady breathing. As for Linda, sleep had never been further away.

3

As soon as she had the house to herself, Linda phoned her mother and the call was immediately answered.

'That was quick.'

'I was passing the phone when it rang. This is very early, Linda, what brings you on?'

'Mum, something has come up and I need your advice rather urgently and Helen's too.'

'Why, what has happened?' Kirsty said sharply.

'Nothing for you to worry about.'

'I doubt that when to me you sound to be in a bit of a state.'

'I am not,' Linda said trying to steady her voice, 'I just need advice.'

'Why not tell me what this is about?'

'Not over the phone. Mum, if you have nothing arranged how about coming here for coffee? When I ring off I'm going to phone Helen but the chances are she will be tied up.'

'Look, darling, I have a better idea. Why not come to me and let me phone Helen. Curiosity will very likely win the day and she'll cancel whatever it is she has arranged.'

Linda was smiling. 'You could be right. Thanks, Mum, I'll leave everything in your capable hands and believe it or not just talking to you has helped.'

Kirsty Cameron was thoughtful as she replaced the receiver. Linda wasn't the type to panic although panic was perhaps too strong a word. Anxious or worried would better describe it. Certainly she, herself, was worried. She phoned Helen.

'Mum, can't it wait? I'm on my way out.'

'You usually are or I've missed you. Linda is just off the phone, some sort of crisis, I gather, and she wants our advice – yours and mine.'

'What sort of crisis?'

'She didn't say.'

'Mum, she must have said something.'

'If she did I didn't hear it.'

'You don't think there is something wrong, I mean with their marriage? That would be a crisis.'

'No, I don't think that for a single moment. That is one very strong marriage.'

'I have to agree but one is always being surprised. Look at Bob and Janet . . .'

'I haven't time to look at Bob and Janet. Linda is coming to the cottage for coffee and you are invited, though I gather you won't manage.'

'It is very inconvenient but, as I always say, family first. I'll give my apologies and be right over. Anything you need? Shall I bring biscuits?'

'No, thank you, that won't be necessary. My cupboard is not completely bare. There is a sultana cake and some short-bread fingers I bought at the church sale on Saturday. Not as good as I make myself but they have to be eaten.'

'I'm curious, aren't you?'

'Yes, I am, Helen. I'm curious and worried.'

'Silly to worry until you know there is something to worry about.'

'We can't all be like you, Helen. Worry comes naturally to some of us. I'll ring off and you come when you are ready.' Kirsty put down the phone. It was kept on top of the bureau with a chair beside the bureau where she could sit if it was to be a lengthy call.

At sixty-five years of age, Kirsty Cameron was still an

attractive woman. Her face was lined, but she was comfortable with that. I look my age and what is wrong with that, she would say. Kirsty was most certainly not a hypochondriac, but she took care of herself so as not to be a burden to others. She tried to walk at least a mile a day and ate sparingly of nourishing food.

She kept her cottage neat and tidy and that required no great effort, a person on their own didn't make much dust. Kirsty would never have described herself as houseproud but she did have a routine, though she would think nothing of breaking it. The Hoover was taken round once a week and the bathroom and kitchen given a good clean. As for the rest of the week, a quick dust was all it got. Today it wasn't even going to get that. She had more important things on her mind.

It was at times like this when she wished that John was sitting in his armchair, smoking his pipe, and telling her to calm down. Kirsty missed him dreadfully but she hid her grief. What was the point of making others miserable? Grief should be private. It was five years since she had moved in to the cottage. Five years since she was widowed and it was about that time that the cottage in Sunnybank had come on the market. The home she had shared with her husband was much too big for one person. Much too big for an elderly couple but John had never shown any enthusiasm for moving. Not worth all the upheaval, better to stay put for as long as possible, he had said.

She often thought of John, even talked to him at times. He had been a quietly spoken, kindly man who had doted on his wife and daughters, his 'girls', as he called them. For John to lose his temper was rare, whereas Kirsty was quick to anger but her rage never lasted and she didn't harbour resentment. Theirs had been a good marriage built on love and respect. John had been ten years older than his wife and very protective. She hadn't always appreciated that but it was what she missed.

Linda and Helen arrived in their cars within minutes of each other and were chatting in the sitting-room while their mother busied herself in the kitchen. Their offer of assistance had been refused.

'I think I can manage, thank you. And, Linda, not a word about whatever it is until I am through.'

After a few minutes Kirsty arrived with the tray and Helen was on her feet to take it from her and put it on the sideboard. Linda set the coffee cups on the coffee table and Kirsty poured the coffee. The cake was offered, declined, and the three of them took a shortbread finger.

'Now, Linda, what is this all about?'

Linda bent down to take an envelope from her handbag. 'I want you to read this letter, Mum, then give it to Helen. When you have read it you will know as much about it as I do.'

'My spectacles.' Kirsty got up to look for them and found them on top of the television set. How they had got there she had no idea. She put them on and began to read the letter, taking her time. Then without a word handed it to Helen. Helen read it twice.

'What a dreadful thing to happen,' Helen said, putting the letter back in its envelope and returning it to Linda. 'I seem to recall meeting your friend, Betty, or there again maybe I am confusing—'

'You aren't. You did meet her once and Mum did several times.'

Kirsty was nodding. 'A nice girl and very pretty.'

'Yes.'

'And you are godmother to her daughter—'

'No, that was news to me. Not at any time did Betty ask me to be godmother to Jennifer. Heavens, Mum, we had lost touch and even when we did correspond it was only once in a blue moon. I wasn't at fault, I answered her letters after a few weeks.'

'You were definitely not asked?'

Linda almost choked on her shortbread. 'Not you as well, Helen. I've told you, and why should I lie? There was never any mention of godmother. Matthew has difficulty in believing me too,' she said bitterly.

'Sorry, I didn't mean it that way,' Helen said, patting her sister's hand. 'Only it does seem incredible, doesn't it, that she should give that information to her solicitor?'

Linda nodded miserably. 'It has put me in an intolerable situation, I don't know what to do.'

'I think I can see how it might have happened,' Kirsty said slowly. 'Correct me in case I have got this wrong. Did Betty run off with someone, break off her engagement?'

'She broke off her engagement but she didn't run off with Robert. Don't you remember, I had to go to the wedding on my own? Matthew broke his leg playing rugby.'

'Yes, it's coming back and as I started to say, I can see how it might have happened.' She paused. 'There are no close relatives, I gather?'

'No. Both Betty and Robert were only children.'

'Probably something said on the spur of the moment. Maybe the girl was distressed at the time, worried for the future or the future of her child. Who knows . . .'

'I suppose it could have been something like that.' Linda moistened her lips. 'Maybe I am wrong to feel some respon- sibility for Betty's child but I do. You see, had she asked me to be Jennifer's godmother I would have said yes.'

'But you weren't, Linda, and there lies the difference. You are not responsible for that girl's welfare.'

'What if I feel I am?'

'You shouldn't. Mum, that shortbread isn't bad,' she said, reaching for another piece and putting it on her plate.

'No, it isn't.'

'Linda?'

'Yes, Helen, what?'

'You are not seriously considering taking this girl into your home?'

'This girl, as you call her, has lost her parents in the most tragic of circumstances.'

'No one is disputing that. What about Matthew and the kids?'

'They wouldn't suffer.'

'How can you be so sure? You can't. In your place I would—'

'Walk away.'

'In a manner of speaking, yes. I wouldn't risk upsetting my own family. And you have to remember Betty was only a college friend.'

'My best friend.'

'We all had best friends when we were young,' she said dismissively, 'but that doesn't put us under any obligation.'

'I'm sorry but I think it does.'

'Do you think I could have my say?' Kirsty said mildly.

'Sorry, Mum,' Helen grinned. 'I'll shut up.'

'Would there be any money?'

'Why?' Linda raised her eyebrows.

'Just tell me.'

'I can't know for sure but I would have said it was highly improbable, Robert had difficulty holding down a job.'

'Must be a little when a solicitor is involved.'

'Maybe Betty's grandmother left her something. Mum, I don't see where this is leading.'

'I've forgotten, myself, for the moment.' The three of them laughed.

'How old is Jennifer?'

'She must be fifteen, Helen.'

'Heavens, I thought we were talking about a child. Fifteen-year-olds are just about grown up these days, especially girls.'

'In some ways, maybe. They do need someone to turn to.'

'True, I suppose. What is Matthew saying to all this and have you discussed it with the family?'

'Matthew is not being very helpful. He says it is up to me.'

'He isn't keen?'

'No.'

'And the family?'

'Oh, mixed.' Linda sighed. 'Hannah is being quite awful. She nearly hit the roof when I suggested that she and Heather could go back to sharing a bedroom.'

'You didn't? Heavens, no wonder she nearly hit the roof!' Helen sounded totally shocked. 'What right had you to ask that of them?'

'Every right, I would have thought. I am their mother.' Linda had flushed angrily.

'Now! Now! raised voices won't get us anywhere and I've remembered what I was going to say.' Kirsty paused to take a sip of coffee then replaced the cup on to its saucer. 'Should there be a bit of money the girl could finish her education at boarding-school. It would only be for a couple of years or so and you could have her for the holidays or part of them.'

Helen was nodding her head and Linda's face brightened but only for a moment.

'Mum, that was a brilliant suggestion and it would solve everything but sadly I am all but sure there won't be that kind of money.'

'Worth making enquiries and I imagine the solicitor would tell you. Why don't you phone to find out the true position.'

'Matthew said that and I will.'

'Phoning might not be all that satisfactory. Better to go and see him, talking face to face is so much easier. Would Matthew take time off to go with you?'

'I think it unlikely and to be honest I'm not sure that I would want him there.'

'How about me?'

'Would you come with me, Mum?'

'Of course, you silly girl. I might not be of much help but having company is better than being on your own.'

'That would be marvellous and you would be a big help and you know it. Thanks so much, I'll phone this solicitor when I get home to acknowledge his letter and make an appointment to see him. Have you any days I need to avoid?'

'Nothing I can't postpone – and you will have to fit in with him.'

'His secretary will deal with that,' Helen said knowingly. She paused to drain the rest of her coffee and declined more when asked. 'How will you go? The train journey is a nightmare, so many stops.'

'Helen, I have friends who go regularly to Inverness by train and I haven't heard them complain.'

Helen made a face as though to say, that is me told off.

'My car is dodgy, it's playing up . . .' Linda began.

'Mine isn't. We'll take it and share the wheel.' It was fortunate Kirsty didn't see the look that passed between her daughters.

'OK.'

'We'll have an overnight stay in some small hotel or guest-house. That way we won't have to rush around. Will the family cope without you for one night?'

'Very easily. Matthew can cook, although I would leave something that only needed heating up. The girls will do their bit and if Robin is home first he can stay with his friend's mother. I'll give Tessa a ring.'

Helen was looking at her neat little wrist-watch. Kirsty wondered how she could make out the time on such a small face. To her it was just a blur and, depressingly, another sign of advancing years.

'I really must dash, thanks for the coffee, Mum.' She smiled to Linda. 'You seem to have everything under control and, as you know, I am always there if I should be needed.'

'Where?' Linda grinned.

For a moment Helen looked put out. 'I admit to leading a busy life but if I am needed you can depend on me.'

'I know that, Helen, I wasn't being serious.'

Helen was on her feet and reaching for her handbag and car keys. She was a tall woman of a heavier build than her sister. Although never a slave to fashion she dressed stylishly. The skirt of her dark grey suit was narrow and being long legged she looked good in it. Linda thought her sister carried herself well.

'Keep me in the picture.'

'Of course,' Linda said, 'and thanks for coming.'

'OK if I tell George what is going on?'

'Of course, you didn't have to ask. Not the boys, though, wait until it happens.'

'Or doesn't,' Helen smiled as she opened the door.

Linda was putting the cups on the tray ready to take through to the kitchen. She stopped for a moment and looked at her mother.

'If I should decide to take Jennifer—'

'You are thinking too far ahead. This is a very big step for all concerned and it needs careful consideration.'

'I've done nothing else but think about it. There is just the chance that Jennifer may prefer to stay with this neighbour who has been looking after her. That way she wouldn't have to change schools and lose her friends.'

'In which case we can all breathe a sigh of relief.'

'That sounds so uncharitable, so unfriendly and I hope that we as a family are not that.'

'You aren't, my dear, but no one would think any worse of you and yours for wishing things to remain the same.'

'Nothing ever does.'

'True, but this would make a big upheaval in your lives.'

'Mum, it is just possible that we may have to bring Jennifer home with us. I mean, we don't want to make a return trip if that could be avoided.'

'I'm sure if Jennifer was met at the station she would manage the train journey on her own.'

'I suppose so.'

'You don't care for the idea?'

'No, I don't. We don't know what state she will be in. She wasn't badly hurt but what about the mental damage? It isn't easy to assess that.'

'Linda, Jennifer will have been examined by a specialist and we will find out about that when we go through. Leave the cups – I've all day.'

'Thanks, Mum, thanks for everything. Just as soon as I have something to report I'll be on the phone to you. What did I do with my car keys?'

'In your hand.'

'Oh, God, so they are. Good thing Helen isn't here.'

'It is. I often wonder how we managed to produce such an efficient and energetic daughter. She didn't get it from me or your father.'

'A throw-back.'

'Must be.'

4

The telephone call to Samuel Brady, the solicitor in Inverness, had been disappointing. Linda had chosen a particularly busy time and there had been no opportunity for a talk and a chance to ask questions. They would talk at length when she came through to Inverness. Mr Brady was soft-spoken and very polite. He would be delighted to see her in his office and his secretary would arrange a day and a time to suit. The call was returned to his secretary who sounded extremely efficient. The appointment was made for Wednesday of the following week at three thirty.

Linda was glad of the few days. She felt there was more time needed to discuss the matter. Matthew was heartily sick of the subject. He had worries at work and could do without coming home to more.

'Matthew, I know you have other things on your mind but this isn't going to go away. I mean I can't just ignore a call for help.'

'If that is what it is.' They were having coffee after their meal. It was their time for relaxing and discussing what had to be discussed. Only it was no longer relaxing and the subject never changed.

'Darling, you haven't thought this through.'

'I thought I had.'

Maybe this was the time to put his foot down. Maybe he should have done it before instead of leaving it to his wife and hoping she would make the sensible decision. He should have known she was too soft-hearted.

'I am not hard-hearted and an extra mouth to feed is nothing.'

She smiled. Matthew was coming round, he hadn't wanted to be rushed that was all. 'Matthew, you are anything but hard-hearted.'

'In this case I can't afford to be soft. You see I am thinking ahead. We have our own three to educate and I have high hopes for them.'

'So have I. We have three bright children,' Linda said proudly.

'We want to do our best for them . . .'

Linda was frowning, her coffee forgotten. 'Matthew, where is this leading?'

'I'll tell you where it is leading. You will agree, I think, that we have a reasonable standard of living, but we are by no means well off.'

'Yes, I know that.'

He rubbed his hands over his face and sighed. 'If we were to take this girl into our home, am I expected to fork out for her education? When I say education, I mean further education. When she leaves school.'

'She is fifteen. We wouldn't have to consider that for a year or two.'

'That isn't long.'

'She could leave and get a job in an office or something.'

'She could. What if she turns out to be bright, bright enough for university?'

'Couldn't we cross that bridge when we come to it?'

'No, we need to think about it now.'

'There could be a little money.'

'You must ask. You have that right if we are to take her.'

'This makes us sound so mean.'

'It does not.'

'If there is nothing, can't we apply to some authority or somewhere?' Linda said vaguely.

'I have no doubt we could but I don't want that.'

'You don't want Jennifer.'

'That is right. I don't,' he said tersely.

'Had you said so at the beginning we could have avoided all this. It isn't too late. I'll phone Inverness and cancel the appointment.'

'No, don't do that. Find out what there is to find out. Arrangements may have already been made. You can satisfy yourself that all is well.'

She nodded. 'I would like to meet Betty's daughter.'

'Then do so.'

'She could spend a holiday with us if she wished.'

'Certainly, I have no problem with that.'

It had been Kirsty's suggestion that she time her arrival at Linda's house for shortly after eight thirty and her daughter had gone along with that. By then the children would have left for school and Matthew for the office.

Wednesday saw Kirsty up bright and early. She liked to give herself plenty of time and she also liked to have a plan and work to it. After a breakfast of a soft boiled egg and toast and two cups of tea she cleared the table and washed the dishes. That done and the dishes put away in the cupboard, she made the bed, gave a quick tidy and returned to the kitchen to prepare a flask of coffee for the journey. She remembered to put out sugar and milk. There was a small bottle kept for the purpose and Kirsty filled it or almost filled it with milk, then twisted the top on as tight as she could. As for sugar, Kirsty had a supply. The sugar lumps came from various coffee houses where one's allowance was usually put on the saucer. Kirsty would drop the surplus lumps into her handbag for occasions such as now. She buttered four pieces of gingerbread and placed them in a Tupperware box and from the cupboard she stretched up for a packet of custard creams. If neither of them felt like a biscuit they would do for the return journey.

Linda might be annoyed and consider it a waste of time but she would insist that they stop somewhere for a decent lunch. Then after it they would take a short walk and get some fresh air into their lungs.

Kirsty wanted to look presentable to meet this solicitor. She had the feeling he would be middle-aged and one of the old school who dressed in a dark suit with a white shirt, or maybe a striped one, and a sober tie. She thought that her coffee and cream jersey two-piece would do very nicely. It was warm without being bulky, it didn't crush, which was a big plus, and she felt comfortable in it.

A glance out of the window showed her that the weather was in their favour although that, of course, could change very suddenly and one had to be prepared. Her raincoat and umbrella would go on the back seat of the car. Kirsty gathered everything together and left them in the hall near to the front door. Together with her overnight bag was the small picnic basket which had come in so useful. Helen had bought it for her mother's Christmas and Kirsty had remarked rather tactlessly that it was a welcome change from the usual gifts of scarves, gloves and boxes of handkerchiefs. She had a drawerful of those.

When she was dressed and ready for the journey, Kirsty opened the cottage door. The air was wonderfully fresh and she breathed in deeply. Then she noticed that there were several weeds in the garden and bent down to pull them out. How quickly they appeared, she could have sworn that none had been there yesterday. Her gardener, who was only an odd-job man with a little knowledge of gardening, had pointed out to her that a few of her rose bushes, mainly her Queen

Elizabeths, were past their best and she should think about replacing them. She supposed that he was right. They would be old, they had been planted by the previous owner and possibly she'd had them for a considerable time. Kirsty promised herself that she would do something about it but not yet. Maybe in another year. There had been quite a good show of roses, though admittedly the display hadn't been up to the standard of previous years.

She went back into the house and picking up her overnight bag walked down the path and put it in the boot of the car which had been left at the gate overnight. Then returning she collected the rest and was on the point of locking up the cottage when she remembered her shoes and dashed to the bedroom for her brown courts. How awful if she had forgotten those. She looked down at her feet, at the shabby moccasins which she kept for the car since she was troubled with swollen feet on long journeys. They would have done nothing for her outfit and she would have been embarrassed. Linda and Helen, too, would have seen the funny side. They would have said, who was going to look at her feet? And they would have been wrong. She could remember, long ago, her own mother saying that one could tell what kind of person someone was by noting the footwear. Unpolished, shabby shoes showed the owner to be a slovenly person.

The windows were shut, the door was locked, the brown court shoes on the back seat and she was ready to set out for Linda's house. She parked in the cul-de-sac in front of Hillcrest. Turning the car in a confined space was awkward and Kirsty left that manoeuvre to Linda.

Linda waved from the doorway that she was ready and Kirsty got out of the driving seat and went round to the passenger side. She watched her daughter put a small case in the boot and throw her raincoat on to the back seat. Unlike her mother Linda hadn't given much thought to clothes.

Kirsty thought her lucky, she could look well without making any effort. The grey skirt and long red cardigan was what she would wear to do the shopping.

'Mum, you are looking very elegant,' she said as she slid into the driving seat.

'I like to go to a little trouble.'

'Meaning I don't,' she grinned.

'Not at all, you will pass. It is when you come to my age that one has to go to more trouble. I'm so glad it isn't raining, I do so hate the wipers going. Mine have started to make a grating noise, I should have seen to it but I forgot.'

Linda made a three-point turn effortlessly and they were on their way.

'The forecast is good for the east and the whole of the north so we should be all right. I missed it but Matthew was listening.'

Linda was a good driver and she enjoyed being behind the wheel. She had, however, never mastered the art of map reading and freely admitted to being a rotten navigator. Matthew, manlike, considered himself to be an expert in both. He was a great believer in share and share alike, or so he said. It didn't apply to everything, it didn't apply to driving. Matthew was not prepared to hand over the wheel of the car to his wife. It made him nervous, he said. On family outings she would be seated in the passenger seat with a map spread over her knees and a baffled expression on her face. Tempers would become frayed when they were on an unfamiliar route and it became obvious that they had taken a wrong turning. Matthew would look for a suitable place to stop, snatch the map from his wife's knees and mutter about the hopelessness of women and their total inability to read a simple map. All this was greatly enjoyed by the back-seat passengers. The children welcomed anything that helped to pass a tedious journey.

Linda pulled out to overtake a lorry, its heavy load covered by a yellow tarpaulin that flapped in the light wind.

'Do we need to go at this speed?' Kirsty said nervously. 'Helen is the same, you are too impatient the pair of you.'

Linda thought, here we go. 'Mum, we don't want to be stuck behind that thing. There was absolutely no danger, no risk. I saw my chance and took it. I suppose you would have been happy to stay behind it and let others overtake.' She tried not to sound exasperated.

'Yes, as a matter of fact I would have been perfectly happy to stay behind. The lorry was going at a fair lick and let me remind you, Linda, I do obey the Highway Code. I would have left enough space behind the lorry to accommodate an overtaking car,' she said primly.

Linda grinned. Her mother's driving was a family joke.

Kirsty opened the glove compartment in front of her and rummaged around until she found the tube of Rowntree's fruit gums. She opened the end of the packet and squeezed one up.

'Want one?'

'Yes, please, but make it two.' Linda put out her hand and Kirsty dropped two into it.

'Thanks, I quite like these and I always forget to buy them for the journey.'

They were silent for a few minutes.

'The car should give you no trouble.'

'It's running well.'

'It should. I got the garage to check everything and there is a full tank of petrol.'

'Fine, that saves us having to stop.'

'I can't recall when last it had a good run.'

'This will do the car good. I think that is the trouble with mine. All it gets are short journeys. The garage suggests a decent run once in a while.'

Kirsty looked out at the scenery. In a few short weeks the leaves would be beginning to fall from the trees. She liked the lovely shades of autumn but always felt it to be a sad season. The passing of summer and winter just ahead.

'Linda, you are not worrying are you?'

'Of course I'm worrying, Mum. It is all I have been doing.'

'You shouldn't have been landed with this.'

'I know.'

'Don't do anything silly. If you take her and it doesn't work out . . .'

'I'll be stuck with her.' Linda began to laugh.

'I can't imagine what is amusing.'

'I'm sorry, Mum, it just reminded me of something Robin said.'

Kirsty smiled. She adored her grandson and knew the little lad to come out with something hilariously funny and be utterly amazed when everybody fell about laughing.

'What did my little darling have to say?'

'He wondered if we could send Jennifer back if we didn't like her.'

Kirsty laughed. 'If only it were so simple. The wee soul has hit the nail on the head and that is what you have to remember, Linda. There is no turning back. Taking the girl is a commitment.'

'I know. Away from the house I seem to be able to think more clearly. I am asking too much of my family and I have all but decided to step back. If it would help, and Jennifer wishes it, we could keep in touch.'

Kirsty felt an overwhelming sense of relief. Linda was beginning to see sense. This trip hadn't been necessary or maybe it was. Linda wouldn't be happy until she met Betty's daughter and satisfied herself that she was all right and that the neighbour or someone else would take care of her. In this day and age there were kindly people who would take charge.

'Yes, dear, and that is all that can be expected of you.' She paused. 'In half an hour we will look for a lay-by. I brought a flask of coffee and gingerbread.'

'You shouldn't have bothered. We could have gone in somewhere for a quick coffee.'

'We can stop for lunch . . .'

'No, Mum, a snack yes, lunch no. I want to get on. We are making good time but that could change if we meet road-works.'

'Linda, we are stopping for a proper lunch and that is an end to it,' Kirsty said in the tone of voice she had used when they were children. 'If you are going to be awkward I shall insist you take a rest and I take over the driving. You will remember it is my car?'

'Blackmail,' Linda muttered.

'Yes, if that is what it takes.'

'OK, you win, lunch it is.'

Kirsty smiled to herself. She usually managed to get her own way.

'Damn! That tractor has just come out and on this single carriageway we haven't a hope of passing.'

'Then relax and stop banging your hand on the wheel. No doubt he is only going to the next farm and will be disappearing before long. There, what did I tell you, he is signalling to go left.'

'Thank heaven for that.' Linda acknowledged the signal, smiled and in a little while they were doing a steady fifty.

Kirsty was looking for a stopping place. There weren't many on this road and the one they passed was already occupied.

'Linda, slow down, this could be one we are coming to.'

'There is no sign to indicate it is.'

'That doesn't matter, there looks to be plenty of room.'

'You could be right,' Linda said, slowing down then signal-ling her intention.

'Coffee in the open air, is there anything quite like it?'

Linda raised her eyes to the sky before opening the boot and taking out the old tartan car rug and spreading it over the grass. She loved her mother dearly but at times she could be a real trial. Linda knew what it would be. Lunch as near to twelve thirty as possible then a walk to stretch the legs. It was exasperating but better to give in.

The coffee was very welcome and so was the gingerbread. There was a coolish breeze but it was pleasant to sit outside, though not for too long.

'That was lovely, Mum,' Linda said as she turned her cup upside down and emptied the last few drops on to the grass.

'Yes, I enjoyed it too and I feel quite refreshed. I'm afraid you'll have to haul me up,' Kirsty said, holding out her hand.

Linda did, but not without difficulty.

'What happened to the picnic chairs?'

'They take up a lot of room in the boot so I didn't bother.'

Linda folded up the tartan rug and Kirsty packed everything away in the picnic basket. Before getting back in the car Kirsty took a look around.

'Nothing left. We have cleared up behind us. What a pity everybody doesn't do that. What a difference it would make.'

'I agree but sadly it won't happen. A perfect world, we aren't going to live in that.'

'I'm not looking for perfection, I don't think I would want that. What I would like to see is consideration for other people.'

'Yes, well, here we go, are you all set?'

'I'm fine. I gather you want to do all the driving?' Kirsty smiled.

'Yes, Mum. This is a change for me. Matthew does all the long journeys.'

'I know, dear, your father was the same. He wasn't a very good driver, but he thought he was.'

Linda grinned. She remembered a few near misses with none of them her father's fault.

'Mum, start paying attention, will you?' Linda said as they reached the outskirts of Inverness. 'How do we get to this guest-house or don't you know?'

'I know it is fairly central which was why I chose it.' Kirsty had taken the brochure from her handbag and was discovering that the print was too small. She would need her spectacles. She got them out of their case and put them on. 'Here we are,' she said, preparing to read it aloud. 'The Laurel Guest-house blah, blah, blah, is very conveniently situated being only five minutes walking distance from the centre of town.' She peered above her spectacles. 'Mind you, I don't set much store by their five minutes. More like double that unless one went like the clappers.'

'Mum, stop exaggerating.'

'I'm not. Think of all the holiday hotels that advertise themselves as being close to the beach when in fact it is a long walk, especially so for a mother with little tots.'

'You didn't by any chance buy a map of Inverness, did you?'

'Never thought about it. I've a good tongue in my head and we can stop someone and ask for directions.'

'We'll have to, I haven't a clue where we are going. You were here with Dad.'

'That was a very long time ago and there will have been lots of changes since then. What I do recall is a very pretty town with lots of flowers everywhere and lovely walks. One in particular sticks in my mind. Your father and I used to walk along by the river bank – the River Ness – you see there is nothing wrong with my memory,' she said proudly.

'No, there isn't. We'll ask this woman coming along with her shopping basket. She'll be local and likely to know.' Linda slowed down, wound down the window and called to the woman who was almost alongside the car.

'Excuse me, I wonder if you could help us?'

She came over, her face wreathed in smiles. 'Lost, are you?'

'We are looking for the Laurel Guest-house, do you happen to know it?'

'I do and you are going the right way. Keep on this road then turn left at the second opening. You'll find The Laurels half-way along.'

'Thank you very much.'

'Glad to be of help. Finding your way in a strange town isn't easy. Enjoy your stay,' she added.

'What a very nice woman,' Kirsty said when they were on their way. 'It makes such a difference when folk are pleasant.'

The Laurel Guest-house had a particularly nice frontage and stood out from the other large houses, all of which at one time had been family homes. The difficulty in getting servants had changed all that. Young women had more opportunities open to them and were less willing to take on the drudgery which had been the lot of the maid for so long. The result was that people were being forced to move to smaller houses and the big ones were being bought over to be turned into boarding houses or guest-houses.

Linda switched off the engine and for a few minutes they looked out of the window. The garden was on a slope and probably because of that it had been made into a rockery. Huge stones that looked to weigh a ton were covered with rock plants of every kind and ferns and other greenery grew between the stones.

'This looks very nice, Mum,' Linda said as she made a move to get out.

'I've chosen well, have I?'

'Too early to say but certainly by the outside appearance.'

Tubs of colourful plants were at either side of the heavy door which was wide open and held that way by a solid-looking brass figure.

Linda had opened the boot and from it taken the overnight bags. Kirsty had gone on ahead and was holding open the glass door until Linda, a bag in one hand and a case in the other, was inside. The hall was surprisingly large and it had a reception area. Linda was about to press down on the bell when a woman came from the back premises and took up a position behind the desk. She was well built, of medium height with cropped auburn hair and to Kirsty she looked to be of a similar age to Linda. She wore a green, wrap-over skirt and an oatmeal, crew-necked jumper.

'Good afternoon, ladies, how can I help you?' she smiled.

Kirsty took over. 'I'm Mrs Cameron and I telephoned to book a room for myself and my daughter.'

The woman dropped her eyes to the book. 'Yes, here we are, a twin-bedded room.'

'Yes.' Single rooms might have suited Linda better, Kirsty thought after she had made the booking, but why waste money when it was for one night only?

'I'll show you to your room,' the woman said as she stretched over to the board and took a key from its hook. 'Allow me.' She took the case from Linda and led the way. 'Did you have a good journey?' she asked, turning her head.

'Yes, very pleasant, the roads weren't too busy.'

They followed her up a thickly carpeted stair and then along a passageway. Kirsty breathed in the faint perfume of air freshener. After passing several doors the woman stopped at one and using the key unlocked the door. The window was open by a few inches and the white net curtains stirred in the breeze. As well as net curtains there were lined floral ones which would be closed at night.

'I'll shut the window. That, I think, should be enough fresh air. I'm sorry, I should have introduced myself, I'm Mrs Sinclair and my husband and I took over The Laurels about two years ago.'

'Are you doing well?' Kirsty asked as Linda wandered over to the window to look out at the view. There wasn't much to see. It was mostly grass cut short and there were toys scattered around which made Linda think the owner had a young family. In a corner, near to a garden shed, there was washing flapping on the line. It was mostly sheets and pillowcases but Linda could see two tiny pyjama suits and various other items of children's wear. Looking beyond the garden one could see the outline of hills in the distance.

'We are doing quite well and we shouldn't complain,' Mrs Sinclair said in answer to Kirsty's question. 'Mind you, if we had to depend on holidaymakers we couldn't survive. The season is so short and we are at the mercy of the weather. If the sun is shining, Inverness looks very inviting and tourists will stop for one night, maybe two.'

'If it is raining they keep on going,' Kirsty said sympathetically.

'I'm afraid so. With us being so close to the centre and yet cut off from the noise, we do get our share of businessmen and representatives. Some have become regulars so, as I said, we can't complain.'

Linda turned back from the window. 'The toys – you have a young family?'

'Yes. They have the freedom of the back garden but they know what is out of bounds. My guests never see them, I make sure of that. I'm not saying they are badly behaved, and they are no worse than anyone else's.'

'I'm sure they aren't,' Kirsty smiled.

'Not everyone likes children, Mrs Cameron, and we want to keep everyone happy. We have to if we want them to return and now let me tell you about breakfast. We start serving at seven thirty but there is no hurry. Come down when you are ready. Some of our guests like to get off to an early start.'

'Between eight thirty and nine would suit us, wouldn't it, Mum?'

'Yes.'

'That's fine and, as I say, come down when you are ready. The bathroom is next door and if there is anything you want, please don't hesitate to ask.'

'Maybe you could tell us how we get to Paterson & Watson, the solicitors,' Linda asked.

'Paterson & Watson? It isn't far but I would advise you to leave the car. Parking is a problem in the town and it is getting worse.'

'Like everywhere else. We will leave the car and use our legs.'

Mrs Sinclair gave them instructions. 'You shouldn't have any problem finding it but before you go out collect a map from the desk. You might find it helpful.'

'I'm sure we will, many thanks.'

The woman went away closing the door behind her and Kirsty and Linda had a look at the room.

'You know, Linda, I do like this. Everything is so clean and fresh and when I see that I know the kitchen will be the same.'

'A bit olde worlde, isn't it?' Linda smiled.

'Part of its charm.'

The single beds had white candlewick covers. Beside each was a bedside cabinet and a lamp with a pretty shade and bobble fringes. The wardrobe was very big but they would not be using it. Not for one night. The kidney-shaped dressing-table was covered with a crochet mat which for Kirsty brought back memories. Her own mother much preferred to spend her evenings with a crochet hook rather than knitting needles. She had tried to interest her daughter but without success. Kirsty fell heir to a huge supply when they had gone out of fashion. Helen had persuaded her mother to get rid of the lot and they had gone to a sale of work where they would be sold and the money received go to a good cause. Helen bought her mother lace covers to take their place.

'I rather wish I had hung on to mine.'

'That was Helen, don't blame me.'

'I wasn't, and the fault was mine for allowing myself to be persuaded.'

'If you want to freshen up you had better get a move on.'

'Yes, of course, I was forgetting the time. I'll go first.' She collected her sponge bag and disappeared.

Linda took what she required from her case then sat down in one of the comfortable chairs. She wondered what she was doing here and why she had thought it necessary. Only she hadn't when she thought about it. Matthew had decided she wouldn't be happy until she knew that all was well with Betty's daughter.

When they set off for Paterson & Watson, Linda had gone quiet and Kirsty noticed.

'No use getting yourself all tensed up.'

'I'm not.'

'You are here, Linda, because of the letter and your need to explain the situation face to face. A written reply would not have been very satisfactory,' she said firmly.

'I know all that but I can't help feeling nervous. Thank goodness I have you, Mum.'

'We explain the situation and that is all that will be necessary.'

'I hope so but I have a horrible feeling that it isn't going to be that easy.'

5

Linda and her mother had decided that twenty-five minutes would give them ample time to reach their destination since Mrs Sinclair had assured them they could do it comfortably in fifteen. They also decided it was better to arrive a few minutes early rather than rushing in at the last minute. When they set out the sun had gone behind the clouds and the air was fresh and cool. Inverness town centre was busy with shoppers but there wasn't the frantic rushing around one found in so many other towns. Here it was more relaxed and it was pleasant walking about and glancing at the window displays. Nice if there had been more time to linger and perhaps be tempted to buy.

'Going by the directions we should be nearly there,' Kirsty said.

'I think we are. According to the numbers that big building just ahead could be it. Yes, I'm right,' Linda said a few moments later.

'Very impressive,' Kirsty remarked when they got near enough to read the brass plates. 'At one time this must have been a beautiful mansion house and then converted into offices. Shame really.'

'Sign of the times, Mum. Not many folk can keep up that style.'

They went up the stone steps and entered a large entrance hall. Paterson & Watson, solicitors, had their offices on the ground floor.

'That's a relief, no stairs to climb.'

'I thought you were hobbling a bit. Poor you, have you got sore feet?'

'No, Linda, I do not have sore feet, it is not long since I paid a visit to the chiropodist. What I do have is slightly swollen ankles after sitting so long in the car. They will come all right.'

'Why didn't you keep on your old shoes?' Linda asked, though she knew the answer.

'And look a mess, certainly not.'

'Pride comes before a fall.'

'Pay attention, what do we do? Knock or what?'

'If the door is unlocked we go in.' Linda turned the knob and the door opened. As they went in a glass panel slid sideways from what appeared to be a reception-cum-office. A head appeared.

'Yes?'

'I have an appointment with Mr Brady.'

'And you are?'

'Mrs Linda Chalmers.'

'Your appointment is for three thirty.'

'Yes.'

'Mr Brady is with a client at the moment. If you would take a seat in the waiting-room I'll let you know when he is free.'

'Thank you.'

'The waiting-room is to your left.' The smile had been long in coming but when it did it lit up her rather plain face.

The glass panel slid back and they went along to the waiting-room which was unoccupied. It was a small drab room and the oblong table took up most of the floor space. On it were several ancient-looking magazines and an empty ashtray. Four high-backed wooden chairs were arranged hard against the wall and they went over to claim two.

'I sincerely hope we are not kept waiting long,' Kirsty said with what sounded like a sniff. 'What a dreary, depressing place and look at those curtains. I wouldn't insult a jumble sale with them.'

'Stop it, Mother. It's a waiting-room and it serves the purpose.'

'Clients deserve better than this.'

'It could be worse.'

'Not much. When do you think that window was last cleaned?'

'I don't know and what is more I do not care. You are the limit, Mother, now will you stop it?'

'No, I won't, this helps to pass the time.'

Linda smiled. There were times when her mother could be more exasperating than a child.

'I know what you are thinking.'

'Do you?'

'Yes, outspokenness is—'

'Acceptable from a senior citizen,' Linda interrupted. 'It is not, the same rules apply to you as to the rest of us.'

'Kirsty, that is you told off.'

'As regards the windows, the likelihood is that the whole building will have a contract with a firm of window cleaners.'

'High time they were putting in an appearance.'

The door opened quietly. 'Mr Brady will see you now.'

'Thank you.' They got up and followed her.

When they were shown in to his office, Samuel Brady got to his feet and came from behind the desk to shake hands. He was a portly man.

'Mr Brady, this is my mother, Mrs Cameron,' Linda said.

'How do you do, Mrs Cameron, did you have a good journey?' he asked with a smile.

'Yes, thank you, it was very pleasant.'

'Please be seated, ladies.' He indicated two chairs positioned so as to be facing him when he was behind the desk.

Kirsty had been studying the solicitor and thought him to be in his middle or late fifties. He was well dressed. His wife, she thought, took good care of him, he had that look. The charcoal grey suit was tailored to fit and had been recently pressed. She couldn't see his feet but Kirsty imagined him to be wearing black, highly polished leather shoes. Advancing years had brought with them a slight paunch and a receding hairline.

So much for the man. She dismissed him for the moment and gave her attention to the office. In sharp contrast to the dreary waiting-room no expense had been spared here. The office was high ceilinged with moulded cornices and was spacious. The wall-to-wall carpeting was deep crimson and of top quality. A cream embossed paper covered the walls and on one hung a painting of a harbour scene. Another had floor-to-ceiling bookcases with glass doors, the shelves filled with mostly leatherbound books. A table in the corner had bundles of files on it with an overflow on the floor. Dominating the office was the handsome desk placed to get maximum light from the double window and on it was an open file which Mr Brady appeared to have been studying or consulting. There were twin upright pen stands and a flat marble stand. Beside the telephone was a notepad. What took Kirsty's interest was the framed photograph only the back of which could be seen by the client. Kirsty longed to turn it round. She felt sure it would be a family photo. Her son-in-law, George, had one of Helen and the two boys on his desk in the office. Helen had said jokingly that it was there to remind him he had a wife and family at home. George was a workaholic.

Mr Brady was talking in a low voice that had Kirsty straining to hear. There wasn't much wrong with her hearing but she did wish that people would speak up and not drop their voice at the end as though the strength had gone from it.

'Such a dreadful tragedy,' he was saying in a hushed voice. 'This must have come as a terrible shock to you, Mrs Chalmers.'

'It was a shock,' Linda said quietly, 'as was the letter I received from you. Betty – Mrs Marshall – was a college friend, but we had lost touch a long time ago.'

He nodded. 'It happens. We are all guilty of it but good friends are friends for life, as they say.' His eyes dropped to the file and the spectacles slid down his nose. After a moment he looked up. 'Are you to be staying in Inverness for a few days or must you return home today?'

'We are staying overnight.'

'Fine.'

Linda wondered why it should be fine and what difference it would make to Mr Brady whether or not they stayed in Inverness overnight.

'I say fine because there is someone very anxious to make your acquaintance.'

'You mean Jennifer?'

'The daughter? No, although I have no doubt she is. I speak of Mrs McDonald, the kindly neighbour who, when there was no one else, took the girl into her home and cared for her.' He waited for Linda to say something and when she didn't he continued. 'The woman is becoming very concerned and has phoned this office several times to find out if I had heard from you.'

'Why should she do that?'

'Because, Mrs Chalmers, she is one very worried woman and there is some anger too which under the circumstances is hardly surprising.'

Linda was shaking her head. 'I can't see what this has to do with me.'

'Mrs McDonald is booked to go to New Zealand, where she has family. As she has said more than once, she did her Christian duty but she did not expect to be landed with the girl. That was her own expression, I hasten to add.' He sighed. 'The woman hates the thought of the girl going into care until such time as her education is finished and she is able to look after herself. Sadly that might well be the case. And that, ladies, is the position.' He leaned back in his swivel chair.

Linda was looking distressed and Kirsty thought there were a few matters they ought to get straight.

'Mr Brady,' Kirsty said firmly, 'my daughter tried to explain the situation to you over the telephone but you didn't have the time to listen.'

'Time is in short supply and telephone conversations, I find, are not always satisfactory. One needs to come face to face.'

Kirsty nodded. 'There seems to be some misunderstanding. My daughter is in no way responsible for this unfortunate child and I am at a loss to understand why this Mrs McDonald should think she is.'

'No relatives have come forward and your daughter's name is the only one mentioned.'

'That doesn't mean anything.'

'Legally it doesn't, I agree.'

'Are you suggesting that my daughter is responsible in some other way?'

'That is something for your daughter to decide.' The man shrugged. 'One makes promises that perhaps one wishes one hadn't. I am, of course, referring to the fact that the late Mrs Marshall named your daughter as her child's godmother.'

'And this is where it all goes wrong, Mr Brady,' Linda came in quickly. 'I was never asked to be godmother to Betty's daughter. The matter was never brought up.'

'Then why—?'

'I can't answer that. Her intention may have been to ask me, it must have been that, but she never got round to it.'

'I see. I see,' he said thoughtfully. 'This is indeed very awkward for you.'

'I feel desperately sorry for Jennifer, Mr Brady, but I have a husband and a family to consider and they must come first.'

'Of course.'

'May I ask you something, Mr Brady?'

'By all means, Mrs Cameron.'

'Is there any money?'

Linda looked shocked and the solicitor startled.

'I only ask because should there be enough the girl could finish her education at boarding-school and possibly spend some of the holidays with my daughter. They don't all cost the earth, do they?'

He smiled. 'There is very little money and certainly not enough to cover boarding-school fees.'

'What about the house?' Kirsty wasn't easily put off, 'Wouldn't that fetch something?'

'The house in question is rented. I see that the rent has been paid until the end of this month and then it will have to be cleared of furniture.'

'Who does that?'

'We can see to it.' He sounded weary, which he was. The solicitor had had a trying day and the sooner this matter was settled the better he would be pleased. Mrs McDonald had his sympathy but she was becoming a nuisance. As for these two ladies, he had some sympathy for them too. The younger woman was in a difficult position. He rather thought that she would like to take responsibility for her friend's daughter but was afraid to in case it caused problems at home. Idly he wondered what his own wife would do if she should be placed in similar circumstances. No, he didn't have to wonder. Marjory would have the good sense not to get involved.

'Could I perhaps suggest that you go and see Mrs McDonald and meet the girl?' He closed the file and got up to indicate that the time allotted to them was up.

Linda got quickly to her feet and Kirsty more slowly.

'Yes, I think we should do that, Mother.' Then turning to Mr Brady, 'Is it far, do you know? I've left the car in Forest Road.'

'If you prefer to leave the car where it is, a bus will take you there. My secretary is knowledgeable about buses and she will keep you right. Excuse me.' He went to open the door next to his and they heard voices. A small, grey-haired woman in a tweed skirt and a pale blue twinset came into the hall. She looked very efficient.

'I'll leave you with Miss McNab. She will give you all the information you need.' His hand shot out. They shook hands and then he was gone.

'You wish to know how to get to Glen Road?'

'If that is where Mrs McDonald lives, yes.'

'Number twenty-eight Glen Road is the address. I've written it down for you. It is very easy to forget an address.' She handed Linda a slip of paper. 'I suppose one could say it is walking distance from here but it is a fair step and most of it is uphill.'

'The bus or some form of transport,' Kirsty said hastily.

'The bus would be best. It passes the end of Glen Road and from there it is a short walk. Several buses go in that direction so be sure to ask before you get on.'

'We will and tell me, please, where is the bus stop?' Linda asked.

'Turn left and you will see it.'

'Thank you, you have been very helpful.'

'All part of the service,' she smiled and left them to return to her office.

'Mum, did you get the feeling that we had overstayed our welcome? I don't mean he was rude, he wasn't.'

'No, he wasn't but he didn't want to spend any more time on this particular case.'

'Not enough in it for him?'

'I didn't say that, though it could well be. The fact is there isn't much he can do. Jennifer is nothing to do with him. His job is to wind up Betty's affairs.'

They were silent for a few moments.

'I am not looking forward to this next bit, Mum. I've got a funny feeling in my stomach.'

'A sick feeling? So have I.'

'I wish none of this was happening,' Linda said wretchedly. 'We shouldn't have come to Inverness, it was a mistake. A letter could have said all I needed to say. Matthew was right.'

'A bit late in the day for those thoughts.'

'Matthew wasn't against me coming to Inverness, in fact he was in favour. He thought I would be happier if I met Jennifer and satisfied myself that she was all right.'

'Isn't that all we are doing?'

'No, not any more. I thought, deep down, that this neighbour would go on caring for Jennifer. That there would be some money so that she wasn't out of pocket.'

'No chance of that now, not with the woman going off to New Zealand.'

'This bus coming might do us. Come on, hurry.'

'Does this take us to Glen Road?' Linda asked the driver.

'We pass the end of Glen Road.'

They got on and Linda paid the fares.

'I'll give you a shout when we get there.'

'Thank you.'

The bus was well filled and they had to take separate seats.

Glen Road turned out to be a rather shabby thoroughfare with terraced houses down both sides. Some of the small front gardens were well kept and others were overgrown and badly neglected.

'We are looking for number twenty-eight,' Kirsty said, referring to the piece of paper she had taken from Linda.

'A bit to go, about halfway down, I reckon.'

When they arrived at number twenty-eight they were relieved to see it was well looked after. The grass was cut and the edges trimmed and there was a border of flowers. The brass nameplate was polished and showed the name McDonald.

'We've come to the right house.' Linda took a deep breath and rang the bell. In a few moments it was answered by a stout, homely looking woman.

'Mrs McDonald?' Linda asked in a questioning voice.

'Yes, I am Mrs McDonald.' She wheezed as she spoke.

'Mr Brady suggested we call. I am Linda Chalmers and this is my mother, Mrs Cameron.'

'Come away in. You are very welcome.'

They stepped into a narrow passageway with doors leading off and a carpeted stair to the right of entering.

'We'll go along to the sitting-room.' She led the way to a square-shaped, average size room. There was a three-piece suite in moquette with the settee facing the coal fire which was not lit but was ready to put a match to. There were four plump cushions with matching embroidered covers, one for each chair and two for the settee. An old-fashioned piano with its equally old-fashioned piano stool took up a lot of space. There was a sheet of music on the stand. 'Do sit down.'

'Thank you.' Kirsty sat on the settee and Linda joined her.

'Jennifer is doing some shopping for me. She shouldn't be long but this will give us a chance to talk.'

'How is Jennifer?' Linda asked.

'She was very lucky, she got off with cuts and bruises.'

'How is she otherwise? This must have been so awful for her.'

'Oh, it was, poor lass. Shock does different things to different people.'

Kirsty wondered what she meant by that.

'She doesn't say much but then she never did have a lot to say.'

'A quiet girl.'

'Not so friendly as her mother but then I always had a soft

spot for Betty. She smiled and shook her head. 'Even living next door to them I never got further than passing the time of day with her husband. Standoffish I would have called him. Betty was so different. She was a really nice young woman and very obliging. When the weather was bad or if I wasn't in the best of health she would do my shopping and maybe make a cup of tea. She never knew her own mother, just her grand-mother, and I think she liked coming in here and having an older person to talk to.'

'She was a lovely person. Is Jennifer like her?'

'In appearance she is. They were a good-looking couple but then you would know that.'

'I didn't know Robert very well.'

'No one around here did. Poor lass, she didn't have her sorrows to seek with that husband. Times I wondered how she put up with him but that is easy to say. Not so easy if you don't have somewhere to go and I don't think Betty had. I'm not a gossip so I'll say no more. It is Jennifer you are interested in. She is quiet, as I said, and the quiet ones don't make trouble. Do you have a family, Mrs Chalmers?'

'Three. Hannah is thirteen, Heather eleven and Robin is eight.'

'That's grand. It's young company Jennifer needs.'

Kirsty leaned forward. 'Mrs McDonald, this is all very difficult—'

'Please, Mum—'

'All right, Linda, you explain the situation to Mrs McDo-nald.'

The smile was replaced by a frown. 'What explaining is there to do? Someone will have to take Jennifer, and soon. Did Mr Brady not tell you?'

'That you are going to New Zealand, yes, he did.'

'Then you can understand I have preparations to make and I would like to be on my own to do them.'

'I quite understand.'

'I hope you do, Mrs Chalmers. That girl is depending on you. Why agree to be godmother when you are not prepared to do your part?' Her colour had risen and the wheezing was getting worse.

'Please calm down, Mrs McDonald.' Linda was getting alarmed.

'Let my daughter explain and without interruptions if you please.'

The woman looked outraged but she kept quiet.

Linda moistened her lips. 'Betty and I were best friends when we were at college and we did keep up for a few years after that. Then there was no correspondence and we lost touch. She had moved and I didn't have her address.' She paused. 'Getting that letter from the solicitor was more than a surprise, it was a shock. You see, Mrs McDonald, I had never at any time agreed to be godmother to her daughter. She didn't ask me. Presumably she had intended to, then forgotten. She wouldn't have expected Jennifer to be left without one parent.'

Mrs Mcdonald gave a huge sigh. 'That's it then. I hate to think of Jennifer going to strangers—'

'We are strangers, Mrs McDonald.'

'That is so, Mrs Cameron, but you will admit it is rather different. Your daughter knew her mother. Jennifer is fifteen, she would be off your hands in a year or two.'

Linda bit her lip.

'And think about it this way, your children might quite like to have an older sister.'

Linda thought she wouldn't put money on that. 'There are other problems,' she said, beginning to sound desperate. 'We don't have a spare room.'

The eyebrows shot up. 'Is that such a problem?'

'No, but it would mean the girls sharing—' She stopped. She was sounding pathetic and that is what she was.

There was the noise of a key turning and with a surprising show of speed, the woman was on her feet and making for the door. They heard her calling.

'Jennifer, leave everything in the kitchen and I'll see to them later. We have visitors, so come through.'

All eyes turned to the door and Linda caught her breath. Betty had been very pretty but this girl with her high cheek-bones was beautiful. There was a stillness about her that was at odds with her fifteen years.

'Jennifer, this lady is Mrs Chalmers, your mother's friend from long ago.'

'My godmother,' she said in a low husky voice.

'And the other lady is Mrs Cameron.'

'My mother,' Linda put in, then smiled to Jennifer. 'You are very like your mother.'

'I'm supposed to take after both of my parents.'

'Yes, I'm sure there is a bit of your father there too.'

'I am going to leave you and make a cup of tea. Jennifer, did you remember the fruit loaf?'

'Yes.'

'You will take a cup of tea?' The woman looked first at Kirsty then at Linda.

'A cup of tea would be very nice, thank you,' Kirsty said and Linda agreed.

'I'll get the kettle on and leave you to get to know each other.'

Jennifer sat down in the chair Mrs McDonald had vacated. She wore a dark skirt and a white blouse open at the neck. There was none of the schoolgirl awkwardness. This was a graceful young woman, tall for her age, and perfectly calm. If she was nervous it certainly didn't show. Had she got over the shock of losing her parents or were her feelings well hidden? Something about the girl made Linda feel uncomfortable and that in turn made her feel guilty. We all have our own way of coping with grief and if this was Jennifer's she was being very brave. She was only fifteen, a child-woman, alone in a world that could be cruel, unspeakably cruel in this case. How could she turn her back? She couldn't.

Linda sought for something to say. 'Do you play the piano, Jennifer?'

'No.'

She didn't waste words, Linda thought and hid a smile. She would try something else.

'How about school? Have you been attending—'

She shrugged. 'I'm supposed to go back on Monday but I won't now, not with you coming for me.'

Linda and her mother shared a quick hopeless look.

'Nothing is settled—'

The girl didn't hear or didn't want to hear. She carried on talking.

'Mrs McDonald can't hide her relief, well you can see how pleased she is.'

'Yes.'

'She is going to New Zealand and she was worried in case you didn't turn up.'

'Were you worried?' Kirsty asked.

'Me? No, I wasn't worried. Worry is a waste of time and effort, that's what my dad used to say. My mum was always worrying.'

'Some of us can't help worrying.'

'You could if you tried. You and Mum were best friends.'

'Yes, when we were at college. We kept up for a year or two then we lost touch.'

'Mum wasn't much of a correspondent.'

'No, she wasn't. You must miss her, you must miss your parents terribly.'

'It happened so there is no use going on about it.'

Linda was shocked.

'Don't look so shocked, what am I supposed to do? Things work out, that was another of Dad's sayings, and it is working out for me.'

'Is it, Jennifer? Is it working out for you?'

'You are taking me, you aren't backing out, are you?'

Linda closed her eyes. There was no way out. She would have to phone Matthew and prepare him. Surely when she explained he would understand. She prayed that he would.

'Yes, Jennifer, you can make your home with us.'

Kirsty said nothing. She was making a study of this young girl who was causing so much stir in their lives. It was early days but she hadn't taken to the girl and that worried her. Linda took after John, she was too soft-hearted for her own good.

There was no denying that Jennifer was a beauty. In a few years she would be stunning. The gods had been kind to her or maybe it was having good-looking parents. Her blue-black hair was thick and shining with just a hint of a wave. She had neat features, a long slender neck and a creamy complexion. When they had shaken hands Kirsty had looked into pale blue eyes fringed with black lashes. The eyes were beautiful but cold.

Kirsty thought about her granddaughter, Hannah, and her heart went out to the child. Of course she would be envious, especially as she was unhappy with her own appearance. The young suffered very often in silence and children could be so cruel, unbelievably cruel at times. Why did people set such store on good appearance? It was the initial attraction but if there was no more than looks then one quickly got tired of a pretty face. The less attractive had to make an effort and the positively ugly could become fascinating with their lively and interesting conversation.

Kirsty thought how lucky she was with her grandchildren.

They were nice ordinary youngsters and she wouldn't wish them any different. How was this beautiful stranger going to fit in? There was no telling, it was a gamble.

Mrs McDonald arrived with a laden tray and began to manoeuvre her bulk through the half-open door. Kirsty expected Jennifer to jump up and give a hand, but she didn't budge from the chair and it was left to Linda to assist.

'Thank you, Mrs Chalmers. Perhaps if you took the tray from me I would get the table out. I should have had it done.'

Linda obliged and the woman got a nest of tables from beside the window and set one in each place. That done she took the tray, put it on the table and began serving the tea.

'That's real good fruit loaf. We do well for bakers in Inverness. There was a time when I did all my own baking and the baker's shop only saw me when I wanted bread.'

'I was the same,' Kirsty smiled. 'Now that I am on my own I take things easy and buy what I need.'

The fruit loaf was praised and they were both persuaded to take another piece.

'When do you go back home, if you don't mind me asking?'

'Tomorrow.'

'I'm glad you are not going tonight, it would have meant a rush. Not that we wouldn't have managed but this will make things easier. Jennifer will have time to collect her bits and pieces and anything that is forgotten I can send on. You can leave your address or I can get it from Mr Brady.'

'I'll leave it but remind me if I forget,' Linda said.

'So much on your mind?'

'Yes, you could say that.'

Kirsty got to her feet. 'Thank you for the tea, that was very enjoyable, and now we must be getting on our way.'

'Yes, we must.' Linda got to her feet. 'We'll come for Jennifer some time about eleven.'

'She'll be ready and in case you didn't know the house has to be emptied, but the solicitor is to see to that.'

'He made mention of it.'

'Jennifer, see the ladies to the bus stop.'

'I was going to do that.' She didn't say, 'I didn't need you to tell me,' but it was certainly implied.

Once again when the bus came they had to take separate seats. Linda's thoughts were in turmoil. What had she done? If this caused unhappiness in the family, how would she ever forgive herself?

They got off the bus and walked the few yards to the guest-house.

'Linda, stop looking so worried. What is done is done.'

'I know, that is what worries me. But what else could I have done?'

'I don't know, dear.'

'You would have done the same?'

'Perhaps. Again I don't know.'

'You didn't like her, did you?'

'I found her strange.'

'Maybe that is not surprising after what she has come through.'

'Very true, Linda. I suppose if she had dissolved in tears or shown some emotion, I would have warmed to her. Maybe she isn't the tearful type, there are some folk like that. They feel just as deeply but they don't show it.'

'Have you some coins, Mum? I noticed there was a pay-phone in the hall. I do have some, but this could be a lengthy call.'

'Matthew?'

'Yes, I want to get that over.'

'Matthew will understand.'

'I hope so but I am not at all sure.'

'There you are, that is all the change I have.'

'That's plenty, thanks. I hope Matthew answers and not one of the children. I couldn't face their questions just now.'

She was lucky, it was Matthew who picked up the phone.

6

'Hello, darling, it's me.' Linda sounded a lot more cheerful than she felt.

'Thought it might be. How is it going? Where are you speaking from and when do you get back?'

'Heavens,' she laughed. 'You mean you aren't coping?'

'Of course I am, although I'm really not cut out for this.'

'I thought one word from you and our lot did what they were told.'

'More like one word from me and they do what they damned well like. Only joking, all is well on the home front.'

'That's a relief and now, to answer your questions, I am speaking from the guest-house, which incidentally is very comfortable and reasonably central. We'll be home tomorrow, probably late afternoon.'

'I'll take the afternoon off and bring work home.'

'You don't need to do that, Matthew.'

'I know but I'll do it.'

'And Matthew—' she faltered.

'Oh, God, don't say it. She's coming here, that's it, isn't it?'

Linda immediately was on the defensive. 'There was nothing else I could do.'

'Nothing else you wanted to do, you mean.'

'That's not fair.'

'What has fair got to do with it? Kirsty has let me down. I honestly thought she would have made you see sense.' There was a long pause. 'This is going to be very upsetting, particularly for Hannah.'

'Hannah will have to learn that she can't get all her own way. And let me remind you, Matthew, since you seem to have forgotten,' she said, her voice shaking, 'you were the one who suggested I go through to Inverness and see for myself that all was well for Betty's daughter.'

'I don't deny it but that didn't give you a licence to bring her here.'

'I understood it did.' She dropped more coins into the box.

'Then you misunderstood.'

'Matthew, I could do no other. Will you please stop talking and give me a chance to explain.'

'If the deed is done explanations can wait.'

'No, they can't, you need to know now.'

'OK, I'm listening,' he said resignedly.

Linda took a deep breath. 'Once we left the solicitor's office Mum and I went to see this neighbour, a Mrs McDonald, who has been looking after Jennifer since the accident. It turns out that the woman is booked to go to New Zealand, where she has family.'

'I see.'

'No, you don't. I am perfectly well aware that Jennifer could go into a hostel or some such place while she finishes her schooling. I also know that girls of that age are easily led. She could get into bad company.'

'Or she could be perfectly content.'

'That is true, Matthew, but I couldn't take that chance, not with Betty's daughter.'

'You would rather take a chance with the happiness of your own family.'

Linda gasped. 'You know that isn't true. This could work out very well and you, I think, are trying to make difficulties.'

'I'm facing facts and you are not. You didn't tell me what the solicitor chap had to say.'

'Mr Brady didn't say very much. His job, after all, is to wind up the estate. Jennifer has his sympathy but obviously her welfare is not his responsibility. Mum asked Mr Brady if there was any money. I couldn't have done that but she did.'

'The answer being none, I suppose.'

'Hardly any, and certainly not enough to cover fees for a couple of years at boarding-school. And before you ask, Betty and Robert were living in a rented house and I don't imagine the contents will fetch very much.'

'There must have been money at one time.'

'I'm sure of it. Betty may have been forced to make withdrawals since Robert didn't appear to be much of a provider. Her grandmother, I do remember, had a lovely home – hang on, Matthew, while I feed this machine again.'

'You could have reversed the charges.'

'It's all right, I've still a pile of coins. Where was I? Oh, yes, Betty's grandmother. She owned her house and they lived very comfortably. Betty wanted for nothing.'

'What is she like this girl you are bringing home to live with us?'

'She looks a lot like her mother.'

'I want to know what she is like not what she looks like.'

'Jennifer is quiet which, I suppose, is understandable. None of us was completely at ease.'

'Did your arrival take her by surprise or was she prepared?'

'Prepared. Mr Brady had informed Mrs McDonald that I was coming through to Inverness and at some point there must have been mention of me being godmother because Mrs McDonald, who is quite elderly by the way, told me in no uncertain terms that I should be prepared to take some responsibility.'

'I hope you enlightened her about the true position.'

'I tried to.'

'Which means you didn't make a very good job of it.'

'Maybe I didn't sound very convincing,' Linda said wearily.

'I see,' he said again but this time heavily.

'Matthew, we can't blame the poor soul.'

'I'm not.'

'Neither am I. As she pointed out to us she did what she saw as her Christian duty by looking after Jennifer after the accident since there was no one else. Now she wants everything settled quickly so that she can prepare for her holiday.'

'And this is us landed with the girl.'

'I wish you wouldn't talk like that, it isn't a bit like you.'

'You could put it down to a new experience,' he said sarcastically, then was immediately ashamed. 'Sorry. I didn't mean that. Actually what I was wondering about was the sleeping arrangements. Do I bring the spare bed down from the attic and put it in Heather's room?'

Linda sighed with relief. She had hoped he would come round and here he was.

'That would be tremendously helpful, darling. The mattress is fine, I checked, but it will need to be aired. So, if you could put it in our bedroom. Would you do that?'

'Where do I put it? On the floor?'

'On top of the bed once you are out of it. No, on second thoughts don't go to all that bother. I have a better idea. I'm sure Robin wouldn't mind for one night sleeping on the camp-bed and letting Jennifer have his room.'

'Absolutely not,' Matthew said in a very firm voice. 'I'll get the bed down.'

'The girls will give you a hand.'

'If I need them.'

'Tell me, Matthew, why is everything so quiet? Where are the children?'

'Out.'

'Out where?'

'On their way to the fish and chip shop or maybe on their way back by now.'

'I left food, all you had to do was heat it up.'

'I know. Someone mentioned fish and chips.'

'And that won over my casserole?'

'I'm afraid so. There was only one dissenting voice and that was mine.'

'Pull the other one. In fact, Matthew Chalmers, I wouldn't put it past you to have been the one to suggest it.'

'Not mad, are you?'

'Of course not. Why would I be mad?'

'The table is only half-set and the kettle isn't on.'

'Maybe you should do that before they get back. Come to think about it, why does it take three to carry the fish and chips home?'

'Good question. I imagine it was to see that no one cheated and ate some of the chips on the way home.'

'Of course I should have thought of that,' she laughed.

'I didn't object, I get peace for a short while.'

'Matthew, I do feel terrible about all this but you do understand—'

'Leave it, Linda, she's coming and we'll have to make the best of it.'

'Everything will work out, I feel sure it will.'

'We'll see. I'll tell the kids you phoned.'

'Give them my love and Gran's too.'

'Sure. I'll break the news to them as well but not until we've had our fish and chips, wouldn't want to put them off.'

There was silence.

'That was meant to be a joke.'

'Was it? I'll ring off and let you get the kettle on.'

'Take care both of you and I'll see you when you come.'

'Yes. Goodbye, darling.'

'Goodbye, sweetheart.'

Linda replaced the receiver gently and went to find Kirsty. Her mother was talking to one of the guests but excused herself when she saw that her daughter was off the phone.

'Did it go well?' she asked anxiously.

'Not very well, not to begin with. I tried to explain but it wasn't easy.'

'No, it wouldn't be.'

'In the end he was accepting reluctantly that I had no choice. You believe that, don't you, that I had no choice?'

'We always have to make a choice, Linda. You had a difficult one to make.'

It wasn't the answer she wanted or had expected and Linda felt let down.

'There will be difficulties. Hannah could be awkward but the other two will accept Jennifer. In fact, I do not see the awkwardness lasting for any length of time. Hannah will come round. It will be in her own time but it will happen. Who knows, they might become good friends.'

'We can but hope,' Kirsty smiled. 'Pity Jennifer hadn't been younger than Hannah.'

'I can't see what difference that would make,' Linda said a little impatiently.

'Just a thought. How is Matthew coping?'

'Mum, there isn't much for him to do.'

'Tomorrow morning will be the testing time. Have you got an alarm clock with a loud ring?'

'We do, it would waken the dead. All my careful preparations, I could have saved myself the trouble. Trust a man to take the easy way out. When I phoned the three of them were on their way to the fish and chip shop.'

'And why not?' Kirsty laughed. 'Don't take it to heart.'

'I'm not, believe me I'm not. All I want is for everyone to be happy,' and she added silently, 'I hope I have done nothing to spoil that.'

'We should be thinking about food. Where do you suggest we eat, Linda? Do we go out or have our meal here? They do dinners on request.'

'I'm easy, Mum, you say what suits you.'

'I would prefer to eat here, I think. While you were on the phone to Matthew I had a glance at the dinner menu. Not much of a choice, I have to say, but one wouldn't expect there to be.'

'What is on offer?'

'The starter is tomato soup or grapefruit and orange segments and the main course is roast lamb, mint sauce, roast potatoes and vegetables. The alternative to that is a selection of cold meats and salad served with chipped potatoes.'

'And the pudding, if you can remember?'

'The sweet is home-made almond tart and custard, which will suit me very nicely. There is some kind of sponge and, of course, ice cream.'

'That sounds reasonably good.'

'Coffee, cheese and biscuits to follow.'

'We could have left it too late to order.'

'I hope not.'

'I'll enquire, Mum, and you go upstairs and have a lie-down.'

'Don't worry, I intend to. This, I can tell you, has been quite a day.'

'I couldn't agree more.'

Kirsty went upstairs and Linda pinged the bell at reception, which brought Mrs Sinclair through from the back.

'Mrs Chalmers, what can I do for you?' she smiled.

'Is it possible to book for dinner or are we too late?'

'No, you aren't. Will that be for two?'

'Yes.'

'Would seven o'clock suit you?'

'Seven o'clock would be perfect, thank you.'

Kirsty was lying stretched out on the bed, her shoes under a nearby chair.

'You look comfortable.'

'I am.'

'Dinner is booked for seven o'clock.'

'Oh, good! Very good. I really didn't feel like going out.'

Linda removed her shoes and skirt and lay down on the other single bed. She put her hands behind her head and gazed at the ceiling.

'Life is strange, isn't it, Mum?'

'Life is full of surprises, my dear, one can never be sure of anything in this world. It is wise to take each day as it comes.'

'I'm lucky to be married to Matthew and I should remember that.'

'Matthew is lucky to be married to you.'

'Thanks, that was nice of you.'

'You won't know it but I frequently give thanks that both of my daughters are happily married.'

'Do you, Mum?' She was smiling.

'Yes, I do. I was blessed with a happy marriage and I wanted no less for you two. Your father was a good man and I don't think I appreciated him enough when he was alive.'

'You still miss him,' Linda said softly.

'I shall always miss your father, Linda, but I have my memories. No one can take those away. Grieving has its place, as I have said before, and when my turn comes I want the mourning period to be short.'

'This is a bit depressing, what brought it on? You aren't usually in this kind of mood.'

'I know and just as well. What brought it on? I don't really know. Your father always said that life had to go on and I think I was trying to get that over to you.'

'Mission accomplished,' Linda giggled and Kirsty joined in the laughter.

'It is good to be able to laugh even in the midst of worries. As for myself, I have a lot to be thankful for. I have my grand-children who are a source of pride and comfort to me. They are so different from one another but equally loveable.'

'Sometimes they are a worry.'

'Of course. Whoever said it was easy to bring up children didn't know what they were talking about.'

'Or never had any of their own,' Linda added.

'Exactly. Linda?'

'What?'

'Do you mind if I get forty winks?'

'Sorry, I'll keep quiet.'

Feeling refreshed after their rest, Kirsty and Linda went downstairs at seven o'clock. Four of the tables in the dining-room were set for breakfast. The cups, white with a narrow blue band were turned upside down on their saucers. The only other guests for dinner were two middle-aged businessmen who had reached the coffee stage. They broke off their conversation to smile to the ladies as Kirsty and Linda passed their table on the way to their own. Each table was covered with a fresh blue and white tablecloth and blue linen napkins, neatly folded, were placed to the side of the cutlery. Linda and her mother sat down and Kirsty picked up her table-mat to study it. The view was of a Scottish castle.

'I've got Glamis Castle. What have you got?'

Linda looked at hers without picking it up. 'Mine is Stirling Castle. I expect they are all different.'

'Plenty to choose from. We aren't short of castles in Scot-land.'

They had chosen the same starter and main course. Tomato soup followed by roast lamb. The soup arrived piping hot and a young girl of perhaps seventeen came with a basket of warmed rolls. They each took one and put it on their plate. The butter dish was already on the table with curls of butter on it. A glass of red wine would have been welcome but it wasn't on offer. Instead they made do with iced cold water and watched it being poured into the glasses.

'Linda, I hoped it would be and it is. This is home-made tomato soup. You can taste the difference to the tinned variety.'

'Delicious,' Linda agreed as she took a spoonful.

'I'm hungry and that, for me, is surprising. Usually I can't face more than one good meal a day.'

'The change of air has given you an appetite.'

'Must have.'

They sat back while the empty soup plates were removed by the girl. In a few minutes a plate of roast lamb was set before them and it was the owner herself who served the vegetables.

'Enjoy your meal, ladies. I'll leave the vegetable dish should you want more.'

The lamb was tender, cooked to perfection, and the roast potatoes were the way Kirsty liked them. They finished what was on their plate and almost sighed with contentment.

'I shouldn't even think about almond tart.'

'Go on, spoil yourself.'

'I'm going to and if I suffer from overindulgence I have only myself to blame.'

'I'm going to choose Charlotte sponge.'

Mrs Sinclair had been talking to the two businessmen and when they left she began clearing their table and then setting it for breakfast with a clean tablecloth.

'I wonder who does the cooking,' Kirsty whispered. 'Do you think it might be the husband?'

Linda nodded. 'I should think it very possible. Could be he trained as a chef—'

'Both of them trained, maybe, and that was where they met.'

'They deserve to get on. That meal would have put many a hotel to shame.'

'Was everything to your satisfaction?'

'Mrs Sinclair, that was a delicious meal.'

'I'm so glad you enjoyed it.'

'Do you mind me asking, who does the cooking?'

'I don't mind in the least, Mrs Cameron. My husband does the cooking and I do the baking. We did our training together and although I admit to Angus being the more imaginative cook, he likes experimenting with sauces, I have a lighter hand with pastry.'

'Melt-in-the-mouth pastry.'

'Thank you. Where would you like to have your coffee? Here or in the visitors' lounge? The fire is burning well and you would have the place to yourselves.'

Linda looked across at Kirsty.

'I'm much too lazy to move or maybe it is because I am too full,' Kirsty laughed.

'You would like it served at the table?'

'Yes, please, unless it is keeping you back?'

'Not at all. I'll brush those crumbs away, then bring your coffee.' She used a small brush and tray and a few minutes later brought the coffee. Neither of them wanted cheese and biscuits.

'Thank you, that's lovely,' Kirsty said when the cream was added to the coffee. 'We'll have this, then go through to the lounge.'

'Just as you please.'

The visitors' lounge was small with rather too much in it. There was a large three-seater settee and several comfortable chairs. Against one wall was a well-filled bookcase with one shelf holding mostly paperbacks. These had been left behind by guests who had bought them for holiday reading and then left them for someone else. The mantelpiece had a pewter jug on either side and a handsome marble clock in the middle. The hands didn't move, it was purely decorative. Linda thought it was very old and would cost too much to mend.

Kirsty took advantage of the embroidered stool and placed her feet on it. She had eaten too much and was leaning back in her chair with her eyes closed.

'Mum, are you asleep?'

'Of course not, I've already had my forty winks.' She opened her eyes.

'I need to talk, do you mind?'

'That is what mothers are for.'

'This is still unreal. I can't believe we are going to collect Jennifer tomorrow.'

'Then you had better believe it.'

'I shouldn't be asking this, but what do you think of Jennifer? Be honest.'

Kirsty was careful. 'It is too early to form an opinion, but I didn't care for her manner. She wasn't very nice to Mrs McDonald.'

'No, she wasn't. I don't think they are getting on too well together.'

'Could be faults on both sides.'

'True, but she should be grateful to the woman for what she has done.'

'Yes.'

'There is school to think about. I'll have a chat with the headmistress and I imagine Miss Dempster will get in touch with the school Jennifer was attending.'

'I wonder what she plans to do with her life? At fifteen she must have some ideas.'

'Not necessarily, Mum, some of them haven't a clue.'

'I'm going to call it a day,' Kirsty said, getting to her feet. 'It is after my bedtime but you stay down and read. Shame to waste the fire.'

'No, I am going to follow your example. An early night will make a change.' She began to plump up the cushions.

'What are you doing that for?'

'Habit, I suppose. Come on, I've got your handbag as well as my own.'

Kirsty was usually slow to get to sleep in a strange bed but after half an hour she was in the land of nod with her mouth slightly open. Linda was faring less well. Her brain was too active and in the still of the night she was plagued by uncertainties. What if she had made a dreadful mistake? If she had then she and she alone would be to blame. The really worrying part she kept to herself. It wasn't just Jennifer's manner, it was more than that. She hadn't taken to the girl. There was a strangeness about her that was disturbing.

In appearance she resembled her mother, but that was all. Betty had been open and friendly whereas Jennifer was closed and secretive. Sleep came fitfully and Linda had been dreaming. In the morning she tried to hold on to the dream but it was slipping away. That distressed Linda because it seemed to be terribly important that she recall the dream. It had something to do with Matthew and he was drifting further and further away until he was lost to sight. It was silly to let a dream upset her but it had. She got up quietly without disturbing her mother and after putting on her dressing-gown and slippers she went along to the bathroom.

By the time they had eaten breakfast and paid the bill it was nearly ten o'clock. Mrs Sinclair was busy but took the time to carry Kirsty's luggage to the car. Linda had opened the boot and stood beside it. They shook hands and hoped to meet again.

Linda had fallen silent as they drove away. She was feeling nervous to the point of sickness and Kirsty, seeing her daughter's set face, said nothing. In a short time they were slowing down at the gate. A curtain at one of the windows twitched and in a few moments the door opened. Kirsty got out first and waited until Linda had locked the car door. They went along the path together.

'Good morning,' Mrs McDonald's face was wreathed in smiles. 'Not a bad day for your journey home. No sun but then the sun can be a nuisance when driving, or so I am led to believe. Come in. Come in. Here's me talking and keeping you standing at the door.'

'Is Jennifer ready?' Linda asked.

'She is.' The woman pointed to a collection of luggage at the bottom of the stairs. 'I hope you have room for all that lot. I told her you might not.'

'We should manage.'

'Would you take a cup of tea before you set off?'

'No, thank you, we would like to get on our way.'

A door shut and all eyes turned to the top of the stairs. Jennifer stood there for a few moments without moving.

Mrs McDonald drew in her breath sharply. 'I said to wear your navy trench coat or your school blazer.'

'I packed them and anyway, what is wrong with what I am wearing?'

Kirsty and Linda wondered that too. The girl had on an off-white boxy jacket.

'You know fine what is wrong, you don't need to be told.'

'This was my mum's coat and now it is mine. I sometimes wore her clothes and she didn't mind.'

'That was before but I see I am wasting my breath. You had better hurry, the ladies are anxious to be on their way.'

'I'm ready.' She ran down the stairs.

'Oh, I nearly forgot and I went especially for it. Just a minute.' Mrs McDonald went away and returned with a small wrapped loaf. 'That's a fruit loaf to take with you,' she beamed.

'How very kind of you,' Linda said. 'We shall enjoy that when we get home.'

'You must be looking forward to your holiday.'

'I am, Mrs Cameron, but I'm nervous too. I'm a bit old to be gallivanting to the other side of the world but my family assure me I'll be fine.'

'Of course you will and it will be a wonderful experience.'

'Jennifer, I will give you a hand with your luggage. Some of it will go in the boot and the rest will go beside you on the back seat.'

'Am I sitting in the back?'

'You are,' Linda said curtly.

'That's OK. I thought you might need directions.'

Linda bit her lip. She had been in the wrong, the girl was only trying to help.

'I'll ask if I need help but I think I should manage. Shouldn't you be saying goodbye to Mrs McDonald?'

'She's coming.'

The woman had been standing at the open door, then decided to come down to the car.

'Is that you all set?'

'I think so.'

'Safe journey and, Jennifer, you be a good girl.'

'I'm not a child.'

'Times you act like one.' She smiled to take the sting out.

'Have a good holiday,' Jennifer said as she got in to the back of the car.

'Thank you. Goodbye everybody.'

They were on their way. Jennifer was leaning forward.

'Are you all right, Jennifer?'

'Yes. There is a quicker way out of the traffic, my dad always used it.'

'Fine. You give me directions from here.'

7

Linda kept hoping that Jennifer would open up on the journey home, that once she was away from Mrs McDonald the girl would be fine. There had been tension between the two. Jennifer could be nervous and apprehensive about what was ahead and who could blame her for that? The unknown was always a bit scary. Only she hadn't appeared nervous or apprehensive, on the contrary she appeared to be perfectly composed. If anyone is nervous it is me, Linda told herself. Kirsty soon lost patience. After several attempts to draw the girl out she had given up. It was not very encouraging to have one's questions answered by yes or no and very little else. For a while Kirsty and Linda carried on their own conversation then fell silent. Each was busy with her own thoughts.

Kirsty was more than annoyed, she was angry and she was worried. Jennifer was a strange, moody girl with little or no consideration for others. Unless there was a big improvement, Linda was in for a hard time and the once happy family would be put under a lot of strain.

Linda refused to think along those lines. It had begun to bother her that in the time they had been together, Jennifer had not shed a single tear. Nor had there been a break in her voice when her parents were mentioned. She remembered her own anguish when her beloved father had died. For weeks after she couldn't talk about him without dissolving into tears. Admittedly everybody wasn't the same. Helen had suffered just as much but she broke down less often.

Now, when it was too late, Linda wished that she had asked some questions. Mrs McDonald might have been more forth-coming if questions had been put directly to her. The little she had divulged was her genuine fondness for Betty. That hadn't extended to Betty's husband. She hadn't liked Robert Mar-shall and neither had the neighbours. How stupid and naïve she had been to expect Jennifer to have her mother's lovely nature. Matthew had been more far-seeing. He had suggested that the girl could take after her father and reminded his wife that she hadn't liked or trusted Robert. She had chosen to ignore that. Although, when she thought about it, she doubted if that would have made any difference. She would still have offered Jennifer a home.

They made two stops, the first for coffee. Jennifer had a glass of lemonade and a Mars bar. At twelve thirty they had a snack lunch. Kirsty did not suggest that they linger. There was no mention of a short walk to stretch their legs. She seemed to be as anxious as Linda to be on their way and Linda took advantage. She got behind the wheel and back on the road.

Jennifer had perked up in the coffee shop and again in the café. She hadn't suddenly become talkative but she was showing an interest in what was going on around her. A few miles further on Jennifer must have been feeling the car hot because she removed her boxy jacket and placed it care-fully over the assortment of bags on the seat. She wore a long-sleeved blouse in a pretty floral pattern and a navy pleated skirt that Kirsty thought was too short.

After the snack and on the way to the car Linda had asked Jennifer if she had enjoyed her lunch. She had chosen sausage roll, chips and peas which would probably have been her own children's choice of meal.

'Yes, it was OK, thanks.'

'Jennifer, you aren't scared, are you?'

'No, why should I be?'

'No reason at all. You are very quiet and I wondered.'

Kirsty had joined them. She wanted to give the girl a good shake. Couldn't she see how hard Linda was trying? No, possibly not, she was too interested in herself.

Several times in the car Kirsty had nodded off. In the back Jennifer had searched the bags until she found what she was looking for – a fashion magazine. For the remainder of the journey she appeared engrossed.

Kirsty stirred. 'I must have dropped off,' she said apologetically.

'You have had a good long sleep, Mum, and there is no need to apologise.'

'A short nap, not a long sleep.'

'Have it your own way,' Linda grinned.

'Heavens, you must be right. I recognise where we are, we are nearly home.'

'Jennifer,' Linda half turned her head, 'we are nearly home.'

'What?'

'This is us approaching Abbotsfield, your new home.'

'Not many shops,' she said after a few minutes.

'I told you we lived in a village.'

'There are more shops here than where I live.'

'Mum lives in the back of beyond.'

'Maybe it is but it is what I like. I have a delightful cottage, Jennifer, which you will see one day soon.'

'Have you ever been in Dundee? Do you know it at all?'

'I've been there, Mrs Chalmers, but I don't remember anything about it.'

'Dundee is only a few miles from where we are and it is where I do my big shopping.'

Kirsty was consulting her watch. 'We've made very good time, Linda, you could be home before Matthew.'

'Matthew should be in the house. He was taking work home.'

'How thoughtful and so like Matthew. Jennifer, you will love your new family. They are delightful.'

She didn't answer, perhaps she didn't hear.

Linda slowed down. 'This is where we live, in this small cul-de-sac.'

'Which house is yours?'

Kirsty pointed.

'It's a big house,' Jennifer said, sounding impressed.

'Not really, dear. It looks bigger than it actually is.' Linda felt like giving a huge sigh of relief. Jennifer was at least showing an interest in where she was to live.

'You've gone beyond, why aren't you stopping?'

'Because my daughter is turning the car to save me an awkward manoeuvre. It will be facing the way I go out.'

Linda reversed to the gate and switched off.

'Better to empty the car before we go in. I don't want to be late in getting home.'

'Surely you'll stay for a meal, Mum?'

'No, thank you, dear, I won't. What I had on the journey will do me. I'll make myself a cup of tea but that will be all.'

Linda opened the boot and emptied it of everything except her mother's overnight bag and the picnic basket, which had not been in use for the return journey. The three of them were busy with the bags when the door opened, there was a flood of light and a small figure came running down the drive.

'Mummy! Mummy! Mummy!' he cried and went into his mother's outstretched arms.

'Nice to be missed,' Kirsty smiled as Robin left his mother and came over to give his grandmother a big hug. For a few moments they had forgotten the girl. Linda took her arm and brought her over.

'Jennifer, this is Robin. Robin, say hello to Jennifer.'

'Hello,' he smiled and remembering his manners stretched

out his hand. 'You're pretty,' he said when they had shaken hands.

'Am I?' It had been her first genuine smile. The smile lit up her dark eyes and revealed small, white perfect teeth.

'Yes, you are. My sisters are pretty but I don't tell them that.' Kirsty ruffled his hair affectionately.

'Robin, don't go back empty-handed. Take one of Jennifer's bags and leave it at the bottom of the stairs.'

'I can manage more than one.'

'Of course you can,' Kirsty said, loading him up with the lightest.

'Daddy's home but he's on the phone.' He staggered along with his load and managed to make himself sound exhausted.

Hannah and Heather appeared at the door. Heather went swiftly down the drive and Hannah followed more slowly.

'I'll help,' Heather said, taking her mother's case, and was about to put the boxy jacket over her arm when Jennifer snatched it from her with an exclamation of annoyance.

'I'll take my own jacket.'

Heather looked taken aback. 'Sorry,' she muttered and was about to move away when Linda reached out to stop her.

'Hannah,' she said, getting the girls together. 'I want you to meet Jennifer.' She smiled to Jennifer. 'My two daughters, Hannah and Heather.'

'How do you do?' Heather said, trying to sound grown-up and not quite managing a smile. She was still smarting from the snub. She had only been trying to help. What was wrong with carrying the jacket into the house?

Hannah was taking her time and Linda raised her eyebrows warningly. She muttered something and they shook hands. It was a case of disliking each other on sight.

The luggage was all indoors and everyone was in the sitting-room. No one was completely at ease except perhaps Robin. The foot of the stairs was littered with bags and there was barely room to pass. Matthew had come off the phone and joined them. His smile was for his wife and he kissed her before greeting his mother-in-law.

'Nice to see you safely home.'

'Nice to be back,' Kirsty smiled. 'And I must say, the house is looking presentable.'

'That's my training. A place for everything and everything in its place,' he grinned.

'Gran, that is not true. You should have heard Dad giving the orders,' Heather said, then fell silent.

'Matthew, this is Jennifer,' Linda said softly and didn't realise that she was looking at him imploringly.

He took the message to heart. He had had time to think everything over. Linda had been placed in a very difficult situation and although he did not approve of her action he thought it his duty to be supportive. Maybe if they all made a special effort it would work out. He should set an example.

'Welcome to Hillcrest, Jennifer,' he said, kissing her cheek. 'You'll get used to us, we are really not too bad, are we, Kirsty?'

Kirsty didn't make a joke of it as he expected.

'Jennifer,' she said quietly and firmly, 'no one can take the place of your parents but you are very lucky to have Matthew and Linda—'

'And me and Hannah and Heather.'

'Yes, Robin, you and Hannah and Heather. I know you will do your best to make Jennifer feel at home and, Jennifer, you have your part to play. You must learn to be helpful and fit in with family life.'

'She will, won't you, Jennifer?' Matthew was feeling sorry for the girl.

'Yes, of course.' The smile she turned on Matthew was radiant and Linda couldn't have been more pleased. Kirsty was disturbed. Her eyes narrowed. Linda had gone out of her way for this girl and her efforts had hardly merited a smile never mind a word of thanks. Hannah and Heather hadn't come off much better. Matthew, admittedly, had given a short welcoming speech and for that he had been honoured with a dazzling smile. Her son-in-law had looked surprised and delighted. It was all a question of being able to handle the situation, she could hear him saying.

The phone rang. Hannah and Heather made a move but Matthew stopped them.

'It will be for me. I'm expecting a call from the office.'

'Another one?'

'Yes, Heather, another one. That is the price I pay for taking a half day off.'

'Linda, I'll go now. I don't like driving in the grey dark.'

'No, I know you don't. Take care and phone to let me know as soon as you get in the house.'

'I always do.'

'Yes, you do, but that was just a reminder. Hannah and Heather, go down to the car with Gran and close the gate.'

They needed no second bidding. This was a chance to get their grandmother on her own.

'She is nice looking,' Heather said carefully.

'Jennifer?'

'Yes. I don't think she is very nice, though.' Heather wondered if she should have said that and to show her uncertainty she kept going over the side of her shoe.

'Don't do that, dear, you will ruin your shoes. And isn't it rather early to form an opinion?'

'You didn't see the way she snatched her jacket from me. What did she think I was going to do with it?'

'That particular garment belonged to her mother and—'

'Oh, I see, I'm sorry, now I feel rotten about it.'

'Don't, you weren't to know, and there was no need to snatch the jacket from you.'

'I don't like her,' Hannah said quietly. 'I didn't expect to and I don't.'

'That is silly and unkind to form an opinion before you met the girl. I'm surprised at you, Hannah.'

'All right, I was wrong to form an opinion before I met her but it doesn't alter anything. I can always tell if I am going to like a person and I most certainly do not like Jennifer. And I am pretty sure she doesn't like me.'

'Then you will have to stop being childish and make a special effort to like each other.'

'Why?'

'That should be obvious. Because she is going to be part of the family whether you like it or not.'

'It is all Mum's fault.'

'I wish now that I hadn't said she could share my room,' Heather said gloomily.

'Really, what a pair of miseries.'

'Sorry, Gran, we aren't really miseries but we are not very happy.'

'Tell me this, Gran.'

'Can't it wait? I'm anxious to be on my way home.'

'It won't take a minute,' Hannah said. 'I was only going to ask if you liked her.'

Kirsty felt trapped. She wouldn't lie to her granddaughter and then again she couldn't tell the truth. The truth being that she didn't like Jennifer. The girl was plain disagreeable but she could hardly say so if she wanted to improve matters for Linda.

'I'm sure I shall once I get to know her better. Poor lass, it would be surprising if she didn't feel strange. We should all give her a chance.'

'OK,' Heather smiled. Hannah remained silent.

Kirsty got behind the wheel, waved to the girls and drove away.

Heather and Hannah waved until the car was out of sight, then walked slowly to the door.

'Did she really snatch her coat from you?'

'It was a jacket.'

'Well, did she?'

'Yes. Didn't you see her?'

'No.'

'Mum did, she couldn't have missed seeing it but she didn't say a word.'

'That is going to be the way it is from now on. You wait and see. Mum will take Jennifer's part every time.'

'That isn't fair.'

'She knows that. I mean, Mum knows it isn't fair but it isn't going to stop her.'

'This is going to be awful, isn't it?'

'Yes.'

'What about Dad? He'll be on our side.'

'Are you blind or something?' Hannah said witheringly as they stepped inside. She dropped her voice. 'That one knows how to play her cards.'

'What does that mean?'

'It means, Heather, that she is going all out to try and charm Dad.'

'Suck up to him, you mean?'

'You could put it that way. I mean, she didn't give us much of a smile but when it came to Dad she nearly split her face smiling.'

'You two took your time and Gran wanted to get on her way.'

'Sorry, we were only talking.'

Linda put her hand to her brow. 'I've got a beastly headache and I didn't mean that. Gran probably kept you talking rather than the other way round.'

'Shall I get the bottle of aspirins?'

'No, thank you, Hannah, I've already swallowed two. It says instant relief and it usually is but not this time. Another minute or two and I'll be fine.'

'What can I do to help? Shall I set the table?'

'No. Maybe you would do that, Hannah?'

'Sure. Where are we eating?'

'Here in the kitchen to save time. Remember to set six places.'

It was a good thing she had been reminded. Hannah would have set it for five without thinking. An extra chair would be required. There was one but it would have to be cleared. Whatever it was that didn't have a home found its way over to the spare chair.

'Mum, what about me?'

'I'll tell you in a minute.'

Matthew was having a long session on the phone. Some problem must have arisen when he wasn't in the office to deal with it, Linda thought. Her own problems were here and now and had to be solved. Robin was upstairs, probably crawling about the floor with a Dinky toy and making the appropriate noises. Jennifer was having a good look at everything.

Linda's kitchen was big, roomy and old-fashioned and she loved it. She had no wish to modernise but if she wanted a time-saving gadget she bought it. Helen's kitchen could have been taken straight out of *Ideal Home*. She couldn't understand Linda's reluctance to modernise hers. It had huge potential. She had even gone as far as to get her husband to plan the perfect kitchen for Linda. George, a peace-loving man, obeyed but knew it to be a waste of time. His sympathy was with his sister-in-law. She was happy with her kitchen, so why change it? To tear out the cupboards and replace them with modern units, he agreed with Linda, would be the equivalent of tearing the heart out of the kitchen. His wife didn't know and would have been astounded to learn that George hated the clinical and streamlined look of theirs.

The potatoes were beginning to boil and Linda turned down the gas.

'Jennifer.'

'What?'

'You can do your unpacking later, though goodness knows where we are going to put everything. Don't worry, we'll find somewhere,' she said hastily when the dark eyes looked at her questioningly. 'First and foremost we must get your bed ready. Heather, dear, you know where everything is kept. Sheets and pillowcases in the linen cupboard and I put two blankets and a quilt on top of the wardrobe.'

'Come on, Jennifer.'

'You have fifteen minutes before the meal is on the table,' Linda smiled, 'that should give you enough time to get the bed ready.'

'Where am I sleeping, Mrs Chalmers?'

Linda thought that Jennifer couldn't go on addressing her as Mrs Chalmers. Maybe Aunt Linda and Uncle Matthew would be best. They would have to talk about that.

'Where are you sleeping? You will be sharing a room with Heather.'

The girl looked startled and upset. 'I've always had my own room.'

'I don't doubt it. You are an only child.'

'I couldn't possibly sleep with someone in the same room.'

Linda's head had stopped throbbing and she felt better able to cope. She had to be very careful, this was a testing time. She could feel Hannah's and Heather's eyes on her. They were waiting to hear what she was going to say. Linda moistened her lips. She had not only to win but to be seen to win. There must be no wavering.

'You will soon get used to sharing, Jennifer.'

'No, I won't. It will be impossible for me to get to sleep.'

'Nonsense,' Linda said briskly, 'at your age there is no problem getting to sleep.'

'Sisters can sleep in the same room, that is different.'

Hannah gasped and dropped a fork on the floor.

'That has nothing to do with it.'

'Of course it has, it has everything to do with it. Why can't Hannah and Heather share?'

'Jennifer, I am not going to answer that. What I am going to tell you is this. There are certain rules in this house that you will be required to obey.' Linda didn't know when she had felt so angry. The nerve of the girl. 'You, Jennifer, are going to share a room with Heather and that is all there is to it. You cannot dictate. My family do not dictate to their parents.' Linda took a deep breath, pleased with herself so far. 'You have come to live with us because you have no other place to go.' That was cruel but she felt it was deserved. 'That said, you are here and we want you to be happy.'

'I don't snore, Jennifer,' Heather said, trying to bring a smile to the set face. It didn't. 'Are you coming upstairs?'

'On you go, Jennifer.'

Jennifer went slowly upstairs.

'Thanks, Mum,' Hannah said softly, 'you stood up to her.'

'You didn't think I would?'

'I wasn't sure.'

'This is going to be awful for me,' Jennifer muttered.

'I can't say I'm looking forward to it.'

'Why couldn't you sleep with your sister?'

'Hannah likes her own room.'

'So do I. Why should she get what she wants.'

'Why should you get what you want?'

'Because I am fifteen.'

'That doesn't matter.'

'It does matter. I think Hannah is mean.'

'My sister is not mean,' Heather said furiously. She had often told Hannah she was but that was different. No one else was going to say it.

'She is. You are both children and I am fifteen.'

'So you said and you shouldn't repeat yourself.'

'It means, Heather, that I am the eldest of this family.'

'You are not family.'

'I thought I was. Your father welcomed me into this family.'

Heather didn't know what to say.

'I could always tell Mr Chalmers that you are not making me welcome.'

'We are trying to make you welcome.'

'It doesn't look that way to me. However, it appears to me that I shall have to put up with this for the time being. Go and get the sheets and pillowcases, then leave me. I prefer to make my own bed.'

'Suits me.'

'Where is Jennifer?' Linda said when Heather came down on her own.

'She wanted to make her own bed.'

'Then let her,' Hannah said.

'Don't worry, I left her to it.'

Linda went to the foot of the stairs. 'Jennifer, the meal is on the table. Leave what you are doing and come down.'

'I'll be down shortly.'

'Her meal will be cold.'

'Her fault if she can't come down when she is told,' Hannah said. 'You say that to us often enough.'

'Now! Now!'

'You do, Mummy, you do say that to us,' Robin said gleefully.

Matthew put down his fork and knife when Jennifer entered.

'There you are, Jennifer, I'm afraid we didn't wait, we are a hungry lot,' Matthew apologised.

Jennifer smiled and took her place at the table. 'I'm sorry, Mr Chalmers, I was doing some tidying up.'

'Linda, we can't have Jennifer calling us Mr and Mrs Chalmers, what do you suggest?'

'Some of the girls in my old school called their parents by their Christian name.'

'I would not approve of that.'

'My mum didn't approve either but Dad thought it was OK.' She swallowed a mouthful of the food. 'When I wanted to annoy Mum I called her Betty.'

'No one in my class calls their parents by their Christian name.'

'Of course not, Heather, you are only a child.'

'And I suppose you think yourself grown-up.'

Matthew was laughing. 'Order! Order! Let the lady of the house speak.'

'Thank you, dear.' Linda smiled to her husband. 'Jennifer, you will please address us as Aunt and Uncle. That should be the easiest way out of the difficulty.' She paused. 'After the meal while Hannah and Heather are clearing the table we will go upstairs and find a temporary place for your belongings.'

'Isn't Helen—?' Matthew began.

'Yes, Helen has offered us a wardrobe, which will save us buying one. I shall have to make arrangements to bring it over.'

It had been a long tiring day for Linda and she was glad to close the bedroom door. She didn't feel like sleeping but she did feel like talking.

'Where did you find my cuff-link?' Matthew asked. He had noticed it on the bedside cabinet.

'Under the bed.'

'What was it doing there?'

'Gathering dust. You were lucky the Hoover didn't swallow

it. Matthew, you were on the phone for ages. Is anything wrong at the office?'

'Nothing that can't be sorted out. Our new recruit hasn't a lot of confidence in himself.'

'You picked the wrong one.'

'No, not at all,' Matthew said, getting in to his side of the bed. 'He's conscientious and the rest will follow. You've had a tiring day?'

'Yes, but I don't feel like sleeping.'

'Are you OK?'

'I don't know. Don't put out the light, not yet.'

'What is bothering you? Not that little skirmish at the table?'

'No, that didn't trouble me. Yes, it did, but not in the way you think. Matthew, from the first moment Mum and I were introduced to Jennifer she had hardly a word to say for herself. I told you she was quiet but she isn't, is she?'

'Isn't that a good sign – that she is coming out of her shell?'

'I don't know. I'm not sure about anything any more.'

'What is all this?' Matthew said, turning his head on the pillow. 'You wanted to give Betty's daughter a home and here she is. Of course they will bicker, our two are at it all the time.'

'They don't mean it.'

'And Jennifer does?'

'I think she is going to be difficult. I think I have made a dreadful mistake.'

'Bit late in the day to find that out.'

'I know.'

'What brought this on? Is there something you are not telling me?'

'It isn't going to work, I should have listened to you.'

'Yes, you should but you didn't. Actually, you know, I think you are worrying about nothing. We all need time to adjust and it has to be harder for Jennifer.'

'I can't have her dictating to me and I told her that.'

'About what? Dictating about what?'

'Where she should sleep.'

'Ah.'

'She made it very clear that she expected to have her own bedroom.'

'And you made it equally clear that she would have to share?'

'Yes, I did. Surely you are not going to suggest that I should have done otherwise?'

'Tricky situation. I can see her point.'

'Can you indeed?' She sat up and gave him a sharp look.

'She is fifteen and a very mature fifteen, I would say.'

'You would?'

'She could pass for older.'

'What has that got to do with it?'

'Rather a lot, I would have thought.'

Linda couldn't believe what she was hearing. 'Should I insist that Hannah and Heather share a room?' she said sarcastically.

The sarcasm was lost. 'Not insist, that would be going about it in the wrong way.'

'Do tell me how I should go about it?'

'God, you are being awkward. Ask nicely and they may surprise you and agree.'

'That wouldn't be a surprise that would be a shock. It won't happen, I can tell you.'

'Pardon me if I am being a bit slow but didn't the suggestion come from you that our two should share?'

'I was wrong and I admit it.'

Matthew yawned. 'So where do we go from here, you tell me that.'

'The awful truth is that I don't know. It is all my fault and I have to find the solution.'

'Make her welcome, that is what I am doing.'

'So I noticed, so we all noticed. You didn't want her and now you do.'

'I am making the best of the situation and I would suggest you did the same.'

'A situation I forced on you?'

'You did, no question about that. You forced it on me, you forced it on us.' Matthew was getting exasperated. He was sitting up and raking his fingers through his hair. 'I am going out of my way to welcome this stranger in to our home and suddenly that is wrong, although before you left for Inverness it was what you wanted. If you want to know, I like her. I find her very pleasant. She doesn't take after her mother and you are blaming her for that.'

Linda kept silent, there was nothing she could say.

'And now, do you mind if I switch off the light and try to get some sleep?'

'Switch it off by all means.'

This was the time when they cuddled in. Linda wanted to. She was cold and she missed the warmth of her husband's body but she couldn't bring herself to snuggle in. Instead she kept to her side of the bed feeling more miserable than she ever remembered.

8

Linda had been dreading the morning and that was silly. Matthew didn't harbour resentment and it was as though last night's angry words had never been spoken. He was his usual self, reluctant to leave the warm bed and grumpy for the first few minutes after making the move. Linda was recalling her grandmother's good advice on the eve of her wedding.

'There will be times,' the old woman had said, 'when you will be angry with your husband and he with you. That need not be bad, you can't always see eye to eye and voicing your differences clears the air. What you must never do, however, is let the sun go down on your wrath. You must make up, Linda, be friends again, that is terribly important and you must agree to differ about whatever it was that caused the anger. Don't let pride stand in the way. Life is too short, don't waste it.'

Last night she had forgotten that advice. She must make sure it didn't happen again.

The house was quiet with everyone gone except Jennifer. She was having a lie-in since she wouldn't be going to school. With no one around, Linda decided it would be a good time to phone Miss Dempster, the headmistress, and find out if Jennifer could be enrolled. She didn't anticipate any problem. Linda dialled the number and the secretary put the call through to Miss Dempster.

'Good morning, Mrs Chalmers.'

Linda liked the woman. Miss Dempster was in her fifties, no one on the staff knew how far into them, and she wasn't prepared to say. Her iron grey hair was cut short and she had a narrow face. Her clipped voice could be off-putting and it did manage to upset some parents.

'Good morning, Miss Dempster.' Linda told her the reason for the phone call.

She listened in silence until Linda had finished.

'Poor girl, how dreadful for her and how fortunate that she has you. Perhaps you could bring her to see me tomorrow morning. Let me see what would be a suitable time.' There was a pause. 'Could we say nine forty-five?'

'Thank you, Miss Dempster, that would suit very well.'

'You say the girl is fifteen?'

'Yes.'

'She might prefer to be seen on her own, or on the other hand she may feel the need for some support after what she has been through. I would suggest you leave it to Jennifer, Mrs Chalmers.'

'That is what I will do and thank you again.'

Linda replaced the receiver, glad that she had got that settled. She had timed it well. There was the sound of a door opening and then another one opening and shutting. Jennifer was up and in the bathroom and would shortly be downstairs looking for her breakfast. There was cereal and she would put a couple of slices of bread in the toaster. The family had a cooked breakfast at the weekend when there was time to eat it. She hoped Jennifer would fall in with the family routine.

Kirsty's suggestion that a plate of steaming hot porridge was a good way to start the school day had not proved popular. The children much preferred cereal and Matthew said with a shudder that his porridge days were long gone. Linda didn't push it, she hadn't much cared for porridge oats.

'There you are, Jennifer, good morning. Did you sleep well?'

'Not bad.'

'Cereal and toast is what we have on weekdays and a cooked breakfast at the weekend.'

'That's all right,' she said, sitting down at the table. 'Mum only did a cooked breakfast on Sunday morning.'

'Help yourself to cornflakes and there is plenty of milk.'

'Who takes Rice Krispies?'

'Robin.'

'I quite like them mixed with cornflakes.'

'Then do that. Heather likes a banana sliced up in hers.'

Jennifer nodded and Linda made the tea. When she was on her feet she took down an extra cup and saucer from the cupboard shelf. The one she had been using was with the washing-up.

'I'm going to join you. This will be a chance for us to talk.'

Jennifer went on eating her cereal.

'I'm just off the phone to Miss Dempster. She is the headmistress and, let me say, I have always found her very approachable.'

The toaster popped and Linda put both pieces of toast in the toast rack.

'Were you talking about me?'

'Yes.' Linda thought that obvious.

'What did you say?'

'What do you mean?'

'I just want to know what you said.'

'Jennifer, I told Miss Dempster about the accident and that you are making your home with us. I don't see what else I could have said.'

'That's OK.'

'The headmistress wants to see you in her office tomorrow morning at nine forty-five.'

'Quarter to ten. How will I get there?'

'I'll drive you.'

She looked up sharply. 'I'll see her on my own.'

'I expected you would want that.'

'You'll have to show me where I get the bus.'

'I'll do that and give you all the information you need. When school comes out you will probably catch the same bus as Hannah and Heather. If you miss it you will have twenty minutes to wait.'

'Mrs Chalmers—'

'Couldn't you make that Aunt Linda?'

'I don't think so. Not yet, maybe later.'

'I hope you will. Sorry, what were you going to say?'

'Any more toast? These slices are not very big.'

'I'll pop another one in the toaster.' Linda got up to take the lid off the bread bin. 'One enough?' she asked as she held the bread aloft.

'Yes.' She drank some tea then put her cup down. 'Mrs McDonald—'

Linda came in swiftly. She didn't want her miscalling the woman.

'She was very kind to you, Jennifer. Not many neighbours would have done what she did and you have to remember she is elderly.'

'I know all that, you don't have to remind me. And for your information she didn't do it for me. We hardly ever spoke. Mum was good to her. She used to go in to keep her company and do her shopping if she didn't feel like going out.'

Linda nodded. That sounded like Betty.

Jennifer smiled. 'She couldn't stand Dad and it was mutual. He called her a nosey old gasbag.'

'That was unkind.'

Jennifer shrugged. 'She was funny about some things or plain daft. I could wear Mum's jewellery if I wanted. I didn't actually want to but she thought that was all right. Not clothes, though, she said it was unlucky to wear a dead person's clothes and the Salvation Army was the place for them. Presumably it wasn't unlucky for them.'

Linda smiled.

'I didn't care where they went. But not that off-white jacket. Mum bought it not long ago. I was with her and I tried it on in the shop. It fitted me and I got to wear it a few times.' She stopped and looked across at Linda. 'You saw for yourself, you saw the way she was when she saw me wearing Mum's jacket.'

'Yes.'

'Do you think it will bring me bad luck?' She raised her eyebrows.

'No, I don't, I'm not superstitious.'

'Could be I've had my share of that.' She choked over a piece of toast and quickly drank some tea.

'All right, dear?' Linda had an urge to comfort the girl, put her arms around her but knew it wouldn't be welcomed. Better to change the subject, she would do that.

'Jennifer, you do have your school uniform with you?'

'Yes. I brought nearly all my clothes and what I left was ready for throwing out.'

'When that wardrobe arrives from my sister you will get everything sorted out. In the meantime I'll find a temporary home for the blankets and give you the hamper to store your belongings.'

She nodded. 'You had better know there is hardly any money,' the girl said abruptly.

'You don't have to worry about that, Jennifer,' Linda said hastily.

'Mum had money, quite a lot. She told me that most of her savings had gone. I shouldn't call it her savings, the money she was left would have come from my grandmother, no my great-grandmother.'

'Yes, your great-grandmother. I met the old lady and remember her as being very charming.'

'Was she?' she said without interest. 'I do know a bit about my own affairs. I have Mrs McDonald to thank for that. She said I would be entitled to any money there was and that would include the proceeds from the sale of the furniture. The car wasn't Dad's, it was company-owned and anyway it was a write-off.'

Linda was amazed as well as shocked at the matter-of-fact way the girl spoke.

'I'm sure you will be entitled to everything once the expenses are met.'

'What expenses?' she said sharply.

'Solicitors charge for their work, Jennifer.'

'What is left after that, I get?'

'It will be held in trust for you.'

'Will you claim some of it for keeping me?'

'Of course not. We wouldn't dream of accepting a penny.'

Linda got up and began clearing the table, and after a small hesitation Jennifer pushed back her cup and saucer and got up to give a hand.

'Something else you should know.'

Linda half turned her head.

'You had better know now, Mrs Chalmers, that I will be leaving school at sixteen. That means I will be going at the summer holidays.'

'Was that decided before – before—'

'Before they died?'

'Is this distressing you? We can stop if it is.'

'No reason to stop.'

'You are not distressed?'

'You've asked that already and the answer is, not much. Why?'

'I was going to talk about your mother,' Linda said quietly as she filled the basin with hot water, added washing-up liquid and began to wash the dishes.

'Talk about her if you want to.'

'She was bright and she was a very good student. I rather thought she would have wanted her daughter to have a good education.'

'Maybe she did. This tea towel is soaking wet.'

'It can't be but take a fresh one from the drawer. Second one down.'

'They have machines for doing this. Mum said if she got prize money for something that is what she would spend it on. Dad said it encouraged laziness.'

'Did your father give any assistance?'

'Of course not, he would have said that was women's work.'

'And what are your thoughts on the subject?' Linda smiled.

'If women don't go out to work then I suppose he was right but if they are both working then maybe they should share the chores. Mum thought that.'

'When dishwashing machines become more popular and are not so expensive then I would hope to persuade my husband to buy one for me. Jennifer, we were talking about you leaving school at sixteen.'

'Mum would have wanted me to stay on at school and work for my Highers but she wasn't going to force me.'

'No, Betty wouldn't do that. She would want your happiness above all else.'

'You know a lot about my Mum.'

'While we were at college I did. We were best friends.'

'Mum was engaged to be married, she broke it off when she met Dad.'

'Yes, I know.'

'Did you know him? Mum said he was called Alan.'

'Yes, I knew Alan.'

'Did you like him?'

'I did, very much. Everybody liked Alan.'

'What about my dad? You must have known him as well.'

'I had met your father but I didn't know Robert.'

Jennifer was silent for a few moments. 'Before we got on to this we were talking about me leaving school at the summer holidays.'

'Is that what you want?'

'I just said so, didn't I?' she said cheekily.

'I think you say things you don't mean, Jennifer. You like to shock, don't you?'

She shrugged. 'Maybe I do but I am serious about this.'

'What would you want to do?'

'I haven't made up my mind.'

'You must have some idea.'

'Something to do with fashion,' she said reluctantly.

Linda nodded, remembering the fashion magazine she had spent so much time poring over in the car.

'Dad was all for it. He said staying on at school could be a waste of time. He said I had the figure and the looks to be a fashion model,' she said proudly. 'And he said that fashion houses offered training to young girls with the right looks and what is more, the younger the better.'

'To be honest, dear, I am a bit out of my depth here. The little I do know is that it is extremely difficult to break into the fashion world.'

'Meaning you don't think I stand a chance,' Jennifer said, flushing angrily.

'Meaning nothing of the kind. What a prickly creature you are. If your heart is set on a modelling career then we must investigate the possibilities.'

'Thanks. My Dad was handsome, everybody said so.'

'Yes, he was, your father was a very handsome man.' And knew it too, she could have added. 'Your parents were a good-looking couple. Your mother was very pretty.'

'Prettier than me?'

'I wouldn't say that. Betty was nice, she had a lovely nature.'

'And I haven't?'

'No. I am going to be honest. You do not have your mother's lovely nature, in fact your manner leaves much to be desired.'

'Does it?'

'You were rude to my mother and I did not like that. You barely answered when she spoke to you.' Linda wrung out the dishcloth and poured away the water. 'We had gone to a lot of trouble for you, young lady, and although we were willing to make allowances we thought you behaved very badly. It isn't clever to be rude.'

It wasn't a sneer but it was near enough.

'My mother was stupid.'

'Betty was far from that.'

'I don't mean she wasn't intelligent, she was cleverer than my dad and he knew it and didn't like it.' Linda had returned to her chair at the table and Jennifer did the same. 'When I said Mum was stupid I meant she was too soft and willing to forgive.' She looked thoughtful for a few moments and Linda didn't break the silence. 'I hated her when she was quiet and submissive and afraid for her when she wasn't,' Jennifer said very quietly.

'Oh, Jennifer.' Linda felt a lump in her throat.

It was as though she hadn't heard Linda, almost as though she was talking to herself. 'She was stupid in some ways. I could see it and she couldn't. Dad would have preferred it if she had stuck up for herself, she did occasionally, but not very often. I knew how to.'

Linda smiled. 'I could believe that.'

'I could handle my dad and give as good as I got and I think he liked me for it.' She smiled. 'He used to say I took after him, that I was a chip off the old block.'

'Maybe you are but with a little of your mother as well.'

'Do you and Mr Chalmers quarrel? No, I don't suppose you do.'

'We disagree as most couples do from time to time but, no, we don't quarrel.' Linda didn't like to think how close they had come to it.

'My parents quarrelled a lot.'

'That must have been distressing for you.'

'I got used to it, I suppose.'

'My grandmother gave me some good advice before I got married. She said never to let the sun go down on your wrath – always to make up.'

'That is just old-fashioned rubbish,' she said rudely.

'No, you would do well to remember it for the future.'

Jennifer raised her eyes to the ceiling. 'When they quarrelled—'

'Not in front of you?'

'They would have forgotten I was there. Most of the time I didn't bother to listen. Mum had a jealous streak and she got mad if Dad got too friendly with some woman. Mostly it was the woman chasing after Dad and he got a kick out of thinking he was irresistible.' She giggled. 'When Mum accused him of being unfaithful he never bothered to deny it, though some of the time I think he was just having her on. I tried to tell her but she could never see it.'

'That was cruel of your father.' Linda's heart went out to Betty. There had been very little happiness in that marriage.

Jennifer shrugged.

'Thank you for being so open, and now I think enough has been said.' Linda had a suspicion that Jennifer might later regret what she had said.

'In other words, I've said too much. You don't want to hear any more?'

'I didn't say that or at least it wasn't what I meant. If you find it helpful to talk about your parents then I am happy to listen. My worry was that you might regret—'

'I won't regret any of this if I have your word that you will not repeat it.'

'You have my word, Jennifer.'

'OK, and I don't want you thinking it was all bad because it wasn't. Sometimes they were happy.' She smiled. 'Dad could be lots of fun when he was in the mood.'

'I'm sure there were good times and you should dwell on those.'

'That is the kind of stupid remark my mother would have made. I don't dwell on anything, I remember what happened.'

Linda thought of all the chores that had to be done but decided to forget about them. She didn't think this outpouring would ever happen again and she was interested, very interested to hear from Betty's daughter what her friend's life had been like.

'I'm going to tell you this even though I don't think I should. You are too easily shocked.'

'No, Jennifer, I don't believe that I am very easily shocked. Try me,' she smiled.

There was no answering smile. 'I remember the time when Dad saw red. It was when Mum brought up Alan. She told him that breaking off her engagement to Alan had been the biggest mistake of her life and that marriage to my dad had brought her nothing but misery and humiliation. That was when he hit her.'

Linda was stunned. She knew it happened, there were a lot of violent men, but for her it was hard to imagine anyone striking Betty. She was so delicate, so fragile-looking.

'She could have got out of the way, she saw it coming but she didn't move. In a strange sort of way, and she told me this herself, she saw it as giving her the upper hand.'

'I'm afraid I don't follow.'

'I don't suppose you do.' It wasn't said in a cheeky manner just a statement of fact. You see, Mrs Chalmers, that allowed

Mum to turn round and say that Alan, unlike Dad, was a gentleman. That no matter how provoked he would be quite incapable of hitting a woman.'

'Was your mother badly hurt?'

'If you mean did she require hospital treatment then the answer is no. She looked a mess, her face I mean. She was all blotchy and her eye turned black. It cleared up but it took about a week and in all that time she never put a foot outside the door. Dad and I got in what was necessary.'

'He was sorry.'

'I'm sure he was. Maybe he said so. I don't know.'

'Poor Betty. Poor you for that matter.'

'You are shocked.'

'Yes.'

'Aren't you wishing now that you had never agreed to be my godmother?'

Linda thought she should seize the opportunity to find out how much Jennifer knew.

'Did your mother tell you that you had a godmother?'

'As a matter of fact she did not and I've wondered why. Could be she forgot but it is a funny thing to forget.'

Linda nodded her head in agreement.

'Godmothers usually send Christmas and birthday gifts. You didn't.'

'Don't try and make me out to be mean,' Linda laughed. 'Your parents moved house, moved several times I think, but I had no address. For her own reasons your mother did not keep me up to date with her movements.'

'So even if you had wanted, you couldn't have sent me anything?'

'I would have been happy to send you a gift but with no address that would have been difficult.'

Jennifer was looking thoughtful. 'It could have been that she didn't want Dad to know, about the godmother business

I mean. He didn't like Mum keeping up with her old friends.'

'When did you find out?'

She shook her head.

'When were you told?'

'I don't know, I don't remember.' She paused. 'It could have been Mrs McDonald, though I can't imagine how she should know.'

'That might have been the solicitor,' Linda suggested.

'Think so?'

'A possibility.'

'Doesn't matter, does it? You are and that is that.'

Linda got to her feet. 'Jennifer, I am terribly far behind with the housework. Would you like to go to the village for me? I do need one or two things.'

'I don't mind.'

'Thank you. I'll make out a short list and if you say it is for me the shop assistant will know what to give you.'

'Which direction?' she asked, scraping back her chair.

'Left at the road end then just keep on. There is a small bank of shops. Take the chance to have a walk around and see our pretty little village. With the sun shining you will be seeing it at its best.'

Jennifer had not long gone with a basket over her arm when the phone rang. Linda muttered in annoyance, then went to answer it.

'It's me.'

'Hello, Helen. Keep it short, will you, I've hardly done a stroke of work.'

'If you will gossip—'

'I wasn't. I was talking to Jennifer or rather she was doing most of the talking.'

'She's here then. That's what I phoned to find out.'

'Of course you couldn't know. I seem to be incapable of coherent thought at the moment.'

'You are forgiven. Last night I was late in getting home. I wanted to ring you but George said I was being selfish and that the news would keep until the morning. So here I am and dying to know how you got on.'

'Which means you haven't been in touch with Mum.'

'I'll do that later.'

'Helen, the details will have to wait. Jennifer is here as you now know.'

'I have to say, I am surprised. Somehow with Mum there I didn't think it would happen.'

'Matthew had that line of thought too,' Linda said dryly.

'Is the poor man mortified to have another female in the house?'

'Matthew has come to accept the situation.'

'Must have come as a shock you arriving home with the girl.'

'Helen, use your intelligence. Of course I phoned to prepare him.'

'Very wise.' She paused. 'May I ask, how did he take it?'

'He offered to bring the spare bed down from the attic.'

'Not too bothered or just resigned?'

'Resigned,' Linda said heavily.

'That was a shame expecting him to lug the bed down,' she said, sounding angry.

'He offered.'

'Because he is a big softie. Surely you could have had all that done just in case it was required.'

'In my shoes you would have.'

'Too true, I like to be prepared.'

'Well I am not like you as we both know. Had the bed not been required it would have been wasted effort.'

'The wardrobe, you will want that?'

'Urgently.'

'Leave it to me, I'll arrange transport.'

'Shouldn't that be me?'

'You have enough on your plate. This will be my small contribution.'

'I'm very grateful, thanks, Helen.'

'What does she look like?'

'A beauty.'

'Honestly?'

'Honestly. She is a lovely-looking girl with dark eyes and wonderful thick blue-black hair. Mind you, that is not surprising. She had a good start with handsome parents.'

'Doesn't always work out that way. The offspring of marvellous-looking parents can be plain—'

'And by the same token, ugly parents can produce a beauty,' Linda laughed. 'Our Jennifer is one of the lucky ones. Lucky in that way,' she said, remembering the tragedy.

'Are my boys safe?'

'I'm not so sure,' Linda said. 'Matthew, I can tell you, was quite captivated by the dazzling smile she gave him.'

'I take it the others didn't get that.'

'No, and it was noticed by Hannah and Heather.'

'A young lady who prefers the opposite sex.'

'Helen,' Linda protested. 'She is only fifteen.'

'Heavens, today's fifteen-year-olds know it all. Or think they do. Is Jennifer friendly?'

'It wouldn't be a word I would use to describe her. Mum and I had an uphill job getting anything out of her. Eventually we gave up. Mum, I know, was itching to give her a good shake.'

'She would, she hates rudeness. That said, you have to make some allowances after what the girl has come through.'

'We were not forgetful of that, Helen.' She paused. 'This morning she opened up to me and needed no encouragement. It was as though she needed to talk to someone and I was there.'

'Did you learn much, serious stuff I mean?'

'Yes, I did, but it was given in confidence.'

'Fair enough, I won't try to worm it out of you. Just tell me one thing. Are there any serious defects in her character that we need to look out for?'

'All I will say is that the poor girl has had a very difficult life, and if at times she is moody it is not surprising. That doesn't mean I let her off. I told her that both Mother and I resented her rudeness and that kind of behaviour is not acceptable.'

'What about school?'

'All taken care of. Jennifer has an appointment with Miss Dempster for tomorrow morning. You must come over and meet the new member of the family, all of you. I'll arrange something.'

'You have more than enough to do without entertaining us. Actually I was about to suggest we have a family get-together in our house. How about Sunday lunch?'

'This coming Sunday?'

'If that is convenient.'

'I'm sure it is.'

'I'm suggesting Sunday lunch because it is the one time I can almost guarantee the boys to be at home. They would hate to miss the roast beef and Yorkshire pudding. Mum won't be doing anything I shouldn't think. I'll phone her after this.'

'Do that. Bye, Helen, I must ring off.' She put the phone down.

Jennifer had returned with the shopping and Linda was making the beds before dashing around with a duster, promising faithfully to lift all the ornaments the next time rather than dusting round them. Jennifer had gone to Heather's bedroom to sort out her clothes before putting them in the hamper. This was awful, she thought glumly, but it would have to do until the wardrobe arrived. What was worse, very much worse, was having to share a bedroom. She valued her privacy and she wasn't going to get much of that in this house.

Jennifer had never wanted sisters or brothers. She had always thought that being an only child had advantages. There was no need to share and when she wanted to be alone she could. Mrs Chalmers was sorry for her, that was plain to see. Her parents quarrelling had not upset her all that much. When it did all she had to do was remove herself. The row would be heated and then over. They would have made up and her mum would have dried her tears. Dad probably had gone to the local for a drink and when he came back it would be with a peace offering. A box of Mum's favourite chocolates and a bar of something for her.

Life would run smoothly for a while. Her mum, she knew, felt guilty about their daughter seeing this darker side of their marriage.

'You must not think that all marriages are like ours, Jennifer,' she said on one occasion when they were alone. 'Your dad and I are a badly matched couple.'

'You must have loved Dad when you married him.'

'I confused love with infatuation. Your father had looks and charm and those were what I fell for.'

'He still has,' his daughter said loyally.

'Yes. The difference is that I see through the charm. You must not make the same mistake, my dear. I want you to know true happiness.'

'Maybe we don't want the same things.'

Her mother had frowned. 'You want to be happy, don't you?'

'If I'm successful I'll be happy. The two for me go together.'

'Your father has filled your head with a lot of nonsense about modelling. He sees the glamour without the hard work. Success in that world comes to very few, and for the others it can be a soul-destroying business.'

'Dad says it pays to be ruthless—'

'Get what you want through fair means or foul, yes, that would be his advice.'

'Maybe I agree with Dad.'

Her mother sounded tired and depressed. 'There is a lot of your father in you.'

'He said you kept him back.'

'Kept him back from what?'

'Making a success of his life.'

'What does he know about success?' Betty said bitterly. 'He has known nothing but failure. Time and time again I have come to his rescue. His hare-brained ideas have been costly and that is where most of my money has gone, digging him out. He wouldn't tell you that?'

'No.'

'I wanted that money to give you a good start in life. My wish, as you know, is for you to stay on at school and work for your Highers. You have it in you if only you would put your mind to it.'

'Why should I slog? I'll use my good appearance and marry for money.'

'I hope you are joking.'

'I'm not, Mum. You don't live in the real world, Dad does.'

'Talking to you is a waste of time. You think at fifteen you know it all.'

'No, I don't know it all but I'll learn by my mistakes. You did.'

'Yes, when it was too late,' Betty said despairingly.

Linda was reasonably organised and the preparations for the meal under way. Robin was first home and flushed and happy to have been rewarded with a star for his work.

'Clever you, darling.'

'Did you ever get a star, Mummy?'

'No, I didn't. I just wasn't as clever as you.'

'But you are good at some things.'

'Oh, I think so. On you go, dear, and change out of your school clothes.'

Half an hour later when Hannah and Heather appeared, Jennifer had finished packing the hamper and was in the sitting-room watching television.

Heather came downstairs from the bedroom and into the kitchen, looking unusually glum.

'What a long face, something wrong at school?'

'No. What is that hamper thing doing in my bedroom?'

'That hamper thing as you call it, Heather, is holding Jennifer's belongings until such time as the wardrobe arrives from your Aunt Helen.'

'There soon won't be enough room to swing a cat,' Heather grumbled.

'You are getting to be as big a moan as your sister.'

Heather grinned. 'That would be impossible.'

Linda gave her younger daughter a quick hug. 'Darling, be nice to Jennifer.'

'Why should I, when she isn't nice to me?'

'The poor girl hasn't had your advantages.'

Heather gave a deep sigh. 'Hannah said she would come up with a sob story.'

'Hannah is being very unkind.'

'It could be a sob story, how do you know it isn't?'

'Apart from losing both parents she has had a difficult life.'

'What if she has? She doesn't have to take it out on us.'

'I know, dear, it isn't very easy for you, for any of us but we must do our best.'

'OK.'

'If Aunt Helen can arrange it we are all invited there for Sunday lunch.'

'Is this to introduce Jennifer?'

'Yes.'

'I bet you anything Hannah refuses to go.'

'Your sister will be there even if I have to drag her.'

9

'That smells good, darling.'

'It should.' Helen turned to smile at her husband. 'It is top quality beef. The butcher, bless him, gave me a particularly nice piece when I told him I was having the family for lunch. Extended family is what I should have said.'

'What is an extended family?' The Hunters' younger son, sixteen-year-old Simon, slouched into the kitchen yawning and then straddled one of the wooden chairs. It would, he knew, annoy his mother. The admonition died on Helen's lips. What was the use? Simon was going through that awkward stage when he wanted to annoy.

Her son was waiting to be told off and when it didn't happen he seemed disappointed.

'It is not fair, Mater,' he grumbled.

'Don't call me Mater, I don't like it. George, darling, I can't get to the oven if you are to stand there.'

'Sorry,' her husband said, removing himself quickly. George was nice, everybody had a good word for him. He had a gentle lazy manner that hid an exceptionally quick brain. George Hunter looked older than his years with his grey thinning hair and his fondness for cardigans. He always wore them about the house and the shabbier they were the more attached to them he became. Like a lot of tall thin men George was round-shouldered.

'I said it's not fair,' Simon repeated.

'I heard you the first time and for goodness sake, what are you doing coming down dressed like that?'

'What I am wearing is perfectly suitable for what I intend doing.'

'Which is?'

'Mum, you don't listen, you never do. I told you I was going over to help Mike clean out their garage. And I promised to be at his house no later than half past one.'

'Out of the question,' Helen said dismissively as she went quickly and purposefully about the kitchen preparing for this lunch which was to introduce Jennifer to the Hunter side of the family.

'Why should it be out of the question?'

'Because I said so.'

'That is not a reason and I could skip afters,' he said hopefully.

'You will not skip anything, Simon. What you will do is go now, this minute, and phone Mike. Explain the situation.'

'He is going to be mad after me promising.'

'I am not sure that I approve of you doing that kind of work on a Sunday. If you want to clean out a garage you can start with ours.'

'There is nothing to clean out or clear out. You never accumulate, you throw away.'

George hid a smile. Simon had a point there. Helen was very good at throwing away what she considered rubbish without asking first.

'Helen, your son asked you a question which you have not as yet answered.'

'What was that, Dad?'

'You wanted to know the meaning of the extended family.'

'So I did. OK, Mum, what is it?'

'An extended family?'

'Yes.'

'Cousins, aunts and uncles, half-cousins, people who are related but who are not close family is the best I can do.

Honestly, I am trying to concentrate on preparing a meal. Thank heaven I made an early start.'

'I know it. I just know it, this lunch will go on for ever. Talk, talk, talk. And this girl, it will be awful, I won't know what to say.'

'That will make a change,' George smiled.

'You should be on my side, Dad, and let me remind you about that time when we were having our little talk. You said that when you were my age if a girl as much as looked at you, you got all embarrassed and tongue-tied.'

'That, my son, was in the dim and distant past. We didn't carry on the way you youngsters do.'

'I bet she'll be all silly and giggly,' Simon said disgustedly.

'Jennifer is neither silly nor giggly from what I hear. There has been a great tragedy in her life.'

'I know, you told us. That's tough on her but I can't do anything about it.'

'You can be kind.'

'No one will notice if I slip away.'

'Simon, you are trying my patience.'

George was shaking his head. He was always amused at the clashes between his wife and the boys.

'Simon, lad, you should know by this time that you are fighting a losing battle. Far better to give in gracefully.'

Helen laughed. She was pleased that she could laugh at herself. There were times, she knew, when she sounded like a sergeant-major barking commands. But was it any wonder, with three easygoing males in the house? They could be so exasperating.

'Where is that brother of yours?'

'How should I know? I am not my brother's keeper.'

'Surely he can't still be in bed?'

'I think it very probable,' George said mildly. 'One of the Sunday papers has disappeared.'

'Reading the newspaper in bed.' She closed her eyes in despair. 'The sheet will be filthy. That print comes off and it is not easy to remove from the bedclothes. And as for breakfast, if he can't come down for it at a reasonable time he can make his own or do without.' She put the baking bowl on the table with unnecessary force.

'I don't think Nigel will be too bothered about missing breakfast, dear, I rather think he indulged too freely at that rugby do.'

Helen stopped with the egg box in her hand. 'George, you can't mean – he wasn't drinking – it wouldn't be allowed – would it?'

'Nothing for you to get het up about. Boys will be boys.'

'That is you all over, you are so easygoing, you take nothing seriously. Surely it is your responsibility—'

'To keep them on the straight and narrow?'

'Yes, as a matter of fact that is what I think. I can't be expected to do everything. Surely that is a father's job.'

'No one expects you to do more than you do. Trust them, my dear, that is what I do.'

'Again the easy way out.'

'Believe me, Helen, it is far from easy. One frequently wants to interfere and one shouldn't. Doing nothing is by far the best way and our two will respect us for that.'

'Too true, Dad. Thanks a million.'

'Are you still there? I'd thought you'd gone. Didn't your mother say something about phoning Mike?'

'Seems I have no choice. I'm beginning to think I should forego the roast beef and Yorkshire pud, the price is too high.' He went away, muttering to himself.

'That boy is becoming impossible. Where do you think I went wrong with his upbringing?'

'You didn't. You've made a fine job of both of them and you know, dear, small acts of rebellion are all part of growing up.

Be pleased that they are showing some independence. If they weren't I would be worried.' He looked at his wife with tenderness. 'When it really counts they won't let us down.'

'No, you are right as usual,' Helen said, showing some exasperation. 'I wonder about this girl we are going to meet. When I was talking to Mum on the phone she was a bit cagey and I had the distinct feeling that she wasn't too happy. Maybe Linda has taken on too much.'

'I imagine that your mother is very wisely leaving it to you to form your own opinion.'

'What if she doesn't fit in? Linda is going to feel terribly guilty, because she and she alone is responsible.'

'Dearest, if I had to be sorry for anyone it would be for this girl, Jennifer. Remember, everyone and everything is strange to her. Poor thing, she has lost her parents, her home, her friends and if she is moody and withdrawn then is it any wonder? We are going to play our part, Helen, and welcome her warmly into our home.'

'Why are you always so damned nice?'

'The nature of the beast. But here I am keeping you back. If I can't be of any assistance I'll make myself scarce.'

'You do that, I get on better if I have the kitchen to myself. What you can do is make sure that Simon changes into something respectable.'

'Would it matter? After all it is only family.'

'George,' she said warningly.

'It would matter, I can see that. If he appears—'

'In scruffy clothes I'll kill him and probably you as well,' Helen laughed.

Over at Hillcrest, with no Sunday lunch to prepare, Linda was having a relaxing morning with her feet up and reading one of the Sunday papers. She was enjoying the novelty of having nothing to do.

'Mummy.'

'Yes, dear?'

'You know this, I won't have anything to play with because Aunt Helen has given me all Simon's toys.'

'Then take a few with you.'

'How many?'

'One or two.'

'Not three?'

'If you want take three.'

'How about my double-decker bus and three Dinky toys?'

'That adds up to four.'

'I know.'

'All right. Robin, I am trying to read the paper.'

'Is that the one with the comic?'

'Yes.'

'Does Aunt Helen get that paper?'

'I don't know.'

'When you finish reading give me the comic.'

'Robin?'

'Please.'

'That's better.'

'I'll need a bag for the toys.'

'You know where the bags are kept.'

'Do I?'

'Yes, you do. In the cupboard. You have to learn to do things for yourself.' Linda always folded the carrier bags and put them in a large bag which hung at the back of the cupboard door. Robin would haul them all out before he got one to satisfy him, and leave the mess for her to clear up. She got up and went to see how he was getting on.

'If one bag isn't enough take two but do not leave a mess for me to clear up.'

'I wasn't going to.'

She smiled. Robin was the most contented of children, he

didn't have to be entertained. Give him his double-decker bus and he would crawl about the floor announcing the various destinations. Robin and his bus had become a family joke. There had been one occasion when he had been inconsolable and it was a long time before they discovered the reason. Linda had noticed the carpet getting worn at the door and had decided to change it round. The carpet had a pattern of squares and Robin had one particular square beside the leg of the table that had become the bus depot. To find that it was no longer there had upset him terribly and more so because he couldn't explain.

Linda went back to her Sunday paper and Matthew mumbled something about taking the car out and she nodded without paying much attention.

Matthew was proud of his car which he had only had for a few months. Being senior management meant he was entitled to a new car every two years. Provided it was within the price range it was left to the employee to make his choice of model. Matthew had gone for a big roomy car and he was thinking how very fortunate that had been. Robin was no longer content to squeeze up, he demanded parity with his sisters, and there was Jennifer now.

By twelve thirty the family was ready to leave. Linda had been waiting for Hannah to be difficult but she was making no fuss. She and her cousin, Simon, had a good rapport and she would be looking forward to seeing him. Linda was glad to see that Hannah had taken care over her appearance. She had shampooed her hair and it hung soft and silky to her shoulders. In her navy skirt and pale blue angora jumper she looked lovely.

'Darling, you do look nice.'

Hannah smiled but said nothing.

'What about me?' Heather said. Their younger daughter had no interest in clothes and put on what was laid out.

'You'll do, dear,' her mother smiled.

'Hannah's cast-offs.'

'Nothing of the kind. Hannah only wore that pinafore dress two or three times before she outgrew it.'

'Which means it is still a cast-off. It was not bought for me.'

'Yes, Heather, all right it is a cast-off.'

'Are you lot coming?' Matthew shouted from the doorway.

'In a minute, darling. Heather, run upstairs and tell Jennifer to get a move on.'

'I'm here.'

'Oh, there you are. On you go, all of you, and I'll lock up.' Linda double-locked the back door. The trees had lost most of their leaves and Matthew would be moaning about the never-ending job of clearing the leaves whereas she didn't mind how long they lay. Today there was some warmth in the sun and a fairly gusty wind was sending the leaves rolling along.

Linda got in the front of the car beside her husband.

'Are we collecting Kirsty?'

'No, Mum said she would take her car.'

'Just as well or it would be a real squeeze up.'

'I'm not sitting on anybody's knees. I'm too big.'

'You are still the smallest so it would have to be you, Robin,' Heather said.

'You're too fat, you would flatten—'

'Now! Now! Behave, all of you.'

Matthew switched on the engine. 'OK, full steam ahead.'

Robin giggled. 'We're not on a train, Daddy.'

'What is my foot coming against?' Jennifer said.

'My toys. Don't kick them,' Robin screamed. 'They'll break.'

'Heavens! What a state to get into. My foot only touched them.'

'Robin, take them beside you. That is what you should have done in the first place.'

There was very little talk for the rest of the journey.

When the car stopped at the gate Helen and her mother were standing at the open door ready to receive their guests. Matthew had decided to leave the car where it was rather than park it in the drive. There were already two cars there – Helen's and Kirsty's. Robin was the first out, clutching his precious toys. His grandmother got the first hug, then it was Helen's turn.

'How is my favourite young man?' she smiled.

'Am I?' he grinned.

'You are but don't tell anyone.'

'Where is Simon?'

'In the house somewhere, go and find him.' Robin was off like a shot.

Hannah and Heather got out of the car and walked together to the door. Jennifer was taking her time and it was obvious she was waiting for Matthew.

'On you go,' he said. 'This is a very respectable area but I am still going to lock up.'

Jennifer smiled and moved away. She wore her off-white boxy jacket over a red skirt and a shocking pink blouse. Linda thought it a startling combination, and with the girl's dark colouring it looked eye-catching. She remembered Betty having good dress sense and this she must have handed on to her daughter. Jennifer did not have a lot of clothes but there was a clever mix and match which made it seem she had more.

Kirsty had gone inside leaving Helen and Linda. Helen wore the welcoming smile and had the easy manner of the perfect hostess.

Linda made the introductions.

'How do you do, Mrs Hunter?' Jennifer said charmingly. 'Thank you for inviting me to your home, it was very kind of you.'

'We wanted to meet you, Jennifer.' Helen had been slightly

taken aback by the girl's cool composure and even more by her appearance. Pretty did not do her justice, she was beautiful. 'Come in and let me close the door. Everybody will be in the sitting-room, I imagine. Give me your jacket and I'll put it in the cloakroom. I do like it. I have a weakness for these casual but smart jackets.'

Linda laughed. 'Helen, you have a weakness for clothes, full stop.'

Jennifer took off her jacket and gave it to Helen. Linda thought she should wait and the three of them go in together.

'Linda, what are you waiting for? Anyone would think you were a stranger.'

'This way we'll make an entrance,' she laughed.

'With our lot it would be wasted.' She led the way through the wide hall to where the sounds of talk and laughter could be heard. There was a moment of silence when they entered. George went forward.

'This is my husband, Jennifer.'

George took her hand in both of his. 'How very pleased I am to meet you, my dear. We welcome you warmly.'

'Thank you.'

'And these two lads are Nigel and Simon.'

Nigel was the first to greet Jennifer. 'Hello, great to see you,' he grinned.

'Hello, too,' she said, looking shy.

'Simon,' George said, giving his younger son a slight push.

'Hello, Je-Jennifer,' he stammered and blushed to the roots of his hair.

'Hello, Simon.'

'Helen, my dear, we are all present and correct and ready for something to eat. Shall we make a move to the dining-room?'

'Yes, do that. Please, everybody, go through to the dining-room and I'll check that all is well in the kitchen.'

'Want a hand?'

'No, Mum, this is a day of rest for you.'

'Most of my days are.'

'I'll come.'

'Yes, Linda, thank you. I could do with your assistance.'

It wasn't the truth, as Linda knew. Helen was always very well prepared. She would want to talk about Jennifer.

The first course was soup.

'Shall I do the carrying?'

'Yes, but not for a minute. Linda, she is gorgeous, a knockout. Did you see my two? Simon in particular.'

'I did tell you.'

'You said pretty. Heavens, in a year or two she will be stunning. That hair and those eyes, not forgetting the legs. She'll have every boy in the school after her.'

'She might at that.'

'You don't sound too happy.'

'I'm not. She isn't always so charming, in fact she can be very difficult, rude even.'

'You are making allowances after all that has happened to her?'

'Of course, Helen. No, it is more than that. I can't put my finger on it. She is a strange girl. Come on with the soup or they will wonder what the hold-up is.'

'Fascinating creature but we'll leave Jennifer for the moment and concentrate on the meal.'

The soup was served and the warmed rolls handed round. George was being the perfect host and making sure that everyone was included in the conversation. He was very good with Robin and the child adored him. Hannah was smiling, but it was strained and Linda could see the pain behind the smile. She knew the reason, too. She and her cousin, Simon, were special friends. In an argument he nearly always took her side and she would go, even on the coldest day, to cheer him on the playing fields. How the young could suffer in silence, they would rather that than have people feeling sorry for them. Pride was very important.

If it hadn't been for Hannah, Linda thought, she would have found it amusing. Simon was listening to every word Jennifer said and she was being quite talkative. He could hardly bear to take his eyes off her.

'How is the new car behaving, Matthew?'

'Very pleased with it, George. I thought it might be difficult to handle but it isn't.'

'Great-looking car, wouldn't mind a shot at the wheel, Uncle Matthew.'

'Sorry, old son, company car, couldn't risk it. Insurance doesn't cover third party.'

Nigel nodded. He had only very recently passed his driving test but it was nice to pretend that he had that kind of confidence.

'Everyone finished?'

'Yes, Helen, I think so,' Kirsty said. 'Speaking for myself, that was a wonderful meal and I thoroughly enjoyed it.'

There was a murmur of agreement.

'George, who does the washing-up?' Kirsty asked him.

'Nobody,' his wife answered for him. 'Linda and I will take the dishes through to the kitchen and leave them for later.

'You will excuse me, folks,' Nigel said.

'Of course, Nigel,' his uncle grinned. 'A heavy date, is it?'

'I would be so lucky.'

'Yes, Nigel, you are excused,' his mother said, 'and that goes for you as well, Simon.'

'I'm in no hurry.'

George spluttered and got out his handkerchief.

'What about Mike?' Helen said, raising her eyebrows, 'Won't he be expecting you?'

'Sort of.' His eyes turned to Jennifer. 'I was going to help
Mike to clean out the garage but any time will do for that.'

Helen hurried from the room before she burst into laughter.

Simon had seen the way Jennifer looked at Nigel and was
glad that his big brother had had the sense to make himself
scarce. He had a girlfriend.

He sidled over to Jennifer. 'It's hot in here. Want to go out
for a bit?'

'I wouldn't mind,' she smiled.

'Need a coat?'

'No, it shouldn't be too cold.'

They went out the front door then walked round to the back
of the house with its large lawns and many flower beds. At the
foot of the garden there was a summer-house with cushioned
seats.

'Want to sit down for a while?'

'Yes.'

'This is very nice,' Jennifer said, sitting down and leaning
back.

'Not much used. Dad got it for Mum but she leads such a
busy life that she doesn't have much time to sit around. She
doesn't potter about the garden and neither does the old man
but they like to see everything nice.'

'Which means a gardener.'

'A gardener and a few assistants.'

'Are your parents wealthy?'

Simon was surprised at the question. 'I wouldn't say so,
comfortably off probably describes it.'

'You have a lovely home.'

'Not bad.'

'What does your father do?'

'Dad is an architect.'

'With his own business? Am I asking too many questions?'

'No.'

'It is just I am interested. Are you going to be an architect?'

'Not me. I want to study languages. With a bit of luck, I might get into the Foreign Office.' He laughed. 'It takes more than luck, I'll have to work hard if I am to be given the chance. Nigel will follow Dad, he wants to be an architect.'

'Has Nigel got a girlfriend?'

'Yes,' he said shortly, 'he does. Why?'

'Mr Chalmers said something about a heavy date.'

'Do you call Aunt Linda and Uncle Matthew Mr and Mrs Chalmers?'

'Yes, I do. Mrs Chalmers wanted me to call her Aunt and her husband Uncle. I couldn't.'

'Why not?'

'Because they are not my aunt and uncle, it is as simple as that.'

'Even so they are looking after you.'

'Mrs Chalmers happens to be my godmother so she couldn't do much else.'

'I don't agree but never mind that.' He smiled. 'I'm glad.'

'Glad about what?'

'That you are here and I am getting to know you.'

She gave him a sideways look. 'Actually, you know, I could call Mr Chalmers Matthew, I wouldn't have a problem with that.'

'Maybe you wouldn't, Jennifer, but I bet Hannah and Heather and not forgetting Robin would take a dim view of it.'

Jennifer made a face. 'I have to share a room with Heather and that is just awful. You have your own bedroom?'

'Yes.'

'Did you ever share with your brother?'

'No, it was never necessary although on holidays it wasn't unknown. Sharing with Nigel would not have bothered me, although I prefer my own space.'

'Lucky you to get what you wanted. Never in all my life

have I had to share and it is all Hannah's fault. She won't share with her sister. Honestly, Simon, she really is very, very selfish.'

'No, Jennifer, you are wrong about Hannah.' He couldn't have her saying that when it was so untrue. 'She is not selfish, anything but.'

'How would you know?'

'She is my cousin.'

'You don't live in the same house.'

'True.'

'You think I am making this up,' Jennifer said haughtily.

'No, I don't think that, not for a moment. It is just that I know Hannah very well and you don't.'

'Is Nigel serious about his girlfriend?'

Simon felt a spark of anger. 'Why do you want to know?'

'I just do.'

'The answer is, I wouldn't know.'

'You are angry.'

'I'm jealous, I don't want you fancying my brother.'

'Simon,' she said softly, 'I am interested in you and Nigel and your parents.'

'I would be happier if you were interested in me and not the rest of my family,' he said with his attractive grin.

'Shouldn't we be getting back?'

'Are you cold?'

'A bit.'

'Sorry. Come on then and we'll get back to the house.'

10

Matthew had agreed to be left in charge of the house so that Linda and Jennifer could take the car into Dundee and see about a school uniform. She was all right for white blouses and had two pair of good school shoes. All that was required was a blazer and a skirt. At least it would do for the time being. That shouldn't take them long, and then they could go to the supermarket and stock up. Being a Saturday it would be busy, but that couldn't be helped.

'That was a waste of money, Mrs Chalmers,' Jennifer said as they left the shop with a large carrier bag. 'I won't be wearing uniform for very much longer.'

'Even so you need a school blazer for the time you are to be there and you could change your mind and stay on for another year.'

'Not a chance.' She smiled, 'I needn't worry, if you can afford to waste it you must have plenty of money.'

'I wouldn't say that,' Linda smiled back. 'We have enough for our needs but we certainly cannot afford to go mad. Come along, there is time for a coffee before we go to the supermarket.'

The restaurant Linda chose was moderately busy but there were a few unoccupied tables. It was not self-service and the waitress was quickly over to take their order.

'White coffee and a fruit scone, please. What about you, Jennifer?'

'The same and a doughnut.'

The waitress looked confused. 'You want a scone and a doughnut?'

'No, I want coffee and a doughnut.'

'I thought I made myself perfectly clear,' Jennifer said when the waitress had gone.

'No, you didn't, Jennifer. The same and a doughnut meant what I was having plus a doughnut.'

'Not to me.'

'No, you knew what you wanted. It doesn't matter and before I forget yet again I wanted you to know that you will find a writing pad and envelopes in the bureau. I don't keep it locked. You might wish to drop a line to your friends and let them know where you are.'

'No, thank you.'

'Jennifer, don't lose touch, that would be a mistake and it is nice to keep up with school friends. Did you have a special friend?'

'No.' She paused. 'Don't run away with the idea that I had no friends—'

'Not for a moment did I think that.'

'I had friends but no one I particularly want to keep up with.'

The coffee arrived and nothing more was said until Jennifer had cut her doughnut into four pieces and Linda had split her scone and was spreading it with butter.

'Dad could never keep money,' she said, changing the subject.

'Some people are like that.'

'He was. He liked to blow the lot on luxuries we couldn't afford. I have to say, it was nice while it lasted.' She laughed and the laugh was filled with amusement.

Linda smiled but kept silent. She bit into her scone and watched Jennifer. She ate quickly and finished her doughnut before Linda had swallowed her second bite. Then she licked the sugar from her fingers.

'Mum used to say that with Dad it was as though there was no tomorrow.' She gulped. 'Maybe he had – I've forgotten the word.'

'A premonition.'

'Yes.' She drank a mouthful of coffee and put her cup down with a clatter. 'Perhaps he knew there wouldn't be many tomorrows. Do you believe in premonitions, Mrs Chalmers?'

'No, Jennifer, I don't but many people do. They find it easier to accept. I remember an old neighbour of ours who had a habit of saying that what was for you wouldn't go past you. She really believed that our future was predetermined.'

'Like the car accident was meant to happen, she would have thought that?'

'Yes, I believe she would.'

'She could be right.'

Linda was shaking her head. 'I don't think so, I think we have to take responsibility for our own actions.'

Linda was taken aback at the show of anger on the young face. 'I might have known you would think that,' Jennifer said furiously.

'Dear me, I only expressed an opinion.'

'Sorry,' she muttered. 'Do you want to go now?'

'In a few minutes.' She thought Jennifer needed time to recover from that totally unwarranted outburst. For that matter she was a little shaken herself.

Jennifer was making an effort. 'Mum hated being hard-up. She said she had never been used to penny-pinching.'

'Your mother had good qualifications. Why didn't she go in for teaching? There is always a demand and the school hours would have been very suitable.'

'She wanted to teach but there was something about her not having a teacher training certificate.'

'She could have got that easily enough.'

'By going back to college – takes a year, doesn't it?'

'I think so.'

'Dad would have been dead against it and his word was law. I told you my mother was soft. So you see, Mrs Chalmers,' Jennifer said flippantly, 'that is the way it was in our house.'

'Yes, I do see that and now we should be getting on our way.' Linda caught the waitress's eye and got the bill. She paid it and they left.

'That was nice coffee or perhaps I was just in the mood for it.'

'It was OK.'

'We must do the shopping as quickly as possible. You take charge of the trolley while I select what we need.'

'Mum and I did it that way.'

They could have been any mother and daughter out together for the shopping. Jennifer was a strange mixture, Linda thought. One could never be sure where one was with her. Being an only child she would be used to getting all the attention, maybe that was why sharing was difficult for her. Life could have been a lot easier all round if she had been given her own bedroom. She and Hannah would not be at each other's throats. Well there was nothing she could do about that. And in due course it would work out. They all needed time to adjust. Matthew was the most surprising after his early reluctance to give the girl a home. If there was a problem and anyone at fault he was inclined to blame Hannah.

Linda dried her hands and went to answer the phone.

'Helen, what is it?' she said, recognising the voice.

'An awkward time?'

'You could say that.'

'Sorry, but I think this is important.'

'What is?' Linda said resignedly.

'Mother. I'm concerned about her.'

'Why are you concerned about Mother?'

'Aren't you?'

'No. Should I be?'

'You must have noticed that she isn't looking well.'

Linda thought back to the previous week when she had seen her mother. She hadn't looked unwell and she hadn't complained, not then or when they had spoken on the phone. Linda began to feel guilty – the uncaring daughter. Her mother had had a heavy cold but appeared to have got over it.

'Maybe she did look a little tired but that isn't surpring after a heavy cold.'

'To me she looks completely run down and in need of a holiday. I want her to have a few days away.'

'You've mentioned this to Mum?'

'Yes.'

'And I gather she didn't think much of the idea.'

'That is where you come in, I need your support.'

'Helen, you can't go pushing people into doing what they don't want and especially Mum. She hates it.'

'I have watched her and she is only picking at her food.'

'Even at the best of times she has a small appetite.'

'I've been checking, and there are some very good coach tours. Folk these days, and particularly the elderly, do not mind paying the extra for first-class accommodation and tour companies have finally discovered that.'

'Surely it is too late in the season.'

'Nonsense. October is a lovely bracing month and think of the wonderful autumn colours.'

'True,' Linda said carefully. 'What exactly have you in mind?'

'One I particularly like is for a few days in Skye. In fact I have made a provisional booking.'

'You are taking a lot on yourself.'

'If you weren't listening I did say provisional.'

'OK, tell me more.'

'Eight-day tour.'

'When does it leave?'

'Thursday, a week today.'

'If it is all that popular, why isn't it completely booked up?'

'There are only a few seats left. Linda, are you trying to be awkward?'

'Not at all, just trying to get the facts right.'

'Very well, here are the facts for you. I called in to the travel agent's to find that a few seats are still available. The very helpful assistant suggested a provisional booking and a phone call by Saturday to confirm or cancel.'

'Helen, I appreciate all that but I can't help feeling this is terribly rushed.'

'Honestly, you and Mother are a pair. What is wrong with booking at the last minute? This holiday would set her up for the winter.'

'Helen, I am not against the holiday.'

'Then back me up. Tell her the change would do her good. She would have company and the comfort of the best hotels. And a big plus, tell her she will have a window seat.'

Helen was a trial at times but she did put herself about. Nothing was too much trouble, Linda thought with affection.

'I'll do my best but I'm not sure it will be enough. When Mum says no she usually means it.'

'Thanks anyway, we can but try.'

'Linda, not you as well. I am not ill, in fact I feel perfectly well.'

'No one suggested you were.'

'Pardon me, I understood from Helen that I was almost at death's door.'

'Don't exaggerate.'

Rather than phone and to put her own mind at rest, Linda had decided to drive over to the cottage and check on her mother's health. She didn't look ill but she did look tired. Helen could be right and the change would do her good.

'You are tired so don't deny it. October month, according to the forecast, is to be dry with higher than average temperatures.'

'And you believe all they say?'

'They do get it right for a lot of the time and they are the experts.'

'I have never been on a coach tour and I am not at all sure that I would want to. If I should wish to go away for a few days there is the car.'

'Be honest, driving for you is not the pleasure it once was.'

'That is because there are too many cars on the road and too many idiots behind the wheel.'

'All you have to do is pack a case. Helen has made a provisional booking—'

'Has she indeed?'

'Mum, she has put herself to no end of trouble—'

'I know, dear, you both do and I am an ungrateful old woman.'

'You are not old.'

'Just getting older like everyone else.'

'You will go?'

'If it means that much to you.' She smiled and patted Linda's knee.

'It does.'

'Go and make a cup of tea. I feel the need for one and no doubt you do too.'

Linda got up and went through to the small kitchen to put the kettle on. She was smiling to herself when she went back in to the sitting-room. Helen was going to be pleased.

'What do I take? Winter woollies?' Kirsty asked.

'You must keep warm, that is important. Take something dressy for the evenings, most folk will, I think.'

'What have I got that would be suitable?'

'I would suggest a long skirt and different tops. Ring the changes, you have some lovely blouses.'

'Fine, we've settled that. I've always had a notion to see Skye. It isn't called the misty island for nothing. People do go and come back disappointed because they saw nothing of its beauty for the swirling mist.'

'The chances are you will get lovely clear days.'

'How long do I have?'

'Two days travelling and six days in Skye.'

'My hearing isn't perfect but I can hear that kettle.'

'Sorry, I'll go and make the tea.'

'Look in the tins and see what there is.'

'Not for me, just the tea.'

'The tea will do me. I nibble too many biscuits.'

They drank their tea in front of the fire.

'What time do I leave the house to catch this coach?'

'You had better set out at quarter to eight. There could be a build-up of traffic about that time. One of us will come for you, and meet you on your return.'

'That you will not. I put my foot down. You both have busy mornings and I am not going to inconvenience you. No, Linda, kindly do not interrupt. I am having my own way or I will not go at all. I shall order a taxi.' She paused. 'That said, I would appreciate someone meeting me on the return journey.'

'Of course, one of us will be there.'

'Tell that bossy sister of yours that I am ordering a taxi and my alarm clock will get me up in plenty of time.'

II

Kirsty had been up very early. She didn't want to be rushing around the cottage getting all hot and bothered. That was no way to start a holiday, a holiday that she didn't want. However, since she had allowed herself to be persuaded she thought she should make the best of it.

After a breakfast of toast and home-made marmalade and while she was drinking her second cup of tea, Kirsty picked up the morning newspaper which always arrived very early. She was thinking that had it been a smaller newspaper she could have folded it up and put it in the outside pouch of her shoulder-bag. She could have read it on the journey. A quick glance at the headlines would have to do.

Her soft-topped suitcase was the one she usually took on holiday since it was a good in-between size. Kirsty had packed it the previous night and it was lying open on the spare bed ready for the last-minute things, and anything else that suddenly came to mind. She had taken Linda's advice and packed a long skirt which did not take up much room and had the advantage of not crushing. The skirt was a cotton and wool mixture in several shades of blue which looked lovely with her cream-coloured silk jumper and equally nice with her blouses. She would feel dressed without in any way being overdressed.

About to close the case Kirsty thought again about the newspaper and went to fetch it from the kitchen where it had been left. One never knew, she could be missing something important in the middle pages. When she gave the matter more thought, what was to stop her reading the paper in the hotel bedroom, stretched out on the bed? There was something wicked and hugely enjoyable about doing on holiday what one would not do at home.

After folding the newspaper she placed it on top of her raincoat and shut the case. Two labels had been provided by the holiday company and Helen had filled in the necessary details. Kirsty tied one label on to the handle, one side was for the outgoing journey and the other for the return. The extra label was not required but she would put it in her shoulder-bag in case the other one got torn or ripped off. She tried to imagine what it would feel like to lose one's luggage. Quite dreadful, she thought, and so much worse at the start of the holiday. She would be so miserable that all she would want was to go home. How awful not to have even a change of underwear. She could afford to buy replacements but many couldn't and apart from that what a bother. Kirsty wondered why she was having these silly thoughts. No one was going to lose their luggage on a coach or it was very, very improbable. There was hardly a need to lock her case but she would. The suitcases and bags would be transferred from the coach to the hotel where the porters would take charge. The next time one saw one's belongings would be at the bedroom door. These days everything was so well organised. Oh, dear, she had forgotten something. Why hadn't she bought a book? She had fully intended getting herself a couple of paperbacks. Still it wasn't a tragedy. The choice might be limited but she would get something on one of the stops.

Kirsty seldom wore trousers though she possessed several pairs. This was one time when she thought she should wear them. She was wearing well-cut navy trousers, a long-sleeved striped blouse and a short camel coat. At sixty-five years of age Kirsty Cameron was still an attractive woman and being tall and slim she looked well in trousers. In her younger days not many

women would be seen in trousers or slacks, as they were sometimes called. Times were changing. These were the eighties and
women of all shapes and sizes were relishing the freedom they
gave. Kirsty felt comfortable in hers but she never felt properly
dressed unless she wore a skirt or dress. The classic suit she used
to call a costume, was still her favourite.

She was ready. The windows were shut, the curtains half
drawn. The back door was locked. She would be going out the
front door then double-locking it. One couldn't be too careful
even in this almost crime-free area. The milk and the newspapers were cancelled and Mrs Grieve in the next cottage had
a spare set of keys. If the taxi was up to time and that was what
they were paid to be, then she should be making a move. She
would go outside, double-lock the door and make her way to
the gate. Rather than dig out her purse, which so easily got lost
in the depths of her shoulder-bag, Kirsty had enough money
in her coat pocket to pay the taxi fare and give a tip, the size of
which would depend upon how highly she rated the driver's
helpfulness. Carrying her case she was just closing the gate
behind her when the taxi drew up.

The man was quickly out of his cab and taking possession of
the case.

'Good morning, that was nice timing.'

'It was,' she smiled. Kirsty settled herself in the back and the
driver, after dealing with the suitcase, got behind the wheel
and they were off.

'This you going on holiday?'

'Yes.'

'And where would you be heading?'

'The Isle of Skye.'

'A fine place if you get the weather.'

'So I'm told.'

'The wife and I were there a year or two back. Never saw a
blessed thing the whole week. Just a blanket of mist.'

'Disappointing for you.'

'It was but for all that we had a fine holiday. Good food, good accommodation and friendly folk.'

'Only the scenery missing and that is really what people go for.'

'You could be lucky. The weather seems settled, though when it's fine in the east it doesn't follow it will be that way in the west.' He stopped talking and began to whistle softly. 'Recognise it?'

'I do. The Skye Boat song.'

When they arrived at the picking-up point the coach was waiting with several people standing about. The driver carried her case and put it with the others waiting to go in the hold. Kirsty paid her fare and added a generous tip. He had been helpful and entertaining besides.

'Many thanks.' He looked highly delighted. 'Have a good holiday and I'll keep my fingers crossed for the weather.'

'You do that,' she smiled.

The driver of the coach referred to his clipboard and ticked off the names. Kirsty got her seat number and boarded the coach to claim it. She saw no point in standing around when she could be comfortably seated. A number of others had the same idea. Helen had said that hers was a window seat but one could never be sure of getting what one had asked for. Couples had no problems but singles were different. They could be asked to move and it would be difficult to refuse.

So far so good, the window seat was hers and towards the front of the coach, which was where she preferred to be. She saw by her watch that the time of departure was close and those who stood outside broke off their conversation and got on to the coach. Kirsty kept waiting for someone to claim the seat beside her and when no one did she began to be hopeful that no one would. All around was the cheerful talk and laughter of those about to leave for a few days' holiday.

Her shoulder-bag, which was big and roomy and with several divisions, could have gone on the rack above her head. The problem was she might want something out of it, indeed she probably would, and that could be awkward with a moving vehicle. How much more convenient if she could have her bag on the seat beside her. Meantime it would stay on the floor at her feet.

The driver came on and did a head count then he introduced himself as Fred. He was a jovial, pleasant-faced man who looked to be in his late forties. He gave a welcoming speech and cracked a few jokes that drew laughter. The weather, he said, should remain fine according to the forecast and hopefully they would leave on time.

No one complained about a wait of five minutes, even ten minutes but when it came close to twenty the good-natured banter was turning to annoyance and even anger.

'How many are we waiting for?' a voice called from the back of the coach.

'Only one.'

'Not good enough. Why should we be held up for one? I say we have waited long enough and we should just go. If whoever it is turns up when we've gone then too bad, it will be a lesson for the future.'

A few murmured agreement. Most kept quiet. Someone spotted a taxi drawing up and Fred, looking visibly relieved, went outside. All necks were craned to see the latecomer. He was a tall, white-haired, distinguished-looking gentleman who after paying the taxi driver took his suitcase and handed it to Fred. Then he got on the coach and straightaway apologised in a very pleasant voice for the lateness of his arrival.

'Thank you for waiting. I rather thought you would have gone. Truly the fault was not mine. I wouldn't allow my daughter to run me here because she is not always reliable when it comes to timekeeping. A taxi I felt I could trust.

Mostly I can but this time I was badly let down. Again I apologise.'

'Not to worry, sir, we'll make up the time,' Fred said as he got behind the wheel.

'Now where do I sit?' he said, peering at the numbers. 'Ah, here we are, this is my seat.' He smiled to Kirsty, who had been praying the man would go further down the coach. There were several seats with one occupant. A shabby briefcase went on the rack followed by a golfing jacket which he had been wearing. In his long-sleeved pullover and open-necked shirt he looked as though he were going on holiday.

'Not a very good start,' he whispered as he sat down. 'I have well and truly blotted my copybook.'

'A few minutes ago you were deeply unpopular but I should think you are forgiven.'

'I'm relieved to hear it.'

Kirsty smiled. 'Just make sure that you are up to time on the stops we make.'

'Heaven forbid that I should be late. Dear lady, I will be a model traveller and one of the first to be back on the coach. What am I kicking?'

Kirsty put her hand down and felt nothing. 'My bag, it was beside my feet.'

'Not to worry, I'll get it,' he said, stretching his long corduroy-covered legs and capturing the leather bag between his feet. 'There you are,' he said triumphantly, 'nothing breakable I hope.'

'No.'

The couple in front turned round.

'Sorry for all that but the lady's bag slipped away.'

'Got it now?'

'Yes, thankyou,' Kirsty said.

A moment or two later there was the rustle of paper and the woman half turned to offer them a butterscotch.

They both took one. 'Thank you,' Kirsty smiled and popped it into her mouth.

'How very kind, I do like these.' He was holding Kirsty's bag. 'Best place for this is on the rack out of harm's way. Anything you want out of it?' he said helpfully.

'No, I don't think so.' She had an insane desire to laugh and turned her head to hide her amusement. She hoped he wouldn't prove to be one of those tiresome people who didn't know when to stop talking.

As though reading her thoughts the man let his head rest on the back of the seat and closed his eyes.

Kirsty studied the passing scenery. There was something very lovely about this time of the year, she thought, but there was a hint of sadness too. Autumn was saying goodbye to summer with the harshness of winter approaching.

The first stop would be for coffee and she would be glad of a cup after her early breakfast. They would make several stops with a fairly lengthy one for lunch. Fred was not only entitled but he was required to take his full rest periods and since it was in the interests of safety no one would quarrel with that.

A few miles on the road and Fred decided there should be music and they were treated to a selection of Scottish dance music played by Jimmie Shand and his band.

The man opened his eyes.

'That gets the feet tapping.'

'It does. Jimmie Shand is the best, don't you think?'

'I do.'

Kirsty felt guilty. She hadn't been very friendly and that wasn't like her. It could be that Helen and Linda were right and she was a bit run down and it was making her irritable. She would try to make amends.

'Have you been to Skye before?'

'No, I haven't.'

'What made you choose it?'

'I didn't. Workmen and painters and God knows who else have taken over my house and my daughter wanted me out of the way.'

'She booked you on this holiday?'

'Yes. And why, may I ask, are you smiling?'

'I was packed off as well. My daughters, I have two, decided that their mother was in need of a change. What they meant by that was that I was getting crabbit. All that I am suffering from is the after-effects of a heavy cold.'

'Difficult to throw off sometimes and I cannot imagine you being crabbit, as you put it.'

'How kind but then you don't know me. Look, isn't that lovely, the sun shining on the water? I get the advantage of the view and you don't.'

'Not at all, I can see perfectly well from where I am. So your two daughters booked you on this holiday?'

'Helen, my older daughter, did. You couldn't find anyone more kind-hearted but oh dear me, Helen is bossy.'

'Lottie is inclined to be that way and I confess to life being easier if I just give in. I do unless I feel very strongly about something, then I dig in my heels.'

'Quite right too. You live alone?'

'Yes. My wife died about four years ago. I have a woman, a Mrs Brady, who comes in each day to do for me, as the saying goes, and Lottie drives over two or three times a week to see if her old dad is coping. You see, I am well looked after.'

'My husband died five years ago and like you I live alone. Not in the family house, I sold it and bought a small cottage.'

'A good move?'

'Yes. I like where I am. It is a bit cut off but I drive and I manage very well. It is easier for a woman on her own, she is used to cooking and looking after the house.' She stopped. 'Did you hear what Fred said?'

'No. I was too busy listening to you.'

They had been talking quietly but their voices must have carried because two heads turned to face them.

'We are to be stopping in a few minutes.'

'Good. I could do with a coffee.'

'Fred said it would have to be a quick one. Fifteen minutes, twenty at the most. He emphasised that,' the woman said.

'It puts the timetable all out,' her husband put in, 'if folk are not punctual.' The coach stopped and the couple made a quick move.

'Were they having a dig at me, do you think? If so I can't blame them.'

'No, I'm sure they weren't. Actually he looked embarrassed as though he wished the words unsaid. Don't we all make that kind of blunder and to start and apologise would only make matters worse.'

'Your bag, you'll want it,' he said, taking it from the rack.

'Thanks. Your jacket?'

'I should survive without it.'

The service was speedy, the coffee was good and in less than twenty minutes everyone was back on the coach.

When they reached the Isle of Skye and the coach pulled in to the front of the hotel in Kyleakin it was gloaming. That lovely word that so beautifully describes the grey dark. Twinkling lights went the length of the hotel making it look like fairyland and drew gasps of delight from the weary travellers. Once inside the weariness fell away like a cloak. A huge log fire blazed in the entrance hall and a soft-voiced woman introduced herself as the manageress and welcomed everyone to the hotel. Each guest was issued with a card showing their name and the number of the room allocated to them. The keys were spread out on the reception desk ready to be collected. As for the luggage, those who wished to carry their own could do so. The porters would deal with the rest as soon as possible.

Kirsty got her key. She was on the first floor. Several of the guests, not all of them from the coach tour, were waiting for the lift. She thought she shouldn't wait with only one flight of stairs to climb. The wide stairway was thickly carpeted and very soon she was outside room fifteen and inserting the key in the lock. In the past she had had problems with hotel keys but this one turned without any difficulty. Once inside she looked about her. The room was not very large but had everything expected of a good hotel. A quick look into the bathroom assured her there was both a bath and a shower. Though she much preferred to soak in a bath she would forego that since there wasn't a lot of time. A quick shower would have to do.

There was a light tap at the door and when she went to open it her case was there but no one in sight. She brought it in, unlocked it and took out what she required for the evening.

Looking at herself in the full-length mirror, Kirsty was pleased with what she saw. The skirt had been expensive, ridiculously so she had thought at the time but she was glad that Helen had insisted she buy it. With it she wore her pale blue, frilly-necked blouse. Kirsty went easy on the make-up, she disliked to see older women with a heavily made-up face. And most of all she hated to see them wearing bright red lipstick. A mouth that was a slash of red made her think of a clown.

As she took a final look in the mirror Kirsty wondered at herself taking so much trouble over her appearance. Could she be doing it for someone? Of course not, the thought made her blush.

Kirsty hoped her travelling companion would be down before her and he was. As soon as she got to the door of the dining-room she saw him. Most of the tables had been set with four places and the man was alone at one. He had changed into a dark suit and with his thick white hair and its tendency to curl he looked very handsome. Kirsty was surprised and not a little alarmed to experience a funny little thrill of pleasure. He wasn't looking her way and with a smile on her face she walked forward, all set to join him. Only she was too late. Three women, she thought of them as the lively trio, were claiming the seats. Kirsty felt foolish and for a moment, it seemed much longer, she didn't know what to do. Desperately looking about she saw a couple at a nearby table and asked if she might join them.

'Of course, please do.' The man half rose while Kirsty sat down.

'We have finished studying the menu,' he said, handing it to Kirsty, 'and as usual there is a good choice.'

'You have been here before?'

'Many times to Skye, and once before to this hotel.'

His wife spoke. 'As my little grandchild would say, Gran's most favourite place.'

'This is my first visit.'

'You will love it. The scenery has to be seen to be believed.' She broke off when the waiter arrived at their table and wanted to know what they would like to drink.

'Nothing for us,' the man said.

'Iced water, dear,' his wife said reproachfully.

'The water will be coming shortly, madam.' He turned his attention to Kirsty.

Red wine didn't agree with her but Kirsty enjoyed a glass of white provided it wasn't too dry. The waiter made a suggestion and she nodded.

The meal could not have been faulted and the service was quick. Coffee, they were informed, would be served in the lounge. As it turned out the guests helped themselves. Occasionally Kirsty heard peals of laughter coming from that other table and when she sneaked a look the man was smiling broadly and obviously enjoying himself. All of a sudden she felt depressed and very alone. She shouldn't have come, this was not her kind of holiday.

The couple were in no hurry to leave the dining-room and Kirsty excused herself. She would have her coffee and then retire to her room. A tap on her shoulder made her turn round and there he was.

'Could we have our coffee together or have you made other arrangements?'

'We could and I haven't. I'll drink my coffee and then retire.'

'My dear lady, I can't allow you to do that on the first night of the holiday.'

'I can't see how you are going to stop me.'

'Sadly I can't if you are determined. You deserted me for dinner—'

'I like that. From what I could see you were having a very merry time.'

He closed his eyes. 'I felt I had to contribute from time to time but it was quite an effort. Three nice ladies but much too exhausting for me. Look, over there is a table with two chairs. You commandeer it, if you will, and I'll get in line for the coffee.'

Kirsty put her evening bag on one of the chairs and went to join him. A waitress came periodically to check the coffee pots and bring fresh when it was required. One woman who declared she had a strong wrist had taken charge of the coffee and dutifully each guest held up a cup to be filled.

Later, sitting at the table stirring their coffee they smiled across to one another. 'We should introduce ourselves. I am David Harris.'

'And I am Kirsty Cameron.'

'I do like that name. May I use it or do you prefer your title?'

'Kirsty will do.'

'Thank you. Am I allowed to say how charming you look?'

'Of course you are and what a nice compliment. At my age the best we can hope for is, doesn't she look well for her age.'

He threw back his head and laughed, a good hearty laugh. 'You know, Kirsty Cameron, I do believe I am going to enjoy this holiday. And now I think we should have a drink. What will you have?'

'I'm not sure I want anything. I don't drink much and I've had a glass of white wine.'

'Please have something.'

'All right, make it a sherry, thank you.'

When David came back he was carrying a small dish of salted nuts and the barman was behind him with the sherry and whisky and a small jug of water. Fred waited until the barman had gone before coming to their table.

'Is everything to your satisfaction?' he smiled.

'Very much so,' Kirsty said, 'and that also applies to the meal, it was delicious.'

'This hotel has an excellent reputation and when possible we use it.'

'A good kitchen,' David smiled.

'The staff wouldn't dare produce anything short of excellent. They both respect and fear the chef.'

'A good chef is worth his weight in gold.'

'And doesn't he know it. Wish I had that kind of talent. Those fellows can make their demands and know they will be met. And now about tomorrow. I'm taking names for the tour to Dunvegan Castle. We make it optional since so many have already done it.'

'Apparently it is a must,' David said to Kirsty. 'I have heard it described as the jewel in the crown of the Isle of Skye.'

'Yes, Fred, it looks as though you can add two names.'

'Mrs Cameron and Mr Harris.' He added the names to his list. 'I won't take the money just now, I'll get it on the coach.' He went on to the next table.

'David, are you retired?'

'Semi-retired.'

'What kind of job allows you to do that?'

'I'm a solicitor. I do some consultancy work but that is all. My office is in Dundee and my home is in Broughty Ferry.'

'My home is in Sunnybank. You won't know it.'

'I know of it. I've seen the sign pointing that way but I've never been there.' He smiled. 'My loss, I am sure.'

'It is rather pretty.'

'Do we ask questions of one another or would those not be welcome?'

'I don't mind. After all I will only tell you what I want to and I take it you will do the same.'

He nodded. 'We could start with family.'

'You have a daughter, is she an only child?'

'No. I have a son.' A shadow crossed his face. 'Geoffrey has been a worry. He was bright enough at school and I suppose I hoped that one day he would join me but there was no pressure put on him. When he refused to go to university my wife and I accepted that. No, that isn't quite true. I accepted it, but Jessica found it more difficult.'

'I could understand that,' Kirsty said gently.

'As I saw it Geoffrey's trouble was that he didn't know what he wanted. He drifted from one dead-end job to another – you don't want to hear this?'

'I do but only if you want to tell me. Sometimes talking to a stranger helps. Most families have their problems. Is your son married?'

'No. There was a girl in his life, a very nice, sensible girl and we had high hopes that she might be the making of Geoffrey. Sadly it didn't work out and they parted company.'

'Where is Geoffrey now?'

'I have no idea,' he said quietly. 'The last time we had a conversation he spoke about making a new life for himself in Canada. He seemed to be really keen and I was so pleased. To give him his due he has never asked me for money but I insisted he take his fare and enough to live on until he got a job. All I asked in return was that he wrote occasionally to let me know how he was getting on. Kirsty, that was almost two years ago and not as much as a postcard to me or to his sister.'

'David, how very sad.' She touched his hand in sympathy.

'Where did we go wrong? Isn't that what all parents ask themselves?'

'You didn't I am sure.'

'He wasn't neglected in any way. If anyone was neglected it was Lottie. Geoffrey got all the mothering because he seemed to be the one in need. Lottie, my daughter, was so different, so strong and independent. Thinking back I have to shoulder a lot of the blame for not being there when they were young and I was needed. Instead I made it my main concern to get ahead in my profession.'

'To give them a good standard of living.'

'Yes.'

'You couldn't be blamed for that.'

'Your turn, Kirsty, but I don't imagine you have problems.'

'Show me a family that doesn't.' She paused. 'I suppose I must consider myself lucky and as a family we get along well. Only very recently has that changed. It concerns a recent addition to the family—'

'A late baby?'

'Oh, dear me, no. That would indeed be a shock but if it were to happen we would all be delighted. The addition to our family, David, is an exceptionally pretty girl of fifteen who I am sorry to say I cannot bring myself to like. You are bewildered and no wonder. I won't go into the details, that would take too long and you would probably get bored.'

'No fear of that.'

'Very well, I'll tell you the essentials. My daughter's best friend from college days was killed with her husband in a car accident. Their daughter, Jennifer, a back-seat passenger, was

lucky and suffered only cuts and bruises.' Kirsty paused and
wondered why she was telling all this to a stranger, even a
sympathetic stranger. Because he is a stranger, she told herself.
'My daughter, Linda, and Jennifer's mother hadn't kept up for
years and for reasons I won't go into just now, Linda was
informed of the accident and made to feel responsible for the
girl.'

'What about family?'

'No one close. Both parents were only children and apparently there was no one or no one willing to come forward. A
kindly neighbour had taken temporary charge of the girl.'
Kirsty took a sip of her sherry. 'Linda, my soft-hearted
daughter, felt she should take Jennifer and give her a home
but her husband was against it. The family weren't keen either,
they didn't want their cosy little world to change. Matthew, my
son-in-law, came up with the suggestion that Linda should go
through to Inverness and find out the true position from the
solicitor. For all we knew the girl could be traumatised and in
need of professional help.'

'None of this had been made known to your daughter?'

'No.'

'Linda went through to Inverness.'

'We went, I accompanied her. The kindly neighbour was
going off to New Zealand to visit family and needless to say
was anxious to get the girl off her hands. She was under the
impression that Linda was Jennifer's godmother.'

'And she wasn't?'

'No. Linda knew about the birth, they kept in touch at that
time but at no time was she asked to be the child's godmother.'

'Had she been, there was still no obligation—'

'She knew that, we knew that. Linda was confused and
worried. She felt she was letting her friend down and another
thing, had she been asked to be the child's godmother she
would have agreed and considered it an honour to be asked.'

'I like the sound of your daughter.'

'She is a darling. Anyway, back to this story before I lose the thread. Linda phoned Matthew and he reluctantly agreed to give the girl a home.'

'How was Jennifer taking all this?'

'As her right. Linda was her godmother after all.' Kirsty shrugged.

'Linda's husband is causing problems?'

'Far from it. He is quite captivated by the girl and has gone out of his way to make her welcome. Linda has three of a family and Hannah, the eldest, and Jennifer can't stand each other. Hannah, poor darling, is jealous and miserable. So there you have it, David.'

'Not an easy one.'

'No. I have a horrible feeling that Jennifer is going to cause trouble between Linda and Matthew but if she does she will have me to deal with.'

'What does your other daughter have to say?'

'She thought taking Jennifer was a mistake and told her sister so. Since she chose to ignore good advice all she can do now is make the best of it.' Kirsty finished her sherry and put down the glass. 'David, I am going upstairs, this is late for me.'

'I couldn't get you another drink?'

'No, thank you.' She got up. 'I'll say goodnight.'

'I'll have another drink then go up. Goodnight, Kirsty, see you at breakfast.' He had risen to his feet and watched her walk away. How nice to have made a friend at the start of the holiday. Such a charming and interesting lady. The time away from home wasn't going to drag and he wouldn't be wandering about like a lost soul. Tomorrow they would explore Dunvegan Castle together.

12

Kirsty awakened refreshed and ready for the day ahead. The morning dawned bright and clear with not a cloud in the sky. Even so folk came out of the hotel carrying coats and umbrellas. Nothing was certain, particularly the Scottish climate, and it was always better to be prepared. The coach when it was unoccupied would be locked, they were assured by Fred, and their belongings safe. The driver had been pleasantly surprised by the number of people deciding to go on the tour to Dunvegan Castle. For several of them it was to be a second visit. At nine o'clock they were ready to go. Although Fred said there was no necessity to keep to the seats they had occupied on the journey to Skye, most of them did and that included Kirsty and David.

'Aren't we lucky to be getting such a lovely day for the start of our holiday?' Kirsty smiled to David as she settled herself in the window seat.

'Very lucky and it could last. According to the forecast, and the locals are seldom wrong, the good weather is to continue for the next few days.' He broke off. 'What about that bag of yours?'

It was on her knees. 'That bag of mine is not going on the rack,' Kirsty said firmly, 'the seat in front of us is not taken and I shall put it there.'

'Very good. I see my services are not required.' David settled himself while Fred did a head count.

'All present and correct,' their driver said as he got behind the wheel and they were off.

'I should have gone to one of the empty seats and given you more room.'

'Is that what you want to do?' Kirsty turned her attention away from the window.

'I most certainly do not but as a gentleman I felt it was expected of me.'

'David, I appreciate your thoughtfulness but I am perfectly happy with your company. One thing I think I ought to say—'

'Go on,' he said when she hesitated.

'Please don't feel you have to keep up a conversation, nothing is more tiring. I appreciate the occasional silences and I am sure you do too.'

'I couldn't have put it better myself.' They looked out at the scenery, which was spectacular, and Fred obligingly stopped the coach for those who wanted to get out and take photographs.

'Kirsty, what do you know about this castle we are about to visit?'

'Next to nothing.'

'You mean, all those leaflets lying about in the hotel and you haven't taken the trouble to read them?'

'David, I prefer to read about places once I have been to see them rather than before.'

'Extraordinary and so like a woman.' He was shaking his head.

'You, I gather,' she said with a sniff that made him laugh, 'are cognisant with the history.'

'I felt it my duty to read the leaflets put there for the guests.'

'If you are trying to make me feel guilty you are failing but since you are dying to share your knowledge I am prepared to listen.'

'We will be getting a conducted tour of the castle so I shall keep it brief.'

'Unless I am near to the front I don't always hear the guide. Not all of them have clear, carrying voices,' she added.

He nodded in agreement. 'Let me begin by telling you that Dunvegan Castle is believed to be the oldest inhabited castle in North Scotland and for over seven centuries has been the home of the chief of the clan Macleod.'

'I wonder what it must be like to live in a castle?'

'Interesting, I would think.'

'Horribly cold, I imagine.'

'No. The part of the castle used as living quarters will be well heated. The aristocracy like their comfort.'

'Quite right too. All the same they must feel very cut off.'

'No they won't, they will be used to it. You wouldn't want to change places?'

'I would not. They can keep their castle and I'll stick to my cosy little cottage. Look, David, isn't that lovely?' she said, pointing to a cascading waterfall.

'Beautiful,' he said softly. 'We forget what Scotland has to offer.'

'We moan about the rain and it is because we have so much of it that the countryside looks so fresh and green.'

'One little gem I have for you and I had very nearly forgotten.'

'Oh, I must hear this.'

'Apparently Flora MacDonald was given as a keepsake a lock of hair clipped from Bonnie Prince Charlie's head, and it is now preserved in a locket in the castle.'

'Thank you, that will be something to tell my grandchildren. And now if you would forget history for a few minutes and tell me if there is a gift shop I would be much obliged.'

'A gift shop.' He closed his eyes.

'David, I will steep myself in history for some of the time but I have a family who will expect me to bring them a gift or souvenir of my holiday. It struck me that I might get something unusual.'

'I believe I read that there are two shops, one for souvenirs, books, stationery and the like. There is also a craft shop.'

'Splendid. I shall get all I need in one go.'

'Why do you bother?'

'It isn't a bother, I enjoy it. I gather you don't.'

'Please don't think I am a skinflint.'

'I am perfectly sure you are not.'

'Thank you, that's a relief. I just draw the line buying gifts on holiday.'

'You have grandchildren?'

'Yes. Three. I remember them at Christmas and for their birthdays' and they get pocket money. On the first day of the month or near enough they come and see their grandfather and get their pocket money, which they can spend or save. I never ask.'

'The first of the month – unusual, I would say, but rather nice. Your idea?'

'No, my wife's and I went along with it.'

'I grant you the children do well, but what about your daughter?'

'What about Lottie?'

'Surely you are going to take her something.'

'It never crossed my mind.'

'Then it should,' Kirsty said severely. 'Here you are enjoying yourself and that poor young woman is hard at it getting your house ready for your return.'

'She brought it on herself. I was perfectly happy with the house in the state it was.'

'Once you see the changes you will be delighted.'

'How do you know?'

'I just do,' she said infuriatingly.

He gave a deep sigh. 'All right, Kirsty, you have won your case. Any suggestions as to what I should take to Lottie.'

'Has she a sweet tooth?'

'She does.'

'How about a box of chocolates, not any old chocolates but a luxury box?'

He nodded. 'Will you help me choose?'

'I would be delighted to.'

'Excellent,' he said, looking pleased. 'Once the chocolates are bought, I'll remove myself and leave you to browse around to your heart's content.'

'What will you do?'

'What will I do? Oh, don't worry about me, I'll be happy wandering around. What I might do when I think about it is have a look at the rare books of historical interest. I may never get another opportunity.'

Kirsty and David stayed together for the official tour of the castle, then made for the gift shop. The box of chocolates Kirsty selected was very expensive, she was slightly shocked herself, but was glad to see that David's face hadn't changed colour. He paid up and they waited while it was carefully wrapped and handed over.

'Good, that is Lottie taken care of.' He looked pleased that the matter had been taken care of so quickly.

Men, she thought with affection, most of them didn't mind parting with the money, it was the choosing that they couldn't be bothered with. The craft shop was a joy and she took a lot of time over the choosing of two pottery dishes for Helen and Linda. After that it was a return to the gift shop for the rest. Candies for the children – there would be frowns about the damage to teeth but not to bother. Mothers made such a song and dance these days. In moderation there was nothing wrong with sweets. Her sons-in-law had a weakness for fudge so that again was no bother. Last of all she bought a tea towel for her neighbour with a picture of Dunvegan Castle printed on it. A glance at her watch showed her it would soon be time to join the coach. From the top of the steps she watched the tourists strolling around the gardens. Some were taking a rest on the seats and a few hardy souls were sitting on the cold steps.

At the door of the gift shop she saw David's tall figure bent over the postcard stand and she watched him select a few.

'Good for you,' Kirsty smiled as she joined him, 'you are going to send a few postcards.'

'I feel I should, folk are good at remembering me. Have you bought yours?'

'Yes, but not here. I'm only going to send two and I got those from the hotel.'

'I didn't see any on sale.'

'Shows you are not very observant.'

'Mrs Cameron, I couldn't help overhearing,' one of their party said. 'The stand disappears from time to time—'

David beamed. 'How kind of you, I'm not so blind after all.' The three of them spoke for a few minutes.

'I think we could have done with more time, there is so much to see.'

Kirsty and David agreed. 'Not easy to please everyone,' Kirsty said, 'and I think Fred does very well.'

David and the lady nodded in agreement, then the three of them made their way back to the coach.

All too soon it was the last day. Everyone agreed the holiday had been a great success and the splendour of Skye not exaggerated. The weather had played a big part with a cloudless sky each day. The chef had excelled himself for the final dinner and appeared from behind the scenes to accept his well-earned praise.

Kirsty and David were sitting in the lounge with their coffee and a drink. They were both unusually quiet.

'I expected to be looking forward to my return home and instead I find that I am not. All due to you, Kirsty.' He smiled and patted her hand. 'You made it special.'

'Thank you. Neither of us was looking forward to our holiday and here we are almost reluctant to return home. Still, as they say, all good things must come to an end.'

'I'm not so sure about that, Kirsty. Good things don't necessarily have to end. That is, not unless you want them to.'

Kirsty was feeling a bit tremulous and her throat was tight. David was leaving it to her and she wasn't sure. This was a holiday friendship and did she want it to continue? Or more important would it be wise? She was very drawn to this man. He was courteous, good company and with a sense of humour not unlike her own. Yes, she did want to see him and no, she didn't think it a good idea.

'You haven't answered my question,' David said softly, 'are you finding it so very difficult?'

'Not easy and I was thinking.'

'What were you thinking?'

'I am going to miss you, David.' She sighed. 'Once we are back home and take up our usual life the holiday will fade—'

'Of course it will. Kirsty, that coffee must be stone cold. Let me get you another.'

'Too late. The waitress has cleared away the coffee things.'

'Even so I can surely get you a coffee—'

'No, thank you, David, I don't really want one. This is lukewarm and it will do me.'

'If you are sure—'

'I am.'

'Then back to what we were talking about. This is no big deal, as our young folk would say. What is wrong with the occasional chat over the phone and perhaps once in a while a meal together? Not too many miles separate our homes and I happen to enjoy driving.'

'Yes, please, that sounds ideal.' Kirsty saw no reason to hide her pleasure and thought that this was one of the joys of being with David. She could be as outspoken as she wished. In other words, she could be herself.

'My suggestion meets with your approval?'

'Haven't I just said so?' she smiled

'I wanted to be sure.' She saw him reach into his pocket, take out his wallet, and from it a card. Then he found a pen, uncapped it and wrote something on the back of the card.

'My business card, Kirsty,' he said, handing it to her. On the reverse side I have written my home address and telephone number.'

'Thank you. Do you want mine?'

He raised his eyebrows. 'Of course I want yours. I was hoping you would offer and I wouldn't have to ask.'

'Sadly I cannot stretch to a visiting card. I wouldn't have much call to use them but a page out of my diary will have to do.'

'No, you mustn't.' He produced another card. 'Use that.'

Kirsty wrote her address and telephone number.

'Thank you.' He looked at it, then put it in his wallet.

'We could have done this tomorrow. We have all day.'

'A large part of it will be spent on the coach and leaving it to the end would not have been a good idea. We might have forgotten. Heaven forbid but it could happen. Is your packing done by the way?'

'Most of it.'

'Cases outside the bedroom door by eight thirty.'

'I won't have any bother with that. Six thirty and it might have been a different story.'

The first rain they had seen since leaving home splattered the coach windows. Some looked up at the darkened sky but not many were complaining. They had, after all, been very lucky with the weather and, as someone said, had it been a bright and sunny morning there would have been a greater reluctance to leave.

'Folks, pay attention, please. One person has omitted to settle the bill for the extras and if whoever it is would see to that—'

'Oh, heavens, Fred,' a portly gentleman heaved himself out of his seat. 'I clean forgot the drinks, I had them put on the bill last night. I am sorry.'

'Not to worry, you would be surprised at how many do forget and just need a reminder. And speaking of forgetting, may I draw your attention to those keys? Please do not take them home with you. It is a great inconvenience to the hotel.'

Two women were seen to dig into their handbags and rather sheepishly hand over their keys to Fred.

'Thank you, ladies, you may hang your heads in shame while I nip in with these. Then once Mr Whyte gets back, we'll get on our way.'

'Here he is,' someone said helpfully.

'Fine.'

When Fred reappeared at the hotel door he was accompanied by some of the staff who had come out to wave goodbye to their guests.

Kirsty's eyes went to David's briefcase on the rack.

'Forgive me asking, David, but I can't help being curious. Why did you bring a briefcase on holiday?'

'Because I had fully intended doing a little work.'

'And have you? Or should that be, why haven't you?'

'I haven't and the fault, my dear Kirsty, is entirely yours. Had you not been such good company I would have made headway with some of my papers.'

They smiled the contented easy smile of two people comfortable with each other.

Fred made good time on the return journey since there was no slowing down for roadworks. In the coach the talk was mostly of home. Some had ordered taxis while others had friends or relatives meeting them.

As the coach arrived at its destination people were craning their necks to see their loved ones and when eye contact was established there was much waving. Fred had the hold open and with assistance was taking out the luggage and placing it on the pavement. Kirsty saw hers and picked it up.

'David, I've got mine and I see Helen's car. There she is, she has seen me.' Kirsty gave a wave to her daughter. 'Goodbye David,' she said and hurried away. David, she thought, had looked taken aback at the speed of her departure, but she didn't think she could have done anything else. She hadn't wanted to introduce David. David didn't belong here, he belonged to her holiday. They had exchanged telephone numbers but whether they made use of them remained to be seen.

'Mum, the coach was right up to time,' Helen smiled as she kissed her mother's cheek and relieved her of the suitcase.

'Yes, it was a good journey.'

'And I have to say, you are looking well,' Helen said, sounding satisfied. 'I was right, it was a holiday you were needing.' They were beside the car. 'In you go and I'll put this in the boot.' She banged the boot shut and slipped behind the wheel. 'Seems I'm blocked. I'll make a three-point turn and we'll get away.' Helen did the manoeuvre effortlessly and then they were passing the coach. David was standing surrounded by luggage and obviously helping some ladies to find theirs. They looked up at the approach of the car and waved to Kirsty. David gave a salute.

'A jolly company by the look of them.'

'Yes, Helen, everybody was very friendly.'

Helen glanced sideways. 'Glad I persuaded you?'

'Yes, I am.'

13

'Was the hotel up to standard?' Helen asked.

'You obviously haven't had my postcard.'

'No.'

'Yes, the hotel was excellent and, to be honest, I couldn't have faulted anything. The food was well cooked and nicely presented and thank goodness we were not served the huge helpings which always manage to put me off.' She smiled. 'It made for a pleasant change, not having to apologise for leaving half of the food on my plate.'

'There is no need to apologise, I keep telling you that. It is all paid for.'

'Even so it doesn't look nice and it makes me feel guilty. My generation doesn't like to see waste.'

'Speaking of food, I did some shopping for you.'

'Thoughtful, my dear, but unnecessary, there are plenty of tins in the cupboard.'

Helen ignored that. 'A nice piece of cold ham and tomatoes and some home baking from Linda.'

'Thank you. Mrs Grieve has my spare keys and she was to put milk in the fridge and get me a small loaf.'

'Good. Save you going out tomorrow unless you want to.'

'You spoil me.'

'And why shouldn't we? You were always there for us and now it is our turn to be there for you. By the way, did you meet up with anyone in particular?'

'Yes, I did.'

Helen turned to give her mother a smile. 'I'm so pleased. Linda and I were hoping you would. We didn't like to think of you being on your own.'

'I was never that and now, please, I want to hear the family news.'

'Nothing much to report. You've only been away eight days not eight weeks,' Helen laughed.

'A lot can happen in a few days,' Kirsty said and for some reason felt herself blushing.

'Everybody is fine. George is busy as usual and that goes for me too. The boys are working or pretending to do so. They disappear to their bedrooms and try to tell George and me that they work best to a background of music.'

'I shouldn't worry and be fair, Helen, you have never had any trouble. Nigel sails through his exams.'

'Yes, he does. Nigel is one of the lucky ones. Not so Simon, he has to work.'

'Which he does.'

'I think so, Mum. Simon knows he has to if he wants to get on.'

'And now, tell me, what is happening at Hillcrest?'

'All is well as far as I know. Linda hasn't said anything to the contrary.'

'I meant Jennifer of course. Is she causing problems?'

'No more than usual.'

'And what am I supposed to take out of that?'

'Mum, you worry too much.'

'I can't help it. None of us has been the same since that girl arrived.'

'Don't include my lot.'

'You may not escape unscathed,' Kirsty said sharply.

'You're joking.'

'Simon—'

'Simon thinks Jennifer is gorgeous. So do the majority of his classmates.'

'Boys of Simon's age can be very impressionable.'

Helen laughed. 'He thinks he is one up on his friends. Jennifer likes to have an older boy waiting for her at the school gate and Simon fills the bill for the moment.'

'She will drop him when she sees someone else she fancies.'

'That is more than likely and he'll get over it. Mum, for goodness sake it is all part of growing up.'

'I know that and I wouldn't normally be worried, it is only that Jennifer is—'

'A very sleek little number, was how one of the mothers described her.'

Kirsty sighed. 'Already she is causing trouble between Linda and Matthew. No, I shouldn't say trouble but irritation.'

'In what way?'

'Your poor sister has got herself in a no-win situation with Matthew.'

'How do you arrive at that?'

'Matthew agreed to have Jennifer live with them to please Linda. He was totally against it.'

'I know all that,' Helen said impatiently.

'Matthew is human enough to be chuffed that a pretty young girl has taken—'

'A shine to him,' Helen finished for her.'

'Don't laugh. It should be funny only it isn't, not to Linda.'

'She can't be—'

'Why not? Wouldn't you be jealous if a strikingly lovely young girl were to take a fancy to George. And don't say it couldn't happen—'

'OK, I take your point. If my opinion were to be asked I would say to leave well alone. Matthew isn't stupid and the last thing he will want to do is hurt Linda.'

'Of course you are right and things have a way of working out.' She shook her head sadly. 'It's the girl herself. I want to like her but I can't.'

'I don't find her hard to like. To me, Mum, she is just a moody teenager with a tragedy behind her.'

'That is what concerns me.'

'Because she doesn't show her grief? It could be that she is unable to do so,' Helen said gently. 'Remember that course I did and grief management was part of it?'

Kirsty nodded. She didn't but then Helen went to so many courses.

'Some people genuinely cannot show their feelings. Instead they bottle it up and that is so much worse. Here we are almost home,' she said, making a right turn. A few minutes later the car stopped outside the cottage door. One of the front windows was showing a light. Mrs Grieve had said she would switch it on since it would be quite dark before Kirsty was home. It looked very welcoming.

'No matter how pleasant the holiday, coming home is lovely.'

'I know. George always says that. He likes his own bed.' Helen held the car door open for her mother and Kirsty went ahead to open the house. Helen opened the boot, got the suitcase and followed. Kirsty had gone straight to the kitchen. There was a note under the loaf of bread. The biro had been coming to the end of its life and the writing was difficult to read. Eventually she mastered it. The woman hoped that Kirsty had enjoyed her holiday. The weather here had been mixed. The man to read the meter had called and she had let him in. The letters were on the hall table but none of them seemed to be important. Kirsty wondered how she could make that out without a close scrutiny. Today's newspaper was with the letters and she didn't want it back.

'She is a good soul for all her annoying little ways.'

'You do the same for her and maybe some of your ways are annoying to her.'

'I wouldn't wonder. I bought her a dish towel, one with a

picture of Dunvegan Castle. I wish now I had bought one for myself. Don't run away. I have something for you.' The case was in the bedroom where Helen had put it on the bed and opened it to save her mother the trouble.

'Thank you, dear, that will make it easy to unpack.' She thrust her hand under the clothes and brought out a small package. 'There you are,' she said, handing it over.

'Thank you, I love surprises.'

'Probably not a bit of use but I had to bring something.'

'No, you didn't.' She removed the tissue paper. 'Mum, it's gorgeous, such lovely colours. I adore pottery and one can never have too much.'

'Linda is getting the same.'

'She will love it. And now if you don't mind I must go.'

'No time to drink a cup of tea?'

'I'm afraid not.'

'Off you go then and take care.'

Kirsty went to the door and stood there until the car had gone, then she shut the door and turned the key. In the sitting-room the fire was set to put a match to, and she would do that tomorrow. Meantime she would make do with the small electric heater she kept handy. With both bars on it gave out a good heat. In the kitchen the kettle boiled and she made the tea. Suddenly deciding she was hungry Kirsty cut a slice of ham and made a sandwich. There was a little mustard left in the jar and she spread it on the ham. She put everything on a tray and carried it through to the sitting-room. This was cosy and she was going to enjoy it.

While she ate the sandwich and drank her tea Kirsty wondered at the surprises life had for us. When she had left for this coach holiday she had never dreamt that she would meet someone like David. What would he be doing now? Being fussed over by his daughter, she rather thought. Would the young woman be pleased with her box of chocolates? But of course she would. Kirsty did hope that David wouldn't spoil the woman's pleasure by mentioning her own part in it. How much nicer to believe that the thought had been her father's.

Would he phone as he promised to do or would it be a case of out of sight out of mind? No, she didn't believe that. When David made a promise he would keep it. She had his phone number but the first move would have to come from him and if it didn't – end of story.

The phone rang a few minutes before ten o'clock when Kirsty was in her dressing-gown. So sure was she that it would be Linda that she lifted the phone and said, 'Hello, dear.'

There was silence and then a voice with a hint of laughter in it spoke. 'Would I be speaking to Mrs Kirsty Cameron?'

'David, isn't it?'

'Yes. I gather by that endearment that you were expecting someone else to ring.'

'Yes, I thought it was Linda. I tried her number earlier but each time I got the engaged signal. No doubt the girls were phoning their friends and then talking for ever.' She dragged a chair nearer to the phone and sat down. 'Did your daughter meet you?'

'Lottie did and was reasonably up to time.'

'The house – how is it looking?'

'All right, I suppose.'

'Not exactly enthusiastic, are you?'

'I can't see anything to get excited about.'

'You could try to look pleased.'

'Whose side are you on?'

'Lottie's, of course. We women have to stick together.'

'So it would seem. The kitchen is all changed, everything is in the wrong place. It will take me twice as long to do any-thing,' he said gloomily.

'Oh, poor you. How awful if you actually have to look for something.'

'Never mind, if I didn't look sufficiently impressed the chocolates made up for it. I think I could say that Lottie's face lit up when I handed over the box.'

'I'm so glad.'

'All thanks to you.'

'I hope you didn't mention my part—'

'I might so easily have done so but I didn't.'

'Thank goodness for that. Had you, it would have taken half the pleasure away.'

'Was that a yawn?'

'No,' she lied.

'You are not annoyed at me ringing you so soon or when I think about it, should that be so late in the evening?'

'An unexpected pleasure, David.'

'Tact and kindness.'

'No, the truth. I am too old to bother about tact.'

'Then I can expect a truthful answer?'

'To what?' She was smiling.

'One evening soon will you have dinner with me?'

'I would love to.'

'Which evening next week would suit you?'

'Most are free, what about the middle of the week?'

'Wednesday is fine. I'll come for you about seven o'clock.'

'David, I drive, we could meet halfway.'

'We might do that on another occasion but not this time. I know how to get to your village and only need directions to your cottage.'

'Very simple. Turn left at the church and mine is the third cottage along. I'll have the light on and I'll be looking out for you.'

'Splendid. Kirsty, I shall look forward to seeing you on Wednesday evening, and now I must let you get your beauty sleep.'

'Meaning I need it?'

'Meaning you need it less than anyone I know. Stop fishing for compliments.'

They were both laughing when Kirsty put the phone down. She must ring Linda, she thought, and was about to do so when the phone rang.

'Mum, are you in bed?'

'Not quite but I am in my dressing-gown.'

'You must have been trying to get through—'

'I—'

'Several times, I have no doubt, and the line engaged. Not Hannah this time and in any case a tap on the shoulder and a warning look does the trick. Not so with Jennifer. I tried several times to catch her eye—'

'And she ignored you?'

'Or wasn't aware—'

'Stuff and nonsense. You are going to have a horrendous telephone bill and Matthew is going to have something to say.'

'If he does he will say it to the wrong person.'

'What do you mean?'

'Nothing, I was just thinking out loud. What I want to hear is how the holiday went.'

'Linda, I enjoyed my holiday very much. Sorry I didn't post the cards earlier. I had them written and in my handbag. Probably arrive tomorrow morning.'

'You sound chirpy.'

'I feel the holiday has done me good and I am honest enough to say so.'

'Skye was lovely?'

'The scenery was spectacular, we saw Skye at its best.'

'Cheerful company?'

'Everyone was very friendly.'

'Did you mix?'

'What a cheek. Of course I did. I am not standoffish.'

'No one suggested you were but you do tend to wait for the other person to make the first move.'

'Like you?'

'Yes, like me.'

'Linda, you don't sound like yourself. Is anything worrying you?'

'No. What could be worrying me? I have a lot to be thankful for and I keep reminding myself of that.'

'Taking Jennifer was a mistake, wasn't it?'

'Sometimes I do have regrets but I know, too, that had I turned my back I would have been plagued with guilt. Hard to know which would have been worse. I wish I understood the girl. Sometimes I think I am getting close, then the shutter goes down.'

'Patience, my dear, although in your shoes I would be fast running out of it.'

'So am I, fast running out of it. There are times when I could cheerfully strangle her and at other times, Mum, I feel an overwhelming pity for Betty's daughter. Sorry, I am keeping you talking and you must be tired.'

'Beginning to be. All that travelling is tiring even with plenty of stops.'

'Off to bed then and sleep well.'

'I'm sure I shall.'

14

Kirsty slept very well and awoke refreshed and ready for the day ahead. After having her breakfast she unpacked the case, hung up what required to be hung up and put aside what was for the washing machine. Handwashing was recommended for the silk blouses, which she found to be a nuisance and perhaps unnecessary. On the occasion when one had mistakenly gone into the machine it had come out none the worse.

The phone rang and she frowned. Who would be calling her at this time of the morning? Not Helen or Linda, she had seen Helen and spoken on the phone to Linda. Kirsty crossed the room, picked up the receiver and found the caller was Helen.

'Mum, this is just a very quick call. I imagine you are free on Wednesday evening but I wanted to confirm it before getting you a ticket for the concert.'

Kirsty closed her eyes. 'You did say Wednesday?'

'Yes.'

'I'm very sorry, Helen but Wednesday is not suitable for me.'

'Why ever not?'

'Must I account for everything I do?' A sharpness had crept into her voice.

Helen was obviously taken aback. 'Of course you don't. All I meant was that it isn't like you. You usually say where you are going.'

Yes, I do, she thought and it made her think again. Was she in danger of losing her independence and requiring permission from her daughters, or should that be approval, before she made a firm decision? No, it wasn't as bad as that but it could be going that way. She didn't want to be called into question about where she went and what she did.

'As it happens I have been invited to have dinner that evening.'

'Oh!'

'Dinner with a friend.'

'Which friend is this, if I am allowed to ask?'

Helen was like a dog with a bone, she never let go. 'No one you know, someone I met on holiday.'

'How very nice. You are going to keep up the friendship?'

'Perhaps.'

'She can't live so very far away from you.'

'Broughty Ferry as it happens and it isn't a woman.'

Kirsty thought she heard the sharp intake of breath but it could have been her imagination. 'Not a woman, you mean—'

'I mean I am having dinner with a man. It has to be one or the other.'

'Don't be facetious, Mum, it doesn't suit you.'

'Do you have to sound so incredulous? Is there some reason why your mother should not have a friend from the opposite sex?'

'Stop it, Mother, what on earth has got into you? You are beginning to worry me.'

'I can't imagine why.'

'Please don't be angry.' Helen was almost pleading. 'Of course you have every right to have dinner with whom you please.'

'Yes, I do. My friend, David, is a particularly nice person.'

'I'm sure he is.'

'You are not sure of anything. David, for your information is a thorough gentleman, a widower who lives alone and we just happen to enjoy each other's company.'

'That was good.'

Kirsty took pity on Helen. She was dying to ask questions and afraid to with her mother in this mood.

'We sat together on the coach.'

'Oh! I would have expected you to share with another lady. What I mean is, with singles they usually put them beside one of their own sex.'

'I wouldn't know about that not having been on a coach tour before.' She smiled. 'Someone must have slipped up or there again when I think about it there were no unaccompanied men.'

'And of course you chatted.'

'Of course.'

'I'm getting myself tied in knots.'

'No need for that, ask what you want. I have the choice to answer or not.'

Helen bristled. 'Really, this is a bit much.'

'I'm joking.' She hadn't been.

'You are in a peculiar mood and that makes me concerned.'

'Why?'

'Because I don't want you doing something you may regret.'

'That is highly unlikely.'

'It could happen. When a man and a woman enjoy each other's company there has to be a spark.'

'What utter nonsense. Let me remind you that you are talking to your mother. There is such a thing as platonic friendship and that applies to any age.'

'No, you are wrong. The experts have disproved that.'

'So-called experts. Only the two people concerned know what is there, and what isn't. Heavens, why are we talking all this drivel? All I am doing is having dinner with a gentleman friend. It may be the first of many or on the other hand this might be the one and only.'

Helen wasn't usually lost for words but she appeared to be. Kirsty broke the silence.

'This is my life, dear, and how I choose to live it is for me to decide.'

'I won't argue with that. All I ask is that you be careful.'

'Careful of what?'

'I don't want to see you hurt.'

'Darling, I am a big girl and I have lived long enough to look after myself.'

'I am going to be horribly late for my appointment. This call was to last a few minutes and no more.'

'Then off you go and not waste any more of your time. Goodbye, dear.' She put the phone down. Then she smiled and shook her head. She knew exactly what would happen. Since Helen was late for her appointment she wouldn't turn up. Instead she would phone her apologies, arrange another appointment and then drive over to see her sister.

When the back door opened Linda turned from the sink to see who it could be.

'Helen, what brings you?'

'You shouldn't leave your door unlocked, I could have been anyone.'

'True. I do take awful chances,' she smiled. 'Now that I get a good look at you, is that heightened colour or out of a box?'

'It is not out of a box. Any coffee going?'

'No, but I'll make instant if that will do.'

'It will have to,' she said, sitting down at the kitchen table. 'I'm in deep shock.'

'Something's happened?' Linda asked as she got down two mugs from the shelf. Helen usually turned up her nose at mugs but at the moment it didn't look as though she would notice.

'Thanks,' she said when the coffee was put in front of her. Linda sat down and stirred her own. 'Something serious?'

'Deadly serious. Mother has taken up with a man.'

Linda spluttered over her coffee. 'You must be joking?'

'I only wish I were. This is someone she met on holiday.'

Linda felt both hurt and annoyed. 'How strange that she should tell you and not say a word to me.'

'I didn't get preferential treatment. Mother had no intention of telling me either. It only came out because I wanted to confirm that she was free on Wednesday evening to go to the concert. By the way I got you a ticket.'

Linda nodded. 'And she isn't free on Wednesday evening, Mother has a prior engagement?'

'Yes, and not very forthcoming about it.'

'Helen, she would be embarrassed.'

'Plain shirty would describe it better. To begin with I thought she was having dinner with a new friend she had made on holiday, a woman, of course.'

'When she said it was a man, that threw you?'

'Wouldn't it have thrown you?' Helen was feeling a little deflated. Linda wasn't showing enough shock.

'No. I would have been surprised but no more than that.' She paused. 'Tell me about this man who has entered Mother's life.'

'Not a lot I can tell you. As I said, she wasn't very forthcoming. His name is David and they sat together on the coach. His home is in Broughty Ferry and he is a widower.'

'Is it so very awful, Helen?'

'Mother taking up with a man at her time of life, do you mean?'

'Yes.'

'Awful is too strong a word but I can't help feeling a bit upset and if I am honest a little scared too.'

'What is there to be scared about?'

'Sensible women can be taken in by a charmer. Some go on these tours just to see who they can meet.'

'I thought that was more likely to be women.'

'Not necessarily.'

'Whoever he is, he will have to be pretty good if he is to hoodwink our mother.'

'I can only hope you are right.'

'Helen, I'm sure all this worrying is unnecessary. This could be friendship pure and simple and we must remember that she is entitled to a life of her own.'

'So she informed me in no uncertain terms.'

Linda laughed. 'That put you in your place.'

Helen frowned. 'What do you suggest we do?'

Linda stared. 'We do nothing. Leave it alone, Helen. Most holiday friendships don't last.'

'We can but hope.'

Linda couldn't resist it. 'Don't forget, you were the one who was so keen for Mother to go on that coach tour.'

'Don't remind me,' she groaned.

On her way home Helen was thoughtful. Linda was probably right and she was worrying unnecessarily. Two elderly people striking up a friendship while on holiday was hardly unusual. It happened all the time, what made this different was the secrecy surrounding it. Her mother had always been open about her life because there had never been any reason to be otherwise – until now. Another thought surfaced and Helen could live with this one. The most likely explanation was that the arrangement with this David had been made on the spur of the moment and the poor love was regretting having agreed to it. Of course, being Mother, she would keep to the arrangement rather than hurt his feelings and during the evening away from the holiday atmosphere they would both come down to earth, realise they had little in common and be relieved to part company. Helen felt almost cheerful as she let herself into the house. Tonight was the flower arranging class but she would give it a miss. That wouldn't be hard to do. Although some of the flower arrangements were very impressive, Helen could not come to terms with what she called the mutilation. It was painful to see a beautiful long-stemmed flower reduced to a few inches to complete the effect. She much preferred her flowers in a vase.

George was sitting smoking his pipe in his favourite chair.

'Not going out this evening, dear?'

'No.'

'Why not?'

'Because I didn't feel like it,' she said, more sharply than she intended.

'A bit under the weather, are you?'

'I am not. I felt like staying at home, that is all, and please don't make it sound as though I were never at home.'

'Sorry. Maybe you want to talk,' he said, putting aside the paper.

'Yes, George, I think I do.' She sat down in the armchair. 'Actually it is Mother.'

'I thought she was fine, good holiday and all that. What is wrong with Ma?'

'Nothing is actually wrong and please, George, do not call her Ma, she doesn't like it.'

George looked bewildered. 'But I've always called her that and she has never complained.'

'No, she hasn't, but that doesn't mean she likes it.'

'What should I call her?'

'Matthew uses her Christian name. Call her Kirsty like he does.'

'Won't be easy but I'll try and remember. Don't know what is wrong with Ma,' he muttered.

'Mum is seeing a man, someone she met on holiday. He lives in Broughty Ferry.'

George was smiling. 'Good for the old girl.'

'I don't agree.'

'Why not?'

'Obvious, I would have thought. At mother's age it is a bit ridiculous.'

'I'm very surprised you should think that. What has age got to do with it? Happiness is the right of everyone.'

'Fair enough. Mum is happy as she is.'

'How do you know?'

'Because she is content. She has us.'

'Is she content? How can you possibly know? She gives all the signs of being happy and contented but she may have secret longings for something more.'

'Such as?' Helen said sarcastically.

'Such as what has happened. A new relationship.'

'I can't believe what I am hearing.'

He smiled. 'Your mother is a very attractive older woman with a quick mind. I enjoy our talks and presumably someone else does also.'

'You are all for this man entertaining my mother.'

'If you want to put it that way. Give your mother some credit.'

'She wouldn't be the first intelligent older woman to be taken in by a – a—'

'The word you are looking for, my dear, is bounder. Kirsty would recognise one a mile away. I'll get us a drink,' he said, getting up, 'then we can talk about something else.'

'That is rather nice,' Helen said, taking a sip from her glass. What is it?'

'Ask no questions, drink and enjoy.'

'Simon. Maybe we should talk about our younger son.'

'What has he been up to?'

'First love, he's got that far-away look.'

'Has he?'

'Does it disturb you?'

'No, why should it? All part of growing up.'

'The girl he has fallen for is Jennifer.'

'Our Jennifer?'

'Yes.' Helen was surprised at the 'our Jennifer'. As far as George was concerned, Jennifer was part of the family.

'You don't mind?'

'Why should I? In fact I am rather pleased. Simon could be good for her. That is one very vulnerable child, Helen.'

'You men. Charm and a pretty face, and you fall for it.'

'That happens to be true. I fell for your charm and your pretty face.'

'Be serious.'

'I am.'

'Simon is besotted,' Helen said quietly. 'Jennifer will drop our son when she gets tired of him.'

'More than likely.'

'Don't you care about Simon being hurt?'

'Simon will get over it. He is made of sterner stuff than you think. Of course he'll hurt, he'll hurt badly but he will recover. A quick recovery, I would think. Or it will be if we all leave him alone.'

15

Sunnybank, the village where Kirsty lived, had a post office and a general store situated between the church and the school but until a year ago no hairdresser. To have one's hair done it had been necessary to make the trip to a neighbouring village or make the longer journey into town. All that had changed thanks, in part, to Charlie Aitken. When it reached Charlie's ears that the incomer to the village was an experienced hairdresser and that she was looking for premises he was quick off the mark. His was a small shoe repair business with premises much too large for his needs. He pointed out the advantages to a clearly interested Moira Duncan. It would be a simple job to divide the shop, he said, and he saw no problem in having separate entrances.

Moira saw its potential and discussed it with her husband, who was in the building trade and had connections with joiners and other tradesmen. He was very enthusiastic and since it could be done on the cheap, the work went ahead quickly.

Thrilled to have her own business, Moira wanted a catchy though appropriate name above the door. She pondered long and hard and considered suggestions from the villagers, some of which were quite good, some very bad and a few bordering on the hilarious. None had hit the right note and in any case it was too late. Everyone spoke about going to Moira's. In time it became Moira's Hairdressing Salon.

Kirsty had made an appointment for Wednesday at nine

o'clock, which was when the salon opened for business. Moira arrived at least a half-hour before then to have the water hot and the premises heated.

Kirsty was early. 'Good morning, Mrs Cameron, you are bright and early,' Moira said in her usual cheerful manner. 'What is the weather to be?'

'I think the rain should stay off. It usually does when I remember to take an umbrella.'

'I find that too,' Moira said as she folded towels and put them in a neat pile. 'Let me have your coat.'

Kirsty took it off and handed it over for Moira to put on a coathanger and then hang it on a peg. She collected a large pink cape and enveloped Kirsty in it. She tied the tapes, reached for a towel and led the way to the wash-basin.

'You don't like leaning back?'

'Moira, you know I don't. That time you persuaded me to try I had a painful neck for the rest of the day.'

'The secret is to get yourself into a really comfortable position and obviously you did not. Mind you, I have a few ladies like you, my mother among them.'

'I'm glad I am not the only awkward customer.'

'Mrs Cameron, you could never be that. We will stick to what you prefer.'

'Yes, please.'

'That water too hot?'

'No, it isn't, it is just right.'

Kirsty enjoyed this bit. Moira prided herself on being a professional who had attended classes and understood the bones of the head and the correct way to massage the scalp. She had very strong fingers and after the shampoo Kirsty would feel her scalp tingling.

Moira Duncan was in her early forties. She was plump and jolly, had a lovely face and didn't worry too much about her own hair. Her excuse, if she felt the need to give one, was that she was much too busy. All she had time for was a shampoo and a quick dry. Everybody liked her. She listened to gossip but never spread it.

With the shampoo over and after a very thorough rinsing, Moira dabbed the hair dry with a towel then taking a fresh one led Kirsty to the chair facing the mirror. After another rub with the towel she brought the comb through Kirsty's hair.

'Is it the usual, Mrs Cameron?'

'Yes, please.'

'We couldn't do something a little bit different?'

'No.'

'Do you want any off?'

'I'll leave it to you.'

'Then I say, yes. A regular cut is good for the hair. Don't worry, this is just a tidy up,' she said when Kirsty looked alarmed.

'The merest whisper,' Kirsty laughed.

'I promise. Just the ends. Is this you going somewhere special?' Moira asked as the scissors came out.

'Well—'

'That means you are.'

'I've been invited out to dinner, that is all.'

'To dinner, how very nice. In some posh restaurant, is it?'

'I have no idea, it is to be a surprise.'

'Better and better.' All the time Moira was talking her busy fingers never stopped. 'Mrs Cameron, are you holding out on us?'

'Why would I do a thing like that?'

'Swept back but slightly to the side – this side?'

'Yes.'

'One day we are going to have a new style, aren't we?'

'No. I am too set in my ways for change.'

'Nonsense. It is like a pick-me-up. We were talking about your date.'

'I never mentioned anything about a date.'

'A dinner date.'

'I said nothing about a date, you are putting words in my mouth.'

'Mrs Cameron, you are by your own admission going out to dinner and you don't know where you will be eating. That can only be a man,' she said triumphantly.

'At my age.'

'You, my dear Mrs Cameron, could be described as a very attractive older woman.'

'Someone who has worn well,' Kirsty smiled.

'Yes, most definitely.'

'How kind. And older woman is right. I am a bit old for romance.'

'Never. Women are never too old to have a bit of romance in their life.'

'Moira, you are a good hairdresser and a terrible blether.'

Moira just laughed. 'You have lovely hair.'

'Once I thought of it as my crowning glory but sadly it isn't as thick as it used to be.'

'That, I am rather afraid, is one of the disadvantages of advancing years. Hair gets thinner. You are one of the lucky ones to start off with a good head of hair. Spare some sympathy for those women with the thin, flyaway kind. They can't afford to lose any.'

'Why don't you clever people come up with something that stops the thinning process? Men suffer more, and they are losing their hair at an earlier and earlier age.'

'We do our best with special shampoos and the like—'

'A waste of money.'

'In most cases I have to agree although, there again, if folk think it is making a difference they will happily buy it.'

'I'm sure.'

'I wish I knew the answer. If I could crack that one and

come up with the magic formula I would make my fortune. Spray?'

'No, thank you.'

'You don't need it.'

The pink cape was removed and then Moira held the mirror to catch a different view. 'How is that?'

'Lovely, thank you.' Kirsty got out her purse and Moira went for her coat. There was no need to ask how much. There was a board at the desk listing the charges. Kirsty felt the woman undercharged for her work although it would be wrong of her to say so. Others wouldn't thank her. Instead she added a generous tip.

'Thank you very much, Mrs Cameron. See you next week and remember to have a lovely evening,' she added as the bell pinged and the next lady arrived. The three of them spoke pleasantries and then Kirsty left.

On her way home Kirsty got a few groceries and then made her way to the cottage. All of a sudden she began to worry about the evening ahead. She was apprehensive and there was a funny little feeling in the pit of her stomach. Why hadn't she given the matter more thought? Then she wouldn't be in this predicament. She would have said no to David. On holiday none of us is completely natural. We make that special effort to sound interesting and take more care over our appearance. Then when we are back home, we slide into our old ways. Maybe they would both be disappointed, David's expectations and her own too high. If that were to be so, they would quickly realise it. They would make the best of things and part company with the vague promise of getting in touch sometime and arranging something. And all the time both of them knowing full well that there would be no next time.

And that, she thought, would come as a huge relief to Helen and Linda. The poor darlings were worried. They hadn't said very much at all, not after her own outburst when she had told them that how she lived her life was up to her, and that though it was highly improbable she would do anything outrageous the possibility was always there. That had been sheer devilment on her part, and irresistible. Worth it too, to see the expression on their faces. Kirsty grinned. She ought to feel ashamed of herself, but she didn't. To be able to shock at her age was something.

Once inside the cottage and her coat off she went to hang it on the coatstand. John's raincoat still hung there, she could never bring herself to remove it. When the removal men brought the coatstand complete with raincoat she had found it comforting. A little bit of John had come with her. What would he think of her seeing David Harris? She had never done anything like this before, never wanted to. Somehow she didn't think he would mind. John had wanted her happiness.

With the shopping away Kirsty made herself a cup of coffee. She ate sparingly at the best of times and today she would have very little. There was dinner to look forward to. People ate too much, she often thought. During the war when food was rationed, folk were much healthier. Doctors recognised it, and it became a well-known fact, but one quickly forgotten as luxuries denied for so long began to appear on the shop shelves. Restaurants were opening up in towns and in the country as eating out became one of the pleasures of life. Cost was not a problem, people were willing to splash out.

Kirsty drank her coffee and turned her thoughts to what she should wear for this evening with David. The choice wasn't all that difficult, she didn't have a wardrobe full of clothes. Maybe she should wear her aquamarine fine woollen two-piece with the silver thread running through it. Thank goodness the dry-cleaners had got that stain out. Robin had come charging over to her when she had been carrying a plate of soup. Only a few splashes had reached her skirt, but she thought it ruined. The dry-cleaners were doubtful if the stains could be removed but agreed to try. It was successful and Kirsty was overjoyed. She had paid a lot of money for the outfit and it was a favourite.

Now to footwear. Should she wear her black patent court shoes? The heel was a good bit higher than she was accustomed to wear and she wouldn't be able to walk any distance. Not that that would matter, she wouldn't be doing much walking and she did feel elegant in high heels.

Fine, that was her more or less organised, but it was the next part that was tricky. This was a new experience and there was no one she could ask for advice. Should she be dressed, her coat on and ready to leave the cottage the minute the car stopped, or should she wait for David to come knocking at her door or ring the bell? And then what? Ask him in for a drink? David was driving and the offer shouldn't be made. There was coffee, but she didn't think so. Kirsty had spirits in the house, she kept a selection in the sideboard cupboard. It was nice to be able to offer her sons-in-law a drink, or a helpful neighbour.

Why on earth was she putting herself through all this? She would do what she thought the occasion demanded. Darkness had fallen and there were no street lights. What light there was came from the cottage windows. David should be putting in an appearance if he was up to time. She hoped he hadn't got lost. Her mohair shawl was over the back of the chair and she draped it over her shoulders, then went to the window. In a few minutes she was relieved to see headlights as a car turned into the lane. If it was David he would be peering ahead and if she had the door open he would see her. The open door let out a flood of light and the car slowed down, then stopped. Remembering her footwear she stopped herself running down the path and waved instead.

David opened the car door and got out. She waited for him where she stood.

'You managed to find me,' she said stupidly.

'Yes, Kirsty, I had no problem getting here. And let me say how wonderful it is to see you again.'

'Thank you, and it is lovely to see you too. Would you like to come in and say hello to my cottage or would you rather we left that for another time?' She wished she hadn't said that, it was presuming a lot.

'A treat in store for me. For now, though, I think we should be getting on our way. I have booked a table at The Stables for seven thirty and we'll need all our time.'

'I'm ready, I've just to lock up.'

'The light, do you leave it on?'

'Yes, I do.'

'Very wise.'

David saw Kirsty settled before going round to the driver's side.

'Have you eaten at The Stables?'

'No, I haven't, but my daughter has. She and George were singing its praises.'

'Good. I like it and I thought you would.'

Kirsty wondered how she would feel if they were to find Helen and George dining there and then remembered the concert and breathed a sigh of relief.

'I'm sure I shall. It was very expensive, even by Helen's standards, and she rather wished that David had chosen somewhere more modest.

'There is a tartan rug,' he began.

'David, I do not want to cover my legs with a car rug. I am trying to forget my age, so kindly do not treat me as though I were an old woman in need of a rug over my legs.'

'Oh dear.'

'That said, I may be glad of it on the journey home.'

'The older one gets, the quicker the years pass. You don't like that.'

'I hate it. Don't you?'

'Sometimes, yes. At other times I find it rather nice. The pace is slower, and one has more time to appreciate what is going on around.'

'I must try and remember that.'

'Everything well with the family?'

'I think so, there are tiny ripples from time to time but nothing too serious.'

'You are there to give advice.'

'I try not to give too much of that. In any case, it wouldn't be heeded. The young do pretty much as they wish these days.'

'We were born too soon.'

'Do you believe that?'

'No, I think we were happier because life was a lot simpler.'

'David, don't think you have to make conversation when you are driving.'

'Thank you. In daylight I don't mind chatting but I need to give more concentration at night. Not so long ago I wouldn't have admitted to that.'

They were silent, a pleasant restful silence that lasted for most of the journey.

'Almost there, Kirsty. We turn off here and I'll go slowly because we are coming to an unmade road.'

They bumped their way to where a number of cars were parked. As they walked from the car to the restaurant, Kirsty gave a small shiver and drew her mohair shawl around her. Coming out of the heated car she felt it cold even for the short distance. David didn't have a coat, but then men didn't feel the cold so much. He opened one door and then another and they were into the welcome warmth. A smiling waiter came over to greet them and once he had checked the name with his list, led them to a corner table. Kirsty was surprised that they hadn't been asked to have a drink in the cocktail bar while they studied the menu. Since they hadn't presumably The Stables did not have a cocktail bar.

The smartly dressed waiter made to take her shawl but Kirsty declined to be parted from it and instead placed it over the back of her chair. If she had need of it then it was there. Once they were seated each was handed a very large menu.

'Can I get you something to drink?' the waiter asked.

'Kirsty, what would you like?'

'No, thank you, David, I would rather not.'

'I won't either,' David smiled to the young man. 'You could, however, bring the wine list.'

'The wine waiter will be over directly.' He gave a small bow and departed.

'David, this is very nice, very nice indeed,' she said, looking about her. The thick carpet was in muted browns and cream, the tables were covered in snowy white tablecloths and in the centre was a long thin candle in its elegant holder. The candle was lit as soon as the table was occupied. The slim-hipped waiters, silent as moths, were quick and attentive. There was no music, just the drone of conversation and the occasional burst of laughter.

The wine waiter, an older man, arrived at their table, handed David a leatherbound book that appeared to have numerous pages.

'That, by the look of it, is an evening's reading.'

David smiled. 'Most of it I can skip. With so many countries producing wine the restaurants are obliged to stock them. I'm not very adventurous, I tend to keep to the tried and trusted. That said, I should ask if you have a preference.'

'David, you know perfectly well I don't. All that palaver people have sniffing and tasting looks ridiculous to me but I accept I am ignorant on the subject.'

'There are those who are very knowledgeable, Kirsty, there is an art in it.'

'So I am led to believe. I am the despair of George and Matthew, who cannot believe that I cannot tell a good wine from—'

'Plonk,' he smiled.

'That's the word, I couldn't remember it. What a size of a menu,' she said as she began to study it. David saw her smile.

'Don't tell me there is something amusing in the menu.'

'Something omitted. Nothing on my menu is priced.'

'They do that here. You choose exactly what you want, Kirsty. In other words, the price does not dictate.'

'I'm not likely to go mad, but some might, and have the man go pale with shock.'

'I don't think so. The food here is excellent and I don't think you could go wrong with any of the dishes. I'm not going to choose for you so take your time and decide what you should have.'

Eventually they gave their order to one waiter, while another one arrived to pick up the stiffly starched napkin, shake it out of its folds and place it over Kirsty's knees. David was given the same treatment. The wine arrived. David nodded his satisfaction and two glasses were poured.

'Kirsty, I am so glad our friendship didn't finish with the holiday,' David said softly and his eyes crinkled in the way she found so attractive.

'So am I. Although if I am to be honest—'

'Which I hope you are going to be.'

'Admit it, you must. When on holiday we are not our true selves.'

'You mean, we make a special effort.'

'Yes.'

'Some do, some don't. Do I seem different to you?'

'No, you don't. I thought you might.'

The starters arrived and they sat back.

'I didn't expect you to change and you haven't,' David said as he picked up his spoon.

'How glad I am that I starved myself. This is absolutely delicious.'

The wine was very pleasant, she thought, and she made no demur when her glass was topped up more than once. She felt happy and relaxed and soothed by the atmosphere. As the evening progressed she was saying more than she intended.

'My daughters know that I am having dinner with you but they don't know where.'

'You told them about us, I wondered if you would.'

'I didn't mean to. It was one of those awful occasions when one is caught out, you might say.'

'Oh.'

'Helen phoned to ask if she should get me a ticket for this concert and guess when the concert was to take place.'

'Wednesday evening of course.'

'Yes, Wednesday evening.'

'Very awkward for you.'

'It was. When I told her that I had been asked out to dinner, then the questions began. My daughters have my best interests at heart, which is not always a blessing. I resented being questioned and I'm afraid I let fly.'

'That I do not believe, you are too dignified for that.'

Kirsty let it go.

'You were annoyed.'

'I was beyond that, I was furious. Mind you, I did hang on to some dignity, but I told them that how I lived my life was my own business. I did not interfere in theirs.'

'Is that true?'

'Occasionally I overstep the mark, but only if I think they are making a big mistake.'

'Which is probably what they are afraid of with you.'

'Could be, and how silly. What about your daughter, what about Lottie?'

'I have said nothing as yet, but one day soon I shall want her to meet the very charming lady I met on holiday.'

'Will she mind?'

'I think she will be delighted.'

'Don't be too sure. Aren't daughters supposed to be very protective of their fathers?'

'Lottie will approve of our friendship.'

Kirsty noted the use of the word friendship and was reassured. There was always the danger of the one becoming serious and embarrassing the other. This wouldn't happen with them. They would be friends.

David gave a sigh of deep satisfaction at how the evening had gone.

'We must do this again, Kirsty,' David said when they had reached the coffee stage.

'That would be lovely but next time it will be my treat.'

For a moment he looked cross and his thick eyebrows were drawn together.

'No,' he said very, very firmly. 'I am old-fashioned in that way and, let me say, the same applies to going Dutch. That is perfectly acceptable for teenagers and young adults but not for elderly gentlemen like me.'

Kirsty was frowning. 'I can't keep taking all the time. It was the same on holiday. You hardly allowed me to pay for anything.'

'Kirsty, that was my pleasure, I had your delightful company.'

She knew it was better to say no more on the subject. David was the perfect, old-fashioned gentleman, as he had made clear.

16

Kirsty walked over to the window and smiled to herself when she saw David's car draw up at the gate. They had talked on the telephone several times and had gone out together but not for an expensive meal. Kirsty hadn't wanted that. She told David that The Stables had been lovely and that she had very much enjoyed the evening but that kind of meal was for special occasions.

'Meaning you do not want to repeat the experience,' he had said.

'Meaning nothing of the kind, David. Getting dressed up once in a while would be rather nice, but keep it to that – once in a while.'

'What would you like?'

'Just a moment, David, while I bring over a chair and take the weight off my legs.' She kept a chair reasonably close to the telephone for long calls and David's were sometimes that. Hauling it over she sat down. 'That's better, why stand when I can sit? What were we talking about?'

'What you would like us to do.'

'I thought maybe a run in the country—'

'A run in the car, I sincerely hope, is what you had in mind?'

They were both laughing. 'I think my running days are long gone, and you won't be so sprightly as you once were.'

'Sadly that is very true. A round of golf is about all I manage.'

'A run somewhere and stop for a bar lunch. Perhaps that doesn't appeal to you,' she added.

'On the contrary, it does appeal to me. Just going where the mood takes us is how I like it. Don't get the wrong idea about me, Kirsty, I have simple tastes.'

'Speaking of simple tastes, you haven't sampled my cooking.'

'And you think I should?' She heard the laughter in his voice.

'If you are prepared to take the risk—'

'Kirsty, if that is an invitation to your home I am more than happy to accept.'

And here he was arriving at her cottage in time for lunch. Once before David had been in her home but only very briefly while she collected her coat.

She took off her apron and went to open the door. A pale sun was shining and to be approaching the end of the year it was surprisingly mild.

David was carrying something in his hand and had stopped to look at her garden. Before going to meet him, she put the sneck on and closed the door. No use having a warm house and letting the heat out. David was always well dressed but not in a bandbox way. He managed to look comfortable in whatever he wore. Today he had on a tweed suit that he had probably had for years. Good-quality tweed would give a lifetime of wear.

There was no peck on the cheek for her, just a warm smile that reached his eyes. Kirsty was glad. Not that a peck on the cheek amounted to much, but it might to one or two of the villagers looking for something to talk about. It would be a mistake to hand them a gift when there was nothing worthy of gossip.

The plain truth, and Kirsty was always honest with herself, was that she liked being with David and to lose him now would make a big gap in her life. For her he was the ideal companion. She found his company stimulating without being tiring and they could laugh at the same things. That was important, she didn't think she would want to be with someone who did not have a sense of humour. There was just a little niggling worry. She knew that there was a real danger that she might be looking forward too much to these outings. That was not to be confused with a romantic involvement. They were past that age. Not that everyone would agree. There were those who maintained that romance never died. It changed but it didn't die. That there was no age limit to experiencing those special kind of feelings. Maybe they were right. She wasn't completely sure and since she wasn't, then it was time to step back. David might feel that way too. He had his life and she had hers and that was the way it should be, the way it should remain. The last thing she wanted was David worried that their friendship was drifting into something more.

When an opportunity arose she must make it clear that all she wanted was companionship.

'Don't the gardens look weary at this time of year? Not all gardens, I know, but mine for sure.'

He nodded. 'My own garden looks tired and untidy. I don't wish for snow because when it starts it forgets to stop but a blanket of the stuff over the garden transforms it. I look out of the window and think how beautiful.'

'I go along with that. What I hate is the slush that follows. Never mind, when winter comes spring is just around the corner.'

'Nice thought. Do you manage the garden on your own?'

'It isn't very big as you can see and no, I don't. I do have some help. An odd-job man who does the digging when that is necessary and he cuts the grass. I ought to make the effort to do a bit more. I have the time but not the inclination.'

'Don't feel guilty, I manage not to. You and I, Kirsty, are at an age when we can happily look at others doing the work. I was never much of a gardener.'

'Harold is no gardener but to get one of those is well nigh impossible and heaven alone knows what the charge would be.'

He nodded. 'Like any scarce commodity the cost goes up and up.'

She smiled at that. 'Harold is a nice old soul. I say old, but I have no idea how old he is. He never rushes just works methodically. Unfortunately he hardly knows a weed from a flower, or should that be a flower from a weed, but he is obliging. I tell him what I want done and he does it to the best of his ability.'

'You can't ask for more than that.'

Kirsty was becoming concerned about the meal. 'Shall we go indoors?' she said, moving away.

'You are cold. No coat.' She had on a warm skirt and a pale green, long-sleeved sweater. 'I am so sorry to have kept you out here. How thoughtless of me.'

'Don't apologise, there is no need. Had I been cold I would have said so. My concern is for the lunch and I don't want you sitting down to a burnt offering.'

'You've gone to a lot of trouble—'

She had, but she didn't want David to know that. 'I have not, all you are getting is plain fare.'

They were at the door and she could see that David was about to lower his head.

'Let me remind you there is no need to stoop.'

'I know, I should have remembered.'

'It's instinctive for tall people to duck. You are about the same height as my sons-in-law and before I offered for the cottage I had them walk through the doorways to check the headroom.'

'Had they been lower you wouldn't have bought it?'

'Probably not. I didn't want to be responsible for anyone bashing their head. However, George and Matthew gave it the thumbs up and I went ahead with the offer.' She laughed. 'That said, it hasn't stopped them stooping when they come in the door. Linda said they do that to tease me. David, excuse me for a minute or two while I check on the meal. You go ahead into the sitting-room.'

There was a fire burning in the old-fashioned grate and David was standing in front of it when Kirsty joined him.

'Ten minutes and then I'll serve the meal.'

'No prizes for guessing what it is,' David said, handing her the parcel he had been carrying.

'Thank you, David, that was kind of you,' she said as she began to remove the wrapping. 'I am not going to say you shouldn't have done it because I think that so ungracious and no way to accept a gift. Ah, how very nice. I do have a bottle of wine bought for the occasion. Good quality plonk is how Matthew, Linda's husband, describes what I buy. We'll have yours, it will be so much better. You won't mind opening it, will you?'

'A pleasure.'

'I'll take it through and put it on the sideboard for you to deal with later. Which reminds me, I must put out the cork-screw. I have three, two of them I find quite useless and I don't know why I don't throw them away.'

'Not many people have a fire, a real fire, these days,' David said on her return.

'Have you?'

He shook his head. 'When we put in central heating we went over completely to electricity. Removing the fireplace in the lounge was a mistake and I do regret that. No complaints about comfort, the house is beautifully warm but no focal point, Kirsty.'

'You didn't know where to sit?'

'Exactly. I didn't. The answer was, of course, a coal-effect bar fire which is attractive. In the summer months when the central heating is off and the evenings are cool it is handy to be able to switch on a bar of the fire. And after saying all that, I must admit to envying you your coal fire.'

'Not the work involved, though?'

'That was why we got rid of it.'

'Labour saving. I'm all for that myself and I only light the fire when I have company and in the coldest weather. Like you, I have my electric fire and various heaters. Some things I might economise on, David, but heat isn't one. I hate feeling cold and see no reason why I should be. That is the ten minutes up and we'll go through to the dining-room.' They got to their feet at the same time. 'While I get the soup through to the table, perhaps you would see to the wine.'

The bottle was on the sideboard where Kirsty had said it would be. She was right about the corkscrews, two of them should go straight into the bin – cheap and useless. The other, similar to one he had at home, did its job and the cork came out clean. It always amazed him that so many of his friends seemed to think that the perfect gift for the widower living on his own, was the latest in corkscrews. He must present one of them to Kirsty.

The photographs on the sideboard were getting his attention. Most of them were of children at different stages of their development. It was the one in the silver frame that he was interested in.

Kirsty came up behind him. 'John and I when we got engaged. I don't know why I favour that one before our wedding photo, but I do.'

'It is very good.' Kirsty looked very young and very lovely. The man was a lot older, he thought.

'How old were you then, if I am allowed to ask?'

'Nineteen. John was ten years older and always very protective,' she said quietly.

Kirsty served the soup at the table and David poured the

wine into the crystal glasses. At one time there had been six but only two remained.

'This is delicious soup.'

'Thank you. Vegetable soup varies so much. This is a recipe that my mother got from her mother, and then it came to me.'

'And in due course it will go to your daughters.'

'I doubt it. They have more sophisticated tastes. That photograph—'

'Yes?'

'John was a lovely person, David, always thinking of us and never of himself. I didn't appreciate him enough when he was alive and it is too late to do so when he is gone.'

'I'm sure you gave him a lot of happiness. He wouldn't have wanted gratitude. That wouldn't have come into it.'

'I suppose you are right.'

When the meal was over, they went through to the sitting-room for coffee.

'This room is really very charming, Kirsty. The cottage has your stamp on it.'

'Meaning it is most definitely me?' she laughed.

'Oh, yes, most definitely you. Such good taste.'

'I took a risk coming to live here. A small village is very different from the outskirts of a town.'

'You've taken to the life?'

'Yes, I have no regrets. Both my daughters heaved a sigh of relief. They gave me one winter and thought that would be enough. That living in the back of beyond was not for me.'

'You proved them wrong.'

'I did.'

'My daughter would love this as a retreat to disappear to when the need arose.'

'I hardly think—'

'No, of course not, but as she would say, one can dream. Actually they are a happy family but Lottie does not have much love for where they live. They have a large, rather characterless house that Lottie frequently describes as a barn, but not in front of her husband. It was Norman's family home and he inherited it on the death of his parents.'

'Your daughter had no say in the matter?'

'Oh, she did, it wasn't forced on her. My son-in-law is a very nice lad. Lottie knew how much the house meant to him, and they were looking to make a move anyway. With three children the villa was too small. Lottie gets a free hand when it comes to improvements and they have made a number of those. As she says herself, she hasn't much to complain about. She says when she gets to my age and she and Norman are old and grey her idea of bliss would be a country cottage like this.'

'When I bought the cottage I brought with me what I wanted and what I thought would suit the house. The rest I bought. Helen calls it a muddle, but a nice muddle, to spare my feelings. She was terribly keen for me to start afresh with everything new but I couldn't have done that.'

'Of course you couldn't. One can't throw away memories. There are special pieces, perhaps of little value, that we would never part with.'

He understood perfectly, Kirsty could see that. They sat for a while in a companionable silence and then she broke it.

'Are you a good cook, David?'

'Never had it to do, so I can't answer that. With the right kind of tuition I might have been. However, Mrs Brady—'

'Who does for you,' she said mischievously.

'Yes, the lady who does for me. Isn't that a dreadful expression? Mrs Brady is a very good housekeeper and works away quietly when I am there. She prepares my meals when required to do so, but I do eat out at my club fairly regularly.'

'You men and your clubs.'

'You women and your coffee mornings.'

She laughed. 'You have a point, I suppose. Speaking of coffee, is that to your liking?'

'It is, thank you.'

'While on the subject of coffee, would you mind terribly coming here and having coffee with Helen and Linda? They are both anxious to meet you.' She said it half fearfully.

'Why should I mind?'

'I thought you might.' Kirsty took a deep breath. 'David, I am going to be completely honest because I don't want there to be any misunderstanding.' She stopped to moisten her lips. To be this outspoken wasn't going to be easy.

He saw her discomfort. 'Perhaps I can help you out,' he said kindly.

'You could try.'

'We are good friends, Kirsty, I would go further and say very good friends and you want to make sure it stays that way?'

She nodded.

'And the fact that your daughters have expressed a wish to see me – you were afraid that I might read more into that than I should?'

'That's about it. I thought it might frighten you away.'

'Oh, dear.' He picked up his cup and drank some coffee. 'Could I fill that up?'

'If you would.'

She did, then filled her own cup.

'Kirsty, let me put your mind at rest. I think we are both happy as things are. We are friends, very good friends, and I like to know that I can pick up the phone and you are there. What I look forward to is a night at the theatre, a meal somewhere, an occasional run in the car – these are the things I look forward to if I have your company. Have I put your mind at rest?'

'Yes. You are very understanding,' she said softly.

'I would very much like to meet your daughters, and it is only natural for them to want to meet me, the man who is seeing their mother. I promise to try and make a good impression,' he smiled.

'You couldn't fail to do that.'

17

Saturday morning turned out to be dry and pleasant and Matthew, dressed in his oldest clothes, was washing the car, flooding the drive and soaking his shoes all at the same time. Too late he realised he should have been wearing wellington boots. Robin, who would have been keen to help and succeed only in being a hindrance, was at his friend's house. The mothers took turn about looking after the boys and the arrangement was found to be very satisfactory. Today Linda was taking the chance to get in some shopping. It was something she didn't mind doing on her own provided she had plenty of time. She enjoyed looking to see what was on offer and reading the labels to find out what they were eating. Helen made a point of studying the ingredients before buying something she hadn't tried before.

Matthew obliged when called upon to push the trolley round the supermarket. But the task was one he so obviously detested that Linda would dash around picking up the first to come to hand and forget half of what she had intended to buy.

When she returned from a successful shopping trip, she found Matthew using one of her new yellow dusters to polish the car and then standing back to admire the gleaming bodywork.

'Heavens! Are you still at it?' she said as she opened the boot of her car.

'You can't rush a job if it is to be properly done. See that shine, Linda, you can see your face in it.'

'Beautiful, I agree,' she laughed.

He went over to look in the boot. 'You have enough food there to feed a regiment.'

'Believe me, it will all be eaten.'

'I suppose you want a hand with the carrier bags?'

'I do. I was waiting for you to offer.'

'My shoes are soaking wet.'

'So I noticed.' She gave a deep sigh. 'They are going to take a bit of drying. Didn't you think to wear your wellingtons?'

'I just forgot and when I did remember, it was too late.' He looked down at the sodden shoes, then began on the shopping and loaded himself with supermarket bags. 'OK if I leave them at the back door?'

'Yes, fine, I'll manage after that. Is everybody out?'

'It would appear so.'

With the shopping now away, Linda felt the usual glow of satisfaction. She liked to have a good stock of food in the house and be prepared for any emergency. First things first, she would have a cup of coffee and Matthew would probably appreciate one after all his hard work. Before starting on the coffee she decided to go upstairs and close the windows. The wind was getting up and she didn't want the dust coming in and giving her more work. Where did it all come from, she often wondered.

Reaching the hall Linda stopped dead and gazed at the mess. The vase, cheap and garish though it was, had been of sentimental value. For so long it had graced the hall table and now it lay in fragments on the floor. Someone must have knocked it over and that someone must have known. Accidents did happen and Linda made a point of never making a fuss. It didn't help, it just made everyone more miserable. What upset her was the fact that the culprit had made no attempt to clear up the mess. It was too bad. She heard Matthew coming in and the closing of the back door.

'Matthew, come and see this,' she shouted.

'In a minute, I'm going to change my shoes.'

Linda stood where she was until Matthew came to stand beside her.

'How did you manage to do that?' he said, stooping to pick up one of the pieces and placing it on the table.

'I didn't. I didn't break it. This is what I found when I came into the hall.' She frowned. 'It wasn't you by any chance?'

'Not guilty. For one thing, I wouldn't have dared venture indoors with soaking wet shoes.'

'You've done it before, come into the house in wet shoes.'

'I repeat, not guilty.'

'No one said anything to you on their way out?' Linda asked, sounding puzzled.

He shook his head.

'It isn't good enough. Someone broke that vase, Matthew, and didn't trouble to tell you.'

'The someone might have been in a tearing hurry.'

'That is no excuse.'

Picking up the largest piece, which showed most of a pink and blue parrot, Matthew looked at it sadly. 'I liked that vase.'

'So did I. I remember when and where you bought it,'

'Cost me a pretty penny for pretty Polly.'

Linda giggled. 'It did nothing of the kind.'

'How can you know?'

'Because, Matthew Chalmers, I never let on before but I knew where you bought the vase. It was in a junk shop. I saw you coming out with your parcel and looking as pleased as Punch.'

'Where were you hiding?'

'Not far away.'

They were both laughing and remembering.

'Many a treasure has been picked up in a junk shop.'

'Sadly ours wasn't of any value.'

'The first time your sister saw it she said it was hideous and she wouldn't give house room to it.'

'Helen has no taste.' They both knew that Helen had excellent taste. 'No use looking at it, I shall have to clear up this mess.'

'Leave it, someone might own up.'

'I can't leave it, it is too risky. Heather has this habit of going about the house in her bare feet and Robin, as you know, is forever on his knees playing with his toy cars.'

'I'll help you.'

'Thanks. I'll go and get the small hard brush and a shovel.'

They picked up the larger pieces, put them on the shovel and brushed the smaller bits out of the carpet. The Hoover should take up the rest.

'Linda?'

'What?'

'Is it worth making a fuss? It wasn't valuable and you are not going to shed tears over it.'

'Matthew, I have no intention of making a fuss. I never make a fuss and you should know that. All I want is for the culprit to own up.'

'Too scared of your wrath,' he grinned.

'What nonsense you do talk.' Linda wasn't amused. 'An apology and that will be the end of the matter.'

When they were seated round the table having their meal, Linda waited for someone to confess but no one did.

'Has someone got something to tell me?' she asked hopefully.

'Like what, Mummy? What kind of something—'

'It concerns a vase, Robin.' She looked at the blank expressions. 'I found the vase from the hall table on the floor and in smithereens.'

'Does that mean it was broken?'

'Yes, Robin, that is exactly what it means.'

'It wasn't me, I didn't break it.'

'Someone did.'

'Was it you, Daddy?' he said cheekily.

'It was not. Had it been me I think I would have owned up.'

'Mummy, tell everybody you are not going to be angry and then someone will own up.'

'Don't be silly, Robin, you know I don't get angry over breakages. Accidents can happen to any of us.'

'They used to happen to me a lot and you never got angry with me. All you said was to be more careful in future.'

'Yes, Heather.'

No one else spoke and everyone seemed to be very intent on what was on their plate.

'Mummy, please may I leave the table?'

'Yes, Robin, you may.'

There was none of the usual delay and the table was quickly cleared, the dishes washed and put away and the family preparing to go their separate ways. Matthew was going out too. He had changed into grey trousers and a sports jacket and was going to visit a sick colleague in hospital.

'Give Eric my love and tell him I hope he makes a speedy recovery.'

'Will do.'

'Don't go empty-handed, you must take something.'

'This,' he said, holding up a car magazine. 'I bought it yesterday.'

'For yourself. You must have read it from cover to cover.'

'Not quite.'

'The point is, Matthew, you didn't buy it for Eric.'

'Sort of, and he isn't to know I've read it.'

'Matthew, you can be the limit. Wait a minute, I've a box of mints in the sideboard. You can take them.' She went to get them and then had a hunt around for a bag to put them in. Eventually she found one of Waterstone's smallest size but big enough for the mints. 'Here you are, tell Eric they are from me.'

'Not true. You got them from somebody, didn't you?'

'I can't remember.'

He went away grinning.

With Matthew having departed she and Robin were alone. He had come into the kitchen where she was getting out the baking things.

'No, Robin, don't eat that, it will be sour.'

'Why is it sour?'

'Cooking apples always are. If you want an apple get one from the fruit dish.'

The child didn't answer and kept close to her.

'Is something the matter, Robin?'

'No.'

'You don't look very cheerful.'

'That is because I'm worried, I don't know what to do.'

'I knew it, there is something worrying you.'

'Telling tales is bad, you always say that.'

'Yes, Robin, telling tales is not nice.'

He remained silent and looked down at his feet.

'You don't tell tales, do you?'

'I do not,' he said indignantly.

'I was sure you didn't.'

'You see, Mummy—' he stopped.

'No, I don't, Robin, and I won't unless you tell me.'

'I can't.'

'Why not?'

'Because that would be telling tales.'

'Yes, I see your difficulty,' she said, trying not to smile.

'I can tell you what it is about.'

'Well, that is always a beginning.'

'I know who broke the vase but I can't tell you who it was.'

'No, you can't. I can see that.' Linda was all but sure that the culprit was Jennifer. Her own children would have owned up.

'Mummy, I know, I know,' he said, jumping up and down with sudden excitement. 'If I told you who it wasn't that would let you know who it was without me telling tales. That's right, isn't it?'

'Yes, I should think that would be all right.' Linda was impressed. She thought that was smart thinking for a young child. When the children came out with some gem, she liked to share it with Matthew. It was something to chuckle over in the evening.

'It wasn't me.'

'No.'

'It wasn't you.'

'No.'

'It wasn't Daddy. He said so, didn't he, you heard him and Daddy wouldn't tell a lie.'

'Of course your daddy wouldn't tell a lie and he would be very annoyed if he was to hear you say that.'

'Do grown-ups never tell lies?'

'I can't speak for everybody. Your parents don't.' The occasional little white one, which really didn't count.

'Why are you putting sugar on the apples?'

'To sweeten them. If I didn't, you wouldn't eat my apple tart.'

'I was still telling you something.' He made it sound as though it were her fault.

'Carry on, I'm listening,' Linda said as she rolled out the remaining pastry to make jam tarts.

'It wasn't Heather, she said so, and I know it wasn't Hannah. You know now, don't you? You know who it was,' he said triumphantly.

Linda frowned. 'Where were you when this was happening? You haven't told me that.'

'I was going to. I was under the table in the dining-room playing with my motor transporter and I saw her legs because the door was wide open. She didn't mean it,' the child said anxiously.

'No, it would be an accident. I knew that.'

'It was, Mummy. When I came from under the table I saw her put her hand over her mouth, like this.' He gave a demonstration.

'How did it happen?'

'I forgot to tell you that bit. She was swinging her bag and it must have caught—'

'Why didn't you speak, let her know you were there?'

'I didn't want to, that's why,' he said, close to tears.

'It's all right, darling.' Linda wanted to give her small son a big hug but her hands were covered in flour.

'If it had been Hannah or Heather I would have, but Jennifer —' He stopped and looked distressed. 'I've said her name and I didn't mean to.'

'Don't worry, it doesn't matter.'

'Sometimes I like Jennifer but she isn't always nice.'

Linda couldn't disagree with that.

'Do you always like her?'

'Most of the time I do,' she said carefully. 'We have to remember that life has not been easy for her and we have to make allowances.'

'What are you going to do now that you know?'

'Nothing. I am going to do nothing, Robin.'

'That isn't fair,' Robin said indignantly. 'If that was one of us you wouldn't half give us a telling off. Not for breaking the vase,' he said hastily, 'only for not owning up. You are just like Daddy,' he added.

Linda washed and dried her hands. 'Why am I like Daddy?' she said quietly.

'Because you are.'

'That is no answer.'

'You let Jennifer off, and so does Daddy. Hannah said that and so did Heather.'

'That is nonsense.'

'It isn't nonsense if you aren't going to do anything.'

'I will in my own good time.'

'You won't say it was me,' Robin said fearfully.

'I won't, I promise, now please get out of my way while I check the oven.'

'Will I get a jam tart when they come out?'

'You might if you are a good boy.'

There was no further mention of the broken vase and who was responsible. If an opportunity arose, Linda thought, she might speak to Jennifer about it but then again, it was in the past and maybe that is where it should remain. Matthew hadn't forgotten and she was quite touched when he came home with a replacement.

'Sorry I couldn't get anything like the original,' he said as Linda removed the packaging.

'This is lovely, much, much nicer. Thank you, darling, that was sweet of you.'

'Cost a lot more.'

'You mean you didn't buy it in a junk shop?' Linda laughed.

'Certainly not. A man in my position can't be seen going into a junk shop.'

Linda looked up when Heather came in. 'Hello, dear, did you find your glove?' Heather was very good at losing a glove. She had a selection of odd gloves in her drawer kept in the hope of matching them up.

'Yes, I did. It was in the cloakroom behind the radiator.'

'In what condition?'

'It's all right, that radiator doesn't work.' Heather sidled over to her mother. 'What do you know, Dad took us right to the school gate.'

'You were cutting it a bit fine to catch the bus.'

'I know, but we could have caught it at the crossroads. Dad always lets us off there only this morning he didn't.'

'And guess why that was?' Hannah said, coming in and dropping her bulging bag on the floor.

'I am not in the mood for guessing.'

'OK then, you tell me this. When did Dad ever take Heather and me all the way to the school gate?'

'I have no idea.' Linda could see that her elder daughter was spoiling for a fight.

'Never, that's how often. Am I right, Heather?'

'Yes.'

'Where is this leading?' Linda said wearily, though she thought she knew.

'Her ladyship—'

'Hannah, if you mean Jennifer then say so.'

'She, Jennifer, put on the charm and boy can she put it on. She sweet-talked Dad into him driving us to the school gate.'

'You and Heather benefited.'

'That is not the point but I can see I am wasting my breath.' There was a defeated look about her elder daughter that tore at Linda's heart. The young were so easily hurt and Hannah was much too sensitive.

'That isn't all, Mum,' Heather said and got an encouraging nod from Hannah. Jennifer always takes the front seat beside Dad.'

'Darlings, if you want the front seat then you will have to be a bit smarter.'

Hannah gave her mother a withering look. 'If you think I would be so childish as rush to claim the front seat then you don't know me.'

'There are times, Hannah, when I don't think I do know you. No, Heather, don't go. Sit down, both of you, and listen to me. Linda turned her own chair round to face them.

Jennifer is difficult, she is not easy to understand but we have to make allowances—'

'We do that all the time.'

'Yes, well, maybe you could try a little harder, Hannah. It isn't easy to feel yourself an outsider. No one enjoys that. We have each other. We belong and that means security. Secure in our love. For Jennifer we are no more than a substitute family and it isn't enough. Maybe she is jealous, maybe she is resentful or maybe the poor girl is just dreadfully unhappy. We don't know.'

'We have tried to make her feel wanted,' Heather said, sounding wretched.

'We have all tried and failed, I'm afraid.'

'Not Dad, he hasn't failed.'

'No, Hannah, your father has had the right approach and we haven't.'

'That is because he is a man.'

'It could be. As for us, we must be patient and try to be understanding. Stop and think for a moment how you would feel in her place.'

'Awful.'

'Yes, Heather. Neither of you would like to be in Jennifer's shoes, would you?'

'No.' They both looked thoughtful and Linda felt she had made some impact.

'Where is Jennifer?'

'I saw her speaking to Simon,' Hannah said. 'Likely she'll be home with the next bus.'

'I wish I was pretty like she is,' Heather said wistfully. 'She has all the boys after her.'

Linda was smiling to herself when the girls went upstairs. She was remembering the afternoon when she had been in Helen's car and they had driven past the school gate when the pupils were coming out. A group of senior girls were laughing and talking. Jennifer was there but standing slightly apart from the others. She stood out not only because of her height but rather because of the graceful way she held herself. There was none of the gawkiness of the very tall schoolgirl embarrassed by her height.

'That's Jennifer over there, isn't it?' Helen said.

'Yes.'

'That skirt she is wearing is ridiculously short and it doesn't seem so long since you bought it. Surely she hasn't shot up in that short space of time?'

Linda was smiling. 'Helen, by the time Jennifer reaches home that skirt will be a decent length and I am not going to say a word because we did the same thing ourselves. Don't you remember when Mum bought us new skirts they were always below the knees—'

'Bought for growth.'

Linda nodded. 'Yes, bought for growth and we hated to see ourselves looking dowdy, so what did we do? The same as Jennifer. We made the skirt shorter by doubling up the waist-band.'

'So we did. I had forgotten.' She slowed down. 'Should we have offered Jennifer a lift?'

'No. We aren't going straight home.'

'Where are we going?'

'I'm short of bread. Could we go round by the baker's?'

'No trouble. Come to think about it, maybe I could do with an extra loaf myself. Those boys of mine eat like a horse with nothing to show for it.'

'I go for the lean, hungry look myself,' Linda grinned. 'And talking of the boys, Simon and Jennifer seem to be hitting it off.'

'Does that surprise you?'

'Helen, nothing surprises me, not these days.'

Helen looked thoughtful. 'Don't get me wrong, I have

nothing against those two seeing each other. I could just wish that Simon wasn't so besotted. His work is beginning to suffer and that is what worries me.'

'Simon is a sensible lad, he won't let that happen.'

'And pray tell me, sister dear, who is sensible when they are in love?'

'Maybe you have a point there.'

'My other worry—'

'Yes?'

'What it will do to Simon when Jennifer drops him, which she will.'

'You can't be sure she will.'

'I am very sure.'

'What is George saying?'

'Nothing particularly helpful. When I spoke to him about it he said to put it down to experience and that it wouldn't do the lad any lasting harm.' She grinned. 'Listen to this next bit, the bold boy said he was talking from experience, that there had been someone in his youth, a girl he idolised.'

'Really! George told you this?'

'He did. Apparently the girl dropped him when someone more exciting came along.'

'Second left here in case you have forgotten.'

'I had.' Helen dropped her speed. 'Good job you spoke.'

'Poor George. Was he devastated or did he get over it and find a new love?'

'Less of the poor George and he found me, didn't he?'

'A match made in heaven, I once heard Mother say.'

'Is there such a thing, would you say?'

A shadow crossed Linda's face. 'No, I don't believe there is.'

'We, you and I didn't do so badly.'

'No, we didn't.'

'Won't Robin be home by now?'

'No, he has a music lesson. I think that Robin is tone deaf

but time will tell. If the others are home before me they know to
go next door for the key.'

'Well organised.'

'Nothing like you but I'm learning.'

Linda couldn't help feeling ruffled. Home life wasn't as simple
as it once had been. The girls were making a mountain out of a
molehill. If Matthew decided to drive the three of them to the
school gate, so what? There was nothing wrong with that. No,
nothing wrong, but unusual. Very unusual or Hannah and
Heather wouldn't have brought the matter up. It was Matthew
who was out of order again. Why did he always do what
Jennifer asked? Was he unable to refuse her anything?
Couldn't he see what he was doing to his own family? His
daughters were getting ever more disgruntled believing, as
they now were, that they meant less to him than the newcomer.
Linda closed her eyes in despair. Whatever she said seemed
only to make matters worse.

What should she do? If indeed she should do anything. Just
let it pass would be more sensible since Matthew was letting
Jennifer get away with anything these days. Perhaps he had
business worries that he was keeping to himself rather than
involve her as he used to. It was like walking a tightrope to
tackle Matthew on the subject of Jennifer. It could so easily put
them at each other's throats, and that was the last thing she
wanted. Linda felt the anger growing within her. It was
monstrous what she was having to put up with. Why couldn't
Matthew understand the harm he was doing by his thoughtless
behaviour? Children didn't forget, nor were they quick to
forgive. They could take the memory of their resentment with
them into later life.

Was Matthew being especially nice to Jennifer because of
his early reluctance to take the orphan girl into his home? It
could be and she could understand that up to a point. But why

go to such extremes and appoint himself her champion as though they were taking sides? Was it any wonder that Jennifer was seeing Matthew as her knight in shining armour?

Not so long ago she would have roared with laughter at the thought of Matthew as the knight in shining armour. Now it wasn't the least bit funny, it was serious. The carefree happy atmosphere they had enjoyed as a family had gone, and in its place had crept jealousy and resentment. To begin with it had only been Hannah but now Heather, her sunny-natured younger daughter, was airing her own disgruntlement. Even Robin, the baby in the family, wasn't too happy. He had noticed that Jennifer was never scolded and, in his own words, got off with anything. Anything including being late down for meals for which she seldom apologised.

This state of affairs couldn't go on. She must have it out with Matthew, a showdown if necessary. She wasn't going to tiptoe round it any longer.

'Matthew, can we talk?'

Was that a sigh? She wasn't sure but at least he had lowered his newspaper so that she could see his face.

'I suppose so. What is it about?'

Linda moistened her lips and wondered why she should be so nervous. She didn't recall another occasion when she had felt so defenceless.

'I don't want you jumping down my throat, Matthew, but there are things that need to be said.'

'Linda, get to the point,' he said grimly.

'You dropped the girls off at the school gate.'

'I did. Anything wrong with that?'

'No. I mean, yes.'

'Make up your mind.'

'Would you please put down that paper and give me all your attention.'

'Very well. Newspaper folded and now on floor.'

It should have been funny but neither of them was prepared to see the funny side of it.

She took a deep breath. 'When the girls are cutting it fine you always drop them off at the crossroads where they catch the bus.'

'That is so.'

'Only this time you didn't.'

'No, I weakened and ran them to the school gate. Rather good of me going out of my way, I would have thought.'

'You weakened, you said. Who persuaded you to go beyond the crossroads?'

'Does it matter?'

'Yes.'

'I can't remember.'

'I'm sure you do. Your two daughters were in the back of the car and it would never have occurred to either of them to suggest you go out of your way and take them to the school gate.'

'Isn't this all very stupid?'

'It should be, I agree, only it isn't. If you want your memory jogged, let me remind you that Jennifer, sitting beside you in the front—'

'Asked me very politely if I would take them to the gate and since I had the time—'

'I thought you hadn't.'

His lips tightened. 'Since I made the time—'

'Oh, I can see how it was and I wouldn't have given it a thought—'

'Then why are you?'

'Because,' Linda said despairingly, 'we are no longer the happy family we once were—'

'Hannah,' he said exasperatedly.

'No, it is the three of them now who are noticing, which has to make it serious.'

'What is there to notice?' He did look puzzled, she had to admit, but was it genuine puzzlement? She could no longer tell.

'What is there to notice, you ask. The way you always take Jennifer's part. Robin, as it happens, says I do it too.'

He was shaking his head. 'You are talking in riddles.'

'The particular incident for Robin was the broken vase.'

'Are you still going on about that?'

'No.'

'There is no proof that Jennifer was the culprit.'

'Don't you believe your own son?'

'It is not a case of whether I do or I don't.'

Linda stared at him. 'I don't believe what I am hearing.'

'You jump to conclusions.'

'And you don't.'

'I look at the whole picture.'

'Oh, for goodness sake don't try to be so smart. The whole picture indeed. We are talking about our family, Matthew, our family.'

'So am I but, unlike you, I am including Jennifer.'

He had her there, she had to admit to herself. 'It was my dearest wish that Jennifer would become part of this family but she very obviously doesn't want that,' Linda said quietly.

'That could be because she needs a bit more kindness and understanding.'

'And you are giving her those?'

'I am trying to.'

'Don't you think I am?'

'If you say so.' He paused and crossed his legs, then glanced down at the newspaper. He wondered how long before he got back to his paper.

'You don't think so,' she persisted.

'I think you are failing to make her feel wanted.'

Linda thought of all the times she had tried and the number of snubs she had received.

'Not through want of trying, I can assure you. You are going out of your way to make her feel special.'

'Yes, I think I would go along with that.'

'I might say it is very noticeable. Not just to the family but to others. I could start with the car and the number of times she is in it.'

'Being obliging. You might try it sometime.'

This wasn't Matthew talking, it couldn't be. What had happened to their once very happy marriage? It was the bit about not being obliging that did it. She felt the anger rising and the colour flooding her face.

'Maybe you should try being more careful. For your information, people are remarking about the times they see the lovely Jennifer in your car. Alone with you in the car, I should add. They made a joke of it, of course, but you know the saying, no smoke without fire.'

Linda saw his face go chalk white and she wished the words unsaid. It was the truth she spoke and though she had laughed along with the others, she hadn't been laughing inside.

'What exactly are you suggesting?' he said in a dangerously quiet voice.

'I am not suggesting anything.'

'I rather think you are and since you have gone this far, you had better finish it.'

'There is nothing more to say,' Linda said quietly, her anger spent and the tears not far away. 'I trust you, Matthew, but I do not trust Jennifer, it is as simple as that. Please do not say she is just a child because she is not. She is a dangerous mixture of woman and child and I have to say, there is something – odd about her,' she added slowly.

'No, she is quiet and withdrawn but no more than that. The girl must have been traumatised with what happened to her.'

'Yes, and I have made allowances.'

'Have you? You excuse Hannah by saying she is at a difficult age.'

Linda managed a smile. 'Hannah is only a child who gets hurt very easily. She would never willingly hurt anyone.'

Matthew's anger seemed to have gone and he was looking at his wife with scared eyes.

'Linda, this is all wrong, what are we doing? We shouldn't be fighting, we never have before this.'

'I know, dear, and I am so sorry. Jennifer has to remain my problem. She is here to stay because of me and I have to work out the best way of keeping our family happy and united. To do that we must pull together, you and I.'

'Yes, we must do that. And as for the nosy neighbours, I am going to be very careful to give them nothing to talk about.'

She smiled. Maybe everything was going to be fine after all.

Matthew had gone back to his newspaper, they were friends again and being a man, the unpleasantness would be quickly forgotten. She got up quietly and left the room. She felt drained as though all the energy had been knocked out of her. Going upstairs she went into the bedroom and lay down on the bed staring at the ceiling and wondering about their future. She had felt in her anger that she was drowning in a sea of trouble with no hope of rescue. Thank God, they had both come to their senses before it got out of hand as these things could.

18

Some people were complete maniacs and shouldn't be allowed to take a car on the road. Matthew cursed under his breath as the papers he had so carefully stacked on the back seat began to shift, then slide off and land on the floor. A lot of time had been spent putting them in order and now they would be in a hopeless mess. It wasn't as though he had left them sitting on the edge, which would have been asking for trouble. The bundle of papers had been placed well back where he had expected them to remain. He hadn't counted on having to brake suddenly to avoid a car that had strayed into his path. What gets into them, he fumed. Was it a death-wish or lack of concentration brought on by lack of sleep? Or just plain carelessness? Whatever the reason, it had given Matthew a nasty fright. He groaned aloud as more of the papers followed the others to the floor. To get them back in order, and no question about it that had to be done, would be a time-consuming task and there were other things crying out for his attention.

Hannah came into his thoughts. He was hoping that she would be at home and not rushing out anywhere. Maybe she would give him a hand. She was quick and careful and he knew he could trust her to do the job right. Still slightly shaken at the near miss, Matthew cut down his speed for the remainder of the journey. It was a relief to turn into the cul-de-sac and then into his own gate. After parking the car in the drive he switched off the engine and collected his briefcase from the front passenger seat. Before going indoors he cast a last despairing glance in the back where the floor was strewn with papers. He opened the back door, which usually remained unlocked when Linda was working in the kitchen.

'Hello, dear,' his wife said, turning from the cooker where she had been checking the pots. 'Is it my imagination or are you looking a bit hot and bothered?'

'If I am, it is no small wonder. I think, I really do, that the world is full of idiots. One of them had the stupidity to stray into my path and force me to step on the brake. There was no excuse, that was what was so infuriating. He wasn't even trying to overtake—'

'What was he doing?'

'Weaving about like a madman.'

'Faulty steering perhaps,' she suggested.

'I very much doubt it. The quick look I got of him, I thought he looked sheepish and no bloody wonder.'

'Language, dear.'

'Some excuse for it, I would say.'

'Probably the man got a fright himself.'

'I should damn well hope so.'

'As long as you are all right,' Linda said soothingly. It must have been a close shave to get Matthew into this state.

'I'm all right now. Sadly I can't say the same for the papers I had on the back seat. The sudden braking did it for them and most are on the floor.'

'What a shame.'

'Is Hannah around?'

'Upstairs, I should think. Why? Do you want her?'

'I was hoping she would give me a hand.'

'I'm sure she will. Give her a shout yourself, I can't leave this.'

'That's OK.' Matthew left the kitchen and called from the foot of the stairs. It required a second shout to bring Hannah to her bedroom door. This was normal practice in the Chalmers' household. The first call was nearly always ignored.

'What is it, Dad?'

'I could do with your assistance, Hannah.'

'Doing what?'

'Come down and you'll see.'

'Be there in a minute.' She was as good as her word. Hannah was curious to know what it could be. She put on her shoes but didn't bother to tie the laces. Then she was running downstairs and into the kitchen. The back door was open, which meant her father must be outside and this was confirmed by her mother pointing to the door. Linda shouted for Hannah to shut the door behind her but she either hadn't heard or didn't want to hear. A cold wind was coming in and with a sigh Linda crossed the kitchen and closed the door. Then she thought better of it. Matthew and possibly Hannah too would be carrying papers, their hands full. She went back to open the door and leave it slightly ajar.

A pair of feet were protruding from the car with the rest of Matthew inside. Hannah went over to have a look.

'What a mess. Did you do that?'

'Not intentionally. I had to brake for an idiot and they went flying.'

'They wouldn't have if you had put them in folders.'

'I am aware of that. Are you here to help or—' he began testily.

'I can't unless you get out. I'll be a lot quicker at collecting them.'

Matthew wriggled himself out. 'Thanks, it's all yours.' He had a small bundle of papers in his hand. 'I'll go in with these and you follow with the rest.'

'Where are you putting them?'

'On the dining-room table would be the best place. I noticed it isn't set so it would appear we are dining in the kitchen.'

'We are. Mum said so. She's been rushed off her feet.'

'Doing what?'

'I don't know.' Hannah was on her knees on the car floor. 'What is going to happen to these? Do they go on the table?'

'For the time being. I was hoping you might put them in order for me, that is if you aren't rushing out anywhere.'

'I'm not.'

'Once the meal is over you can get started.'

'OK.'

'Thanks, Hannah.' Matthew was very relieved. 'I thought I could depend on you.'

Hannah felt a warm glow. This was what she wanted. This was how it used to be.

'Mum, why are we eating in the kitchen?' Heather demanded to know.

'I was pushed for time and this is much quicker.' She smiled across the table to Matthew. 'Which was lucky, as it happened, because your father is to make use of the dining-room table.'

'Correction, Mum. I am the one who is to be using the dining-room table.'

'No, you aren't. You are not allowed to use the table for your homework.'

'Who said it was for homework?'

'Heather,' Matthew said patiently, 'Hannah is not using the table for her homework, she is going to be doing something for me.'

Linda noticed that Jennifer's plate was empty. She ate quickly and was usually finished first.

'More rice pudding, Jennifer?'

'No, thank you.'

'You gave me too much, you always do,' Robin complained. 'I can't eat all this.'

'Yes, you can. You must eat up everything on your plate if you want to grow up big and strong.'

'I don't. I want to be like Simon.'

'He's skinny,' Heather said witheringly.

'Be careful what you say in front of Jennifer,' Matthew said jokingly.

'You mean, because Simon is her boyfriend?'

'He is not my boyfriend, Robin.'

'He is so your boyfriend,' Heather said, 'everyone knows that.'

'Who is everyone?'

'Just everyone.'

'Then everyone is wrong,' she snapped. 'Simon happens to be a friend of mine and that is all.'

'Jennifer, they are only teasing,' Linda said placatingly. 'Ignore them.'

'I wasn't teasing.'

'That is enough, Robin,' his mother said warningly.

Hannah was enjoying seeing Jennifer annoyed. She was particularly pleased to hear that her cousin Simon was no more than a friend. Jennifer wasn't in love with him or anything. She wished the same could be said for Simon but sadly that wasn't the case. One had only to see that stupid besotted look on his face when Jennifer was around. It was sickening.

Could be, of course, that Jennifer's annoyance had nothing to do with Simon and everything to do with her dad asking for her assistance and not Jennifer's. The thought of that really put a smile on Hannah's face.

The job turned out to be long and tedious but at last Hannah had it completed and the papers arranged in order in neat piles on the polished table.

Matthew looked particularly pleased when he came in to see how she was getting on.

'Splendid, Hannah, an absolute first-class job and, do you know, I am feeling very guilty.'

'Why?'

'Because I imagine this to be homework time you were using.'

She shook her head. 'Not really. None of the teachers bother with homework before the exams. We are supposed to be revising.'

'And now you have to go and do that.'

'Not me. I don't believe in doing revision this early. If I did I would have forgotten most of it by the time I was sitting the exam.'

'Not you. It is all stored there in that head of yours.'

'If only,' she grinned.

Linda thought that Hannah was lazy and spent too little time over her schoolwork but Matthew didn't agree. Hannah was one of the lucky ones like her cousin Nigel. They both had retentive memories and learning came easy to them.

She was a nice kid, he thought, looking at his daughter with affection, and maybe he had been neglecting her of late. Linda certainly appeared to think so, which was complete nonsense of course. What his wife failed to see or to realise was that a family unit was different. No matter what, there was a to-getherness. Nothing was going to come between them. In other words, they were secure in their love. Not so Jennifer. No matter how welcome she was made, she remained the odd one out – the cuckoo in the nest. No one could be completely happy in that situation, he could see that clear enough. He wished Linda could. Poor Jennifer was the one in need of love and attention and being difficult was her cry for help. In-security affected people in different ways. He and Linda had almost fallen out over it. No, not almost, they had fallen out and it had left them both appalled and shaken. Linda had not taken that first step to a reconciliation as he would have expected. He had been the one to do that.

Maybe this was a good time to have a talk with Hannah. No one was likely to disturb them in the dining-room. He drew out two chairs and invited Hannah to sit in one while he took the other.

'Come and sit down and we'll have a few minutes' talk.'

Hannah looked surprised but she sat down.

He smiled. 'Tell me your news, what has been happening in your world?' The moment the words were out he thought how stupid they sounded.

'Nothing. Nothing much.'

'Hannah, you haven't been very happy of late, have you?'

She shrugged.

It was something she did often, and it could be irritating. He wouldn't draw her attention to it and spoil the moment. Maybe Linda should have a word, though, and try and get her out of it. He was unaware that he did a lot of shrugging himself.

'You and Jennifer haven't hit it off and I think that is a great pity.'

'I don't like her and she doesn't like me.'

'Neither of you gave friendship a chance.'

Another shrug of the shoulders.

Matthew gave a sigh. 'It has all to do with the fact that we are a bedroom short. Sadly there is nothing to be done about that. The house does not lend itself to structural alterations.'

'Mum should have thought about that before landing Jennifer on us.'

'That is not a very nice thing to say,' Matthew said reprovingly.

'Maybe it isn't but it happens to be true. I could be wrong but I think Mum may be having regrets about doing what she did. A bit late now for regrets.'

'Yes, it is.'

'Dad, Mum doesn't find Jennifer easy to get on with.'

'Did she say so?'

'No, but it is obvious to me.'

'Hannah, have you ever tried to put yourself in Jennifer's place?'

'No, why should I?' Her mother had said the same thing.

'It could be helpful, and I suggest you try.' He paused and wondered if it was worth bothering. Trying to change Hannah's attitude to Jennifer seemed like a lost cause.

'Let me put it this way,' he said eventually. 'Try to imagine yourself suddenly and tragically all alone in the world. No mother, no father, no Heather or Robin, no Gran, no Aunt Helen, Uncle George and your cousins – are you still with me?' he asked as her feet became objects of great interest to her.

'Yes.'

'Nobody to care what happened to you.'

'That neighbour—'

'That neighbour was going off to New Zealand and anxious to have the girl taken off her hands and Jennifer was well aware of that.'

'Mum got dumped with her.'

Matthew told himself he wasn't going to get angry.

'Your mother stepped in and it is to my great shame that I showed reluctance to open our door to Jennifer.'

'Dad, you changed your mind only when you saw her and could see how pretty she was.'

He stared. 'Pretty or plain she would have got the same welcome.'

'Speaking of welcome, that was quite a speech you made when she arrived.'

'You would rather I hadn't?'

'I didn't say that.'

'I am at a loss to understand you.'

'I am not being bitchy.'

'I should hope not. You are too young for that, too young to say it as well.' Heavens! The way children spoke these days.

No wonder grandparents wondered what the world was coming to. He wondered himself.

'You don't understand because she is different with you. We saw it, though.'

'Saw what?'

'The way she almost split her face smiling at you yet she was barely civil to Mum and Gran on the journey from Inverness.'

'She could have been tired and worried about what lay ahead. I happened to say the right thing and straightaway she saw me as a friend.'

More like a soft touch, Hannah thought, but knew better than say it. There was only so far she could go with her dad.

Hannah gave a huge sigh. 'I think I know where this is leading.'

'Do you?'

'You want me to give up my bedroom.'

'I am not going to ask you to do that.'

'No, but you are hoping.'

'I do believe if you could bring yourself to make that sacrifice we would all be happier. That does not, and I repeat does not, mean you are being asked to do so. We, your mother and I, know how much it means to you to have your own room. The decision now, as it always has been, is yours. There is no pressure on you whatsoever.'

Oh, no, pull the other one. 'You could tell me this –'

'Tell you what?'

'Why is it so important that Jennifer should have her own room and don't say it is because she is older, that won't wash.'

'Very well, I will try and explain, though I may not make a very good job of it. In some ways Jennifer is a strange girl. She doesn't show her feelings, but she could be crying inside and you wouldn't know. Some people are like that, Hannah. They cannot show their grief and because they can't, it is so much harder on them. They don't get the sympathy they deserve.'

He paused and was pleased to see he had her attention. 'Jennifer misses her parents dreadfully and in some twisted way she feels guilty because they died and she lived.'

'That is silly. She couldn't help what happened.'

'I have tried to tell her that but she won't accept it. She is the type of person who will give way to her grief at night in the privacy of her own room, where she won't disturb anyone. She will hold it back because of Heather.'

'It would take more than that to disturb Heather.' It was said flippantly, and she thought her father looked disappointed. She felt ashamed.

'I'm sorry, I didn't mean to say that, it just came out. I do know what you are trying to say. I am sorry for Jennifer, I genuinely am, but—'

Matthew gave a rueful smile. 'She is her own worst enemy.'

'Yes, she is, Dad. What happened to her was awful, we all know that, but she could surely be nicer.'

'Yes, I have to agree with what you say. However, I have the feeling that things will improve. We can but hope. Has our little talk helped?'

'Maybe it has.'

'Must get on. Thanks for all your help,' he said, pointing to the neat piles of papers.

'That's OK.'

19

Jennifer was not popular. The girls in her form didn't much care for her but she was envied. Envied for her slim figure, long shapely legs and that wonderful thick, blue-black hair with its hint of a wave. Her classmates knew that there had been some kind of tragedy in her life and they had gone out of their way to be particularly friendly, which made it all the more upsetting when all their efforts were met with a coldness that didn't encourage them to try again. If Jennifer Marshall preferred her own company they would leave her to it. One thing they would say in her favour, she didn't flaunt her good looks. It was as though she was unaware of them or took her beauty for granted.

The boys were not so easily disheartened. When she was in the vicinity there would be a great deal of nudging and some would whistle after her. Usually they were ignored but occasionally Jennifer would turn round and reward them with a smile. The bolder ones tried to date her but always without success. It was Simon Hunter who made the conquest and without even trying. He couldn't get over it and neither could anyone else. Simon was truly amazed that she had actually gone to the part of the playground mostly favoured by the boys for the sole purpose of seeking him out.

Simon quickly came to the right conclusion that the Sunday lunch had done it. The Sunday lunch his mother had given to introduce Jennifer to the family. They had hit it off and he did remember saying something to Jennifer about seeing her around. At the time he hadn't taken himself seriously. He had said it without meaning anything. Presumably Jennifer had taken him seriously, which was great.

Simon had been thrilled and embarrassed. What could the prettiest girl in the school see in him? It was a question others were asking, and who could blame them? He wasn't. All the same, what had made her make the first move? When the answer came to him his face burned in shame. She had known he wouldn't. That he wouldn't have been able to pluck up the courage. He was pathetic.

Simon and his friend, Mike, had never shown much interest in girls. They accepted that they would in due course but there was no hurry. The two lads had been friends since primary school days and were part of the crowd. A gang of them, and that included a few girls, would often be seen laughing and joking inside the Italian café, that is if funds permitted. When they didn't they would hang around outside the café until they were moved on for making too much noise and making a nuisance of themselves.

The more daring might be showing off by smoking a cigarette and inhaling deeply. Simon was not against a quick puff, nor was Mike. Neither of them particularly enjoyed the experience but felt they should. There had to be something going for it when it was frowned on. At eighteen, Nigel, Simon's brother, could do much as he pleased and once in a while he would leave a packet of Players lying about the house. He would make it perfectly clear that he did not approve of his kid brother getting into the habit.

Simon would occasionally pinch one and hide it away for future use, then look the innocent when big brother raised an eyebrow accusingly. Simon was convinced the old meanie had them counted.

Helen said nothing but kept an eye on both of her sons. She took a moderate outlook, she thought, and was tolerant.

Indeed what was the use of going off the deep end? It did no good and perhaps a lot of harm. It was walking a tightrope but Helen was used to that. And it didn't do any harm to remind herself that at Simon's age she had choked over a cigarette behind the bicycle shed. In those days smoking had not been seen as damaging to health. Rather, it was considered the height of sophistication.

Helen didn't think her sons would be so stupid as risk their health and they could hardly fail to get the message that cigarettes kill. Unlike his wife George did have something to say on the subject. He said that cigarette smoking was a filthy habit and not to be encouraged but that there was absolutely nothing wrong in smoking a pipe. It wouldn't shorten his life. The male side of the Hunter family had all been pipe smokers and without exception had all lived to a ripe old age.

Simon Hunter had no conceit about his appearance. Long ago he had accepted that, at best, he was ordinary and that no really good-looking girl would give him a second glance. They would be too busy eyeing up the real talent. Fluttering their eyelashes at David Winters with his great physique and film-star looks. Or Stephen Smart with his swagger, his broad shoulders and the blond hair that fell across his eyes. A few others in his year hadn't fared badly, but those two stood out and knew it.

What most of all upset Simon about his appearance was being so skinny. He was fed up being told he was only skin and bone. It was awful, especially as he ate like a horse. His mother, trying by her way of it to be kind, had said he must give it time and that he would fill out.

Fill out, for Pete's sake, what a stupid thing to say. What did she take him for? Who wanted to fill out? All he wanted was more flesh on the bones. Not a lot to ask, wanting to look like the average human being.

Buying new clothes was nothing short of torture. Everything hung on him. His mother would try not to despair. Simon had reached that stage even before entering the shop. The poor assistant would eventually lose heart but still continue to bring more garments for Simon to try on. Even the school blazer, made to fit every size and shape, failed him. If it fitted in the body the sleeves were too short and could not be lengthened. Trousers, though, were the worst and George, taking pity on his younger son and remembering perhaps when he, too, had been painfully thin – still was for that matter, though it didn't bother him now – had come to the rescue. Simon and the understanding and sympathetic tailor became good friends. George didn't wonder at that when the bills arrived for him to pay.

Simon fancied Jennifer like mad and thought this must be love. Certainly she was never far from his thoughts and poor Mike, bewildered and disgusted with his friend, found himself a new pal. Simon barely noticed. His head was in the clouds and try as he might, he couldn't keep his mind on his work. Several times in class he had been reprimanded.

'Simon,' his form master said with heavy sarcasm. 'You will tell me if I am boring you?'

There was a general titter that became laughter at Simon's baffled expression. For a moment there he had had to wonder where he was. Simon had not been bored, he hadn't heard a single word.

'Sorry, sir,' he mumbled.

'Pay attention,' the master said, raising his voice, 'and that goes for all of you. Unless you want to fail your exam which, believe me, is all too possible.' The teacher didn't mean that. On the whole they were a bright lot but it did them no harm to be given a fright. As for Simon Hunter, he would have to have a word with the lad. It wasn't like him to be so inattentive. He hoped to God it wasn't girl trouble.

The more anxious of the pupils were looking worried. A few adopted a couldn't care less expression but the truth was, they did care. They all cared. Each and every one of them wanted to do well in future life and that meant passing exams.

Simon was well aware of having fallen behind with his work, not seriously, not yet, but he would have to watch it. His concentration had gone, but it would come back. He had no intention of failing his exams and if it became necessary, he would burn the midnight oil. Jennifer had become too important to him, he knew that, and the sad thing was he was almost sure that the love was all on his side. He wished Jennifer could feel for him even a little of what he felt for her. Didn't she know how much he had given up? He was hardly ever with the gang and when he had suggested to Jennifer that she might like to join them, she had shuddered.

Why was life so difficult? Why did he feel so happy some of the time and at others so despondent? Was that what love was all about? Was that the explanation for his mood changes? It wasn't kid's stuff, it was serious. In the playground he didn't want to listen to crude jokes and he would walk away feeling angry and disgusted. OK, it hadn't always been that way. It hadn't bothered him before, and he had laughed along with the others. Now he felt like punching whoever it was on the nose. Simon Hunter was a pain, that was what they were saying, and he couldn't blame them.

When it came to pocket money George Hunter was generous to his sons. Until recently Simon had found it more than adequate to take care of his needs. He had been able to put aside something towards records or whatever he fancied. Not now. Jennifer paid her own way when it came to cinema tickets or a concert but Simon always paid for the refreshments and the chocolate biscuits that were Jennifer's weakness. He enjoyed paying but it did mount up and there were occasions when he had to ask his mother to help out. She never refused but she would frown.

'You will have to learn to live within your means, Simon.'

'I know but—'

'Taking Jennifer out is expensive.'

'I don't pay for everything,' he said hastily. 'Jennifer pays her share, but boys are expected—'

'To pay. Not schoolboys, not in my day. We pooled our resources – it was called going Dutch.'

'Mum, that's dead old-fashioned. These are the eighties.'

She went into her purse and handed him some coins. 'Will that tide you over?'

'Yes, thanks, that's great.'

'Simon, I'm serious. Don't fall behind with your schoolwork.'

'I don't intend to.'

'You already are and your father and I are worried.'

'No need to be. Honest, I'll make it up.'

'Jennifer will be leaving school at the summer holidays and she isn't bothered about schoolwork. She will shortly be looking for a job and when that happens, she won't be dating a schoolboy.'

'Fair enough, but that is a long time away.'

'A few months that is all.'

'Mum, you worry too much.'

'And you not enough.' She shook her head as he sauntered off.

Simon thought he should pluck up courage and find out just how much he meant to Jennifer. If he asked her point blank she would have to say something. In desperation he had blurted it out.

'Jennifer, mind if I ask you a question?'

'No. What do you want to know?'

'I need to know where I stand with you. I mean, we have been going together for a while.'

She took her time to answer. 'Why are you asking me this now?'

'Because, as I said, I want to know where I stand.'

'I like you,' she said slowly. 'I must or I wouldn't be going out with you,' she added reasonably.

'You like me. Could we have a bit more than that, do you think?'

'Simon, what brought this on?'

'Never mind what brought it on, just answer the question.' Simon was becoming annoyed. She wasn't stupid but she was acting like it.

'If you must know, I feel comfortable with you.'

'Comfortable!' He felt insulted.

'Yes, Simon, that is exactly what I feel. I feel comfortable with you and the reason for that is because you don't keep on asking me questions. You don't because you already know the answers.'

He looked mystified for the moment, then his face cleared. 'You mean, about the tragedy and losing your parents?'

'Yes.'

'Surely nobody would—'

'People ask questions all the time, Simon, and they don't take the hint. They ask and ask until they get an answer.'

Simon was shaking his head.

'You don't believe me.'

'Jennifer, you imagine all this. No one would be so insensitive as to badger you with questions and after all this time. What happened is in the past and nobody would bring up the subject, of that I am sure.'

'I can't expect you to understand. Only someone who has been questioned over and over again can come close to understanding the way I feel.' There was a sheen of perspiration on her brow. 'As I said, I feel comfortable with you.'

That was all he was going to get. 'Is that supposed to be a compliment?'

Her lovely blue eyes widened. 'It is a compliment. I chose to be with you.'

'Love doesn't enter into it. You don't love me.'

'I don't love anyone and I never shall.' The words had a very final sound.

Before he fell asleep that night, Simon tried to recall every word of that conversation. He was comfortable to be with. That really stung. Some compliment that was. But wait a minute, it was still a compliment and maybe for the moment he should be satisfied with that. Most people thought there was something strange about Jennifer and her aloofness put them off. Simon wouldn't use the word strange. He preferred to call her unusual. There were times when he sensed a deep unhappiness but he had the good sense not to intrude. She was a very private person.

Simon lay on his back, his hands behind his head, and stared at the ceiling. This wonderful feeling that he couldn't describe had hit him suddenly and he wished there was someone he could talk to, someone who would understand, but there was no one. Even if there had been he would be too embarrassed to bring up the subject. It seemed that this love thing could hit you at any age but not in the same way, that would be impossible. Take his gran, she was pretty old and past it all but here she was going about with a man of her own age, someone she met on holiday. It was a hoot but nice too. His gran was OK.

Simon's brother, Nigel, who never interfered or hardly ever, said he should cool it with Jennifer and get his head down unless he wanted to repeat a year.

He wasn't the one who was cooling off. Twice in recent days Jennifer had made an excuse not to see him and he blamed himself. He shouldn't have been so clumsy. Trying to get her to declare her feelings had been a monumental mistake. He had scared her off. Why hadn't he made do with comfortable? He wished he had but it was too late for regrets, the damage was done. This cooling off was the beginning of the end. Simon could see it coming.

20

'Nigel, your brother looks deeply unhappy. Have you any idea what is the matter with him?'

'I don't know for sure, Dad, but at a guess I would say that Jennifer has given him the old heave-ho.'

'Such horrible expressions you young people use,' Helen said, 'but I have to say if that is Simon's trouble I am delighted. In fact it is the best news I have had in a long time.'

'That is a bit strong, dear,' George lifted his eyebrows.

'I am thinking of his schoolwork.' They had just finished eating. 'Nigel, don't just stand there. Make yourself useful and pile the dishes on the tray.'

'When is this wonder machine arriving?'

'The dishwashing machine should arrive at the beginning of next week. It does not clear the table, it only washes and dries the dishes.'

'Pity.'

George was looking thoughtful. 'Don't be treating this thing lightly, Helen. Our boy is suffering, I would say.'

'George, as his mother I do know that. I also know that Simon will get over it. For heaven's sake they are only a couple of kids.' She drew in a sharp breath. 'Nigel, be careful or that is going to fall. Two cups will go into each other, three will not, not with that set. What was I saying?'

'I don't know,' George smiled.

'Ah, yes, I remember. Simon is hurting, you said, but I am of the opinion that he might be secretly relieved.'

George smiled. 'Missing his pals.'

'Yes.'

'You could be right, dear, and I have no doubt things will work out but in the meantime I suggest that the three of us leave Simon alone. The lad will deal with this in his own way.'

'I go along with that, Dad,' Nigel said as he balanced the tray and Helen closed her eyes. She was better doing everything herself. It was easier on the nerves. 'In his place that is what I would want.'

'And if Simon looks miserable and wretched I, his mother, have to pretend not to notice?'

'I'm afraid so. Difficult for you, dear, but by far the best way.'

'Switch it off, one of you.' The three girls had been watching one of the soaps. Matthew was at a meeting and Robin was in bed with a heavy cold and feeling very sorry for himself. When Linda went upstairs to check on the little lad he was fast asleep with his mouth slightly open. She tucked him in and tiptoed out of the room.

'How is he?' Hannah asked when her mother returned.

'Sound to the world. A good night's sleep and I think he should be fine but I'll keep him indoors tomorrow to be on the safe side.'

'I've caught it from him, I think.'

'No, you haven't, Heather, but you are to stop going about the house in your bare feet. That is the way to catch a chill.'

'It is supposed to be good for your feet.'

'In the summer perhaps.'

'Jennifer.' It was Hannah addressing Jennifer and that was unusual enough to have Linda and Heather look up.

'What?' Jennifer was startled too.

'I have decided that you can have my bedroom and I'll share with Heather.'

'You mean it?'

'I wouldn't be saying it if I didn't.'

'Thank you. Thank you very much.' Jennifer was looking amazed and absolutely delighted.

'Hannah?'

'It's all right, Mum.' She turned to look at Jennifer. 'To-morrow after school?'

'Fine by me. Thanks again.' No one had ever seen her so enthusiastic.

'We can make the change-over then.'

Jennifer nodded happily.

'I'll help,' Heather said. She had got used to Jennifer sharing her room but it would be nice to have her sister and someone to fight with.

Linda was keeping quiet. She would wait until she had Hannah on her own. Of one thing she was certain, the change of heart hadn't come about without pressure from somewhere.

Matthew had returned from his meeting, which he said had been a waste of time. The annoying bit was he had missed the beginning of the football match showing on television but since no goals had been scored it wasn't so bad. He would enjoy the rest. Heather was on the phone to her new friend and giggling about arrangements for the weekend.

Linda saw her chance.

'Hannah, come into the kitchen, please.'

'OK.'

'Sit down. I think you know what this is about?'

A shrug.

'Don't do that, your father doesn't like it and for that matter neither do I.'

The eyes widened. 'Dad said nothing to me.'

'No, he wouldn't, he left that to me.' She paused. 'Why, Hannah, why all of a sudden are you prepared to let Jennifer have your bedroom?'

'I didn't understand before, now I do.'

'Understand what?'

'The reason why Jennifer needs to be on her own.'

'Perhaps you could enlighten me.'

'No need to get angry.'

'I'm not but I am certainly surprised.'

'Dad understands her the way we didn't.'

'He said that?'

Hannah nodded. 'We had a talk –'

'When was this?'

'Mum, does it matter when it was?'

'I'm curious as to when it could have been.'

'That time when I was helping Dad sort out his papers.'

'Yes, I remember now, you were a long time together in the dining-room.'

'Jennifer can't give in to her grief,' she said very seriously.

'Oh.'

'She can't, Mum. She can't show her feelings. Dad said there are some people like that and Jennifer is one. She puts on a show of indifference when all the time she is crying inside.'

'I see.'

'No, you don't. In bed at night is when they can let go and give in to their grief, I mean people like Jennifer. To do that you have to be on your own.'

'Your father said all that?'

'Not in those words but that was what he meant.' She paused. Mum, Dad said to think about it and to try and imagine how I would feel if suddenly I didn't have you or Dad or Heather.' Her voice caught and it took Hannah a moment or two to go on. 'No Gran, or Uncle George or – or—'

'All right. If you were quite alone in the world was what he meant and yes, it would be dreadful but do you know, Hannah, if you were in Jennifer's shoes I am very sure that you would not be so rude and difficult. There are times when I think the girl wants to be disliked.'

'I don't know, I don't know what I would be like. Certainly I would be scared, I know that.' She looked at her mother accusingly. 'You should be pleased I am doing this and you aren't.'

For a moment Linda closed her eyes. It was so unfair. She was being made out to be the unfeeling one and yet all she had ever tried to do was please everybody. She should have known that was impossible. Betty's daughter was in need of a home and she had been desperately anxious to offer one. No one was keen but she had fought her battle and won. Or had she? Wasn't it more likely that she had lost?

She had done her best to welcome Jennifer into the family but not for her to get preferential treatment. Matthew was doing just that and until now Hannah had objected strongly. She took a deep breath and tried to keep calm, to sound reasonable.

'My dearest wish, Hannah, is as it always has been to keep my family happy. I had hoped that Jennifer would settle but she hasn't made much attempt to do so. It would appear that I have gone about it the wrong way and where I have failed your father has succeeded.'

Hannah smiled kindly. 'Don't take it to heart, Mum, usually it is you who is the understanding one but this time it happens to be Dad.'

Linda sighed. There was really nothing more to say. She got up.

'Is that Heather still on the phone?'

'Sounds like it, but not to worry, whoever it is made the call so it won't go on our bill.'

'Even so I think I'll remind her she has talked long enough.'

Somehow Linda got through the rest of the day and if she was quieter than usual no one remarked on it. The girls had gone up to bed, in Heather's case reluctantly. She was never tired at night only in the morning when it was time to get up. Robin had wakened, been given a glass of milk and something to eat and promptly fallen asleep after it. Linda hoped the sleep would last until the morning but knew that to be unlikely. A disturbed night was on the cards.

She looked at the late news with her husband without taking much of it in. Matthew looked at her several times and then got up to switch off the television.

'OK, Linda, I gather I'm in the dog-house. What am I supposed to have done?'

'Would it surprise you to know that Hannah has decided to give Jennifer her bedroom? She is prepared to share with Heather.'

'A little surprised, I must admit, but pleased,' he said carefully. Linda's expression wasn't very encouraging. 'You should be pleased, this is what you wanted.'

'Not when Hannah objected so strongly.'

'She has got over that.'

'I wonder how that came about.'

'A change of heart.'

'Not without pressure from somewhere. You were responsible, weren't you?'

'If I was, what of it?'

Linda didn't bother to answer. She just gave him a steady look.

'There was no pressure put on Hannah, of that I can assure you.'

'Gentle persuasion, could we describe it that way?'

'Yes, I could accept that,' he said quietly. He gave a half-smile. 'Tell me this, Linda, does Hannah look unhappy or resentful over the sacrifice she is making?'

'No, she is enjoying the role of martyr.' She shook her head. 'That was unkind of me. Hannah is showing no resentment.'

'Why all this fuss?'

She shrugged before she could stop herself. They were a family of shruggers, she thought.

'Accept that the matter has been resolved,' he said almost triumphantly. 'The one obstacle to a contented family life has been removed.'

Matthew was being reasonable and she wasn't and that was making her furious. She shouldn't have got herself into this position.

'I am satisfied with the end result but not the way it was achieved.'

'Aren't you being small-minded?'

'Yes, very possibly.'

'You are not small-minded and I am sorry I said that. This hasn't been easy for you but wait and you'll see that all is well. Jennifer will be a changed girl.'

'Of course she will, isn't she getting what she wants? It doesn't take a genius to work that out.'

'Could we leave it there?'

'Certainly. I have no more to say on the matter.'

'Good.'

'I am going up to bed.'

'I won't be long behind you.'

Linda no longer knew what she thought. She was confused and she was tired. She had tried hard and got nowhere. Matthew had used a different approach and with little effort had succeeded. She ought to congratulate Matthew but she couldn't bring herself to do that. Maybe she was suffering from hurt pride, that could be it. But not all. Why did she feel that none of them understood Jennifer and that the girl was hiding something? She sighed, undressed and got into bed. She was tired but had never felt less like sleeping. What she would do was feign sleep when Matthew joined her.

*   *   *

Simon did not give anything up without a fight and that included Jennifer. He hadn't lost her, not yet. Fingering the two tickets in his pocket he smiled. If he was smart he should be able to catch Jennifer before she headed for the bus stop. Her height made her easy to pick out and more than likely she would be on her own. And there she was walking briskly. Simon had to do a sprint to make up on her. His fingers kept playing with the tickets in his pocket while he tried to convince himself that there had been no cooling off. It had only been in his imagination.

Jennifer liked dancing. She had told him in one of the rare times she spoke of her parents that her dad had been a smashing dancer and had taught her all the steps. Simon didn't see Jennifer turning down a chance to go dancing particularly when it was the Tennis Club dance and that was a very special occasion.

'We are in a hurry,' he said, pretending to be out of breath.

'I am in a hurry as it happens.'

'Where are you rushing to?'

'To catch the same bus as Hannah. I want to get home quickly.'

'That makes a change,' he couldn't help saying.

'What makes a change?'

'You hurrying home for one thing and mentioning Hannah's name for another.'

She looked at him sharply and he thought she wasn't going to answer, then she did.

'I want to get home to sort out my things,' she said as they fell into step. 'Hannah is letting me have her bedroom and she is going to share with Heather.'

'How come? What brought this on?' He knew that Hannah was dead keen to keep her own room.

'I have no idea what brought it on. It just came out of the blue.'

'That's great, Jennifer. Great for you, I mean.'

'Yes.'

And very big of Hannah, he thought. Somebody must have put pressure on her. He didn't see his cousin moving out and making way for Jennifer without there being a very good reason.

She was smiling. 'It will be a bit of an upheaval until we get everything sorted out. That's why I want home to get started.'

'Don't worry I won't let you miss your bus. I wanted to let you know I've got two tickets for the Tennis Club dance. Thought you would like to go,' he said smiling foolishly.

'Then you thought wrong, Simon Hunter. And you should have asked me before you bought the tickets.' She tossed her head and her hair danced in the way he loved to see.

Simon's face fell. 'You don't want to go or should that be you don't want to go with me?' Bitterness had crept into his voice.

Jennifer looked at him but remained silent.

'That's it, isn't it? You are going to the dance with someone else.'

'Did I say that?'

'You didn't have to, I'm not stupid.'

'You are being very stupid. I am not going to the dance with you or with anyone else.'

'Even so this is me getting the push?'

'Yes, if you want to put it that way. I have liked being with you, Simon, but I want it to end.'

'What have I done?'

'Nothing. You have done nothing. All I want is to be left alone. Is that too much to ask?'

Simon didn't answer.

'Can't you understand? And as for the tickets, no need to waste them. There are plenty of girls who would love to go with you.'

'I know. I'll have to decide which one I am going to ask.' He turned away, too choked to say any more.

Simon dug his hands deep into his pockets and spying a battered tin can in the gutter began to kick it along the pavement. A woman loaded with shopping tut-tutted at the noise but it didn't stop Simon. He wanted to annoy, that was the way he felt. What was a bit of noise compared to the pain he was feeling? He was at a loose end, not knowing what to do with himself. The gang would take him back but it was too soon for that and he couldn't stand the ribbing. Mike would take his time about welcoming him back, but he would.

If he only knew what had gone wrong. Not knowing troubled him greatly. Jennifer said it was nothing and all she wanted was to be left alone. That didn't ring true. He must have annoyed her. In Simon's book there had to be an explanation for everything.

How unspeakably awful it would have been if Jennifer had left him for Daniel Winters or Stephen Smart. He would have wanted to die. Jennifer hadn't done that to him.

Nobody had remarked that he looked glum or anything, which surprised him. He must be doing better than he imagined. It was good to think that the family hadn't noticed but there was a downside too. He could do with a bit of sympathy and understanding but he couldn't bring himself to ask.

There was a need in him to talk to someone, someone who would understand his unhappiness. But who? None of his pals that was for sure. No sympathy there, more like – told you so – in fact none of us gave you this long with that gorgeous-looking bird. He stopped kicking the tin can. He had it. His gran. He could talk to her without fear of it going any further. Tomorrow was Saturday and he would go over in the morning. If the weather was half decent he would use his bike, if not there was the bus. No one would be all that surprised, he did occasionally visit his gran.

Helen was preparing the leg of lamb for the roasting tin. It was a Saturday morning and Simon had come into the kitchen wearing his anorak and a scarf.

'Off somewhere?' she smiled.

'Thought I might go and see Gran.'

'She will be pleased.'

'I was going to cycle—'

'No, it is too far and you don't know what the weather is going to be. According to the weather forecast snow is on the way with a considerable fall predicted.'

'You don't want to believe all that.'

'Simon, it is as well to be prepared. Take the bus.' She wiped her hands on the towel. 'No use you going empty-handed. I'll give you two jars of marmalade. Tell your gran I made it at the beginning of the week.'

'OK.' Simon didn't give the usual moan about not wanting to carry things. This could be the excuse, not that he needed one but it could be handy in case he thought he did.

'Money in the Toby jug.'

'I'm all right for funds.'

'That makes a change.' She wished she hadn't said that. The reason he was in funds was because he wasn't spending money on Jennifer. Simon dropped his eyes but didn't say anything. Meantime Helen got a strong bag for the marmalade then put it inside another to be on the safe side. 'Don't drop that.'

'Or leave it on the bus,' he grinned. It had happened once before with a cake his mother had baked for Kirsty. He had put it on the seat beside him and forgotten about it. Enquiries had been made but of no avail. Possibly the finder had been hungry.

She could see how hard he was trying to appear his usual

self and Helen could have wept. He was still her baby and his pain was hers. Many would have blamed Jennifer but she didn't. The girl was behaving like any teenager. She didn't want to go on seeing the boy, so what else could she do but break it off?

21

Kirsty had an apron tied round her waist and she was standing at the kitchen sink scraping a carrot with two medium sized potatoes on the draining-board waiting to be peeled. That would do very well with the two loin chops she had bought from the butcher. The rap on the kitchen window startled her and she looked up sharply. Living alone made her nervous about unexpected noises although she would never admit it to her two daughters. The startled expression quickly gave way to a broad smile. Her visitor was Simon, his face half hidden by the hood of his blue and yellow anorak. Drying her hands quickly, Kirsty hurried to the door and opened it.

'Simon, how lovely to see you,' she said, pulling him in and giving him a hug. 'What was wrong with the front door?'

'You don't always hear the bell if you are in the kitchen.'

'I do if people would only press the thing properly. Let me get the door shut and keep the cold out.'

'It's perishing.'

'Yes, snow is in the air I think.'

'Not you as well. Mum said that before I left. That's for you, it's marmalade,' Simon said, giving his grandmother the carrier bag.

'Now isn't that nice, I was down to my last jar. Many thanks, Simon. You will remember to thank your mother?'

He nodded. 'Sure thing.'

'Take off your anorak.'

'Where will I put it?' he asked when it was off.

'Hang it on the hallstand like you always do.'

'Can't, the loop is broken. I forgot to tell Mum.'

'In which case you will need a coathanger.' Kirsty got one from the cupboard and took the anorak from Simon. 'Maybe I could stitch that loop before you leave. On you go in to the sitting-room and get a heat.' Kirsty had been studying her grandson and thought he looked strained and not a bit like himself.

'Everyone well?'

'Yes.'

'Simon, push that chair nearer to the fire. I am going to put the kettle on.'

'You don't need to for me. I'm not bothered.'

Now she knew something was far wrong. 'I thought there was something troubling you. What is the matter, dear?'

'Nothing. Why should anything be the matter?'

'You tell me.'

'If there is it's nothing much.'

'Enough to make you miserable.'

He didn't answer and kept his eyes on the fire.

'Believe it or not I was once young myself.'

He looked up and smiled.

Kirsty took the poker in her hand and began to rearrange the coal, making the flames shoot up the chimney.

'There were times, not many admittedly, when I felt I couldn't talk to my parents and I would go along to see my grandmother. She was a gentle soul, Simon, and quiet-spoken. I did the talking and she listened and I found that putting it into words helped. After I had poured it all out we would discuss whatever it was that was troubling me. She was a great help I do know that.' She patted his knee. 'Trust me, dear, I am a good listener and I promise not to preach.'

'You never do, Gran, preach I mean.'

'I'm glad. I shouldn't like to be guilty of that.'

'You won't think it much but it's all off with Jennifer,' he said dully.

'Oh.'

'When I say all off, it was never more than friendship on Jennifer's side.'

'For you it was more than friendship?'

'A lot more. She was just everything to me. It sounds daft but she was never out of my thoughts.'

'It doesn't sound daft at all.'

'I should have known it was coming. I don't think she gave me more than a passing thought. She did say she liked to be with me.'

'Well, then—'

'Of course she did. I mean you don't go around with someone unless you like the person.'

'I agree with that.' She paused. 'Jennifer was paying you a compliment when she said she enjoyed your company.'

'Comfortable to be with was how she described me. You can imagine how that made me feel.'

'Like an old pair of slippers,' Kirsty laughed.

Simon couldn't keep the laughter back.

'There you are, we can make a joke of it.'

'It's no joke, Gran.'

'I know, dear, but sometimes we have to laugh or we would cry.'

Kirsty was looking at her grandson with affection. The young, especially boys, were so vulnerable, so easily hurt. His pride had to be protected too. No one likes to be thrown over and one's peers could be so cruel. She didn't think the young were deliberately cruel, just thoughtless.

'Going out with an exceptionally pretty girl must have had your school friends envious.'

'You bet. Probably thought Jennifer needed her eyesight tested.'

'Now! Now! We'll have less of that,' Kirsty said severely, 'you are not to put yourself down. I am a woman as well as your grandmother and to me you are a very attractive and presentable young man. And remember, looks are not everything,' she added rather unfortunately.

'Looks are important to most girls.'

'Tell me, were you proud to be seen with Jennifer?'

'What do you think?'

'I'm asking you.'

'Of course I was, who wouldn't be?'

'Rather like a trophy.'

'I'm not with you, Gran.'

'To put it simply, Jennifer was the prize and you the winner.'

'It wasn't like that at all,' Simon said half angrily. 'I happen to love her.'

'I see.'

'What shook me was Jennifer making the first move. She did, Gran, and do you know why?'

'No I don't.'

His Adam's apple wobbled. 'Because she knew I would never get round to it. Too scared of a refusal and making a fool of myself. And she was right.'

'Nothing there to be ashamed about. She made the first move and shall I tell you what I think?'

'You had better, I suppose.'

'When Jennifer used the word comfortable that is precisely what she felt. Some girls welcome attention but Jennifer isn't one of them. She felt safe with you because of the family connection and the bonus was that she also liked you. In a sense you were both getting what you wanted. Jennifer wouldn't be pestered by other boys when she was with you and you, Simon, were delighted to be seen with her.'

'OK, I go along with some of that,' he said sullenly. This

wasn't going the way he had hoped and Simon was beginning to wish he hadn't come.

'Good, we are getting on.'

'No, we aren't. I don't know why I came.'

'Because your mother sent you here with two jars of marmalade.'

'No, that was after I said I was going to see you.'

'Then I am honoured. Simon, dear, I do understand. You came to me for sympathy and I have let you down.'

'It isn't that.'

'Yes, it is and believe me I am not without sympathy but at the moment I think you are more in need of plain speaking.'

'If you say so,' he said grumpily.

'I do. There is no pain like the pain of betrayal but Jennifer has not done that to you. Or have I got this wrong? Has she dropped you to take up with someone else?'

'No. She says she wants to be left alone.'

'Then she has every right to be left alone if that is her wish. And you should respect her wishes.'

'I can't do much else.'

'Simon, I think we are all agreed in our family that Jennifer is not the easiest person to understand,'

He nodded.

'As a matter of interest to me – and don't get me wrong, I am so glad you are here – why didn't you confide in your parents? They are particularly understanding, I would have thought.'

'Because, Gran, I was afraid they wouldn't take it seriously. You know, think it was only kid's stuff.'

'I doubt they would have thought that.' She paused. 'No matter what age we are we all have feelings.' She wasn't looking at him and he thought she might be thinking about that man his mother said she had met on holiday. He couldn't quite get round to the idea that old people like his gran could be in love. Maybe there were different kinds of love, he supposed that was it.

'You know if—' He stopped.

'If what dear?'

'If Jennifer had given me the push because she was going out with someone in my year I think I would have died.'

'No, you would have survived. Life is too precious.'

'I would have felt awful.'

'I don't doubt it but it hasn't happened.'

'No and I have to be glad about that. He grimaced. 'I bought two tickets for the Tennis Club dance and I asked Jennifer to go with me.'

'She refused.'

'Yes and that shook me. I was so sure she would want to go. I mean she likes dancing and she is good.'

Kirsty nodded.

'And before you ask she isn't going with anybody else.'

'That must have been a relief,' she smiled.

'Too true it was.'

'And here you are with two spare tickets.'

'I can't hand them back. Maybe I should tear them up.'

'What a waste.'

'What else can I do?'

'Take another girl. Jennifer isn't the only pebble on the beach.'

'I don't want to take another girl.'

'Fair enough. May I make a suggestion?'

'You can but I doubt if I'll take it.'

'And that is before you hear it, thank you very much.'

'OK, I'm listening.'

'Ask your cousin Hannah.'

'Hannah?'

'Why not? You two have always been the best of friends. She might not accept but there is no harm in asking.'

'She'll think I've got a bit of a nerve. Knowing Hannah she might tell me what to do with the ticket.' Kirsty saw him grin as though that amused him.

'She might well do that but I would hope my granddaughter would not be so rude.'

'Worth thinking about. I could, I suppose, hand back the tickets. They will take a dim view of it but I might get my money back.'

'Ask Hannah first.'

'Yes, I think I might. I mean it isn't like going with a girl. She is only my cousin.'

'Tact is not your middle name, Simon,' Kirsty said drily.

'You offered me tea, is it still going?'

'Yes. Are you hungry?'

'A bit.'

'A good sign, you must be feeling better.'

'Not much but I have to put a face on it.'

'You are feeling less miserable than you were when you arrived?'

'Yes, thanks to you. But I am still miserable.'

'Heartache doesn't disappear as quickly as all that. Before I put the kettle on I am going to talk to you very seriously because I know how worried your parents are.'

'I know what is coming. And honestly, Gran, I am going to get my head down this weekend and do some work.'

'I am very glad to hear it. And Simon –'

'What?'

'Your friends must have felt neglected.'

'Suppose so.'

'Won't it be nice to get back with them?'

'OK, I suppose.'

Hannah was leaving the playing fields and that was Simon hanging about.

'Before you get the wrong idea, he is my cousin,' Hannah said as she broke away from her school friends.

'What are you doing here?' she asked him.

'Waiting for you.'

'Why?'

'Wanted to ask you something.'

'Ask it then.'

'How would you like to come to the Tennis Club dance with me?'

Hannah couldn't imagine anything more wonderful. 'How about Jennifer?'

'That's all off, thought you would have known.'

'No, but then Jennifer doesn't say much.'

'You know now.'

'You are stuck for a partner and that is why you are asking me?'

'Yes.'

'Thanks, you know how to make a girl feel good.'

He laughed. 'You didn't think of that, you read it in one of your girls' papers.'

'I do not read such rubbish,' she said haughtily. 'And as for your second-hand invitation I shall have to give the matter some thought.'

'Don't take too long about it.'

'In case you change your mind.'

'There is always that to it.'

'How about tomorrow?'

'I guess I could wait that long,' he said, beginning to move away.

They were a few yards apart when she shouted, 'Simon.'

He turned back.

'Forget tomorrow, I'll give you your answer now.'

Simon waited for the refusal he felt sure was coming. 'Forget it, Hannah, I just thought you might like to come that is all.'

'I think I need my head examined but I'll go with you.'

'Great. Thanks.'

'I'm only accepting because I am your cousin.'

'You are only being asked because you are my cousin.'

They were both grinning as they walked away.

Hannah was chewing her thumbnail.

'Don't do that, dear. It took me long enough to stop Robin sucking his thumb.'

'It helps me to think. And it is only my nail.' She followed her mother into the kitchen. 'Mum, it's all off between Simon and Jennifer.'

'So I believe.'

'You knew and you didn't tell me.'

'I must have forgotten.'

'Simon has asked me to go with him to the Tennis Club dance.'

'And have you accepted?'

'Yes.' She bit her lip. 'He is only asking me because Jennifer doesn't want to go. Am I making myself cheap?' she asked worriedly.

'What do you think?' Linda said gently.

'If I wasn't Simon's cousin then yes I would be making myself cheap.'

'But you are Simon's cousin.'

'That makes it all right?'

'I would think so.'

'How did it come about, I wonder? Do you think someone asked him to invite me?'

'It is possible.'

'Gran, would you say?'

'Maybe, I don't know.' Linda nodded her head slowly. 'Simon went to see your grandmother.'

'He must be feeling rotten, Mum. Simon was besotted with Jennifer.'

'He'll get over it.'

'I do want to go but I was scared in case I was making myself cheap.'

'You aren't, so stop worrying about it.'

'It's only three weeks away.'

'Yes.'

'Mum, I can't wear that horrible puffy-sleeved dress I had for the school dance.'

'That horrible puffy-sleeved dress was your own choice.'

'I wouldn't be seen dead in it. The shop assistant talked me into it.'

'No she didn't. The choice was yours and yours alone. However, you can have a new dress.'

'I can choose.'

'If you make a better job of it this time.'

'I can choose whatever I want.'

'Within reason.'

'What does that mean? Nothing too revealing?'

Linda could hardly keep her face straight. There was precious little to reveal.

22

The snow that had been forecast began to fall in the late afternoon. At first it was no more than a light dusting, then it began to snow in earnest. The flakes got bigger and fell heavily and evenly, mantling the countryside and the hills. For the children it was a magical scene and they were impatient to be out of doors. Their parents were much less enthusiastic, seeing before them hours of clearing the snow. Also there was a feeling of being hard done by. This was late into February and they had hoped the worst of the winter was over. They should have known better.

Dressed for the weather the girls had trudged to the cross-roads believing that to be the only place they were likely to see a bus. Linda had watched them set off and was glad she had insisted that Jennifer get herself a pair of wellington boots. Robin was to remain at home. His friend's mother had telephoned Linda to say she was keeping her boy off. The weather could get worse, she said, and with the snow drifting some of the teachers might find it difficult to reach the school. Linda agreed.

Matthew, after a few mild expletives concerning the weather, had decided his first priority should be to clear a path round the house. By afternoon there might be an improvement and he would manage to get into the office but he wasn't too bothered if he didn't since he had had the forethought to bring work home with him.

Heather, looking flushed and excited, was the first to burst into the kitchen.

'Mum, no bus, it never came.'

'I'm not surprised,' Linda said as she began clearing the breakfast dishes from the table.

'You sent us,' her younger daughter said accusingly.

'The bus might have been running. You had to make the effort to find out.'

Hannah and Jennifer came in but unlike Heather they had scraped their feet on the wire mat to get rid of some of the snow.

'Mum, we waited for ages and then somebody passing said the bus had got stuck on the hill and we would be better going home.'

'Since you are and dressed for the weather you can help your father clear the snow.'

'Me, too, Mummy.'

'Yes, Robin, there is a little shovel you can use. The garage is open, girls, and you'll find something there to do the job.'

'Are you going to help, Mummy?'

'No, I'm keeping the home fires burning. There will be hot chocolate for everybody once I see a big clearance of snow.' Linda was smiling. This was what brought everyone together, she thought. Neighbours phoning to chat about road conditions and of course the drifts getting higher with each telling. She looked down at the wet floor and went to get the mop, then changed her mind. Before doing that she would phone her mother.

'Mum, how bad is it with you?'

'Linda, I have been standing at the window looking out at this winter wonderland.'

'Matthew isn't calling it that. You are hopeless, Mum, everybody else is moaning and groaning and here you are going into raptures about the snow.'

'If it lasts then it will be a nuisance but that isn't likely, is it?'

'More than likely. Don't you read the papers or listen to the news?'

'I do both but I haven't bothered with the radio and, no surprise, there is no newspaper.'

'No, there wouldn't be. Are you all right?'

'Of course I am. I don't require to put a foot outside the door and—'

'You are as snug as a bug in a rug.'

'That's me, dear. What about you?'

'No school or at least no buses running to get them there. The family are outside giving Matthew a hand. A case of all hands on deck.'

'What fun.'

'Not if this wretched snow doesn't go off.'

'It will.'

'I hope you are right. I've lots to do, Mum, I just wanted to make sure you were all right.'

'I'm fine.'

'I'll ring later. Bye, Mum.'

Kirsty put the phone down and felt all of a sudden, strangely uneasy. The white blanket that appeared to stretch for miles and miles had ceased to be a winter wonderland, it had become a menacing threat. There was no one in the house next door. Her neighbour, Mrs Grieve, had gone down south to see her latest grandchild and would be away for several days. It made Kirsty feel very alone and not a little frightened. She shivered, then chided herself. How silly could one get? The winters of late had not been harsh and it was easy to forget what it was like. No doubt she had experienced severe snow storms but at that time she had been living in the suburbs and, of course, she hadn't been alone.

This was the country and it was all too possible that she could be cut off for days, a prisoner in her cottage, if this snow was to continue.

Linda mopped the floor, then brought her own wellingtons from the cupboard. She put on an old raincoat and covered her head with a scarf. Then she went outside. The flakes were not so big now.

Matthew had made good headway and the girls' efforts were making a difference. Robin was well wrapped up and wore his new red wellingtons, Hannah and Heather's were black. It had never occurred to them to have any other colour until Jennifer came back from a shopping expedition with green wellingtons. She had been relentless in her search for them and eventually Linda, tired of trailing round the shops, had given her the money and told her not to return home without a pair of wellington boots – black, green or whatever.

'Mummy, look at me.'

'Yes, dear.'

'I'm working the hardest.'

'I can see that.'

'I don't take any rests.'

'No, dear.'

'Daddy takes lots of little rests.'

'Daddy has been working hard since before you were up.'

'Hardly,' Matthew grinned, 'but thanks. God, this is hard work. I wasn't cut out for it.' He leaned on his spade. 'I wouldn't mind so much if this was it but I have that sinking feeling that I'll waken up to the same scene tomorrow and maybe the day after that.'

'Heaven forbid,' Linda smiled. 'I phoned Mum.'

'Is she all right?'

'She says so.'

'Daddy, you are still not working.'

'I'll strangle that child.'

'Your own son,' she laughed.

'This is my official break, Robin,' he shouted, 'and I am talking to your mother so be quiet. You are worried about Kirsty?'

'I am a bit.'

'Maybe I could attempt it.'

'No, Matthew. If the buses can't get through you can't. And our car—'

'I know, not much good in these conditions.'

'Mum, that's the phone, shall I get it?'

'No, Hannah, I'm on my way.' Linda was out of breath and taking off her headsquare when she lifted the phone.

'Sorry, is this an inconvenient time?'

'No, Helen, I was outside.'

'This is awful, isn't it?'

'An understatement.'

'Mum said you were on the phone.'

'Yes, she says she is fine but I am not so sure.'

'Why? Did she sound upset?'

'No she didn't but she could be for all that. I do wish her neighbour hadn't been away from home. Mum is bound to feel isolated.'

'Linda, Mum is sensible, she won't do anything stupid or I hope she won't.'

'Anything stupid? What do you mean by that?'

'Well you know if she is short of coal she might try to get to the cellar.'

'I hadn't thought of that, now you have got me worried. Matthew did suggest that he made an attempt to reach Sunnybank but I thought it foolhardy in our car.'

'Absolute madness. How are the roads beside you?'

'Pretty bad. The snow clearers are concentrating on the main roads, which is only sensible but with the wind blowing it back they might not be making much headway.'

'Nigel, poor lad, was up half the night with raging toothache.'

'What a shame. As they say, it is the hell of all diseases.'

'It could be an abscess.'

'Has he tried—'

'Everything. He has tried everything, Linda. Still, if all has gone well he should be in the dentist's chair by now.'

'How was he going to manage that?'

'Nigel phoned his friend, Bobby. George did offer to take him, in fact he tried to insist but Nigel would have none of it.'

'Helen, that daredevil.' Linda sounded shocked. 'I mean, Bobby has been cautioned.'

'I know but that was quite a while ago. It was a bit of showing off and the caution did him good, he is much more careful now.'

'It is to be hoped so.'

'Actually Bobby is a very good driver and if anyone can get through this snow he can.'

'Even so they could get stuck.'

'Yes and I said that. Nigel's reply was that he would prefer to take that chance than put in another night like the last.'

'It's always the same, isn't it? If illness strikes or there is an emergency you can rest assured it will be a Sunday or like now a day when nothing is moving. Oh, just a thought. What if the dentist hasn't turned up?'

'Linda, give us credit for some sense. Of course we checked that the man was there and as for not having an appointment, that caused him some amusement. He said he was twirling his thumbs and looking at a page of cancelled appointments. Hang on, Linda, George is trying to say something.'

Linda waited. She heard the voices but not what they were saying.

'You still there?'

'Yes.'

'George and Simon are preparing to go and see if mother is all right and to try and persuade her to come back with them.'

'That might not be such a good idea. It could be more risky than staying where she is.'

'If they consider that to be the case they won't suggest it.' There was a note of exasperation in Helen's voice. 'And Linda –'

'What?'

'When you are on the phone to Mum don't say anything to her about George and Simon—'

'I had no intention of doing so.' They were becoming short-tempered with each other.

'The only reason I mentioned it was because Mum would start worrying and blame herself if they were to find themselves in difficulties. And before you ask, they have all the essential equipment in the car including not one spade but two.'

'You must be a bit worried yourself.'

'Linda, I cannot afford to give in to worries or nothing would get done. I have a lot of confidence in George. He won't take any unnecessary risks when he has Simon in the car.'

'Food and drink all taken care of?'

'Nothing has been forgotten. Mum will have some food in the house but as we both know she doesn't believe in stocking up.'

'Prefers everything fresh.'

'Fair enough but it is always better to be prepared for an emergency, especially living in the country.'

Linda agreed.

'I do have one worry. The electricity failing, the lines coming down and Mum plunged into darkness.'

'I hadn't thought of that,' Linda sounded horrified. 'And the phone, what if it were to go dead?'

'Exactly, we have to take those into account. By the way, do you know if Mum has candles?'

'I'm not sure. Oh, wait a minute, she may have some in that tin box under the sink.'

'And how does she find that in the dark?'

'A torch.'

'Has she one?'

'She might.'

'With a functioning battery?'

'Probably not. This is getting more worrying by the minute.'

'Calm down, getting in a panic won't help. All that has been taken care of. George has one of those big torches in the car and the boys are bound to have several lying about the house.'

'With batteries?'

'Oh, yes, I would think so. Boys are fairly dependable that way.'

Linda wondered how she managed to think that.

'I must ring off and get on. We'll keep in touch.'

'Yes. Helen, matches, don't forget those.'

'Thank you, I had as it happens.'

Kirsty, wearing a warm skirt and a thick Aran sweater, kept getting up from the chair and wandering aimlessly about the cottage. She couldn't settle to anything. To make matters worse the wind had got up, rattling the windows and whipping the snow against the outbuildings. From the window the sky looked heavy with snow yet to come.

She seemed to be drinking endless cups of tea but couldn't face food. Later on she would try to take something but at the moment it would stick in her throat.

How long she had been dozing in the chair she couldn't have said. The ringing of the bell and the banging on the door awakened her and set her heart racing. Her hand went to her mouth. It could be anyone, perhaps a tramp desperate to get shelter. Harmless maybe or maybe not. How to tell? Safer not to answer and then whoever it was might go away. She almost crept from the sitting-room to the kitchen and half hidden by the curtain she peered out. Someone was there and that someone was wearing a blue and yellow anorak. Kirsty almost cried out in her relief, then she was rushing to unbolt the door.

'Gran, what were you doing? We were making enough noise to waken the dead.'

'I'm sorry, I was dozing in the chair, Simon. George, you look frozen. Come inside quickly and in to the warmth. Don't worry about cleaning your feet.' She was almost weeping.

George gave her a hug, then sat down on a kitchen chair and Simon pulled off his father's boots, then George did the same for him.

'Leave everything in the kitchen and come through to the fire'

They both wore heavy woollen socks. 'What about the stuff in the car, Dad?'

'Later, Simon.' It had been a hazardous journey and it would be the same on the way home. A rest was what he needed right now. Simon was chirpy but he hadn't had to do the driving.

Once she had them both warming themselves at the fire Kirsty went to put on the kettle. They could be drinking a hot cup of tea while she made them something to eat.

'Would bacon and egg do you? It is the quickest to make.'

'Don't go and put yourself to all that trouble.'

'It isn't any trouble and why shouldn't I put myself to some trouble? You've gone to plenty for me.'

'Bacon and egg would be great, Gran.'

Kirsty thought back to the last time Simon had been in the cottage. How fortunate that the young could recover so quickly. Hannah had agreed to be Simon's partner at the dance and for that she took full credit.

'If we are having bacon and egg, Kirsty, I insist that you have the same.'

'Oh, I don't think—'

'I don't care what you think,' he said quietly but firmly. 'You eat or we don't.' He smiled his lopsided smile to take the sting out of the words.

'Very well,' she smiled, 'you've bullied me into it.' Another egg went into the pan.

When all was cooked to perfection they sat round the kitchen table to enjoy it.

'George,' she said after pouring the tea, 'may I ask you something?'

'I should think so,' he smiled.

'You have always called me Ma until recently. Am I permitted to ask the reason for the change?'

'Helen said you disliked being called Ma. Why she couldn't have told me that years ago I have no idea, but then that is Helen.'

'It's true I don't like Ma but from you I didn't mind.'

'I'm just getting used to addressing you as Kirsty so I think I will stick with that.'

'Mum wants you to pack a case and come home with us. You should, Gran.'

'Yes, Kirsty, we would all feel happier. We don't like to think of you on your own.'

'How lucky I am to have such a caring family and I am touched.' She could pack a case and go with them but she wouldn't. That would be giving in. This was her house. She had chosen to live in a cottage in the country and it didn't say much for her if she were to run away when the weather turned nasty.

'No, I won't. This has been quite wonderful of you both to risk these treacherous roads but this is my home and it is where I should be.'

George heard the note of finality in her voice and didn't attempt to dissuade her.

'I can see your mind is made up.'

'Yes, George, it is.'

'Then we must see that you have everything you need and to hand.'

'I should be fine.'

'A power failure, have you thought of that? Are you pre-pared?'

'Candles in a tin box under the sink,' she said almost proudly.

'Matches,' Simon said.

'There should be a box somewhere,' Kirsty said vaguely.

'Won't do, Gran, but not to worry we have everything in the car. Once we get the stuff indoors we'll put everything where you can find it.'

'Yes, Simon.' She was amused. He was looking after her and enjoying it.

'Keep a torch beside you all the time. That is very im-portant, Gran.' He paused. 'You do have one?'

Oh, dear, this was showing her up. She wasn't in the least prepared.

'I'm not sure.'

'It's all right,' Simon said kindly, 'old people are allowed to be forgetful.'

'I'm not sure if that was what I wanted to hear, Simon.'

George was shaking his head. The food and the rest had done wonders and he was feeling much better.

'Forgetful or not, Kirsty, that was a very tasty meal you produced. I really did enjoy it,' he said, putting down his knife and fork.

'Thanks, Gran, it was great.'

'And now to work, on your feet, Simon. We'll get our things on—'

'And bring the stuff in from the car.'

'Yes. I think your mother has thought of everything.'

'I'm sure she has,' Kirsty smiled.

Simon was looking in the coal scuttle. 'Is that all you have?'

'No. I filled a bucket yesterday and put it in the cupboard.'

'It might not last you.'

'Then I switch on a bar of the fire.'

'You won't, not if the lines are down.'

'And I suppose that is a possibility.'

'It has happened already in some places,' George said quietly. He didn't want to alarm Kirsty but he wanted her to be aware of what could happen.

Simon had taken charge of the coal situation. He wouldn't allow his father to help remove the snow piled high against the door of the cellar where the coal was kept. He was a thoughtful lad and he recognised that his father would be apprehensive about the return journey and anyway this was something he could do.

They watched him from the window as Simon made inroads on the snow and eventually had the cellar door opened. He made several journeys with coal and logs until he was satisfied that there was enough to last a week or even longer.

'You have a good boy there, George,' Kirsty said when Simon was out of earshot.

'Yes, I have to agree with that.'

'He seems to have got over Jennifer.'

'Perhaps not altogether but the worst is over. We left him alone, that was my idea and I think it worked.'

'Yes, I think you did the right thing. How about his school-work?'

'Oh, that, everything is fine. He did have me worried and unknown to Helen I had a word with his form master. He was concerned too since Simon is not guilty of being inattentive in class.'

'What had the schoolmaster to say?'

'To leave it a little longer and if Simon didn't snap out of it then there would be the threat of him having to repeat a year.'

'He is working now and that is all that matters.'

'Actually, Kirsty, Simon is working extremely hard so all in all no damage has been done.'

'I'm so glad.'

'None of us should blame Jennifer. The girl had every right to do what she did.'

'You and Matthew have a soft spot for Jennifer.'

'I don't know about Matthew, and remember I am not very often in Jennifer's company, but I get the feeling that something is troubling her.'

'Why doesn't she say what it is? We can't help if we don't know what it is. There is no one more understanding than Linda.'

'Perhaps she feels she can't. Or there again I could be hopelessly wrong. And now if you are sure you will be all right we had better get on our way.'

'Yes, you should. What can I say but many, many thanks for all you have done. You and Simon.'

George kissed Kirsty's cheek. 'Lock your door behind us.'

'I'll do that and please, when you reach home let me know. I won't rest easy until I know you are safely home.'

'Helen will phone the minute we get in.'

They had only been gone for half an hour when the phone rang. She went to answer it.

'Hello, Kirsty.'

'David, it's you,' Kirsty said, smiling happily.

'I was worried, are you all right?'

'Yes, thank you, I am. My son-in-law and Simon are not long gone. They drove through dreadful conditions to get here. It was so good of them.'

'You didn't consider returning with them?'

'They offered and I did think about it, then I decided no I wouldn't. This is my home and this is where I should be.'

'I'm so sorry I couldn't offer my assistance but I am laid low as the saying goes.'

'David, you are ill in bed. Is it the flu?'

'No, it appears I have a touch of pleurisy.'

Kirsty was shocked. 'David, don't make light of it. Pleurisy can be serious.'

'If neglected but I am going to be fine. A week or two in bed should do the trick according to the doctor. I don't see me staying in bed for more than a few days, doctor's orders or not.'

'You will do as you are told. Men, honestly, you can be the absolute limit. The doctor knows best, didn't you get that drummed into you when you were little?'

'Kirsty, you are as good as a tonic.'

'Who is looking after you? Your daughter?'

'No, she has enough to do with her own family. Mrs Brady—'

'Your housekeeper?'

'Yes. She has been kindness itself. The woman has taken up residence here and I am being very well looked after.'

'Why didn't you tell me?' Kirsty felt unreasonably hurt.

'Kirsty, I have not been at death's door. I have just been feeling dreadfully tired, no more than that.'

'Does talking tire you?'

'Not when you are doing the talking.'

'All the same I don't want to be responsible for wearing you out.'

'Kirsty, will you please stop it. Believe me, just hearing your voice does wonders for me. What I want to know is, are you all right?'

How many times had she been asked that? 'I told you, I'm fine. Simon brought in coal and logs and Helen had the car packed with everything I could possibly need.'

'I'm glad.'

'What are conditions like in Broughty Ferry?'

'To be honest we are extremely lucky here. There has been

quite a fall of snow, or so they tell me, but traffic is moving. My newspaper arrived only a little later than usual and was a welcome sight.'

'David, we have talked long enough. I'll ring you tomorrow. Take care, I shall be thinking of you.'

'How very nice. That means we will be thinking of each other.'

'Yes,' she smiled and put down the receiver. Poor David, she hoped he would obey the doctor and not take any chances. Most men made dreadful patients.

Kirsty washed the dishes from the meal and last of all the frying pan. It wasn't used all that often. Once everything was back in its place she went through to the sitting-room and sat in her usual chair. She was well prepared for all eventualities. Simon had asked her for three old saucers and fixed a candle on each. The torch had a reassuring feel to it as she picked it up. Were they getting it easier going back, she hoped so. The window drew her and she was back looking out.

Kirsty gave a slight start as she saw two men approaching the door. One of them saw her at the window and gave a wave. She didn't immediately recognise them and that made her curious rather than alarmed. Kirsty unlocked the door and opened it.

'Hello there, Mrs Chalmers, we just came to check that you are all right,' the small stout man said cheerily.

'Do come in,' she said opening the door wider.

'Just inside the door will do. No need to get your floor wet.' They both stood on the old rug she had put there earlier. 'You don't want to ask but you are wondering who we are.'

'I think I should know you but I can't place—'

'Angus Duncan, Moira's husband.'

'Of course, my hairdresser's husband. We met briefly and I should have remembered.'

'And this is Sam. We are checking on the villagers who are living on their own. Moira said you were and I had better ask about your neighbour, we couldn't raise her.'

'Mrs Grieve is not at home. She's visiting family down south.'

'Well timed, she's escaped this.'

'Yes.'

'You've had callers? Saw the footsteps in the snow.'

'Yes. My son-in-law and my grandson braved the elements. They came from Abbotsfield.'

'Roads are bad that way. Still those with the right vehicle can usually manage.'

'Won't you come in and have a hot drink?' Kirsty was anxious to offer hospitality.

'No. No, but thanks all the same. We have a few more houses to check on and then it is home to a roaring fire I hope.'

'Moira will see to that I know. Again my grateful thanks for your thoughtfulness and for Moira remembering me.'

'Method in her madness,' he said jokingly, 'she likes to look after her customers.'

Kirsty locked up after they had gone. There was so much good in people. They cared and it showed in times like these. She had always liked the village but considered herself a newcomer. That had changed. Now she felt that she truly belonged and it was a nice feeling. They were a small community who looked after each other. She felt safe.

Tonight she would sleep well. George and Simon had arrived home safely. Nigel was home after having spent an uncomfortable twenty minutes in the dentist's chair. The abscess had had to be drained and with that successfully done there should be no more pain, but should there be any discomfort he had tablets to take.

★   ★   ★

The snow continued to fall for six more days but not as relentlessly as before. There was concern when there was a big upsurge in temperature. Flooding could be the next problem and some areas did suffer, but not as badly as they had feared. Life was getting back to normal.

23

'I thought that went rather well.'

'So did I,' Helen nodded her head in agreement, then frowned and muttered a mild oath as the car lurched from one pothole to another. Trying to avoid the worst had her weaving about to the concern and discomfort of her passenger.

'Take it easy, will you?'

'I can't do any better than I'm doing. This lane is in a shocking condition and something should be done about it.'

'I know that, we all know that.' The lane was badly potholed and those holes were filled with muddy water after the overnight rain. 'It will be the usual story – no one prepared to take the responsibility.'

'A lane will be low priority.'

'You can bet on that,' Linda said with feeling.

'It wouldn't cost much in men's time to have a few potholes filled in.'

'Mum doesn't get into a state about it. She adjusts her speed and you should do the same. I do, I have some respect for my car.'

'That is not the point, Linda, If the car came to grief after a few potholes it wouldn't say much for it.'

Linda kept quiet until they were on the main road.

'Mr Harris is very nice.'

'Yes, I found Mum's boyfriend delightful,' Helen said as she got up speed.

'Calling Mr Harris Mum's boyfriend sounds silly but what are the alternatives?' Linda said as she settled herself more comfortably. 'Man friend, gentleman friend, they don't sound right and as for partner—'

'The word no longer means what it once did. Maybe we should stick to friend.'

For this first meeting with David Harris, Linda and Helen had taken care over their appearance. Linda had chosen to wear a crisp blue and white striped cotton blouse with a straight light grey skirt. The narrow leather belt round her slim waist gave the outfit a finished look. There was still that chill wind that wouldn't go away and to keep warm she had taken her navy blue blazer.

Helen had a liking for all shades of brown. She was more stylish than her sister and to get that look she spent a lot more on clothes. Today she favoured a cinnamon-coloured skirt with a small slit at the back and a fine cashmere sweater in cream with a band of brown at cuffs and neck. Unlike Linda she did not change her shoes to drive unless she was making a very long journey. She had no difficulty in driving in three-inch heels and to give credit where credit was due, Helen had never been involved in an accident. On the back seat of the car was her three-quarter-length camel coat bought from Jaeger where a lot of her clothes came from.

Linda was without her own transport and annoyed about it. Matthew had taken hers which was why she was in Helen's car. His almost new car had gone in for its regular service and a fault was discovered. Needless to say the spare part required was not in stock and had to be ordered and needless to say there was no guarantee when that spare part would arrive. Within a day or two or there again it might take a week. Matthew had been furious and complained bitterly about the inconvenience. Linda wondered what inconvenience. If anyone was inconvenienced it was she. She was the one minus her wheels.

'Do you want me to drop you anywhere or is it home, James?'

'Straight home, please.' She paused. 'Could we get back to Mr Harris?'

'By all means.'

'Did you notice how protective Mum was being?'

'Protective of whom?' Helen grinned.

'Not us. We don't need protection.'

'Joking apart Mum was genuinely concerned about her friend.'

'Which was hardly surprising. The poor soul is just getting over pleurisy which can be serious for anyone but particularly so for the elderly.'

'I suppose so.' Helen agreed.

'He was easy to talk to.'

'Yes, he was and it could have been so different. An uphill job finding something to talk about.'

'No doubt his training as a solicitor would have helped.'

'Putting folk at their ease.'

'Retired solicitor I should have said.'

'No, Helen, he hasn't retired completely, he does some consultancy work.'

'You know a lot more about him than I do,' Helen said, sounding peeved.

'No I don't, that is all I do know and Mum must have thought she had told you.'

'Possibly.' Helen paused to watch as a pedestrian took a chance to cross the busy road. 'Some folk take their life in their hands. Complete idiots. What was I going to say?'

'I have no idea. Something about Mr Harris presumably.

'A real charmer, I thought.'

'If you mean that in the nicest possible way then I go along with it.'

'Wouldn't it have been awful if we hadn't liked him?'

'I went expecting to like him, Mum wouldn't have taken up with just anyone.'

'No, not just anyone but you have to remember that love is blind.' Helen gave a little laugh after she said it.

'Do you think they are in love?'

'No, I don't.'

'Neither do I, Helen. I do think there is a lot of affection and they very obviously enjoy each other's company but no more than that.'

'Let's give the lovebirds a rest for a few minutes and talk about something else.'

'Like what?'

'Simon. Is he all right?'

'If you mean has he got over Jennifer I think the answer is yes. Maybe not completely over her but near enough. At that age it has more to do with hurt pride than a broken heart.'

'Don't be so dismissive. Simon was besotted with Jennifer and if you didn't notice you were the only one.'

'OK, so he was besotted with the girl but that state does not last long. What is important to me is that my son is pretty near back to his old self. A little older and a little wiser one might say but no great harm done.'

'Mum was concerned. She said Simon looked miserable and she was so sorry for him.'

'Since we had decided to ignore his misery he went to the cottage for sympathy.'

'Who decided that?'

'George with the backing of Nigel. I wasn't altogether happy but—'

'You went along with it?'

'Yes. In the event I suppose they were right and as for Mum she must have said all the right things because from then on he perked up.'

'Is he back with his school friends?'

'Yes.'

'Good. Everything is more or less back to normal?'

'Whatever normal is.'

'Did you know that it was Mum's suggestion that Simon should ask Hannah to the dance?'

'I didn't but I thought it might be the case. It was sweet of Hannah to accept.'

'My poor daughter was in a quandary.'

'Why was that?'

'She was desperate to accept. You know the way she is about Simon but she was afraid of making herself look cheap.'

Helen turned her head to look at Linda. 'Surely she didn't think that? As well as being good pals they are cousins.'

'That was what I said. She is going and for my sins I am having to stump up for a new ball gown.'

'What is wrong with the one Hannah wore to the school dance?'

'Everything apparently. That horrid thing with the ghastly puffy sleeves, she wasn't going to wear it, she would rather die.'

Helen was laughing. 'Honestly, kids are the limit.'

'Mind you it was her own choice, hers alone. It most certainly wasn't mine and I couldn't blame the shop assistant. She preferred Hannah in some of the others.'

'I'm glad you weakened and promised her a new dress.'

'Worth every penny if it makes her happy.'

'Teenage blues.'

'Perhaps.' She smiled. 'I promised to keep Saturday morning free. Matthew can take charge of the house while we go hunting for something suitable.'

'You can't know how much I envy you, Linda,' Helen said wistfully. 'I would love to have had a daughter, a little girl to dress up. Mind you the chances are she would have turned out to be a proper little tomboy with absolutely no interest in clothes. Incidentally where were you thinking of going?'

'One of the big stores in Dundee.'

'Don't forget the boutiques, you'll get something different there.'

'They won't have the same choice as the big stores.'

'Worth seeing what they have.'

'Sorry, I should have asked about Simon and his school-work. That was suffering wasn't it?'

'That I can tell you was my biggest worry but, thank God, that has sorted itself out. Simon is putting in a lot of hard work.'

'Your worries are over.'

'Are they ever?' Helen smiled a satisfied smile. 'At the moment everything is fine and long may it continue that way.'

'And so say all of us. I'm so glad, Helen,' Linda said quietly. 'You see I can never rid myself of the fact that Jennifer is my responsibility and no one else's and if she steps out of line it is my fault.'

'I have told you before that is ridiculous. No one is respon-sible for another person's behaviour and let us be fair. Although I admit I felt like strangling the girl, Jennifer did nothing wrong.'

'She could have gone about it differently, been gentler, but I am afraid Jennifer has a cruel streak.'

'Aren't you being a little harsh? Young people can be thoughtlessly cruel. You can see it in very young children. We would have been the same, Linda, when it came to boyfriends. When someone more interesting came along we weren't long in dumping the boy we were going with.'

'Just a minute, speak for yourself.'

'I'm talking about when we were sweet sixteen.'

'OK. I'll let that go.'

'All I am trying to say is that Jennifer had every right to end the relationship if it could be described as that,' Helen said on a note of finality. She drove in silence until the car turned into the cul-de-sac and drew to a stop at the gate.

'Thanks, Helen, won't you come in?'

'No, I won't thanks all the same. I have heaps to do.'

'Before I get out let me ask you this. And I am asking this in all seriousness. If Mum and Mr Harris were to make a match of it would you be very upset?'

Helen didn't immediately answer. She was tapping her fingers on the steering wheel while she gave the matter some thought. 'I have to say I would rather it didn't happen but if it did I would not be greatly upset. How about you?'

'The same as you, I think.'

'You don't see it happening?'

'No, I don't, Helen.'

'Neither do I.'

In the cottage the coffee table was cleared with David Harris insisting on giving Kirsty a hand. It was clear from the painstaking care he was taking with the cups and saucers that he had little experience.

'Shall I dry?' David asked when everything had been carried through to the kitchen.

'Certainly not, you didn't come here to work. All I wanted was the food away, the rest can wait and you, my dear David, are still a semi-invalid.'

'I am nothing of the kind.'

'Say what you like you are not fully fit. Whether you want to believe it or not you have had a shake and it takes time to recover. Go and sit down in a comfortable chair and I shall join you in a minute or two.'

'Very well, Kirsty, I shall do as I'm told.'

Kirsty had wanted to postpone this visit. After all there was no urgency. There would be another time for David to meet

Helen and Linda. David had been adamant that he was well enough to drive over to the cottage and the arrangements to stay. Kirsty, seeing how determined he was, had said no more.

The pleurisy, mild though it might have been, had taken its toll and David had lost weight. The suit he wore did not exactly hang on him but it did not fit as well as it should.

'You are very cosy here.'

'Yes, I am, David. I am very fond of my cottage and it would take a lot of persuading to get me to move.'

She felt his eyes on her.

'I think I can understand that. Like you it would take a lot of persuading to get me to move. We get very attached to what we know and love.'

'Yes, we do.'

'That said, you made the move, Kirsty, yet you must have loved the family house?'

'I did and leaving it was a wrench but one I was prepared for. You see, John and I had spoken of a time when one of us would be left and a big house with all the attention it would need, could be a worry. Far better that the one left should look for something smaller and more manageable. This came on the market and I had only to go the once to see it to know it was what I wanted.'

'How fortuitous.'

'Yes, it was.'

'My home is too big, I do know that, but I get round it by closing part of the house. It isn't neglected,' he said hastily, 'my housekeeper gives it an occasional clean. And furthermore, Kirsty, moving to something smaller would mean disposing of such a lot of things and I don't just mean furniture.'

'You mean so many things bring back memories,' she said softly.

'That is exactly what I mean.'

'They travel, David.'

'You mean you can pack up memories and take them along with you?'

'They go with you in your heart.'

'Maybe you are right there. In any case I don't have the energy for a big upheaval and it would most certainly be that. In the end it will be sold but I won't be here to see it.'

'Would Lottie not be interested?'

'I'm sure she would be. She would want it but her husband would be unwilling to move. I think I mentioned to you that Norman inherited the family home.'

'Yes, you did. Lottie isn't madly keen on it.'

'Very true although I think she feels settled now. Norman gave her a free hand to make whatever changes she wanted. Rather than cause any trouble I would rather my house went to strangers.'

'And your son?' Kirsty said quietly.

'Geoffrey has walked away. He won't come back, I am fairly sure of that, but I do believe he will keep in touch even if that is no more than a postcard.'

Kirsty touched his hand in sympathy but made no comment. What was there to say that would help?

'So be it,' he smiled. 'There is always an open door and he knows it. As for the house it will be of no interest to Geoffrey though a share of its value might prove welcome. You don't have to tiptoe round it, Kirsty. I have now accepted that my son wants to live his life in his own way. We all have a choice I like to think and if Geoffrey is happy with his nomad life who am I to say he is wrong?'

'You talk of choices, David. Linda made one I think she is regretting though she hasn't said so. I told you about Jennifer?'

'Yes, you did and I gather things haven't improved a lot.'

'No. Jennifer makes no effort to fit in. She isn't rebellious. If she were I think Linda could handle that better. She just keeps herself to herself. There is something wrong, I feel it in my bones, and one day I am going to try and get to the root of it.'

'Maybe the girl would welcome that.'

'I doubt it.'

'Kirsty, I do feel guilty that as yet you haven't seen my home. It hasn't been intentional I assure you but nevertheless I am at fault. You see I had hoped to arrange a time with Lottie but with her busy life I should have known better. After all my housekeeper will be there to prepare a meal or there again we could eat out. There is nothing to stop us arranging a day that would suit you, Kirsty.'

'David, I would very much like to see your home and yes we can arrange something.'

'Good. I feel a lot better now.'

'I wished I could have been of help when you needed it.'

'My dear lady, you did a lot.'

'I did nothing.'

He was shaking his head. 'Those telephone calls were a life-saver. My only complaint would be that they were too short.'

'I didn't want to tire you out.'

'There was no danger of that and please do not try to make out that my illness was worse than it was. I was never at death's door. It was unpleasant, debilitating and wearisome and I must have been a trial to Mrs Brady who proved to be a tower of strength.'

'Men make dreadful patients, that is well known.'

'And I am no exception. Enough about me. What about you?'

'What about me?'

'You were very brave, Kirsty, living alone in your cottage in that dreadful snowstorm.'

'I was not brave, anything but. When my son-in-law and Simon came to check on me I was too scared to let them in.'

'If you weren't expecting them you were quite right to be wary, you could have been opening your door to anyone.'

'I hid behind the curtain and only when I recognised Simon's anorak did I rush to open the door. They were quite wonderful and I was deeply grateful.'

'You have a supportive family.'

'Very supportive and I am extremely fortunate.'

'It goes both ways. They have your support when it is needed.'

'Yes, I suppose that is true.'

'You weren't tempted to go back with them?'

'I was and they were anxious that I should do so.'

'You decided to stay and battle on alone?' He was smiling.

'I'm ashamed to say how ill-prepared I was. George brought everything I could possibly require, then after they had gone I got a visit from two gentlemen.'

'Did you indeed?'

'My hairdresser's husband and another gentleman. They were checking on all the villagers who lived alone. Wasn't that marvellous?'

'The true country spirit.'

'Yes, David. This has changed me. I think I was a little aloof, not intentionally let me say. I felt I didn't quite belong, that I was still a newcomer.'

'Now you do belong?'

'Now I do belong and it is a lovely feeling.'

'Before I go, Kirsty, let me say how much I liked your daughters. They were charming and friendly just as I expected daughters of yours to be.'

'Too much flattery.'

'Meaning it can't be genuine? Wrong, I speak only the truth.'

'Thank you and from what I gathered you met with their approval.'

'That is a relief.'

She thought he sounded tired and was immediately concerned. 'David, I am not rushing you away but I don't want you overdoing it.'

'Perhaps you are right and I should be making tracks for home.'

They walked together to the car.

'Sorry about the potholes, Helen is always complaining.'

'I'll take it slowly. Goodbye, Kirsty, and many thanks. I'll ring you.'

'Take care.'

'You, too,' he smiled and gave a wave as he drove away.

Kirsty watched the car until it was out of sight. She had another look at the potholes then decided she should do something. Someone had to make the effort. It would be her small contribution to the common good of the village.

Just then she felt very content. The girls liked David and he had thought them charming. She had been vaguely worried that David might have serious intentions whereas she didn't but she no longer thought that. They both wanted the same thing. They wanted companionship but no more than that.

24

'Mum, what about my dress? When are we going for it?' Hannah said in a despairing voice.

'Saturday morning. I hadn't forgotten, dear,' Linda said briskly, 'there hasn't been the time.'

'Is that definite?' Hannah wasn't convinced.

'Saturday morning is definite, you have my word on that. We'll spend the whole morning or however long it takes.'

'That's OK then. Thanks, Mum.' Hannah was smiling and showing her relief.

'We'll make an early start and get into Dundee before the shops get busy.'

The family, apart from Matthew, were together in the sitting-room. Jennifer was there as well. Usually she disappeared to her bedroom but tonight she was sitting in one of the armchairs reading a paperback. The conversation was going on around her.

'Mum, I don't have to go, do I?'

'No, Heather, only if you want.'

'I don't.'

'That's settled then.'

Jennifer put her finger between the pages of her novel to keep her place and looked up.

'Is this you going for a new dress for the Tennis Club dance?'

'Yes, it is,' Hannah said shortly. It was common knowledge that Jennifer had refused Simon's invitation and that Hannah was going in her place. Hannah was finding it embarrassing and was quick to explain that Simon and she were cousins and that was why she was going with him. Only the more she tried to explain the less convincing it sounded. She was second-best or even less than second-best. She wished now that she had said no but it was too late to back down.

'Mum, Hannah got a new party dress for the school dance, why is she getting another?' Heather asked. 'I hardly ever get any new clothes.'

'You are just a poor neglected wee soul,' her mother answered.

Hannah was quick to show her annoyance. 'Heather, will you kindly listen to me and take in what I am about to say. I do not have a party dress. Party dresses are for children like you. What I do have is an evening dress for which I have no further use. If you want it you are welcome.' She crossed her legs and sat back in the chair.

'I don't want it. You looked awful in it and why should I wear your cast-offs?'

Linda thought it was time she intervened. The family seemed to be in a quarrelsome mood this evening.

'Heather, that is quite enough from you. No one is asking you to wear Hannah's cast-offs and in any case nothing of Hannah's would fit you.'

'Meaning?' Heather said, standing up and putting her hands on her hips washer-woman style.

'Meaning whatever you like to take out of it.' Linda was losing patience.

'I know what to take out of it. You are suggesting I am too fat.' There was the hint of tears in her voice.

'You are not fat, dear,' Linda said gently.

'Then I must be skinny.'

That was too much for Hannah who exploded in mirth and Robin, without a clue what it was about, joined in and began to roll about the floor laughing wildly.

'Heather, don't be silly, you are lovely as you are. In fact you are to be envied. It is very nice to be in between, not too fat and not too thin.'

'You are only saying that.'

'Saying it and meaning it.'

'Really?' she said, smiling broadly.

'Really.'

Heather was desperate for reassurance. A few short weeks ago she hadn't bothered about her appearance, now it had become important. Heather had only just discovered boys and one in particular who had actually whistled after her. He wouldn't have done that if he didn't think she looked OK.

'Mummy?'

'Yes, Robin?'

'I want to come on Saturday. I want to come with you and Hannah.'

'You can't, this is not an outing for little boys.'

'But I want to come,' he said outraged.

'No.'

'Why not?'

'Because I said so. You will stay here with Daddy.'

'I don't want to and it isn't fair. Daddy won't play with me. All he does is read the paper.'

Linda tried to keep her face straight. Robin certainly had a point. Five minutes with Robin and his Dinky toys was enough for Matthew. He would have liked a sports-loving son and been happy to kick a ball around but Robin showed no sign of becoming even remotely interested in any ball game.

Robin was looking mutinous and Linda was thinking she would have to take a firmer hand. Matthew had said she was spoiling him and perhaps she was.

'Please, I want to come with you.'

It was hard to say no but she forced herself.

'Robin, the answer is no. You get two comics delivered on

Saturday morning. Content yourself with those. And there is one lesson you will have to learn and that is you cannot have your own way all the time. No one likes a spoilt boy and that is what you are becoming.'

The lower lip was quivering but Linda steeled herself. There was a small tantrum and then having decided he had lost this battle, Robin began to play with his cars. It was unfortunate that it was the Saturday when he would not have his friend's company. The family were motoring north to attend a wedding.

'I'm not doing anything special on Saturday, I'll come and help you choose, Hannah.'

There was a moment of shocked silence. Hannah looked taken aback and then uncomfortable.

'No, thank you, Jennifer, there is no need. I'll have Mum to help me choose.'

'I would like to come.' She turned to Linda. 'Have you any objections, Mrs Chalmers?'

'No, of course not, Jennifer. You are welcome to come,' Linda said, at the same time trying to ignore the black looks coming her way. 'However, I must warn you that we are leaving the house early. No later than half past eight and if you are not dressed and ready by then we go without you.'

'Fair enough, I won't sleep in.' With one graceful movement, Jennifer had risen from her chair and with the paperback in her hand, left the room. They heard her feet on the stairs and then the door shutting.

'See what you've done,' Hannah said furiously. 'Why couldn't you have said no? I don't want her and you knew that.'

'Hannah, you appear to have forgotten that Jennifer is part of this family but if it is of any comfort I don't see Jennifer getting up early to come with us. She is too fond of her bed.'

Hannah didn't look convinced.

'There is no need to look like that. She won't be choosing your dress.'

'Want to bet?'

'If she does it will be your own fault for allowing her to do the choosing. I am paying for the dress and you are to decide what you want.'

'She'll still be there.'

'That is so and I hope you are not going to be difficult. You never know, she might be helpful.'

'I still wish she wasn't coming.'

'Put something in her cocoa to make her sleep,' Heather suggested mischievously.

'That is not nice.'

'Just a thought.'

'And a good one too,' Hannah muttered.

Saturday was bright and sunny and had it not been for the cold wind it would have been very pleasant. Linda and Hannah were breakfasting alone in the kitchen. All was quiet upstairs and Hannah was smiling to herself. Her mother was right and Jennifer was going to sleep on.

The teapot was in Linda's hand and she was about to refill their cups when the door opened and Jennifer appeared. Not in her dressing-gown but dressed.

'Good morning,' she said quietly.

Hannah's mouth fell open. Linda smiled. 'Good morning, Jennifer, you are up bright and early.'

'I said I would and if I make up my mind to waken at a certain time I do.'

'Not many can do that. Most of us depend on the alarm clock. Pop bread into the toaster for yourself and I'll make fresh tea.'

The meal was eaten in silence but that wasn't unusual. No one had much to say at breakfast time.

They were up to time even a few minutes early. Linda had gone upstairs to tell Matthew they were leaving. He was lying on his back and snoring. She gave him a none too gentle shake.

'Matthew, we are leaving now. Remember you are in charge so don't sleep all morning.'

'Fat chance,' he muttered and turned on to his side. Linda smiled and closed the door quietly.

Hannah sat beside her mother in the front seat and Jennifer was in the back, her eyes closed as though to make up for her lost sleep. Linda and Hannah spoke occasionally but for most of the time Linda concentrated on her driving.

'Where are you going to park?' Hannah asked as they reached the city.

'I thought Bell Street, we might be lucky and find a space.'

They did. It was between two badly parked cars and made for an awkward manoeuvre but eventually Linda managed.

'Mum, you haven't left much space.'

'That's their problem. They ought to have been more considerate when parking. Come along.'

Together they walked along Reform Street and into the centre of the town. The first store they tried had a large stock and it looked promising. Most of it, however, was to suit the older and more sophisticated woman. In the end three dresses were put aside. It was unfortunate that the style Hannah preferred was not in the colour she wanted. She tried it on again.

'Mum, what do you think?'

'I think you should make up your own mind.'

'I would value your opinion.'

'I prefer you in the apricot shade.'

'Do you?' Hannah said uncertainly.

Jennifer had not been asked for her opinion and until now hadn't spoken.

'You don't have to decide right away. We have plenty of time and you can always come back if you want.'

Linda nodded. 'Yes, Jennifer, we could do that.' She turned to the assistant who was trying to hide her disappointment. That had been so nearly a sale. 'Thank you for being so helpful and there is a good chance we will be back.'

Two hours later and there was no purchase. The town was busy with shoppers crowding the pavements.

'Nothing else for it but to go back to the first shop,' Hannah said sounding dispirited.

'Yes, dear, it looks that way.' She made to turn back only to find Jennifer missing. 'Where has she gone, where is Jennifer?'

'She was here a minute ago. Oh, here she is.'

'We wondered where you had got to.'

'Come and look at this, Hannah.'

'Look at what?'

'The boutique round the corner.'

'No. Mum and I have decided to go back to the first shop.'

'That would be silly. They had nothing in particular.'

'None of the shops had if it comes to that,' Hannah said grumpily.

'You can surely look, it won't take a minute.'

'Yes, of course,' Linda said wearily.

It was a narrow backstreet and the window they went to look at was small but the display was eye-catching.

'Very nice,' Hannah said, 'but nothing for me.'

'Don't be so dismissive. Just look at that dress in the corner.'

'Red. I don't want red. It would make me look like a pillarbox.'

'That is not red. That shade is called crushed strawberry, an absolutely gorgeous colour. You are pale-skinned and you need something like that, not pastel shades. Pastel shades make you look wishy-washy.'

'Thank you very much,' Hannah said huffily.

'We could go in?' Jennifer looked at Linda.

'Why not since we are here.'

The lady who came forward to meet them looked to be about Linda's age. She wasn't beautiful, her features were too blunt, but she had style. The black skirt she wore fell in soft folds to her calves showing good legs and neat ankles. She had teamed the skirt with a shocking pink blouse. Linda thought she looked fabulous.

'Can I help you or do you want to look around?' She had a pleasant voice.

'My daughter is looking for an evening dress.'

'Me,' Hannah said in case the woman thought it was Jennifer.

'Let me look at you.' She did for a moment or two then nodded and smiled. 'Slim and pretty and easy to fit. No,' when she saw Hannah's face. 'That is not sales talk, my dear. I would never tell someone she was slim and pretty unless she was. Most people prefer the truth to silly compliments that have no one fooled. Do be seated,' she said to Linda and Jennifer.

'Thank you,' Linda said glad to be off her feet.

'Do you mind if I have a look around?' Jennifer asked.

'Not at all, you are very welcome to look.' She turned to Hannah. 'If you would go into the cubicle I'll go and see what I have in your size. Actually you have chosen a good time. My new stock arrived this week.'

All tiredness had gone and Hannah was thinking this was a super place. The woman brought an armful of gowns for Hannah's inspection. They were lovely.

Linda's spirits soared. Hannah was going to be spoiled for choice. One after another was put aside for another inspection.

'Mum, they are perfect, I am definitely going to get something here.'

'Hannah, you really should try on the one in the window.'

'Which one would that be?'

'Jennifer means the red one but I don't want to try it on. Red is not my colour.'

'You know for the moment I had forgotten that dress and I do believe it is in your size.'

'I don't want red.'

'We don't call that red. That is crushed strawberry.'

'I shouldn't worry, Hannah seems to be making up her mind—'

'Not before she sees this one on. I have to say it is one of my favourites.'

'We are putting you to a lot of trouble—'

Linda was ignored as the woman reached into the window for the dress. In the confined space it hadn't been possible to show the full skirt.

'Here we are. Now who could call that red? Slip it on and see what you think.' She helped Hannah into the gown.

'It's lovely, really, really lovely,' Hannah breathed.

'It is, Hannah, it is perfect on you.'

'I agree. There were others you looked pretty in but this one is that little bit special. You have your sister to thank.'

Hannah didn't correct her. 'Thanks, Jennifer.'

Jennifer was looking pleased but not smug. 'I knew it was right for Hannah as soon as I saw it in the window.'

'You have the gift,' the woman said, 'and not too many have that.'

'Mum, you haven't asked how much it is.'

'Neither I have but if it doesn't bankrupt me you are going to have your dress.'

'What a nice mother to have.'

'I know. She's the best.'

'Stand still, please, while I make a slight adjustment. It needs to be taken in a little at the waist. Excuse me and I'll get the pins.'

'How long will the alteration take?' Hannah asked anxiously.

'Wednesday morning? Would that be all right?'

'Mum?'

'Yes, that's fine. I'll call for it.'

Linda was shown the price ticket. It was more than she had expected to pay but not by so very much. In any case it was worth every penny to see the sparkle in Hannah's eyes.

Linda had hoped that Jennifer's part in the purchase of the dress would have brought the two girls closer but nothing had changed. Jennifer appeared at meal times, then removed herself to her bedroom. Only occasionally did she go out and she never said where she was going.

25

'Hannah, I have not forgotten and you don't have to keep reminding me. Your dress will be here on Wednesday when you get home from school.'

'Thanks. I just wanted to make sure.'

'Yes, and now you have.'

Linda had organised her day so that she could spend Wednesday morning in Dundee. She knew there would be little hope of a parking space by the time she got there and didn't waste time looking. Linda wasn't over-fond of multi-store carparks but sometimes needs must and this was one of those times. The first level was full as was the second and she had to go to the one above to find a space. She parked, got her ticket and hurried away down the stairs, glad to be outside.

The woman in the boutique, whom she now knew to be its owner, greeted her warmly.

'Good morning and a pleasant one too. The dress is in its box ready for collection.'

'Thank you.'

'Will you manage it like that or shall I put another string round it?'

'No, it will be fine this way. I won't have anything else to carry.'

'I hope your daughter has a lovely time at the dance. One thing is for sure she will not want for partners,' she smiled.

'Hannah is going with her cousin, Simon. He is a little older and can keep an eye on her.'

'Do you wish you were that age again?'

'I'm not sure,' Linda said thoughtfully. 'Being young is not all sweetness and light. They have their problems.'

'Very true, and they have their mood swings.'

'Oh most definitely they have those.' They were both laughing when the door opened and they turned to see who had come in.

Linda felt her eyes widen in shocked surprise and she could see that same shock on the man's face when he saw her. She registered that he was smartly dressed in a dark business suit, white shirt and a quiet tie in two shades of blue. Matthew had one very similar.

'Alan Stephenson! It is you. I can hardly believe it,' Linda said incredulously.

'Linda. I can't believe it either.' He was shaking his head and smiling.

'Will someone please tell me—'

'Janette, this is just too amazing.'

'I gathered that.'

He turned again to Linda. 'My wife is waiting for me to make the introductions so let me do that. Janette, this is Linda. She and I were students together.'

'Oh, I see.'

'Linda, I'm afraid I don't know your married name.'

'Chalmers.'

The women shook hands.

Linda had been studying the man who had once been engaged to Jennifer's mother. The years had been kind to Alan, he hadn't changed very much. Just the usual with the approach of middle age. There was more flesh on the bones and his face was fuller. He had a good head of hair which was liberally peppered with grey. It was difficult to remember what had been its original colour.

'Would you say Alan had changed? In appearance, I mean.'

'Not very much, Mrs Stephenson. Apart from the hair, that is. What were you – dark brown?'

'I think so,' Alan laughed. 'I cannot remember that far back. As for you, Linda, you haven't changed at all.'

'Flatterer. You are looking at the mother of three children, one of those a teenager. Of course I have changed.'

'Mrs Chalmers, leave the box with me. Why don't you and Alan go through to the back shop and do your reminiscing there. Have a cup of coffee, it is freshly made.'

'Are you sure, Mrs Stephenson, I don't want to be in the way.'

'You aren't and please would you make that Janette since you and Alan go back a long way.'

'Thank you and I'm Linda.'

A customer came in at that moment and Janette shooed her husband and Linda into the back shop.

'You must excuse the clutter,' Alan said as he began moving boxes and stacking them one on top of the other to make more room. 'Janette is used to working in this muddle and doesn't seem to notice.'

Alan saw to the coffee and then sat opposite Linda at the small table. He had put a tin of biscuits in the middle. 'I should look for a plate.'

'Don't, this is fine. I'm still trying to get over the shock of seeing you.'

'It is amazing, isn't it? What brought you to Janette's boutique?'

'Chance again. We were looking for a dress for Hannah, my daughter, a dance dress and not having much success. Then we discovered your wife's boutique and Hannah found her dream dress.'

'Good.'

'The selection of dresses is wonderful, your wife has excellent taste.' He nodded. 'Before Janette opened the boutique

she was the fashion buyer for one of the top Edinburgh stores.'
She heard the pride in his voice.

'May I ask what brought you to Dundee?'

'My job. The company – by the way I am in insurance – was
opening a branch here and I was to be put in charge.'

'Congratulations.'

'To accept or not to accept was the problem facing us. And
to refuse the promotion wouldn't have done my future pro-
spects much good but that said it was a lot to ask of Janette.
She had worked very hard to get to where she was.'

'In the end you made the decision to move.'

'Yes, or rather Janette insisted I did. I wanted the job, of
course I did, but it would have been selfish of me to expect
Janette to make the sacrifice. In the end it worked out very
nicely. Janette had always fancied having her own boutique
but would never have given up her well-paid position to take
that chance. I told her this was her opportunity and I was
willing to help put up the money to get the business started.
And to cut a long story short these premises came on the
market. Janette would have preferred more room, she is very
cramped, but the position was ideal. It is very near the town
centre.'

'Not easy to find.'

'No, you have to know where to look. That is true as we
found out. Janette did a little advertising but not much. It was a
slow beginning but the boutique is doing well now.'

'I'm glad to hear that but not surprised. Satisfied customers
return.'

'And better still they tell their friends.'

'True.'

'Home, by the way, is in the Ninewells district. We bought
an old house that requires a lot done to it and is much too large
for two people. Some would say we were mad.'

'Not at all, not if you fell in love with it. That is what

happened with Matthew and I. The house wasn't too big but it cost a lot more than we wanted to give or could afford to offer.'

'You managed,' he smiled.

'With the help of my mother.'

'Your turn, Linda, tell me how life has treated you.'

'I can't complain, I have a good life and I try to remember that when once in a while things get on top of me. Before I say more I need to ask you something.'

'Ask away.'

'Did you know about Betty and her husband?'

'You mean the accident? Yes I did. My sister saw it in the newspaper and sent on the cutting. Linda, I couldn't get over the horror of it. I mean it was so awful.' He paused. 'You kept up with Betty, didn't you?'

'For a time we did but Betty wasn't much of a correspondent. She never had any news or none that she wanted to share with me.'

'Was she happy with Robert?'

'I don't think she was, Alan. Reading between the lines I would have said they had their problems. To be honest I didn't care for Robert and I don't think he was good to Betty. She was infatuated and didn't discover that until it was too late.'

'He was a handsome hunk.'

'And didn't he know it! We shouldn't speak ill of the dead, or so they say. I think the truth should be told. Betty never said this in so many words but I think she bitterly regretted what she did to you.'

'We all have our regrets, Linda. Mine is that I didn't stay and fight. Perhaps I would have won Betty back or there again maybe not. At the time I thought I was doing what was best. Me hanging around was an embarrassment so I cleared out.'

'Everyone was very upset. We all thought Betty and you were right for each other. Oh, dear, I am being tactless. I shouldn't have said that and you happily married.'

He shook his head. 'No, Linda, you can say anything and Janette wouldn't mind. Our special relationship takes a bit of explaining so it will have to keep until later. I wanted to ask you about the child. She escaped serious injury.'

'Yes, Jennifer was fifteen when it happened.'

'Do you know what became of her?'

'Yes, I do, Alan. Jennifer is living with us. Actually she came to the boutique to help Hannah choose.'

'This is absolutely fascinating.'

'Alan, I must be keeping you back. You have your work to go to.'

'Don't worry about that. You could say the boss has flexi-hours. Seriously, most nights I am there when the staff has gone. That suits me and I can pick up Janette.'

Linda nodded but absentmindedly, her thoughts were on how she would word what she had to tell Alan.

'I'll keep this short,' she said at last. 'Jennifer has no close relatives. Both Betty and Robert were only children and no one came forward to claim Jennifer.'

'Until you did.'

'In a roundabout way. Betty's solicitor wrote to me and that was how I knew about the accident. It had turned out that Betty had left word with him that I was her child's godmother. I wasn't, she hadn't asked me, but had she done so I would have felt honoured.'

'You would have accepted.'

'Yes, without hesitation.'

'With a family of your own that was very good of you and your husband to give Betty's daughter a home. Did your husband mind?'

'At first Matthew was against it and so was the family.'

'All is well now and Jennifer is accepted.'

'If only things were that simple. I'm afraid there have been difficulties. My elder daughter and Jennifer don't hit it off, haven't done so from the start though there might be a little improvement.'

'Happens. Clash of personalities.'

'I wouldn't call it that. Whatever it was it put a strain on family life. The main problem, Alan, was lack of space or rather the want of another room. We have four bedrooms, adequate for our needs until Jennifer arrived. Being an only child she was used to having her own bedroom and expected to have that in our house. My two girls had their own and saw no reason why they should give up their bedroom. For a while Jennifer had no choice but to share with Heather but that has now changed and my two are sharing.'

'Betty's daughter, what is she like?' He seemed eager to know.

'If you mean in appearance she is very like her mother though I would have to say that whereas Betty was very pretty, Jennifer is beautiful, a graceful and very striking-looking girl.'

'The product of handsome parents.'

'In this case, yes. Incidentally I'm sure Janette must have noticed. You don't not notice Jennifer. I didn't mention that she is very tall.'

Janette had come in. 'That was a complete waste of time, that woman had no intention of buying. I think she was just putting off time.'

'Do you get a lot of that?'

'No, I don't for which I should be thankful. I'm curious, I heard you say Janette must have noticed. What would that be?'

'The tall girl who was with Hannah and me.'

'I thought she was your other daughter.'

'No.'

'I do recall her. A graceful beauty or she will be in a year or two.'

The doorbell pinged. 'No rest for the wicked.'

'I should be going,' Linda said half rising.

'Not at all. Not unless you are in a hurry to get somewhere.'

'I'm not.'

'Then sit down and I'll top up that coffee,' Alan said.

'No need to dash away. You and Alan obviously have a lot to say to each other.'

'And a lot to tell you, Janette, when you have the time to listen.'

'I'll make the time. Excuse me while I attend to my customer.'

'What a charming wife you have.'

'She is. Janette is one of the best but before I tell you about us I want to hear about Jennifer.'

'Alan, Jennifer does not have Betty's lovely nature. She can be sullen, rude even and she keeps herself apart from us as much as possible. Not all of us. She and Matthew get along well.'

'Poor girl, she must have been devastated at her loss. To lose both parents.'

'I've no doubt she was devastated and still is but she doesn't show it. Alan, I would have been happier with floods of tears, I would have known how to cope with those.'

'Perhaps she is one of those people who cannot show their grief.'

'Matthew said that.'

Alan's face softened and she knew he was remembering.

'I never forgot Betty and I never will. She was my whole life and I worshipped her. When she broke our engagement I can't put into words what I felt.'

'And then you met Janette.' Linda thought she must say that. Janette was his wife.

'Yes, she was my saviour and she said I was hers. It was a turning point for both of us when we met. Janette had lost her beloved husband about the time of my broken engagement. We were both heartbroken and miserable. Neither of us was looking for love or expecting to find it. There was no question of us falling in love. No one was going to take the place of our first love. What we did find, Linda, was comfort in each other's company. Loneliness can be soul-destroying and since we got on so well and understood each other, marriage seemed a sensible step to take.'

'Which it has proved to be.'

'Yes, it was a wise decision. Over the years love has grown and quite frankly I would be lost without Janette.'

'It was good of you telling me all this.'

'You have been open with me and I returned the compliment.'

Janette came in. 'Is that coffee still drinkable?'

'It should be reasonable,' Alan said, getting up for another cup and saucer.

Linda got up. 'I must go and thank you for being so kind, Janette. This has been a morning I won't forget in a hurry. And as I said, Alan will tell you all about it.'

'I'm sure he'll do that and I am also sure he won't want to lose touch.'

'I was hoping we could arrange a time when you could come to us and meet the family.'

'That would be lovely. We would enjoy that wouldn't we, Alan?'

'Very much.'

'Do you have family?' Linda didn't think so but thought she should ask.

'No, Linda, we don't.'

'Our lot are noisy or at least Robin is.'

'Children need to express themselves.'

'Not by shouting,' Linda laughed. 'I'm joking. They are reasonably well behaved.' She scribbled her address and telephone number on the back of an old envelope and gave it to Janette. 'We are easy to find but I'll give you instructions how to get to Hillcrest when I phone. Perhaps I could have your home telephone number.'

'Here we are.' Janette gave her a card which had the boutique address and phone number. She had added the house number and Alan's work number.'

'Thank you, I'll put this in my purse and I shall be in touch very shortly.'

The three of them were through in the shop and Linda was making her way to the door.

'Don't forget what you came for.'

Linda looked blank for a moment. 'Heavens! I'm almost away without the precious dress,' she said, taking the cardboard box from Janette. 'Thank goodness you reminded me.'

Carrying the box Linda hurried away. Her head was spinning. Fancy meeting Alan Stephenson after all these years and in a boutique of all places.

26

Linda had the dining-room table set and in the kitchen the meal was cooking. Hannah couldn't seem to keep still. She had been thinking about her dress all day and trying to hide her excitement. Showing too much of it was childish and she wanted so much to be grown-up and dignified. Especially when she was going to the dance with Simon. She didn't want duty dances, she wanted Simon to fancy her. Once it hadn't been accepted that cousins could be interested in one another that way or so she had heard, but apparently it was OK now. Cousins even got married.

Hannah got to her feet to follow her mother upstairs and into the bedroom she shared with Heather.

'I put the box on the bed.' They both looked at it. Linda had removed the string.

'I'm dying to see it.'

'So am I but I didn't want to open the box until you were here.'

'Thanks. You take the lid off.'

Linda did. Then she lifted the dress from the sheets of tissue paper and spread it over the other bed. And as she did Hannah caught her breath.

'Mum, it is even lovelier than I remembered. Do I get to try it on now?'

'I don't see why not.' Linda was touched and amused. It had been a very long time since Hannah had shown this amount of excitement about anything.

'I know. Don't tell Dad and I'll come down after you and give him a surprise.'

'I have a better idea. Let us get the meal over first and when everything is cleared away you can come down to the sitting-room and make your entrance.'

'Yes, I could do that.' Hannah's eyes were shining as her fingers lovingly touched the material.

'I have to agree that it is a gorgeous colour and Jennifer was right when she said the colour was perfect with your pale skin.'

'I know that now but I was mad when she said it. I thought she was suggesting I was pale and dull or something like that.'

'Hannah, you've got that all wrong. When I was young, about your age, we all wanted to be pale and interesting. You see that conjured up someone mysterious and delicate.'

'You are having me on,' Hannah said but she was giggling.

'No, I am not having you on. We were being silly, of course we were. What I am trying to get into your head, Hannah, is that you can be highly coloured or pale-skinned and be equally attractive. Beauty means different things to different people, if you get what I mean.'

'I think so.'

'Jennifer has an unfortunate manner which is a pity. And she would do well to think before she spoke.'

That had Hannah laughing. 'She doesn't have much to say at the best of times and if she was to think before she spoke she would never speak at all.' It wasn't said unkindly. Jennifer never chatted like other people.

'Jennifer is much too quiet but we have to accept the way she is. However, we must give credit where credit is due. She does have an eye for fashion and she is genuinely interested. You got the benefit of her expertise and you have to remember you didn't want her there.'

'I know I didn't. She was going to be a pain I thought and I was so wrong.'

'What did you think, that she would put you off?'

'Yes, I did as a matter of fact. Didn't you?'

'No, I did not. It would have been silly of you to allow her to influence you against your better judgement.'

Hannah smiled. 'Only she did, Mum. I was influenced and her judgement was better than mine.'

'Yes, that is true.'

'I *am* grateful to Jennifer for choosing my dress,' Hannah said slowly, 'but there is something about her I don't like and I can't explain what it is. It isn't because she keeps herself aloof, it is more than that. And whether you believe it or not I have tried to be friendly, especially after that talk with Dad.'

'Don't forget you gave up your bedroom and that was very big of you so anything Jennifer has done—'

'Makes us quits, is that what you are trying to say?'

'I suppose I am.' She paused. 'By all means make the effort to be friendly but if Jennifer doesn't want that, leave her alone.'

'Is that what you do?'

'I take her as I find her.'

After the meal was over and the dishes washed, dried and put away, Jennifer excused herself and went upstairs as she usually did. Hannah waited to hear the door shutting before she, too, climbed the stairs. Matthew was sitting in his armchair with his long legs stretched out before him. Heather was holding a book of poetry and from it reading a verse out loud. She then closed the book and for some reason her eyes, and tried to recite the verse from memory. She started off well and then got stuck and her patience gave out.

'This is awful,' she said, throwing down the book. 'I am never going to remember it and anyway I don't see why we have to learn poetry off by heart. It is plain daft when you can read it from the book.'

Matthew did have some sympathy for his younger daughter.

'When we got chunks of that stuff to memorise I used to think the same as you.'

'Did you, Dad?'

'I did,' he said, reaching for his paper.

'Not me. There is something rather nice about being able to recite a few lines of poetry,' Linda said and gave Matthew a playful punch when he made a face.

'Can you still do that, Mum, I mean after all those years?'

Talk of being made to feel old before your time, she thought resignedly.

'Yes, dear, once you really learn something off by heart it stays with you.'

'That is only your mother trying to impress us,' Matthew grinned, then the grin turned into a frown. 'Robin, I do not object to your playing on the floor with your cars but do we have to have a line of them leading from here to the hall? One of us is going to break our neck.'

'Not if you look where you are going.'

Hannah's entrance saved Robin from a severe reprimand for being cheeky. She stood just inside the door for a moment, then walked slowly into the room.

'What do you think, Dad?' Her voice wasn't quite steady.

'What do I think? I am wondering if this gorgeous creature is my daughter.' It was a lovely moment for father and daughter spoiled by Robin.

'Of course it is Hannah. Silly Daddy not to be sure.'

Matthew was experiencing several emotions. He was genuinely astonished. This young woman was his gawky, sometimes sullen, very often awkward, schoolgirl daughter and he didn't think he was ready for the change. She was lovely and he was proud, of course he was, but he couldn't help being saddened. His little girl was growing up and it was all happening too quickly.

'You do like my dress,' Hannah said, giving a little twirl.

'Darling, you look wonderful. Your mother looked like that
when she was young.'

'That was a hundred years ago.'

'Thank you, Robin, you say the nicest things.'

He beamed, thinking he must have got that right. 'Hannah,
did your dress cost a lot of money?'

'Yes, it did but Mum isn't complaining.'

'She isn't the one doing the forking out, that is why.'

Heather was taking her father seriously.

'Will we be very hard up?'

'Looks that way,' Matthew teased.

'Typical, I always come off worst.'

'Heather, your father was only joking.'

'It didn't look like it to me. And if there is no money I am
going to have to wait simply ages before I get a single new thing
to wear.'

'What do you want, Heather? If you would say what it is
instead of these hints.'

'I'm not sure, Mum. Maybe shoes for a start and I don't
mean horrid school shoes.'

'Very well. Since you think you are so hard done by we'll go
and see about new shoes for you.'

'Good.' Heather was looking enormously pleased. That had
been dead easy. She must try that again some time.

'Dad, it is Jennifer I have to thank. She found the boutique
and she made me try this on. I wasn't going to.'

'That was nice of Jennifer and very nice of you to admit
it.'

'Did you think I might not?' Hannah sounded hurt.

'If I did I think I could be forgiven. After all you two have
never hit it off.' He raised his eyebrows. 'Has she gone out?
Jennifer, I mean.'

'No, Matthew, Jennifer is upstairs in her bedroom where she
spends a great deal of her time.'

'And why not if that is what she wants? She isn't doing anyone any harm.'

'Except herself perhaps.'

'I don't get it.' As always when anything was said about Jennifer, Matthew was quick to take her part.

'All I meant was that it can't be good for her being so much on her own. She should be downstairs with us.'

'Could be she only wants a bit of peace. I feel that way myself at times,' he smiled.

'If that was all I wouldn't be worried.' Linda paused and wrinkled her brow. 'To me the girl seems lost in a world of her own.'

He was shaking his head and watching Hannah dancing round the room.

'You'll make yourself dizzy going round and round like that,' he said and turned again to his wife. 'Jennifer is a quiet girl who likes her own company. And that bit about her being lost in a dream world, you can be pretty good at that yourself.'

'Tell me when? Tell me when you have seen me lost in a dream world?'

'When I have been talking to you and you don't bother to answer.'

'If it comes to that I could say the same about you.'

'There you are, then, we all do it.'

Linda sighed and turned away. She wondered why she bothered, she never got anywhere. 'Come along, Hannah, the dress rehearsal is over. I'll come upstairs and help you off with your dress.'

'Where will we put it for safety?'

'In my wardrobe where it won't get crushed.'

Linda had been dying to tell Matthew about her meeting with Alan Stephenson but decided to put it off until they could be alone with no fear of interruptions. The only time that could be was when they retired for the night. She would have to be patient.

As was to be expected this was one of the nights when the family was reluctant to go to bed. To try and hurry them was not advisable, if anything it increased the reluctance. By half past eleven the family was in bed and she had seen to the setting of the breakfast table with the cereal packets to hand. Matthew was switching off the television and unplugging it. Apparently it was safer to do so. Linda went upstairs, undressed and got into bed. A few minutes later and Matthew was getting in at his side.

'Switch off the light, will you?' Matthew said between yawns.

'Not yet. I've been waiting for this moment. I want to talk and I prefer to do that with the light on.' In the darkness Matthew could always feign sleep. He was good at that and come to think about it she wasn't too bad herself.

'Talk about what?'

'Talk about someone I met today, name of Alan Stephenson.'

'Who is he when he is at home?'

'You know perfectly well who Alan Stephenson is. He and Jennifer's mother were engaged to be married.'

'That Alan Stephenson.'

Linda didn't know there was another. 'Yes, Matthew, that Alan Stephenson.'

'Got you. Then what's-his-name arrived on the scene –'

'Robert.'

'I'm with you. And you are going to tell me you met this Alan today—'

'Yes and of all places we met in the boutique where Hannah got her dress.'

'What was he doing there?'

'His wife owns it.'

'I see. Is that all? Can I get some shut-eye?'

'No, I haven't finished. His wife was very charming.'

'Hardly surprising since she had made such a good sale.'

'Alan wasn't there when we bought the dress. That was Saturday and I met Alan on Wednesday when I went to collect it.'

'So.'

'So we talked.'

Why did women always take so long to tell a story? Why couldn't they keep to the point and better still keep it short.

'Janette was very obliging and suggested that Alan and I should have a coffee and a chat in the back shop.'

'Didn't she want to join you?'

'No, she was much too busy. There was stock to put away and she had to attend to any customer who might come in.'

'Go on.'

'I'll better tell you first that Alan never got over Betty, he said as much. She was the love of his life.'

'Not the most tactful of remarks with his wife a few yards away.'

'Janette wouldn't have heard and even if she had it would not have bothered her. I won't go into it now, I'll just tell you that Alan is Janette's second husband and when her first husband died, she was completely devastated.'

'They consoled each other. God, I'm tired.'

'When it is the late-night film you can last out.'

'That's different.' He paused. 'If consoling each other was all they did it wasn't a very solid foundation for marriage. A gamble I would have said.'

'One that paid off. They seem happy together. Matthew, it would have been a case of two lonely people getting together and if neither of them was looking for too much—'

'OK, I get the picture.'

'Alan couldn't believe it when I told him we had Jennifer living with us.'

He sat up, she had his full attention. 'Alan knew about the accident?'

'Yes, he heard about it through his sister. He also knew that Betty's daughter had survived the accident and he was terribly anxious to hear all about her.'

'I'm ahead of you, I think. This is leading up to you inviting them here to meet Jennifer.'

'I wasn't aware it was leading anywhere,' Linda answered sharply, 'but since you mention it, yes, I have invited Alan and Janette though no date was fixed. Do you mind?'

'Of course I don't mind. When have you ever had to ask my permission to invite anyone to the house?'

'I know.' She paused. 'It isn't just to meet Jennifer. They would like to meet you and the family. Janette saw Jennifer briefly but of course it was Hannah who was getting her attention.'

'Go ahead and make a date. Not a Saturday though.'

'I thought Sunday and instead of Sunday lunch we could have the roast beef and Yorkshire pudding in the evening.'

'I am right in thinking they have no family?'

'You are right.'

'Are you going to warn Jennifer, if that is the right word?'

'I will prepare her but I don't anticipate a problem, Matthew. I have a feeling that Jennifer will be very interested to meet Alan. She knows all about her mother's broken engagement. Betty seems to have been very open with her daughter.'

He was nodding. 'Could be interesting to observe how our Jennifer responds.'

Linda took note of the 'our Jennifer'. No one else in the family called her that. Was Matthew concerned, worried even, that Alan Stephenson might become important to Jennifer and as a consequence she would have no further need of him? She was letting her imagination run away with her.

'Yes, I agree it could be interesting and now I think I should tell you about Alan.'

'That could wait. I do have to work tomorrow.'

'This will only take a few minutes and it is better to hear it, then you can't say I didn't tell you.'

'What does he do for a living?'

'That was what I was going to tell you. Alan is with an insurance company. Don't ask me which one, I don't think it was mentioned, but the company has recently opened an office in Dundee and Alan has been put in charge.'

'Where did they live before they came to Dundee?'

'Edinburgh. Janette was the buyer for the fashion department of one of the big stores.'

'Good remuneration, I would imagine. She couldn't have been too keen to give it up.'

'It couldn't have been easy but actually, according to Alan, it has worked out very well. Janette always wanted her own boutique but she would never have taken the risk.'

'Her opportunity.'

'Yes and from all accounts she is doing very well indeed.'

'Do you see the time?' Matthew groaned.

'Yes, you can go to sleep.'

'I am actually going to get some shut-eye?'

'Don't be cheeky.'

'Speaking of cheek,' Matthew was leaning on his elbow, 'that young monkey of ours is becoming much too cheeky and I don't like it.'

'Well, isn't that too bad. Robin was too quiet, you said. Too timid, you said. Unable to stick up for himself. And now you don't like it.'

'Granted the boy needed to toughen up. I was certainly all for that but it is no excuse for cheeking up to his parents.'

'He doesn't mean to.'

'There you go again making excuses.'

'No, I am not. I don't like cheeky children any more than you do and I wouldn't want Robin to become one of them. I shall have a word with him. Incidentally, Matthew, I bet at Robin's age you were cheeky to your parents. I bet you were no angel.'

'Not me. I didn't give my parents cheek. No fear. I wasn't going to invite a clip round the ear.'

They were both laughing when Linda switched off the lamp. Matthew was quickly asleep, she knew by his regular breathing. She wasn't ready for sleep, her brain was too active. It was a good time to make plans. She would telephone Alan and Janette and fix a date. Evening would be the best time to phone when they would be at home or likely to be. She would suggest Sunday and explain that with a young family it was the best day though if Sunday was out of the question they would make it a weekday evening. Saturday was out, Matthew had made that clear.

With the matter settled in her mind Linda snuggled up to the sleeping Matthew and very soon she, too, was asleep.

27

It was Alan who answered the telephone.

'Hello, Alan, it's Linda Chalmers.'

'Linda, how are you?'

'I'm fine, thank you. This is very short notice I know but I wondered if you and Janette might be free on Sunday evening to come and have a meal with us?'

'I'm nearly sure it is but hang on a moment and I'll get Janette.'

Linda heard voices, then Janette was on the line.

'Hello, Linda, Alan is saying something about Sunday –'

'Yes. If you happen to be free on Sunday evening would you like to come for a meal and meet the family?'

'Love to and yes, Sunday evening will suit us nicely. It will be a very pleasant change because until very recently our Sundays have been spent doing up the house. It needed a tremendous lot done to it which, of course, was the reason we could afford it. We did have the professionals in to do the major work but the rest is very amateurish DIY.'

'I'm sure it is nothing of the kind. You are a perfectionist unless I am very much mistaken.'

'Thank you, I do love compliments. The end result isn't all that bad but you can be the judge of that when you come and visit us.'

'I gather you have had a very busy time.'

'Hectic. Most of the time the workmen were left on their own to get on with it while I concentrated on getting the boutique up and running. As well as that, would you believe, Alan had the responsibility for opening the new office and there were problems with that. I would not like to go through it all again.'

'How on earth did you both keep your sanity?'

'With the greatest of difficulty. There were times when we thought we had taken on too much but when you have committed yourself there is nothing for it but to soldier on.'

'In comparison I lead a life of leisure.'

'Not with a family you don't. Actually, Linda, it shouldn't have been like that. Alan and I expected to be much better organised but as you know yourself things don't always run to plan.'

'I do indeed.'

'The house was to be my main concern and once we had that to our satisfaction I was to switch my energies to finding suitable premises to open my boutique.'

'What happened?'

'My solicitor phoned to say that a property had come on the market which largely met my requirements and I should view it as soon as possible. I contacted Alan and we rushed over. It looked nothing, a scruffy little shop tucked away in a side road, but immediately I saw its potential. The situation was better than I could have hoped. It was hidden away but it was in the town centre.'

'What was it? What kind of shop?'

'A barber's. Apparently of very long standing with its regular customers. I don't know but I imagine it was old age or ill health that forced the owner to close.'

'Lucky you to find what you wanted.'

'Very lucky. The one drawback was its size. I had wanted something bigger but one can't have everything.'

'Was Alan in favour?'

'Very much so. He it was who persuaded me to seek

professional advice and that proved to be money well spent. Believe me, not an inch of space has been wasted.'

'I have to say we loved the window and its display and then going inside was so inviting. It lifted our spirits right away.'

'Poor you, were you foot weary?'

'I was and Hannah was downhearted. Some of the dresses we had seen were very nice –'

'None caught the eye?'

'No. Then thanks to Jennifer we found you.'

'I'm so glad you did. And now tell me, when is this dance?'

'Friday.'

'Good. I'll hear all about it on Sunday.'

'I'm sure you will. Hannah is not a particularly excitable girl but about this she is.'

'Her first big affair?'

'Yes. She went to the school dance but apparently that doesn't count, it was just kid's stuff.'

Janette was laughing. 'I have painful memories of being partnered by boys who couldn't dance but thought they could.'

'My experience too. The night would end with ruined shoes and squashed toes. As long as we are on about the dance I should tell you we had a dress rehearsal mainly for Matthew's benefit. Her father's approval matters a lot to Hannah.'

'Fathers and daughters,' Janette said softly. 'What did he say?'

'All the right things. He thought she looked enchanting, a vision of loveliness.'

'How she must have loved that.'

'To be honest, Janette, I think Matthew was taken aback. This couldn't be his gawky schoolgirl daughter.'

'Not gawky.'

'Yes gawky. All skinny arms and legs. The transformation was so sudden and he was seeing his little girl all grown-up.'

'Before he was ready for it.'

'Yes, I think so. Hannah has no conceit about her appearance. She has always been convinced she is plain and the dress gets full marks for changing that.'

'Then your daughter is being silly and I would tell her that. No dress, no matter how beautiful, turns an ugly duckling into a swan. The beauty is there already just waiting to come out. Linda, you make me envious.'

'In what way?'

'Yours is obviously a very happy family.'

'Most of the time we are but the going isn't all smooth. Would you have liked a family, Janette?'

'I'm not sure. Alan and I didn't plan one and I am happy with my life. There are those women who can manage a family and a career but for me it would have to be one or the other. Here, let me say, I am talking about real success, the high-flyer. To reach those heights one would have to be single-minded. There wouldn't be room for anything else. Linda, I'm sorry, I am keeping you talking when you must have things to do.'

'Nothing in particular. This has been a nice little chat and I have enjoyed it. As for Sunday, Janette, could we say seven for seven thirty?'

'That would suit us perfectly.'

'I could have made it later but it would have been awkward. Robin, our youngest, is only eight and with school in the morning I like to have him in bed no later than nine.'

'I quite understand and please, Linda, don't go to any trouble for us. We are happy—'

'To take pot luck, as my father used to say. Don't worry, the meal will be simple. And now I will ring off and look forward to seeing you both on Sunday.'

'Thank you.'

*   *   *

'Jennifer, don't disappear upstairs, not yet.'

The girl stopped and turned round. 'What is it, Mrs Chalmers? Is there something you want to see me about?'

'Yes, there is and with everybody out this could be a good opportunity. We'll go into the sitting-room and have our talk in comfort.'

Linda saw the look of puzzlement on Jennifer's face and perhaps there was a touch of alarm.

Linda sat down in one of the easy chairs and after a slight hesitation Jennifer chose the settee.

'Is something wrong?'

'No, nothing is wrong. Why should you think there was?'

'I'm not sure what to think but this is a bit unusual, isn't it?'

'Yes, I suppose it is. You and I don't have many conversations and more's the pity. However, I won't keep you in suspense. This concerns the lady in the boutique. You remember her?'

'Yes.'

'The lady's married name is Stephenson.'

'So? I can't see what—'

'Let me finish. I was about to tell you that her husband's name is Alan. Alan Stephenson.' She paused then went on. 'That name should mean something to you, Jennifer.'

The girl had become very still. 'Should it?' she said at last.

'Yes, my dear, I think it should.'

She swallowed and moistened her lips. 'My mother was once engaged to someone of that name. It doesn't have to be the same person.'

'It doesn't have to be, only it is, Jennifer. It is the same Alan Stephenson.'

'Is that why you invited them? Was it to meet me?'

'That wasn't the only reason. I was delighted to meet Alan after all those years and as you can imagine there was a lot to talk about.'

'How did it happen?'

'Chance, pure chance. You will remember I was to collect Hannah's dress on Wednesday.'

'Yes.'

'That was when I saw Alan. He came to the boutique to see his wife.' Linda was smiling as she remembered. 'It would be difficult to say which of us was the more surprised.'

Jennifer bit her lip and remained silent.

'It was Mrs Stephenson's suggestion that Alan and I should go through to the back shop and have a coffee and a chat.'

'Is that when my name came up?'

'Yes. We spoke about the accident,' Linda said quietly. 'Alan's sister had given him the news and he told me how shocked and saddened he had been.' Linda looked at Jennifer's set face and was surprised. She seemed more upset talking about the accident now than she had been at the beginning.

'I expect he would have been shocked.'

'He knew there was a daughter and that she had survived the accident. Alan wanted to know what had become of you.'

'And you told him.'

'That you were living with us. Yes, I told Alan that.'

'Another shock for him.'

'He was very surprised, Jennifer, and very anxious to hear about you.'

'I can't think why. He doesn't know me, we have never met.'

'You are Betty's daughter, that is what makes you special to Alan. He was very fond of your mother.'

'Even after what she did to him?'

'You don't stop loving a person because things go wrong. Alan was broken-hearted when Betty broke off their engagement but he was never bitter. Alan is incapable of bitterness. He accepted that Betty's feelings for him had changed and to make it easier for both of them he moved away from the district.'

'You wouldn't have got my dad to do that.' She said it a little defiantly. 'He would have said that was soft.'

'Alan and your father were very different.'

'Mum told me that breaking off her engagement to Alan was the hardest thing she had ever had to do.'

'I could believe that. Betty would never deliberately hurt anyone.'

'Only she did.'

'Yes, Jennifer, she did. Poor Alan was devastated and we were all desperately sorry for him.'

'Not for Mum, you weren't sorry for her.'

'We thought she was making a big mistake but it was none of our business. She wanted Robert and it was her life.'

'Since Alan married he must have got over her.'

'I don't think he ever got over your mother but life must go on. Mrs Stephenson's first husband died so it is possible they helped one another with their loss.'

Jennifer looked thoughtful. 'Mum is dead so I suppose I can say it. She never forgot Alan nor did she forgive herself for what she did. If you want to know, I think that was the cause of the trouble between my parents.'

Linda nodded. She thought that was very possible.

'It could have been,' Jennifer persisted.

'Yes, Jennifer, I think so too.'

'Mum would have been pleased to know that Alan hadn't forgotten her.'

'Yes, I'm sure that is true and it might help you to understand why it is so important for Alan to meet you.'

'You seem to have forgotten his wife, she has feelings.'

From Jennifer that was surprising.

'I think they have an understanding in their marriage and that Janette wouldn't mind at all.'

'You mean they don't come first with each other?'

'I think they do now but neither has forgotten their first love.'

'Could be, I suppose.'

'You saw Mrs Stephenson.'

'Yes, but I didn't pay much attention.'

Linda smiled. 'More interested in the stock.'

'Yes, I was. I thought what she had was terrific.'

'Janette would be pleased to hear that.'

'If I don't make it as a model then maybe one day I will open my own boutique. Getting the money to start up would be the problem or I could do what my dad suggested.' She grinned.

'And what was that if I may ask?'

'Marry for money and don't look so shocked, Mrs Chalmers, my dad was only half serious.'

'I hope he wasn't serious at all. Marrying for money is a recipe for disaster. Don't even think about it, Jennifer.'

'I'm not right now but I can't say that I won't at some time in the future.'

'Jennifer, I think you are being a little monkey and now let us be serious. How do you feel about meeting Alan?'

'I don't know,' Jennifer said slowly. 'The thought of it gives me a funny sort of feeling. I'm not sure that I want to meet the man my mother might have married.'

'Aren't you curious?'

'I suppose I might be.'

'Remember this, there is no pressure on you. This has to be your decision.'

'You think I should, don't you?'

'Yes, Jennifer, I do.'

'Do I get to think about it?'

'Of course.'

'OK, I'll think about it. Is it all right if I go upstairs now?'

'On you go.'

Linda watched her go and felt a lot of satisfaction. That had been a good conversation and a lot had come out, with some surprisingly open comments about her parents. Jennifer might decide to go out on Sunday evening, she hadn't committed herself. They would have to wait. Jennifer was a law unto herself. She knew that there was no pressure on her and that no one would question her decision.

It paid to talk nicely to the butcher and Linda came away from the shop with a prime piece of Scottish beef. The quality of the beef made all the difference.

The preparation for the meal went smoothly. Linda had every confidence in her ability to produce a tasty and well-cooked dinner. She did it every Sunday. Matthew helped her to put the extra leaf in the dining-room table. That way they would all have room to move. Hannah helped her to put on the large white starched tablecloth that the laundry did so beautifully and charged accordingly. Apart from Christmas and the New Year there weren't many occasions when it was used. There were many attractive ways to fold the matching starched napkins and Linda had had several lessons. She made an attempt with one then gave it up. Flat on the side plate they looked quite nice.

Once she would have dictated to the girls what they should wear but not now. All she asked of them was that they should be neat and tidy. More important was deciding what she should wear. Her one dress that could be considered stylish was unsuitable. The full sleeves would be a nuisance when it came to serving the meal. She had several pretty skirts in her wardrobe and a very good selection of blouses. One of the long ones would be dressier and she would wear it with a self-coloured blouse.

For most of that Sunday the weather had been sunshine and showers but with the disappearance of the rain clouds it looked promising for the evening. The visitors were up to time arriving a few minutes after seven. Linda went to open the door with Matthew behind her. When the introductions were made Alan handed Matthew a bottle of wine.

'Thanks. Thanks very much.'

Meantime Linda was admiring the flowers Janette had put in her hand.

'These are beautiful, Janette. I'll leave them on the hall table until I get a vase. And, no, this is not something else.'

'Only chocolate bars for the children, we can't forget them.'

'You are very kind.'

'Better hide them,' Matthew said. 'From Robin that is, our wee lad would exist on chocolate if he got the chance.'

'Why are you saying that, Daddy?'

'Where did you spring from?'

'I didn't spring, I was on the floor playing.'

'I take it this young gentleman is the son of the house,' Alan was saying as Linda put an arm around the small boy.

'Yes, Alan, this is Robin. Robin, I want you to meet Mr and Mrs Stephenson.'

Janette bent down to the child's level. 'Hello, Robin, I'm so pleased to meet you.'

Robin had been all ready to hold out his hand to have it shaken but the lady kissed his cheek. She smelt nice. Usually when he had to tolerate a kiss from a stranger he rubbed at the bit of cheek to get rid of the feeling. He didn't mind with this lady because he had overheard the magic word chocolate. He wasn't daft, he had caught a glimpse of a paper bag, the kind sweetie shops used, before it was removed from sight. Robin left the grown-ups and went back to his toys.

'What a lovely little boy, Linda, and so smart in his grey trousers and open-necked white shirt.'

Linda smiled. 'Boys are certainly a lot easier to dress than girls. For one thing they couldn't care less about clothes. Shall I take your cardigan? The house is quite warm.'

'If you would, thank you.' Janette took off her long, cream-coloured cashmere cardigan and handed it to Linda.

'This is beautiful,' Linda said admiringly.

'A very useful garment I have to say.'

Linda went into the cloakroom with it and draped it over a padded coathanger. When she returned to her guests she silently admired the plain emerald green dress with its scooped neckline that showed Janette's lovely long neck. She wore no jewellery and she looked elegant. Then she thought casually elegant was a better description. In other words she was dressed without being over-dressed.

After Hannah and Heather were introduced the four adults went into the sitting-room for a pre-dinner drink. There was no sign of Jennifer, she was probably still in her bedroom. No one had mentioned her name.

Linda wouldn't call her or ask anyone else to do it. Jennifer knew the time the meal was to be served. She hadn't said she wouldn't be present nor again had she said she would.

They were all seated with one exception. Linda was about to serve the meal when Jennifer entered the room and took her place at the table.

'I do apologise, Mrs Chalmers, I didn't realise the time.'

Linda nodded. That may or may not have been true. The main thing was she had put in an appearance. Linda made the introductions. Shaking hands would have been awkward and instead there were murmurs and smiles.

From the moment the girl stepped into the room Alan's eyes had followed her.

'You are very like your mother.'

Linda thought she heard a break in his voice.

'So I'm told and I'm also told I look a lot like my father.'

There was a lull in the conversation while Linda served the soup and Hannah assisted. Heather handed round the basket of warmed rolls and Matthew filled the four glasses with wine.

'Hannah, do tell me about the dance. Was it a huge success?'

'It was absolutely great, Mrs Stephenson, and my dress was fabulous.'

'And you looked fabulous in it.'

'I wouldn't say so much about that,' Hannah said modestly and dropping her eyes.

'Well, I would. And I bet you didn't miss a dance.'

'I didn't actually and everybody was admiring my dress. They wanted to know where I got it.'

'I hope you told them, Hannah,' Alan smiled.

'I did.'

'Thank you, dear, if I have a rush of customers I'll have you to thank,' Janette laughed.

'Simon said I looked nice so I suppose I must have.'

'Simon being –'

'My cousin, he was my partner.'

'And cousins don't throw away compliments?'

'Simon doesn't or not until now. I think that he thought he would be stuck with me.' Hannah flushed. 'I got asked to dance by boys I didn't know and that was good because I didn't want to sit out.'

'Why should you sit out?'

'Because, Dad, Simon had strict instructions from Aunt Helen not to forget his duty dances.' She giggled. 'He was glad to get them over.'

'Were you at the dance, Jennifer?'

'No, Mr Stephenson, I didn't want to go.'

'Don't you like dancing?'

'Yes, I do. My dad taught me the steps and he was a terrific dancer.'

'Your mother was a very good dancer and so light on her feet.'

'Dad thought she was stiff, didn't let herself go.'

Jennifer was now the centre of attention.

'Tell me, Jennifer, what do you want to do when you leave school?'

'I'm leaving at the summer holidays.'

'Not long to go then.'

'We would rather Jennifer stayed on for another year at least, a good education is so important.'

Janette nodded. 'Yes, it is.'

'It isn't necessary, not for everything,' Jennifer said quickly.

'So what is your ambition, Jennifer?' Alan smiled, looking at her like an indulgent uncle.

'I want to be a model and by that I mean a top model, one who appears on the glossies.'

'With your appearance I would say you had a very good chance. How would you rate Jennifer's chances, Janette?'

'Good. Definitely good.' She smiled across the table to Jennifer. 'You have the height and a good figure. Some girls feel awkward with their height. You don't, which is a point in your favour.'

'Jennifer is pretty,' Heather said. She felt she had been ignored and she wanted to be included in the conversation. 'I wish I was.'

'But you are, my dear. You and Hannah are lovely girls and the nicest thing of all is that neither of you is conceited.'

'Mummy.'

'Yes, Robin?'

'Why is no one talking to me?'

'You've been a good boy and your turn will come.'

'When?'

Janette and Alan were laughing heartily. 'I bet there never is a dull moment in your house,' Janette said through her laughter. 'Robin, I do apologise we have been naughty not to include you.'

'That's all right.' He liked the bit about grown-ups being naughty.

'Tell us what you like doing?'

'Playing with my Dinky cars. I've got a lot. Mr Stephens –'

'Mr Stephenson,' Linda corrected him.

'Mr Stephenson.'

'Yes, Robin?'

'Would you like to see my cars?'

'Robin, I would love to see your cars.'

'Now? I've finished eating.'

'No, Robin,' Matthew said firmly. 'We will excuse you and you can go and play with your toys and when we have finished you can show Mr Stephenson your Dinky models.'

'Will you be long?'

'Robin?' Linda said warningly. 'Off you go and remember it is bed by nine o'clock and no later.'

They heard the sigh as they were meant to do before he left the room.

'He's a delight.'

'He is a pest with those damned cars. If he would keep them to one place but no they are all over the house.'

'Matthew is exaggerating.'

'Linda is always making excuses for him. He can be a cheeky little monkey, the same wee lad.'

'I don't believe that.'

'Robin can be cheeky, Janette, but he doesn't mean to be. Not so long ago he was too quiet and that worried us or at least it worried Matthew.'

'He has to be able to hold his own in the playground.'

'Which he can do now and that is enough about Robin. Matthew, Alan's glass is needing refilled.'

'No, really, that is enough for me. This has been a lovely meal.'

'It has,' his wife agreed. 'I have thoroughly enjoyed it.' She paused and looked from Linda to Jennifer. 'Are your Saturdays fully taken up, Jennifer?'

'No.'

'Would a Saturday job interest you?'

'Depends what it is.'

'Helping me in the boutique. Saturdays can be quite hectic.'

'Helping in the boutique, yes, I think I would like that.'

'If you are agreeable, Linda?'

'Yes. I'm happy about it.'

28

Since it was a spur of the moment decision, Kirsty hadn't phoned to tell Linda of her intention to visit. It was the weather that did it. For too many days the rain had confined her to the house. There was no necessity to go out since the grocer and the butcher had message boys to deliver what she needed. The first dry sunny day was enticing her out of doors and should Linda not be at home, which was very possible, she wouldn't consider it a wasted journey. She would enjoy the run.

She hadn't reached this stage yet but she knew that some folk, as they got older, went out less and less and that was a mistake. She wasn't going to fall into that bad habit. There was no immediate danger since she was active enough but nevertheless it was something to remember for the future.

Kirsty drove sedately and admired the countryside. We shouldn't complain about the amount of rain that fell because without it there wouldn't be the lovely green, green grass, she thought.

Turning into the cul-de-sac she stopped outside the gate of Hillcrest and getting out of the car heard the sound of the lawnmower. Somebody was at home.

Linda showed her delight. 'What a lovely surprise, Mum,' she said, kissing her mother's cheek. 'You should have phoned before you left, I could so easily have been out.'

'I know and I was prepared for that.'

'You wanted the run?'

'I did as a matter of fact. The car needs a few good runs. It is due its service shortly and there is hardly any mileage on the clock since the last one.'

'Don't worry about that. Come into the sitting-room and I'll get the kettle on. Tea or coffee, which would you prefer?'

'I'm easy.'

'You say.'

'Make it tea then,' Kirsty said sitting down. 'I do like tea in the afternoon.'

'You are in luck I did a baking this morning. Just the old faithfuls, scones and sponges.'

'I'll enjoy a home-baked scone and yours are always delicious.'

Linda placed the small table between the two chairs then went through to the kitchen to prepare the tea. The kettle had already been boiling and it wouldn't take long to make a pot of tea. When everything was on the tray Linda carried it through and with Kirsty's assistance transferred the dishes to the table.

The smell of recently cut grass reached Linda and her mother through the open window and the light breeze was gently blowing the curtains.

'Mum, if it is too cold for you, say so and I'll close the window.'

'No, don't do that. We get little enough sunshine and I am enjoying this. I'm also enjoying being waited on.' She breathed in. 'I do so love the smell of newly cut grass.'

'So do I.'

'I see you've managed to get someone to help with the garden. Matthew will be pleased about that.'

'Only temporary I'm afraid. The man is between jobs and was making no promises. If he can fit me in then fine, if not I'll have to look for someone else. Matthew isn't all that keen as you know but he will do it if necessary. I do a spot of weeding and as for the girls the mere mention of gardening and they have something urgent to do that can't wait.'

'You and Helen were like that so you can hardly complain.'

'Yes, I can. They won't know that unless you tell them.'

'Which I promise not to do,' she smiled.

Linda pushed the jam dish nearer.

'Butter and jam, I shouldn't.'

'Go on spoil yourself.'

'I don't need much persuasion,' Kirsty said as she put a liberal amount of jam on the side of her plate.

'When am I going to hear?'

'Hear about what?'

'As if you didn't know. You saw David's home for the first time and met his daughter.'

'I did and spent a very pleasant day.'

'And that is it? That is all I am going to be told?'

'What more do you want?'

'The lot. I'm curious and I make no apology for my curiosity.'

'I'm teasing, dear, I was going to tell you.' She drank some tea and put her cup down. 'I should start with Lottie, I think.'

'You had already spoken to her on the phone.'

'That is so and now I can put a face to the voice.'

'You liked her?'

'I liked her immensely. She has her father's charm.'

'Good-looking like her papa?'

'Pleasant-looking, I would say. There is a strong resemblance between father and daughter.' She paused. 'Sadly as sometimes happens the features that are perfect on a man are not so attractive on a woman.'

'Was she pleased to meet you?'

'I would have said so.'

'There was no resentment, none that surfaced.'

'Why should there have been?' Kirsty sounded nettled.

'Mum, you know what I mean. She could very well resent your closeness to her father.'

Kirsty was frowning. 'You really have got this all wrong.'

'Put me right then.'

'David and I do not have a close relationship. A close friendship would be more accurate.'

'I don't see the two as very different but if I have given offence I do apologise.'

'You haven't. I am being over-sensitive. Since presumably most of this will reach Helen let me put your mind at rest. Lottie told me and I believe her, that she is more than happy for her father to have someone –'

'When that someone is you.'

'I would like to think so. She says her father is happier than he has been in a long time.'

'The same could be said of you, Mum, you must be good for each other.' Was that a blush? Linda couldn't be sure.

'And now if you don't mind I think we have said enough on the subject.'

'The subject of Lottie, yes I agree. The house now, I am dying to hear about that. Are we very posh or just middling of the road?'

'I have to say that David's house is very impressive.'

'I had a feeling it might.'

'Oh, and why was that?'

'Just a feeling, Mum. He does have that lord of the manor look but in the nicest possible way. Excuse me, I am going to close the window, it has got colder.'

'Yes, it has.'

Linda saw to the window then returned to her chair. 'More tea?'

'Yes, please, that was a nice cup.'

Linda filled up her mother's cup then her own. She sat back and waited expectantly.

'The house was very grand and I remember feeling a little

annoyed with David. It was so much grander than he had led
me to expect.'

'He won't think of it as grand if that is what he has been used
to.'

Kirsty smiled. 'You could be right.'

'A small mansion.'

'Not far short of it.'

'Could you take me through it?'

'I'm not very good at describing houses.'

'You can try.'

'Very well,' Kirsty said resignedly, 'I'll do my best. I am not
going to describe the outside of the house except to say it is a
solid, stone-built house.' Kirsty closed her eyes as a way to
remember. 'Stepping inside I was in a large entrance hall, all
wood panelled and with a beautiful wide staircase that curved
upwards.'

'Who did the showing around?'

'David to begin with then Lottie took over. I think she was
enjoying herself showing me the house.'

'And I want to enjoy hearing about it. Start downstairs and
don't be rushing it.'

'Don't you have things you should be doing?' Kirsty said
hopefully.

'Yes, Mother, lots of things are in need of my attention but
they can wait. This can't. If I don't hear now I never will.'

'I'm in the hall —'

'Yes.'

'Cloakroom – just the usual, nothing special about it. There
was a breakfast-room and a large dining-room, rather dull I
thought it. Then David's study. It would appear not many get
to see the inside of it so I was privileged.'

'His den which he guards,' Linda smiled.

'What I saw from the doorway was a very large desk over by
the window and a swivel chair that looked the worse for wear.

Papers were scattered over the desk and from the appearance of the floor that was where he did his filing. Lottie and I had a good laugh and David joined in. Mind you he was quick to point out that he could put his hand on what he wanted which was more than he could do after someone had gone mad with the duster. How am I doing?'

'Very well.'

'The sitting-room I did like and that was where we sat and talked.'

'Big and high ceilinged?'

'Yes, as one would expect. It is a lovely bright room with large windows facing west and getting the benefit of the sunshine.' She paused to drink some tea. 'All the furniture and furnishings throughout the house were very good, of a high quality. Money had not been spared. Nothing but the best and that best bought a very long time ago.'

'Am I right in thinking this is a family house handed down from father to son?'

'Yes. David fell heir to it.'

'A mixed blessing, I would say. I don't know about you, Mum, but I have some sympathy for the wife in a situation like that. She is denied choice. Maybe she has no love for antique furniture but is stuck with what is there because anything more modern would look ridiculous.'

Kirsty nodded. 'There could be some truth in that. David's wife might not have been too happy. He obviously loves his home but she may have longed for something smaller and homelier.'

'You didn't find it homely.'

'I couldn't say I did.'

'Would you make changes?'

'What are you talking about?'

'I'm just wondering what kind of changes you would make if you should ever become mistress of the house.'

Kirsty was not amused. 'Linda, stop right there if you please. You are probably saying this in jest but to me it is in bad taste.'

'Sorry.'

'Let me make this very clear. There will be no marriage between your mother and David Harris because neither of us wishes it. We are very good friends and I hope that will continue. There is also a possibility that we may go on holiday together. Do not read anything into that. If eyebrows should be raised then so be it. I'm too long in the tooth to let that bother me.'

Linda smiled to herself. That wasn't true, it would bother her mother to think she was being talked about.

'Don't you believe me?'

'Of course I do.'

'Some of us move with the times.'

'Like having a modern outlook.'

'Exactly.'

'About the house, have we come to a full stop?'

'I had forgotten what we were talking about.'

'Upstairs, we hadn't got the length of that.'

'Four or five bedrooms, I can't remember. David should do something about the bathroom. It does have a heater but manages to look cold and the bath has clawed feet as well as brass taps.'

'Why doesn't Lottie persuade her father to modernise the bathroom?'

'I gather she has tried. She worked on him about the kitchen until he eventually gave in.' She smiled remembering. 'I knew about that. Lottie booked him on that holiday to get him out of the road.'

'And that was where you two met.'

'Yes. The main bedroom has a dressing-room, did I say that?'

'No, but I sort of thought it might.'

'The garden gets full marks. Not that awful manicured way that some are. This was a garden to enjoy. I loved the trees, old and knarled. A bit like the one we had at home where you two loved to climb and hide from me.'

'Thanks, Mum, I'll let you off now. You've given me a pretty good picture.'

'I will tell you one thing more, Linda. I enjoyed seeing round David's house but it was lovely to get home to my little cottage.'

'You are happy there.'

'It is where I want to spend the rest of my days.'

They were silent for a few moments.

'We haven't spoken about the family.'

'Everybody is well, no complaints or none I have heard.'

'And Jennifer? Is that young lady settling down any better?'

'Jennifer is no trouble. She keeps herself to herself because that is the way she wants it.'

'A young girl shouldn't be like that.'

'I agree. I don't like it.'

Kirsty was shaking her head. 'To my mind there is something not right about it.'

'Matthew doesn't have a problem with it and we agree to differ.'

Kirsty looked at her daughter sharply but said no more on the matter.

'I almost forgot and it was what I wanted to ask. How did the evening go with your friends?'

'It went off very well. They are a lovely couple and Alan was so pleased to meet Jennifer. He couldn't keep his eyes off her.'

'That would be with her resemblance to Betty. More to the point, how did Jennifer behave?'

'Mum, you make her sound like a problem child.'

'Which is precisely what she is.'

'Jennifer was quite talkative, most of it about the boutique and the fashion world. Janette and she got on well. So well in fact that Janette asked if Jennifer would like a Saturday job in the boutique.'

'And was she interested?'

'Yes. She said she would like that very much.'

'A bit of extra pocket money for her to spend.'

'Jennifer spends very little. She saves her money.'

'What for?'

'I have no idea and I wouldn't ask. My two could take a lesson from her. Money burns a hole in their pockets.'

'Simon is quite his old self again according to Helen.'

'Yes and working hard for his exams.'

'Poor lad. The young feel such terrible pain but thankfully it doesn't last very long. Actually I feel rather proud of myself.'

'About what? Let me put the table back and give us more room.' She did that.

'About suggesting to Simon that he should ask Hannah to the dance.'

'You made your granddaughter very happy.'

'I thought it was the dress that did that?'

'It had a lot to do with it,' Linda smiled.

'From what Helen said, Simon was quite bowled over by his cousin looking so lovely. She didn't want for partners.'

'Hannah puts it all down to the magic of the dress.'

'For which she has Jennifer to thank. And you know I have been thinking –'

Linda wondered what was coming.

'I hardly know Jennifer.'

'Nobody knows Jennifer, she is a mystery.'

'We, she and I, have never had a talk on our own and I feel it is time we did.'

'How do you propose arranging that?'

'I don't know. The cottage would be the ideal place, but how to get her there on her own? I suppose I could purposely forget my spectacles and you could ask Jennifer to return them to me.'

Linda was shaking her head. 'Not very original is it, you leaving your spectacles. You do have a spare pair.'

'Jennifer isn't to know that.'

'True. More than likely if I asked her she would make some excuse not to go and it would be left to Hannah or Heather to—'

'Nonsense, you give in too easily.'

'Can't you think of something better?'

'No, I cannot and I am not going to rack my brains. You are supposed to be in charge of the home, Linda.' Kirsty got to her feet and placed the spectacle case on the table. 'Linda, that was delightful, I have enjoyed my afternoon and now I must be like the beggars and be on my way. Just make sure, my dear, that it is Jennifer who returns my spectacles. Go about it the right way and she won't be able to refuse.'

'What is the right way, you tell me?' Linda said gloomily.

'That is for you to decide.'

Linda went out to the car with her mother. 'You will go carefully.'

'I can promise that.'

'Are you going to manage to turn the car?'

'I was going to make an attempt. This is something I should have mastered.'

'Only you haven't,' Linda grinned. 'Out you come and I'll do it for you.'

'Thank you. I'm glad I don't have this to contend with where I am.'

Linda did a three-point turn and then got out and stood while Kirsty got into the driving seat. 'You make it look so easy.'

'It is easy.'

'Not for me.' Kirsty blew a kiss and drove away.

*   *   *

Hannah was going to the library to change her book so she was safely out of the way and as luck would have it Heather was at her friend's house. Linda felt that things were working in her favour.

'Jennifer, may I ask a favour of you?'

Her mother would not have thought much of that as an opening.

She nodded but looked uncertain.

'My mother is becoming very absentminded. She was here in the afternoon and went away without her spectacles. Would you be a dear and take them to her?'

Jennifer didn't immediately answer and it was obvious to Linda that she wasn't at all keen to return the spectacles but was unable to think up an excuse to get out of it.

'I—'

'If you hurry you will get that bus. Take money from the sideboard.'

Jennifer went upstairs to get her blazer and Linda was waiting at the foot of the stairs with the spectacle case.

'Thanks.' She put it in her blazer pocket. 'I'll try and get the same bus back.'

'You will be hard put to manage that. Don't rush, Jennifer, my mother will be so pleased to see you. You can keep her company for a little while.'

Jennifer didn't answer but if her expression was anything to go by she wasn't thrilled at the prospect. The door closed and she was gone.

Linda waited a few minutes then phoned Kirsty.

'Mission accomplished,' she said to her mother's hello.

'What?'

'Jennifer and your spectacles are on their way to the cottage.'

'Very good. I knew you would manage it.'

'I am beginning to get worried. What are you up to?' Linda said suspiciously.

'What am I up to? Nothing at all. No more than a little friendly talk. What a suspicious mind you have.'

'You are up to something, I know you too well.'

'If I am it is nothing at all for you to be concerned about.'

'Seriously, Mum, be careful. Keep it to a friendly chat and no more than that otherwise you could cause an awful lot of trouble.'

'You have my word there will be no trouble. Goodbye, dear.' The phone went down.

29

Kirsty was not good at admitting it but she could doze off very easily, particularly in the early evening while watching television. It was only when she discovered how much of the programme she had missed that she realised she must have slept through the earlier part.

Knowing that Jennifer was on her way she ought to have known better than to sit down in the comfortable chair beside the fire. She should have occupied herself doing something.

The loud ringing of the doorbell made her jump and for a moment or two Kirsty was disorientated. Then realising what it was she got up and hurried to open the door.

Jennifer stood there in her school blazer and with the spectacle case in her hand.

'Jennifer, my dear, come away in. It is lovely to see you and how kind of you to bring my spectacles. In you come and let me close the door.'

'I won't come in, Mrs Cameron. I said I would get the same bus back and I can manage it if I hurry.'

'I wouldn't dream of letting you do that. Surely you can spend a little time with me.'

Looking resigned Jennifer stepped inside and Kirsty shut the door.

'Let me have your blazer and I'll hang it on the hallstand.'

'I would rather keep it on for all the time I will be staying.'

'Even so my house is very warm, you would do better to take it off and then know the benefit when you go out into the cold.'

Jennifer took off her blazer and gave it to Kirsty to hang up.

'Come along in to the sitting-room,' Kirsty said, leading the way. Jennifer followed.

'Sit beside the fire and make yourself at home.'

'Thank you.' Jennifer sat down and Kirsty went to sit in her own chair.

'I was thinking the other day that you and I have never had the chance to talk without others being present.'

Jennifer looked at her but remained silent.

'Tell me about school. How are you getting on?'

'All right.'

'Are you still determined to leave at the summer holidays?'

'Yes.'

'You are thinking about going into the fashion industry if I have got that right.'

'I am considering it.'

'You are very wise not to rush into anything. Keep your options open, my dear.'

'Mrs Cameron, this was an excuse wasn't it?'

'Pardon.'

'There was no urgency—'

'To unite me with my spectacles. Was that what you were going to say?'

'You do have another pair.'

'Do I?'

'Yes, you do. On the chest of drawers. Did you forget to put them out of sight?'

'Perhaps I did, Jennifer,' Kirsty said quietly. 'I thought it was time you and I had a talk.'

'What about?'

'About you, Jennifer.'

Kirsty was shocked to see the girl's face turn chalk white but before she could ask what was the matter the alarm clock went off. Quickly Kirsty got up to press the little nob and silence it, then she went into the kitchen to open the oven door and take out the sultana cake. Without the alarm to remind her she might have forgotten and left the cake to burn. Carefully she removed it from the tin and placed it on the wire tray.

Back in the sitting-room she found Jennifer sitting well forward in her chair with her eyes on the carpet. She didn't look up when Kirsty came in. She appeared to be completely self-absorbed.

'Did I say something to upset you? You went very white.'

The shining blue-black hair swung as she shook her head, then after a few moments she said something that Kirsty didn't catch.

'I'm sorry, I didn't hear that.'

'You know, don't you?'

'Know what?'

Jennifer shook her head impatiently. 'I don't know how you could know. I haven't told anyone.'

'Jennifer, my dear child, I am totally lost.'

'Mrs McDonald —'

'The woman who looked after you.'

'Yes. She said I spoke in my sleep, that I was distressed but she couldn't make out what I was saying.'

Kirsty knew she had to go carefully. A wrong word and Jennifer would go back in her shell.

'A lot of people mutter in their sleep, it doesn't mean much.'

'It might, you can't know. That was why it was so important for me to have my own bedroom.'

'You didn't want to disturb anyone.'

'No, it wasn't that. I was afraid of what I might say in my sleep.'

'Why should that make you afraid?'

'Because of what I did.'

'And what did you do?' Kirsty asked quietly.

The girl said something that again Kirsty didn't catch.

'I'm sorry, my hearing isn't perfect. Would you say that again.' She leaned forward.

'I killed them. I killed my parents.' It was said in no more than a whisper but this time Kirsty did hear. Her scalp prickled and she felt the hairs on her neck stand up.

'Jennifer, you don't know what you are saying.'

'I do.'

Kirsty got out of her chair with difficulty.

'Where are you going?' The head shot up and the voice was high-pitched, on the edge of hysteria.

'Not far. Just into the kitchen to put the kettle on.'

'You were going to phone the police.'

'No I wasn't. Why should I do that. And I might add there is no telephone in the kitchen.'

She had calmed down a little. 'I thought you might consider it your duty.' Jennifer paused for a moment. 'I did kill them.'

'I don't believe you.'

'Then you should. I wouldn't say a thing like that if it wasn't true. Would I?'

'I don't know.' Kirsty was shaking inside but somehow she managed to keep her voice steady. She didn't think she was afraid but she was uneasy. 'What I do know is that we are both in need of a cup of tea.'

'The answer to everything.'

Kirsty heard the bitterness. 'It does help. Jennifer, sit where you are.'

'I am not going to run away. Where would I run to?'

'Let me get the kettle on and make the tea. Once I have that done you are going to tell me what this is all about. I want to know what is troubling you.'

'I've told you.'

Kirsty ignored that. 'All I want from you, Jennifer, is the truth. Is that understood?'

'Yes.' There was a weariness in the droop of her shoulders.

Kirsty left her and went into the kitchen. Her hand was shaking so much that she was having difficulty holding the kettle under the tap and some of the water sprayed out wetting the front of her woollen jumper. Telling herself to keep calm was all very well but it wasn't so easy putting it into practice. The girl was talking nonsense, had to be, but clearly something was very far wrong.

She got the tray out and began to set it with two cups and saucers. Then she walked over to the fridge to take out the carton of milk and pour some into a jug. It was difficult to concentrate and it was like doing everything in slow motion. From the cupboard she took out the sugar bowl which had very little in it and she added more from the sugar canister. Then she stood watching the kettle until it boiled and she made the tea. About to take the tray through to the sitting-room she remembered the coffee table was not in position. When that was done and placed between the two chairs Kirsty went back for the tray.

Somehow she managed to pour tea into the cups without spilling any in the saucer. Not troubling to ask how she took it Kirsty put sugar and milk in Jennifer's cup and a splash of milk in her own.

'Sit back, Jennifer, and let me get this cup in front of you.'

There was no movement.

'Jennifer, will you kindly sit back in your chair,' Kirsty said, raising her voice.

This time she sat back.

'Drink that up.'

Jennifer looked at the cup but made no effort to lift it.

Kirsty did that and put the cup into her hand. Only when Jennifer's finger hooked into the handle of the cup did she let go.

Jennifer drank some of the tea and put the cup back on its saucer. Then she lifted the cup in both hands as though she welcomed the comforting warmth.

Kirsty waited.

'Mrs Cameron –'

'Yes,' she said encouragingly.

'My dad didn't lose control of the car – well, he did, but it wasn't his fault. I made him lose control.'

'Why did you do that?'

'To get him to stop.'

'Stop the car, you mean?'

'No. No. No. To stop him tormenting my mum.'

'Jennifer, it might be easier if you were to go back to the beginning.'

'In the car. I think I should begin there.'

'You do that and take your time.'

'My parents didn't always get on. They argued a lot but you knew that.'

'You mentioned it before.'

'That didn't bother me, I suppose I was so used to it that I could shut myself off. They knew I did that, Mrs Cameron, and that was the reason they didn't worry whether I was there or not.'

'These would be small differences, not serious arguments.'

Jennifer shrugged. 'As I said I didn't pay much attention.'

'This was your parents having a disagreement in the car.'

'Yes, but I forgot to say that Dad stopped at the newsagent's for me to collect my magazine. I had to mention that because that was what I was reading and I only looked up when the voices got louder. And that was when I heard Dad saying he was leaving Mum and it was for good.' She paused to draw a ragged breath. 'To let you understand –' she stopped and bit her lip.

'It's all right, dear, take your time,' Kirsty said gently.

'When my dad lost his temper he would start shouting and swearing. Not my mum though, that wasn't her style. She always tried to be dignified. She once told me that it was very

important to keep her temper under control no matter how
hard that might be because as long as she didn't lose it she had
the upper hand. And you know this, she was right, it made
Dad furious.'

Kirsty nodded.

'You see that was what made it so much worse for me. She lost
her temper completely and it had become a slanging match.'

Kirsty was shocked. 'How awful for you. And how dangerous, this happening in the car.'

'It was dreadful and I was getting scared. Mum was shouting that Dad had lost all her money in his hare-brained
schemes. She said she had been stupid giving into him and
now that there was nothing left he was leaving them and – and
what was she going to do.'

Kirsty was visualising the scene and how it would affect a
young girl. Parents had no right to put their children through
that. They should settle their differences when they were on
their own.

'I had never seen my mum like that, Mrs Cameron, she was
becoming hysterical and –'

Kirsty could see the girl was getting agitated and wondered
if it was time to call a halt. Only if she did it would be an
incomplete story and that wouldn't help any of them.

'That was when it happened.' Her voice dropped. 'That was
when I did it.'

'What was it you did, Jennifer?'

'I didn't mean it to happen, you have to believe me.'

'I do believe you, Jennifer.'

'I only wanted Dad to stop but he wasn't paying any
attention to me and that was when I began to hit him.'

'From the back seat where you were sitting.'

'I was leaning forward.'

'Where did you hit him?'

'Does it matter?' she asked, showing a flash of anger.

'It might.'

'On the shoulder.'

'Not heavy blows, they couldn't be, or I wouldn't have thought so. Can you go on and tell me the rest?'

'Give me a minute and I'll be all right.' She swallowed nervously.

'That tea will be cold but take a mouthful, it might help.'

Jennifer did as she was asked and the cup clattered back on its saucer.

'It's not easy to remember everything but I do know I kept on hitting him and it must have been then that Dad lost control of the car. The rest is hazy.'

'I can understand that.'

'Bits of it I will always remember. I'll never forget the scream. My mother let out the most terrible scream and that was the moment I saw this huge tree and then everything went black.' Jennifer put her hand over her mouth and began to sob. Great racking sobs that seemed to be torn from her.

Kirsty got up to kneel beside the chair and gather the girl in her arms.

'You need to cry to get it all out. Bottling it up was the worst thing you could have done. Oh, my dear, how you have suffered. Why didn't you confide in us?'

'I couldn't.'

'My daughter, Linda, is the most sympathetic of souls.'

'She wouldn't have wanted her family to mix with someone who had killed her parents.'

'Jennifer, accidents happen and this was an accident.'

'I was still responsible. It would have been better if I had been killed too.'

'I will not have you talking like that. Oh, dear –'

'What is the matter?'

'You'll have to help me up. I can't move. It isn't the getting down that is the problem it is getting up.'

Jennifer managed a watery smile as she helped Kirsty to her feet, then her eyes went to the clock.

'Look at the time, Mrs Cameron. I said to Mrs Chalmers I wouldn't be long.'

'Never mind the time, you won't be going anywhere in the state you are in. I shall phone Linda and tell her you will be staying overnight and that I'll drive you home in the morning.'

'What about school?'

'Since you are so desperate to leave in the summer one day won't matter and if you are so keen you can go in for the afternoon.'

'I won't bother.'

The phone rang before Kirsty reached it. 'That will be Linda. She has beat me to it.'

It was Linda.

'Mum, Jennifer hasn't arrived home yet.'

'No, she is still here.'

'Why is she still with you? I don't understand, she was to come straight home.'

'Yes, Jennifer said so but we got talking and I'm afraid we lost all track of time.' Kirsty smiled over to Jennifer who was listening to the conversation.

'What on earth were you talking about?' There was the hint of annoyance in her voice.

'Just this and that,' she said vaguely.

'Would I be right in thinking Jennifer is hearing all this?'

'Yes.'

'You can't say much.'

'No.'

'Actually you know, this is very inconvenient, Mum. I don't want Jennifer walking home alone after the last bus and Matthew isn't home yet.'

'Don't worry about that. I was about to phone you to say

that Jennifer will be staying overnight with me and I'll drive her home sometime in the morning.'

'Surely none of this was necessary?'

'I have to disagree there.'

'What about school?'

'One day off won't matter very much.'

'You are the limit, Mum, do you know that.'

'Yes, dear, and now I'll say goodnight.' She put the phone down.

'Linda was worried about you,' Kirsty said as she went back to her chair.

'Was she annoyed?'

'No, just worried.'

'Will you tell her what I told you?'

'I was hoping you would do that.'

Jennifer was shaking her head. 'No.'

'It would come better from you.'

'And if I can't bring myself to do that?'

'Then it will fall to me. Linda and Matthew must be told. No one else needs to know except them.'

She was working her lower lip with her teeth.

'Jennifer, will you listen to me for a few minutes?'

She nodded.

'What happened that day was a tragic accident. And taking into account all you have told me I am not convinced you were responsible.'

'Thank you for that but I know I was.'

'You cannot know for sure.' She paused. 'You said your mother was becoming hysterical.'

'She was.'

'My dear, when someone reaches that stage they are not responsible for their actions. It is perfectly possible that in her distress she could have grabbed at your father and that would have made him lose control.'

'Do you really think that?'

'It is a possibility but no one will ever know for sure. What you must do is stop tormenting yourself. No good will come of that. If I was the judge, Jennifer, and was asked to apportion blame I would have no hesitation in putting most of the blame on your father. He was largely at fault for what happened. The man should have had the decency to wait until they were at home before telling his wife that their marriage was over.'

Jennifer seemed to be relaxing.

'You are being very kind.'

'I am sorry that none of us knew what you were suffering but along with my sympathy there is some anger. Linda has had to put up with a lot from you and for that there can be no excuse. You seemed to go out of your way to be difficult.'

'I'm sorry. It is hard to explain but I didn't want people to like me – not after what I had done. And if they didn't like me they wouldn't ask me questions.'

'Did we ask you questions?'

'Yes. Mr Chalmers didn't. That is why I felt safe with him.'

Kirsty didn't recall asking many questions but perhaps they did without being aware of it. They were both silent for a few moments.

'Jennifer, in this world we all need someone. Didn't you have someone you could have turned to?'

'No.'

'You should have been helped. The hospital where you were should have arranged counselling to help you through the ordeal. I am very surprised they didn't.'

'They did. Several people came –'

'You didn't co-operate.'

'That's right, I didn't.'

'You were being your own worst enemy.'

'Not the way I saw it. Mrs McDonald had no time for them.

She said in her day there was no such thing as counselling, folk just got on with it. They coped because they had to.'

'In my day too but things have changed – not all of them for the better,' she added.

'I'm telling you everything.'

'I'm glad. For too long you have bottled it all up.'

'You know what really scared me?'

'No.'

'Finding a policeman by my bedside. He had been given permission to question me.'

'Oh.'

'I didn't tell him anything. All I did say was that I couldn't remember.'

'And was that true?'

'At first it was then it all came back and I was so afraid. I'm not stupid—'

'Far from it I'd say.'

'I knew I was too young to go to prison but I thought they might send me away somewhere.'

'My dear child there was no danger of that.'

'I wasn't to know was I?'

'You didn't tell the policeman your parents had been quarrelling before the accident?'

'No, I didn't, I would never have done that. It would have gone into the newspapers and my mother would have hated it.'

'Did he come back again – the policeman, I mean?'

'Yes he did and that last time he told me it was wrong to deliberately hold back information that could help to clear up what had happened.'

'He didn't believe you.'

'I don't think he did. He told me they had ruled out mechanical failure and that no other vehicle was involved.'

'You still said nothing.'

'It was difficult but I kept quiet. For all they knew, Mrs Cameron, my dad could have been ill, his heart or something.'

Kirsty shook her head. 'They know these things, Jennifer.'

'Telling you all this has made me feel funny.'

'In what way?'

'You've made it different, not so bad as it was. That isn't to say I don't feel guilt, I do.'

'That isn't necessarily a bad thing. We do have to take some responsibility for our actions. What you were doing was taking it too far. I would say you have suffered enough and it is time to put this behind you.'

'Thank you.' She paused. 'I don't know why it is I want to tell you this but I do.'

Kirsty was amused. 'Dear me, is this confession time?'

'I do have something to confess. That vase that got broken, you know the one that used to sit on the hall table.'

'Yes. I seem to recall that no one owned up. Is this you admitting to it?'

Jennifer was frowning as though she wished the words unsaid. 'It was an accident.'

'Of course it was an accident. No one in their right mind would go about deliberately breaking vases. Why on earth didn't you confess at the time?'

'I wanted to but the words wouldn't come out and then it was too late.'

'It is never too late.'

'Maybe I did Mrs Chalmers a good turn. She got a much nicer one in its place.'

Cheeky monkey, Kirsty thought. 'That is not the point, Jennifer. Didn't it occur to you that someone else could have been blamed?'

'I wouldn't have let that happen but then it wouldn't. Mrs Chalmers would have known her three would have owned up. She would know it was me.'

'My daughter must have been disappointed in you.'

Jennifer shrugged.

'It would help both my daughter and you if you could bring yourself to say how sorry you are.'

'I'll try but it won't be easy.'

'You don't deserve to get it easy.'

'All right I'll do it.'

'Good girl.' The fire was getting low and Kirsty got up to add coal and top it with a log. 'That should do for the rest of the evening.'

'Mrs Cameron –'

'Yes?'

'Is there anything to eat? I'm hungry.'

Kirsty closed her eyes for a second. 'I do apologise, food simply slipped my memory. Come along with me to the kitchen and see what we can find and after that you can help me get the bed ready for you.'

'OK.'

'Speaking of bed, I'll have to find a nightdress for you.'

'I always wear pyjamas.'

'Not tonight you don't.'

When Linda came off the phone and informed the family that Jennifer was to remain overnight at the cottage there had been outrage.

'I've never stayed all night with Gran,' Robin said enviously. 'I didn't even know she had two beds.'

'You are not the only one who hasn't stayed in the cottage overnight.' Hannah looked over to her mother for an explanation.

'I'm sorry, I'm no wiser than you are.'

'What was Jennifer doing at Gran's cottage?'

'Returning your grandmother's spectacles, Heather. I asked her if she would.'

'Why her? Why didn't you ask Hannah or me?'

'Because neither of you was available.'

'What do you mean not available?'

'You were both otherwise engaged.'

'Were we?' She looked puzzled.

'Yes.' Linda paused. 'When Jennifer left here she fully intended returning with the next bus.'

'What made her change her mind?'

'Heather, how should I know?'

'Could be she had it changed for her?' Hannah said shrewdly. 'I mean I've heard Gran say more than once that she didn't understand Jennifer so maybe she saw this as a way to get her talking. Just a thought,' she said huffily when nobody said anything.

Linda was impressed. 'Good thinking, dear, You might have got that right. Gran didn't say much on the phone, she wouldn't if Jennifer was beside her, but she did say they had been talking and completely forgotten the time.'

'She could very easily get the last bus.'

'I wouldn't have wanted that, Hannah. All right if there was someone to meet her but I didn't know when your father would get in and he hasn't arrived as yet. Anyway is it all that important?'

No one answered which meant they did think it important.

Linda had hoped that would be an end to it but it had been too much to hope.

'That means she is going to skip school unless Gran brings her back very early.'

'I don't see that happening. Gran will appear at some time around ten.'

'Some folk have all the luck.'

'You wouldn't want to miss school, Heather.'

'Only because I can't afford to. I'm not clever like some people and there is another thing.'

'And what might that be?' Linda sighed.

'What will Jennifer do about pyjamas? And she won't have a toothbrush.'

'She may well have to go one night without brushing her teeth.'

'Will they fall out?'

'No, Robin.'

'You told me if I didn't—'

'Shut up, Robin, I was talking to Mum and you interrupted. I was on about pyjamas,' she reminded her mother.

'Your grandmother will be able to supply nightwear.'

'An old granny nightdress you mean.' Heather giggled. 'I wonder what Jennifer will look like in one.'

'Very nice I imagine and let me tell you, my girl, your grandmother would be mortified if she could hear you – old granny nightdress indeed.'

'Aunt Helen buys Gran lovely nightdresses for her Christmas or her birthday,' Hannah put in. If you ask me, Jennifer will look glamorous like she always does.' It wasn't said grudgingly, just a statement of fact.

'I really think that is quite enough about nightwear. Robin, do you see the time?'

'The clock is fast. It always is and that's not fair.'

'Only by a few minutes.'

'Five minutes more, please Mummy.'

'All right but no more than five. You are not very smart at getting up in the morning.'

'That's because I'm not sleepy at night, only in the morning.'

Linda smiled. 'Five minutes and no more.'

The morning saw the usual rush to get ready though with one less for the bathroom it did help. Once the breakfast was over and they were gone Linda relaxed and sitting down at the kitchen table poured herself a cup of tea. There wasn't a lot in the teapot and she had to squeeze it to get a full cup. She needed these precious minutes before starting on the chores. There was no particular rush, Linda was reasonably sure her mother and Jennifer wouldn't put in their appearance before ten o'clock. By then the house would be tidy and she would have set the coffee table in the sitting-room. She would set it for three in the hope that Jennifer would join them.

A few minutes after ten Linda was at the window when the car drew up at the gate. Turning away she put on a welcoming smile and went to stand at the open door. She was dressed for summer in lightweight trousers and a sleeveless cotton top.

'Good morning to you both, isn't this a heavenly day?'

'Perfect,' Kirsty smiled. She wore a duck-egg blue linen dress buttoned down the front. It had three-quarter sleeves which Kirsty didn't much like. It was neither one thing nor another. A bad buy. She wouldn't make the same mistake again. 'Summer has come, let us hope it has decided to stay!'

Linda gave her mother a peck on the cheek and Jennifer would have got the same had she not slipped past and in to the house.

'Coffee is ready, Jennifer,' Linda called after her.

'No, thanks, Mrs Chalmers, I had a late breakfast. Excuse me, I have things to do in my room.'

What things? Linda wanted to say. Instead she frowned. They heard her feet on the stairs then a door closing.

'Honestly, she really is the limit.'

'I know, dear, I don't blame you for being annoyed but on this occasion I think she could be forgiven.'

'You do, do you? That makes a change.'

'It does and I won't try to deny it.'

'Come along to the sitting-room, I have the coffee ready.' She went ahead to push the door wider. 'Sit down, Mum, and I'll go and get the coffee pot.'

'You shouldn't have gone to all this trouble. The kitchen would have been fine.'

Linda bristled. 'I usually go to this bother or haven't you noticed?'

'Oh, dear, we are in a mood.'

Linda took a deep breath. 'Sorry, I really am. It is just that sometimes it gets to me. Why must she keep herself to herself?'

'I think I might have the answer.'

Linda gave her mother a swift look.

'Before I start let me have a drink of your delicious coffee. Helen's coffee is much too strong for me.'

Linda poured the coffee. She was desperate to hear what her mother had to say but it was no use trying to hurry her, she would tell it in her own good time.

'You suit that dress.'

'I like it but I cannot be doing with the sleeves. I keep wanting to pull them down.'

'Why did you buy it?'

'The assistant persuaded me. She said I would get used to three-quarter sleeves. She was wrong, I haven't. I'll wear it this year and then give it to the charity shop. Enough about my dress, that isn't why I am here.'

'Mum, I can't help thinking that Jennifer should be here. I shouldn't have to hear this from you.'

'I wanted her to tell you but she said it would be too difficult.'

'Am I so unapproachable?' she said bitterly.

'Linda, don't take this to heart. You've got it all wrong,' Kirsty said gently and patted Linda's hand. 'Jennifer did not choose to tell me. She blurted it out believing I already knew and then when she realised what she had done she panicked.'

Linda looked puzzled. 'What made her think you knew?'

'I don't know. Something I said but for the life of me I don't know what that was.'

'For heaven's sake, are you going to tell me or not? What is it that she is supposed to have done?'

'Something that will shock you as it did me.'

'You mean something awful,' she faltered.

'Jennifer has suffered more than any child should. And as for that father of hers –'

'Robert is dead,' Linda said quietly.

'Yes, the man is dead and I hope that wherever he is that he will have to answer for his sins.' Kirsty paused and looked at Linda across the table. 'Jennifer believes she was responsible for her parents' death and it is just possible that she was.'

Linda's hand went to her mouth. 'Oh, my God, you can't mean it. I never dreamt it could be anything so awful.'

'You need to hear it all and I'll do my best.'

When she had finished the coffee was cold but neither of them noticed. Linda was looking anguished.

'Poor, poor Jennifer. I feel so wretched.' She paused. 'If only she had confided in me and not suffered alone.'

'Don't blame yourself, there is nothing more you could have done. You did your best to give Jennifer a happy home.'

'I tried to. Then when I wasn't getting anywhere I left her alone. Matthew said to do that.'

'We all, including the children, did our best.'

'I want to think that.'

'Then do, it happens to be the truth.'

'Mum, it is very important that this goes no further than ourselves.'

'I agree.'

'By ourselves I am including Matthew, Helen and George.'

'I would expect that. Of course they need to be told but that isn't a problem. We know we can trust each other.'

Linda was nodding. 'Will Jennifer be more relaxed, I wonder? One would think so and hopefully she won't want to spend so much time on her own.' She waited for her mother to say something.

'She will be happier in herself, I have no doubt,' Kirsty said slowly, 'but don't look for big changes. Jennifer will always be a difficult girl, I think. Some of it will be in her nature and a lot of it the fault of her upbringing.'

'Why do you say that? Betty would have been a good and loving mother.'

'Yes, and trying too hard I expect. You know, over-compensating for what was wrong in the marriage.'

'Possible, I suppose.'

Kirsty gave a rueful smile. 'Jennifer would have done what countless other children have done in similar circumstances. Children are very quick to take advantage.'

'I'm with you. What they don't get from one parent they will get from the other. Little monsters playing one parent off against the other.' She paused, 'What now? Where do we go from here?'

'Carry on as before, I would say.'

'I can't just ignore this. Jennifer knows you are telling me. I have to say something.'

'You do what you think best but make sure she knows the matter is closed.'

'I will.' She looked at her mother thoughtfully. 'There is one thing I am not too happy about.'

Kirsty raised her eyebrows.

'Going back to the accident, I don't think you should have put the blame for it on Betty. In all likelihood she was completely innocent.'

'She could be and I am all but sure that Betty would be prepared to take the blame, or some of it, rather than have her daughter's whole life spoiled by believing that she alone caused the death of her parents. Think about it, Linda, wouldn't you have wanted to spare your daughter?'

'When you put it that way.'

'There is no other way to put it. Not if you want Jennifer to live a normal life and not be burdened with guilt.'

'You are right, of course you are. I'll tell Matthew tonight when we are on our own. He is going to be terribly shocked. Mum, don't drink that, I'll go and make fresh.'

'No, don't do that. I must be going.' She got to her feet. 'You are going to be an angel, aren't you, and turn the car.'

'Yes, and one day I am going to teach you how to do it yourself.'

'I've managed all these years without being able to do a proper three-point turn.'

'That is no excuse,' Linda laughed.

'Call Jennifer down, if you will, then go and do your duty.'

Rather than shout from the foot of the stairs Linda went up to the bedroom and knocked on the door. It was opened almost at once.

'Do you want me?' She looked wary and perhaps a little scared.

'My mother is just leaving and she wants to see you before she goes. And, Jennifer,' Linda said gently. 'I know all about it and you are not to worry. Put it all behind you. My only regret is that you couldn't bring yourself to confide in me.'

'I couldn't, Mrs Chalmers. My mother was your best friend and I killed her. How could I have told you that?'

'Jennifer, it was an accident. Accidents do happen and no one will ever know for sure how it happened.'

'Except me.'

'You saw a part of what happened that is all. Some of it was in your imagination.' On an impulse she gave Jennifer a hug and was encouraged when she didn't draw away. 'My mother is waiting, off you go and see what she wants.'

Jennifer ran downstairs and Linda's passing thought was that her blouse didn't look fresh. Then she remembered it had been worn all the previous day.

'Hello, dear, Linda is turning my car. Are you going to be all right?' she said anxiously.

'Yes, I do feel better and thank you, Mrs Cameron, you have been very kind.'

'You are among friends, Jennifer, don't ever forget that. If you have worries share them, that is what families are for and whether you believe it or not you are part of this family.'

Jennifer nodded and Kirsty took her leave.

Matthew was visibly upset. 'That poor kid. My God, it doesn't bear thinking about what she has come through. The accident was bad enough but to believe she might have been responsible –'

'Matthew, she probably was responsible and she is intelligent enough to know that. Mother tried to shift some of the blame on to Betty –'

'The only one at fault was that bloody fool of a father.'

'I absolutely agree.'

'Linda, we should have done more. Why didn't we?'

'I did try.'

'Not hard enough.'

'Pardon me, Matthew, but you have a very convenient memory. You said to leave her alone.'

'Did I?'

'Yes, you did.'

'Seems I was wrong then.'

'Yes. Or maybe again there was no right or wrong way. We can only be thankful it has come out now.'

'It is to be hoped she can put it all behind her.'

'In time she will. The memory of it will fade. On a lighter note the family were green with envy that Jennifer had got to sleep in the cottage. None of them has.'

'Kirsty can do something about that.'

'My poor mother.'

'Nonsense, I bet Kirsty would love to have them for the odd night. Not together, one at a time,' he grinned. 'How about some sleep? Some of us have to work tomorrow,' he said, slipping further under the bedclothes.

Linda knew she wouldn't sleep for a long time but Matthew was one of the lucky ones who could fall asleep as soon as his head touched the pillow.

30

Life at Hillcrest was going on much as usual with the children already counting the days until the end of term and the beginning of the long summer holidays. Jennifer would be leaving school for good. She hadn't shone. She was an average pupil, according to her report, who could have done better if she had tried harder. Not being interested in further education she had seen no point in putting in greater effort. Rather she would make use of what she had been given – her good appearance, her height and her model figure. Linda had tried to draw her out about her plans for the future but without making much headway though she was pleased to notice the girl studying the situations vacant in the local newspaper.

Linda and her mother had looked for signs of strain from the trauma Jennifer had suffered but found none. There was no noticeable change that they could see. She still preferred her own company. The Saturday job in the boutique, however, was a success and Jennifer was clearly enjoying it.

The month of May had been disappointing with little sunshine and too many squally showers and that disagreeable wind. June was starting well with warm sunshine and clear blue skies. The gardens at Hillcrest had never looked better and that without Matthew having touched a garden tool, which pleased him enormously. To her own and everyone's delight Linda had managed to hold on to her gardener, even managing to extend his hours. She didn't know and thought it best not to ask, but presumed the job he had hoped was his own hadn't materialised. Whatever the truth of the matter the man no longer talked of being between jobs.

A few miles away in a large, stone-built house in Ninewells, Alan and Janette Stephenson were sitting in their living-room. The empty coffee cups had been removed from the table and placed on a tray to be taken to the kitchen when one of them was going there. Cluttered around Janette's feet were samples of material and Alan, who did the books for the boutique, was busy putting the invoices in order. Janette was not methodical when it came to paperwork.

'Business is looking good, dear,' Alan said.

Janette glanced up from her study of the new season's colours.

'Can't complain,' she smiled, 'in fact rather too hectic at times. This lovely sunshine is encouraging folk to buy.'

'No use killing yourself. You need assistance.'

'I know.'

'Then do something about it. Advertise for someone.'

'Actually, Alan, I was thinking about approaching Jennifer to see if she might be interested in working full time for me. I find her such a help on Saturdays.'

'Do it before she gets fixed up elsewhere. The schools will be off in a week or two.'

Janette looked at him thoughtfully. 'You are quite taken with Jennifer, aren't you?' Janette said softly.

'I suppose I am.'

'Because of her resemblance to Betty? It is, isn't it? It has to be.'

'It's true that I find I want to protect her which, of course, is silly and you are going to tell me she doesn't need protecting.'

'I am not. You don't need to be told what you already know.' She paused. 'There has always been complete honesty between us.'

Alan smiled. 'That is what makes our relationship so special. We can each say what we think without fear of hurting the other. So go ahead and say what you want to.'

'Do you see Jennifer as the daughter you might have had?'

He took so long to answer that Janette didn't think he was going to.

'Maybe I do,' he said at last. 'I'm not sure about that, though.'

'Forgive me but you see what you want to see, Alan. I see what is there. Jennifer is not like your gentle Betty. There is a ruthless streak –'

'You don't like her. You don't like Jennifer.'

'I do like her as it happens but that doesn't blind me to her faults, her selfishness. She probably doesn't realise she is selfish, there are people like that.' Janette stopped and thought about what she was going to say next. 'I don't hold it against her, being ruthless I mean. One has to have a bit of it in business if you want to succeed. Your Jennifer—'

'My Jennifer?'

'That is the way you like to think of her. I'm only teasing. Seriously, she is a very beautiful girl and if her ambition is to be a top model then she will need every scrap of that ruthlessness.'

'You exaggerate.'

'No, it is a cutthroat business.'

'When are you going to put your offer to Jennifer?'

'Now that I have discussed the matter with you I shall go ahead and ask her on Saturday.'

Janette waited until it was quiet in the boutique then she made her offer to Jennifer.

'You can think it over. Discuss it with Mr and Mrs Chalmers.'

'No, I don't have to do that. It isn't necessary. I make my own decisions, Mrs Stephenson.'

'And if you make an unwise one?'

'Then I have only myself to blame. I don't see that happening, though.'

'I wish at sixteen that I had had your confidence.'

'I have my father to thank for that. He encouraged me to think for myself and to ignore advice if I didn't like it. That is what he did,' she grinned. 'He said to go after what I wanted and not to let anything or anyone stand in the way.'

'Did he make a success of his own life?'

'No, Dad was one of life's failures, my mother said. I suppose I was to benefit from his mistakes.'

'We all make mistakes in this life.'

Jennifer was becoming restless. 'You want your answer about the boutique.'

'When you are ready to give it.'

'You can have it now. I accept your offer, Mrs Stephenson, and thank you.'

'Good. I'm glad we've got that settled. Since you are about to leave school you must have been looking to see what jobs are on offer.'

'Yes. I have been studying the situations vacant page in the *Dundee Courier*. One of the big stores has vacancies in several departments including fashion.'

'Be careful when you see that. It sounds to me as though that particular store is having difficulty holding on to their staff.'

'That struck me too. The job does have one advantage over the boutique.'

'Oh.' Janette felt deflated then brightened when she heard the reason.

'I would need only one bus to get there.'

'Do you find that a problem – having to get two buses?'

'Not a big problem but hanging around waiting is a nuisance. Not so bad in the summer –' she left the rest of the sentence unsaid.

Janette didn't think there was much she could do about that. 'Jennifer, may I ask about your long-term plans unless you prefer to keep those to yourself?'

'No. You already know what my ambition is. I told you before that I want to be a model. A top model. I like what is involved, all that travelling about. I mean, London and Paris and all those other places. Maybe in time it would get boring but I hardly think so.'

'I wouldn't think so either. It could be a wonderful life and I hope you get the chance to find out,' Janette smiled.

'If I don't get the break and I have to forget modelling then I may think about doing what you did.'

'Becoming a buyer in a fashion store?'

'That or opening my own boutique. It would mean finding a lot of capital, wouldn't it?'

'I'm afraid so.'

'Could be I'll have to find a rich husband to take care of that.'

'You wouldn't go that far?' Janette laughed.

'I might very well go that far.'

Janette was serious. 'Don't even think about it. That, my dear, could be a recipe for disaster. What is success if you are not happy?'

'I don't think love is that important,' Jennifer said carelessly. 'Obviously I wouldn't marry someone I disliked. Great, though, if I could find someone I loved who had money but if it was to be one or the other then I would settle for a rich husband.'

'Jennifer, I think you are having me on.' Janette smiled as she said it but she had the feeling Jennifer meant what she said. She would choose wealth to further her ambition. Two customers had just come in to the boutique which put an end to the conversation.

In the evening Janette repeated most of the conversation to Alan.

'Don't all girls talk about marrying a rich husband?'

'In fun, but I got the impression that Jennifer could be serious.'

'Linda and Matthew will talk sense into her if the need ever arises.'

Janette looked up 'I doubt if Jennifer would pay much attention to what anyone said.'

'Oh, I don't know. She might listen to you,' Alan smiled.

'Why should she?'

'Because you can teach her a lot and she knows that.'

Janette frowned and stopped what she was doing. 'Alan, I am going to phone Linda. She might think it a bit underhand offering Jennifer a full-time job without first mentioning it to her.'

'I don't think Linda would take offence but there is no harm in phoning to keep yourself right. Before you get up –' Janette had half risen but sat down again – 'I am a little concerned about the journey. Jennifer isn't too keen about having to take two buses.'

'I know and that has me slightly worried.'

'Pity she couldn't get a lift.'

'That is not very likely. It would take Matthew out of his way and that would be expecting too much.'

Alan was looking thoughtful.

'Come on, I know that look. You've got an idea.'

'A non-starter I'm afraid.'

'Let me hear it.'

'We have rather a large house.'

'We do, so what?'

'Think, woman.'

'Has this to do with accommodation?'

'Decidedly warm. One of the upstairs rooms could be made into a bedsitter.'

'Very easily,' Janette said, looking interested. 'A lot of the young folk are going for that these days.' She shook her head. 'Not as young as sixteen, though.'

'We would be there for her. You know, keep an eye on her without making it obvious.'

'Do you think Jennifer would be interested?'

'I do.'

'So do I. Linda worries because she spends so much time on her own.'

'That is what the girl likes. She likes her own company at least for some of the time.' Alan was glad that Janette wasn't dismissing his suggestion out of hand. He liked the idea of having Betty's daughter under his roof.

'Would it work?'

'I think so.'

'I'm inclined to agree. All the same we must go carefully, I don't want to hurt anyone.'

'Nor I. Will you put the suggestion to Jennifer?'

'Not until I hear what Linda has to say.' Janette frowned. 'She might think we've got a nerve.'

'Or she might be secretly pleased. She has made no secret of the fact that Jennifer has never really fitted in with the family.'

'As an only child she would find that difficult.'

Janette nodded. 'Linda's girls have had to share a bedroom and I gather there were all sorts of problems at the beginning. Hannah put her foot down and refused to share with her sister and Jennifer was forced to share with Heather and did not like it one bit. Then something happened or something was said and Hannah decided to give up her bedroom to Jennifer.'

'So our suggestion could be well received.'

'We'll have to wait and see.'

Janette chose a time when she thought Linda would be alone in the house.

'Hello, Janette, lucky you caught me,' she said when she went to answer the phone.

'Am I holding you back?'

'No, not at all, it was nothing important, just an outing. How are you both?'

'Very well, thank you. Busy like yourself.'

'Compared to you I am a lady of leisure.'

'Linda, first of all I need to know if you are happy about Jennifer coming to work for me full time.'

'Of course I am. I am delighted and so is Matthew. Jennifer isn't particularly forthcoming but I gather she is looking forward to working in the boutique. She has been helping you on Saturdays so she knows what it is all about.'

'Good, I have got that part over.'

'Is there more to come?'

'Yes and I am getting cold feet about putting forward our suggestion.'

'All you are doing is making me curiouser and curiouser,' Linda laughed. 'Come on out with it.'

'If it doesn't meet with your approval, you will say so? I value our friendship and I wouldn't want to jeopardise it.'

'Janette, I am not going to fall out with you I promise.'

'Here it is then. Jennifer does find one drawback about working in the boutique.'

'She hasn't said anything to us.'

'She doesn't like having to take two buses.'

Linda came in quickly. 'Sorry, but there is no way we can help out there. It is out of Matthew's way and then there would be the return journey. No, the answer has to be a definite no.'

'Linda, you didn't give me a chance to get a word in. No one would expect Matthew to do that. We wondered, Alan and I, if you would allow Jennifer—'

'Jennifer is a law unto herself, she will do what she wants.

She doesn't consider us her guardians. I'm a sort of god-mother.'

'The position is, Linda, that I want to hold on to Jennifer for as long as possible. I could advertise but I doubt if I would find someone as good. We have a lot of room here in our house and if Jennifer would be interested she could have a bedsitter. We would respect her privacy but we would be there for her if she wanted us.'

'Have you asked her?'

'No, and I won't. Not until I know how you feel about it.'

'I have no objections. If Jennifer agrees and I am sure she will—'

'You are?'

'Yes, I have a feeling that what you suggest might be quite perfect for Jennifer. She never wanted to be part of a family. Having her own bedsitter will please her immensely.'

'Your two girls have been very generous. They will be able to have their own bedroom again.'

'Yes.'

Linda was pleased when Jennifer spoke about being offered a bedsitter in Janette's house.

'You would like that,' Linda said as she prepared the vegetables for the evening meal and Jennifer sat watching her.

'I would. I would like it very much.'

'You haven't been very happy here, have you?'

Jennifer looked surprised. 'I haven't been unhappy, it is only that I don't fit in. My own mum didn't understand me at times so it is no small wonder if you don't.'

Linda laughed at that. 'Jennifer, dear, we are all different. Some of us like to be on our own and others can't stand to be. We are going to miss you.'

'Can't I come and see you?'

'I hope you will, we all do.'

Jennifer looked pleased. 'Hannah must come to the boutique when she wants new clothes. She isn't very good at choosing but I won't let her buy something she doesn't suit.'

'Thank you,' Linda said, keeping her face straight. 'You must do the same for Heather.'

'Of course.'

Linda had wondered about Matthew and how he would feel about Jennifer going to live in Ninewells with Alan and Janette. Not that it was going to alter anything but she would prefer it if he was pleased.

'What made you think I might not be pleased?' Matthew said, showing genuine amazement. 'On the contrary this strikes me as being the perfect answer. Everyone appears to be getting something out of it. Jennifer will be happy to have her own bedsitter. Janette is getting the assistant she wants and Alan probably feels happy about having Betty's daughter in his house.'

'And us?'

'We, my darling, are back where we were. You have done your duty by Jennifer, we all have in our own way. Then remember, Linda, that we have three super kids and Alan and Janette are alone. This could work out very happily.'

Linda nodded, too choked for words. They were a family again.

'One day, who knows, Jennifer might be a famous model.'

'Matthew, that could happen and Janette will be there to give advice.'

'Doesn't it all depend on being in the right place at the right time?'

'Absolutely. The top models, according to what I have read, are usually spotted by a model agency and encouraged to have a test to see if they have the potential. I hope it happens for Jennifer.'

'So do I, the kid deserves a break.'

*   *   *

Linda got up in the morning feeling full of energy and decided not to waste it. She would clean out the cupboard under the stairs, something she had promised herself for ages, and throw out what she considered to be rubbish. The problem with that was the family wouldn't agree with her. They couldn't bear to throw anything away.

The phone rang when she had two piles beside her. One lot to go out and the other to be kept. The one for the bin was pathetically small. Getting up from her kneeling position Linda went to answer the telephone.

'Hello.'

'It's me.'

It was early for Helen. 'What brings you on at this time?'

'I wondered if I might invite myself for coffee, that is if you are not going out.'

'I'm not. I have been cleaning out the cupboard under the stairs.'

'The glory hole. We have one of those but I make the boys clean it out. It is full of their junk after all. Do I come?'

'Of course.' Linda had a sudden thought. 'Nothing wrong, is there?'

'No, nothing at all. I thought it would be nice to have a chat, just the two of us.'

'A chat about Jennifer?'

'Yes. I can't get over what that poor girl has come through, is still going through for that matter.'

'Helen, I'll finish what I am doing then get the coffee on. You wouldn't settle for instant, would you?'

'Not unless you are terribly pushed.'

'I'm not. It will be the real thing.'

'Great, I'll be right over.'

Helen hadn't put off any time and before Linda had a chance to change out of her old clothes her sister had arrived.

'That was smart. As you see I haven't had time to change but the coffee is ready.'

'Good, I could do with a cup.' Helen was looking very elegant in cream tailored trousers and a multi-coloured top.

'You look nice and summery.'

'Thank you.'

'Go through and sit down. I'll bring the coffee.'

'Don't tempt me with biscuits.'

'I won't, I'm trying to lose a pound or two before I have a look around Janette's boutique.'

'One day I must pop in.'

'You should. Janette has excellent taste and if you wait a week or so Jennifer might serve you.'

Helen took a sip of her coffee. 'How is she? How is Jennifer?'

'She's fine.'

'She can't be fine, Linda.'

'Jennifer has been coping with this, Helen, and coping in her own way.'

'Sharing her worries must have helped.'

'I'm sure it has and it was just a chance remark that brought it all out.'

'So Mum said. She must have handled it well.'

Linda nodded. 'Believe me, when Jennifer went to the cottage with Mum's spectacles I had misgivings.'

'Why?'

'Because, Helen, Mum was going to give Jennifer a good talking to and I was afraid her interference would do more harm than good.'

'In the event it did a lot of good – Jennifer going over to the cottage, I mean.'

'Yes.'

'This coffee is quite good.'

'Praise indeed,' Linda said as she took a drink of hers.

'All I meant was that I prefer mine stronger than you usually make it.' She paused and looked thoughtful. 'You know, if I had been in Jennifer's position I think I would have gone mad. On the other hand I couldn't see myself doing anything so stupid.'

Linda felt a surge of anger. 'How do you know what you would have done? Our parents didn't quarrel. Jennifer was so used to her parents bickering that for some of the time she hardly noticed.'

Helen looked shamefaced. 'I'm sorry and of course you are right.'

They were both silent for a few moments, then Helen spoke. 'You must be feeling hurt.'

Linda looked puzzled. 'Why should I be feeling hurt?'

'You know, Jennifer leaving Hillcrest and going off to live with Janette and Alan.'

'She isn't, not in the way you are suggesting. Janette and Alan are giving Jennifer a bedsitter in their home. They will respect her privacy but be mindful that the girl is only sixteen and keep an eye on her. I'm happy about the situation and so is Matthew. And something else we are pleased about, Jennifer said that she wants to keep in touch.'

'Fine, I'm glad to hear it and the girls will have their own bedroom.'

'Yes and obviously they are happy about that.'

'Won't they miss Jennifer?'

'Yes, I'm sure they will but it won't upset them. Looking back I see now that I was wrong to try and make Jennifer part of the family.'

'She didn't want that?'

'No, she didn't.'

'That could be the result of being an only child.'

'That is very possible.'

'She is very lovely and with a perfect figure too,' Helen said enviously.

'Betty would have been so proud of her.'

'I'm sure and imagine how thrilled we would be to see Jennifer's face on the cover of *Vogue*.'

'Wouldn't we just.' Linda was smiling happily. The future looked bright for them all.